As a last defiant gesture, he swung the mast over his head.

He laughed, but then suddenly changed and began to scream; the kind of scream that Stroup had not heard since three of his men had dropped into a *punji* trap full of sharpened stakes in Vietnam. Heacox clawed wildly at the sides of the Rangda mask and staggered around the courtyard.

"Jimmy!" Stroup shouted, and caught hold of him. For one moment Stroup found himself staring straight into the face of the goddess. Then Heacox buckled and collapsed and the mast hit the stones of the courtyard with a hollow, wooden sound and rolled away.

As it rolled, the mask left a batik pattern of bright scarlet blood on the ground.

GRAHAM MASTERTON
DEATH TRANCE

TOR
HORROR
A TOM DOHERTY ASSOCIATES BOOK

DEATH TRANCE

Copyright © 1986 by Graham Masterton

Reprinted by arrangement with Wiescka Masterton

First printing: September 1986

A TOR Book

Published by Tom Doherty Associates, Inc.
49 West 24 Street
New York, N.Y. 10010

ISBN: 0-812-52187-0
CAN. ED.: 0-812-52188-9

Printed in the United States

0 9 8 7 6 5 4 3 2 1

Prologue

Bali, 1981

It was just after eight o'clock in the evening when Michael came cycling through the night market.

He steered his antiquated Rudge between the shuffling crowds of tourists and shoppers, between the jumbled arrangement of stalls lit with hundreds and hundreds of glass-funneled gaslights. It was the monsoon season, hot and cloudy, and there were no stars.

Whenever Michael found himself obstructed by early evening diners clustered around the *warong* stands with their white-china bowls of fried noodles, he furiously jangled his bell. Occasionally people would move out of the way for him, but more often he was forced to hop down from the saddle that was far too high for him and manhandle the bicycle through the crowds like a young cowboy trying to wrestle an obstinate steer.

Sometimes he had to half-lift the bicycle onto his left shoulder to get around crates of chickens, bales of batik and baskets of snake-skinned *salak* fruit.

Scarcely anybody took notice of the slight, thin-wristed boy with the old-fashioned bicycle. An occasional American would glance at him, especially one who remembered the half-caste heritage of Vietnam, but then he would look away almost at once. For the boy had tousled hair so blond it was almost white, while his eyes were dark brown and slightly slanted, and there was a curve to his nose and a softness about his mouth that betrayed his mother's Balinese blood.

Two women were standing in his way now, arguing over the price of jackfruit.

"*Aduh! Terlalu mahal! Tidak, saya tidak mau membelinya!*"

Michael jangled his bell and the women moved out of the way, still arguing. He could have been any local boy cycling through the night market on any kind of errand. Only somebody sensitive to the magic that awoke in the city of Denpasar every time the sun sank, only somebody who could recognize the preoccupied expression of a child who had been trained in the spiritual disciplines of Yama—only somebody like that would know where Michael was going, and why.

He cycled on, toward the street called Jalan Mahabharata. The night market was filled with distorted rock 'n' roll blaring from rickety hooked-up speakers, and the rock 'n' roll clashed with the jingling of *ceng-ceng* cymbals and the beating of *kendang* drums. The air was fragrant with chili and rice and with the crackling fat of *babi guling*, the Balinese roast suckling pig. Strident voices chattered and argued, proffering food and fruit and shoes and "guaranteed ancient" root carvings.

An old man with a burned-down cigarette between his lips and a strange, lopsided turban tried to step into Michael's path and stop him. "*Behenti! Behenti!*"

Michael wobbled around him, skipping one foot on the ground to keep his balance and skinning the back of his calf on the serrated edge of one pedal.

The man cried out hoarsely, "You—*puthi anak*—white child! I've seen you before. I know where you go. You should beware of leyaks. You should be careful of whose advice you take. You—*puthi anak!* You should be careful who guides you!"

Michael kept on cycling without looking around to see if the old man was following him, hoping that he wasn't. Nevertheless, he wasn't surprised or distressed. He had been warned from the very beginning that there were others who were sensitive to spirits and that many of these others would recognize him for what he was.

It was usually the old who sniffed him out, those who had retained a nose for the subtle presence of Dewi and Dewa, the male and female deities whose spirits could still be heard whispering in the dead of night, whose movements still left the gentlest of eddies in the morning mists. Few young people had any interest in the spirit world now; they were more interested in Bruce Springsteen, in Prince, and in roaring up and down Jalan Gajamahda on their mopeds, whistling at American girls. The spiritual power of Denpasar was still potent, especially in the older parts of the city, but as far as the young were concerned, the ancient deities had long ago been outshone by red and yellow neon lights and by the garish posters advertising sexy films.

Michael was uncertain of what the old man in the turban had been trying to tell him, but he remembered, as he often did, the words of his father: "Be patient, for there is always an explanation for everything. And whatever happens, you always have your soul, and you will always have me."

"I shall never ever leave you," his father had told him gently on the porch of their house at Sangeh village, with the monsoon rain dripping from the eaves and steam rising from the blue-green fields. "No matter where I travel, no matter what happens to me—even if I die—I shall never leave you."

It had been raining this afternoon in Denpasar. It was November, the second month of the monsoon season, and the temperature was up to eighty-seven degrees. The city felt as if it had been wrapped in hot, wet towels. Michael's face was glossy with sweat and his white short-sleeved shirt clung to his narrow back. Around his waist he wore a scarlet *saput*, or temple scarf, that had once belonged to his father. On his feet he wore grubby Adidas running shoes. Apart from his bicycle, which had been given to him by Mr. Henry at the American consulate, his only other concession to Western culture was a Casio digital wristwatch with a football game on it.

When he reached Jalan Mahabharata, he dismounted. He wheeled his bicycle past a batik stall, where a young girl was sitting sewing by the light of a gaslamp. Her beauty was almost unearthly even though her hair was fastened back with the simplest of combs and she wore nothing more elaborate than a plain dress of white cotton. She raised her eyes as Michael passed. She may have recognized him, but she said nothing.

Farther along the street, the stalls and *warong* stands of the night market gave way to rows of older houses: Dutch colonial frontages with secretive doors and shuttered windows, dark entrances with signs written in Indonesian, shops and dental surgeries. A stray dog tore at a thrown-away chicken carcass. Two young men with slicked-back hair sat astride their Yamaha mopeds, smoking and hooting and singing "hey-hey rock 'n' roh" over and over again. Across the street, outside a derelict laundry, a girl in a tight red-satin skirt waited for somebody, or nobody.

The air along this part of the street was rank with the smell of cheap food and sewage and incense. Tourists avoided the area because it seemed so heavy and threatening. But Michael wheeled his bicycle through the garbage and the fallen frangipani leaves, calm and distant in his demeanor, and unafraid.

There was nothing to fear in the world of men. It was only on the edge of the world of spirits that real fear began.

He reached the gates of an old and neglected temple, the Pura Dalem, the Temple of the Dead. The ancient structure stood between a flaking-walled Dutch apartment house and the "Rumah Makan Rama," the Rama restaurant. Its towers and arches were draped with dense, entangled creeper, and here it was darker and more silent than in any other part of the street. Along the front wall, stone carvings of devils and demons glared with hideous faces bearing long tusks. The gateway was guarded by the effigies of Rangda, the Witch Widow, and Barong Keket, the Lord of the Forests. Their grotesque bodies were thick with moss and their limbs were girded with flowering vines.

The girl in the tight red-satin skirt called across the street, "Are you lonesome, young Charlie?"

But Michael said, *"Tidak,"* which meant "No."

"Mungkin nanti, Charlie?" the girl asked in the same flat tone. "Maybe later?"

Michael nodded to show that he had heard her, but he walked without hesitation up to the corroded green-copper gates of the Pura Dalem and turned the heavy handle. He pushed his bicycle inside and then closed the gates behind him. He was in deep silence here, except for the distant ripping echo of a moped. Oil lamps flickered and smoldered, although the outer courtyard through which Michael had entered remained shadowy and oddly dark. The temple had been looted during the grisly days of the *puputan,* the great suicidal struggle against the Dutch, and the few thatched pavilions that surrounded the courtyard had long since collapsed, leaving nothing but their white skeletal framework. The stone flooring was slippery with moss.

Michael left his bicycle by the outer gate and crossed the courtyard until he reached a smaller gateway embossed with flowers and figures of beasts and guarded by the twin monkey giants of Hanuman. This was the *paduraksa,* the door to the inner courtyard, the gateway to the Kingdom of Death itself.

There was no need for Michael to open the inner door, or even to knock. The high priest always anticipated his arrival and would toll the temple bell three times: three flat, dull, oval-shaped chimes that would reverberate through the temple like the disapproving voice of a demon. A flock of mynah birds scattered into the night from the overhanging frangipani trees and then quickly settled again.

The gates opened and there stood the *pedanda,* the high priest, his smallness and frailty still surprising after five years. He wore a white headdress of knotted cotton, no grander than an ordinary temple priest would have worn, and he was wrapped in simple white robes, almost as if he were ready to be cremated. Michael had often tried to guess how old he was but it was impossible to say for sure; the little man was so thin and wizened, with eyes as impenetrable as pebbles and a wispy white beard. Beneath his wrappings his body seemed to have no substance at all, like the body of a fragile, mummified bird.

"Selamat malam, Michael," the *pedanda* nodded, lightly pressing the palms of his hands together. "Good evening."

"Selamat malam, Pak," Michael replied.

The *pedanda* turned without ceremony and led the way into the inner courtyard. There stood four earthenware braziers, one set at each corner, smoking with incense. The priest appeared to almost float through the smoke as if his feet never touched the ground.

"Ada sesuatu yang menjusahkan?" the *pedanda* asked without turning around. His voice betrayed a hint of amusement. He wanted to know if Michael felt there was anything wrong.

"An old man tried to stop me when I was cycling along Jalan Kartini. He said some strange things."

"Ah," said the *pedanda.* He raised one hand. His fingernails had grown so long that they twisted like corkscrews. His head was angled in an odd way, somehow indicating to Michael that he was pleased.

"The old man sensed your readiness," the *pedanda* explained.

"Am I really ready?" Michael asked.

"Do you have any doubts?"

Incense wafted between them, rolling over in the heavy night air. Michael said, "Yes, naturally I have doubts. Didn't you have doubts before you did it for the first time?"

"Of course," replied the *pedanda.* He had taught Michael to always question him. "But I had to throw away my doubts. Just as you will have to throw away yours." He paused for a moment and then said, *"Silakan duduk."*

Michael obeyed, walking across to the center of the courtyard where two frayed silken mats had been laid out. Carefully, so that he would not wrinkle the silk, he sat down cross-legged, his back rigidly straight and the palms of his hands held outward.

"Tonight you will take your first steps into the world of the spirits," said the *pedanda.* He did not join Michael straightaway as he usually did, but stood watching him with stony eyes, his hands still lightly pressed together as if he were holding a living butterfly between them. *What shall I do now? Release the butterfly, or crush it to death?*

Michael shivered, although he had always promised himself that when the *pedanda* announced that this evening had finally arrived, he would accept it without fear and without sentimental feelings. He had every right to feel afraid, however, because the culmination of his tutorship under the *pedanda* would mean that he could see and talk to any of the dead whom he chose to, just as clearly as if they were still living.

He had every right to feel sentimental too, because once he had seen the dead—once he was able to enter that trancelike state that was the necessary vehicle to such difficult explorations—he would become a priest himself, and after that, he would never see the *pedanda* again. The *pedanda* had taught him everything he could. Now it would be Michael's turn to seek out evil and walk among the ghosts of Bali's ancestors.

The *pedanda* had never shown him any fatherly affection, for all that Michael called him *Pak*. On the contrary, he had often been persnickety and brittle-tempered, and he had even given Michael penances for the slightest mistakes. And when Michael's father had died, the *pedanda* had been unsympathetic. "He is dead? He is lucky. And besides, when you are ready, you will meet him again."

All the same, a strong unspoken understanding had grown up between them, an understanding that in many ways was more valuable to Michael than affection. It was partly based on mutual respect, this understanding, and partly on the mystical sensitivity they shared, a faculty that enabled them both to enter the dream worlds of the deities. They had experienced the reality of the gods at first hand through the trancelike state known in its less highly developed form as *sanghyang*, during which a man could walk on fire or stab himself repeatedly with sharp-bladed knives and remain unhurt.

"You say nothing," the *pedanda* told him. "Are you afraid?"

"*Tidak*," Michael said. "No."

The *pedanda* continued to stare at him without expression. "I have told you what to expect. As you enter the world of the dead, you will also be entering the world of the demons. You will encounter the leyaks, the night vampires who are the acolytes of Rangda. You will see for yourself the butas and the kalas, those who breathe disease into the mouths of babies."

"I am not afraid," Michael said. He glanced at the *pedanda* quickly, a sideways look, to see his reaction.

The *pedanda* came closer and leaned over Michael so that the boy could smell the curious dry, woody smell the priest always seemed to exude.

"Very well, you are not afraid of leyaks. But suppose you came face to face with Rangda herself."

"I should call on Barong Keket to protect me."

The *pedanda* cackled. "You will be afraid, I promise you, even if you are not afraid now. It is right to be afraid of Rangda. My son, even I am afraid of Rangda."

Then the *pedanda* left Michael briefly and returned with a large object concealed beneath an ornately embroidered cloth. He set the object in front of Michael and smiled.

"Do you know what this is?"

"It looks like a mask."

"And what else can you tell me about it?"

Michael licked his lips. "It is very *sakti*." He meant that it was magically powerful, so powerful that it had to be covered by a cloth.

"Would you be frightened if I were to show it to you?" asked the priest.

Michael said nothing. The *pedanda* watched him closely, searching for the slightest twitch of nervousness or spiritual hesitation. After a moment, Michael reached forward, grasped the corner of the cloth and drew it off the mask.

As confident and calm as he was, he felt his insides coldly recoil. For the hideous face staring at him was that of Rangda, the Witch Widow, with bulging eyes, flaring nostrils, and fangs so hooked and long that they crossed over each other. Michael's sensitivity to the presence of evil was so heightened now that he felt the malevolence of Rangda like a freezing fire burning into his bones. Even his teeth felt as if they were phosphorescing in their sockets.

"Now what do you feel?" asked the priest. His face was half hidden by shadow.

Michael stared at the mask for a long time. Although it was nothing more than paper and wood and gilded paint, it exuded extraordinary evil. It looked as if it were ready to snap into sudden life and devour them both.

Michael said, "If Barong Keket does not protect me, the spirit of my father will."

The *pedanda* took the embroidered cloth and covered the mask again, although he left it where it was, resting between them.

"You are ready," he said dryly. "We shall close our eyes and meditate, and then we shall begin."

The *pedanda* sat opposite Michael and bowed his head. The fragrant incense billowed between them, sometimes obscuring the priest altogether so that Michael could not be certain that he was still there. The incense evoked in Michael's consciousness the singing at funerals, the trance dances, and all the secret rituals the *pedanda* had taught him since he was twelve years old. There was another aroma in the incense, however: bitter and pungent, like burning coriander leaves.

"You must think of the dead," the *pedanda* told him. "You must think of the spirits who walk through the city. You must think of the presence of all those who have gone before you: the temple priests who once tended this courtyard, the merchants who cried in the streets outside, the *rajas* and the *perbekels*, the children and the proud young women. They are still with us, and now, when you wish to, you may see them. The crowds of the dead!"

Michael looked around. He was in the first stages of trance, breathing evenly as if he were cautiously entering a clear, cold pool of water. There, lining the walls of the inner courtyard, stood carved stone shrines to the deities of life and death, a shrine to Gunung Alung, the volcano, and another to the spirits of Mount Batur. It was in these shrines that the gods were supposed to sit when they visited the

Pura Dalem. Michael had occasionally wondered if the gods ever came here anymore—the temple was so ruined and the *odalan* festivals were no longer held here—but he realized that it would be heretical to display doubts to the *pedanda*.

The shrines to the greatest deities had eleven layered meru roofs, tapering upward into the darkness. Those to lesser gods had only seven roofs, or five. There were no gifts laid in front of any of these shrines as there were in other temples, no fruit or flowers or bullock's heads or chickens. Here there were nothing but dried leaves that had fallen from the overhanging trees and a few scattered poultry bones. There were no longer any temple priests to cater to the comforts of the gods.

The *pedanda* began to recite to Michael the words that would gradually lift him into a deeper state of trance. Michael kept his eyes open at first but then slowly his eyelids drooped and his body relaxed; gradually his conscious perceptions began to drain away and pour across the courtyard floor like oil.

The *pedanda* began to tap one foot on the stones rhythmically and Michael swayed back and forth in the same rhythm, as if anticipating the arrival of celebrating villagers, the way it would have been when the *odalan* festivals were held in the temple. He swayed as if the *kendang* drums were beating, and the *kempli* gong was banging, and the night was suddenly shrill with the jingling of finger cymbals.

"You can walk now among the dead, who are themselves among us. You can see quite clearly the ghosts of those who have gone before. Your eyes are opened both to this world and the next. You have reached the trance of trances, the trance of the dead, the world within worlds."

Michael pressed his hands against his face and began to sway ever faster. The clangor of drumming and cymbal clashing inside his brain was deafening. *Jhanga-jhanga-jhanga-jhanga-jhanga:* the complicated, unwritten rhythms of gamelan music; the whistling melodies of life and death; the rustling of fire without burning, of knives that refused to cut; the swath in the air made by demons who stole children in the dark.

Great blocks of crimson and black came silently thundering down on top of him. His mind began to burst apart like an endless succession of opening flowers, each one richer and more florid than the last.

The *kendang* drums pounded harder and harder; the cymbals shrilled mercilessly; the gongs reverberated until they set up a continuous ringing of almost intolerable sound.

Michael swayed furiously now, his hands pressed hard against his face. The voice of the *pedanda* reached him through the soundless music, repeating over and over, "Sanghyang Widi, guide us; Sanghyang Widi, guide us; Sanghyang Widi, guide us."

It was now—at the very crescendo of his trance—that Michael would usually have stood up to dance, following the steps untaught by priests or parents, or by anybody mortal, yet known by all who can enter into the *sanghyang*.

But tonight he was suddenly, and unexpectedly, met by silence and stillness. He continued to sway for a short time, but then he became motionless as the silence and the stillness persisted and the imaginary music utterly ceased. He took his hands from his face and there was the *pedanda*, watching him; and there was the inner courtyard of the temple, with its dead leaves and its abandoned shrines; and there was the incense smoke, drifting thickly into the darkness.

"What has happened?" he asked. His voice sounded strange to himself, as if he were speaking from beneath a blanket.

The old man raised one skeletal arm and indicated the courtyard. "Can you not understand what has happened?"

Michael frowned and lifted his head. The smell of burned coriander leaves was stronger than ever. Somewhere a whistle blew, loud and long.

The *pedanda* said, "You know already that your one body consists of three bodies: your mortal body, your *stulasarira;* your emotional body, your *suksmasarira;* and your spiritual body, your *antakaransarira*. Well, your *stulasarira* and your *suksmasarira* have fallen into a sleeping trance, not like the wild and frenzied trance of the *sanghyang*, but more like a dream. Your *antakaransarira*, however, has remained awake. Your spirit can perceive everything now, unhindered by physical or emotional considerations. You will not be concerned by the prospect of hurting yourself. You will not be concerned by anger, or love, or resentment. In this state, you will be able to see the dead."

Michael raised his hands and examined them, then looked back at the *pedanda*. "If I am asleep, how can I move?"

"You forget that your *stulasarira* and your *antakaransarira* are inseparable, even after death. That is why we cremate our dead, so that the *antakaransarira* may at last fly free from its ashes. Your spirit wishes to move your mortal body and so it has, just as your mortal body, when it is awake, can move your spirit."

Michael sat silent; the *pedanda* watched him with a patient smile. Although essentially the temple seemed to be the same, now it possessed a curious dreamlike quality, a subdued luminosity, and the clouds above the meru towers appeared to be moving at unnatural speed.

"You have so many questions and yet you cannot ask them," the *pedanda* said.

Michael shook his head. "I feel that the answers will come by themselves."

"Nonetheless, you must try to put into words everything that you fail to understand."

"Can I feel pain in this trance?" Michael asked. "Can I walk on fire, or stab myself with knives?"

"Try for yourself," smiled the *pedanda,* and from the folds of his plain white robes he produced a wavy-bladed kris, the traditional Balinese dagger. Michael could see by the way the blade shone that it had recently been sharpened. He accepted the weapon cautiously, testing the weight of its decorative handle. For a moment, as the *pedanda* handed it to him, their eyes met and there was a strange, secretive look in the old man's expression that Michael could not remember having noticed before; it was almost a look of resignation.

In the *sanghyang* trance, young boys seven or eight years old could stab their chests with these daggers and the blades would not penetrate their skin. But this was not an ordinary *sanghyang* trance. This was a very different kind of trance, if it was a trance at all. The silence in the courtyard was so deep that Michael could almost have believed the *pedanda* had deceived him. He wondered if perhaps in some unknown way he had failed his initiation and let the old priest down. Perhaps the only honorable course of action left to a student who disappointed the *pedanda* was suicide, and perhaps this was what he was being offered now.

Michael hesitated, and as he did so, a scraggly looking jungle cock stalked into the courtyard, lifted its plumed head and stared at him.

The *pedanda* said, "You are afraid? What are you afraid of? Death?"

"I'm not sure," Michael replied uncertainly.

"To be irresolute is a sin."

"I'm afraid but I don't know why. I'm afraid of you."

"Of me?" smiled the priest. He lifted his hands, their long, twisty fingernails gleaming. "You have no need to be afraid of me. You have no need to be afraid of anything, not even of death. Come, let me show you what death is."

Michael glanced down at the kris in his hand. Then he looked back questioningly at the *pedanda*, who shook his head. "Do not strike now. The question has passed. The question will arise again later, never fear, perhaps in a different way."

The priest rose to his feet gracefully. For one moment he stood staring at the mask of Rangda, with its embroidered covering. Then he turned and glided across the courtyard, back through the *paduraksa* gate, across the outer courtyard and into the street. Michael followed him closely, aware of a strange slowness in the way in which his limbs responded, as if he were wading through warm and murky water. The streets seemed to be deserted except for the cigarette ends that glowed in doorways, the murmur of deep, blurry voices and a soft rustling sound that filled the air.

The *pedanda* guided him along to the end of the street. Michael felt as if he were pursuing a figure in a dream. He was conscious for the first time in over a year that he was half-Western, that he was only half-entitled to know the secrets the *pedanda* was revealing to him. Although he had advanced even farther in his spiritual studies than most full-blooded Balinese boys, he always felt that he was holding something back, some small, skeptical part of his spirit that would always be white.

Now the *pedanda* reached a bronze door set into a crumbling stone wall. He opened it and Michael followed him through. To his surprise, he found himself in a small cemetery thickly overgrown with weeds and garish green moss, curtained with creeper that hung from the trees, silent, neglected, its shrines broken and its pathways long choked up, but elegant all the same, in the saddest and most regretful of ways. The high wall surrounding it must have at one time shielded the graveyard from the sight of every building around it, but now the little cemetery was overlooked by three or four office blocks and an illuminated sign that read "Udaya Tours." In the middle distance, a scarlet sign said, "Qantas."

The *pedanda* stood still. "I have never shown you this place before," he said. "This is the graveyard for a hundred and fifty families who died in the *puputan*, slaughtered by the Dutch and by the *rajas*. Families without names, children without parents. They were cremated and so their *antakaransariras* were freed, but they have remained here out of sorrow."

Michael walked slowly between the lines of weed-tangled shrines. The carving on each stone was sinuous and curving in the style of Ida Bagus Njana, depicting demons and dancers and ghosts and scowling warriors. Each shrine represented one dead family.

Then he stood still, uncertain of why the *pedanda* had brought him here. The Qantas sign shone brightly: an uncompromising message that the past was long past and that Bali was now regularly visited by 747s as well as by demons.

When Michael turned back to talk to the *pedanda*, his scalp prickled in shock, for the priest was still standing by the cemetery gate, his hands clasped, his head slightly raised, but right behind Michael a family had gathered in complete silence. A father, a mother, two grown-up daughters and a young son, no more than eight years old. They wore traditional grave clothes and their heads were bound with white scarves. All were staring at him, not moving, and although he could see them quite distinctly, they seemed to have no more reality than the evening air. He stared back at them. He knew without a doubt that they were dead.

Slowly the family turned and walked away between the shrines, fading from sight as they passed the *pedanda*. Then, as he looked around, Michael saw other figures standing equally silent among the creepers: a pale-faced young girl, her black hair fastened with gilded combs; a man who kept his hands clasped over his face; an old woman who kept raising her hand as if she were waving to somebody miles and miles away; children with frightened faces and eye sockets as dark as ink.

The *pedanda* came through the graveyard and stood close to Michael, still smiling. "All these people have been dead for many years. They still remain, however, and they always shall. We refuse to accept the presence of spirits only because we cannot see them except in trances."

"Will they speak?" Michael asked. In spite of the humidity, he felt intensely cold and he was shivering.

"They will speak if they believe you can help them, but they are frightened and suspicious. They feel helpless without their mortal bodies, as if they are invalids."

There was a young girl of twelve or thirteen standing by one of the nearer shrines. She reminded Michael of the girl he had seen sewing at the batik stall. He approached her carefully until he was standing only three feet from her. She stared back at him with wide brown eyes.

"Can you speak?" Michael asked. "My name is Michael. *Nama saya* Michael. *Siapa nama saudara?*"

There was an achingly long silence while the girl kept her eyes on Michael, regarding him with curiosity and suspicion. Something in her expression told him that she had suffered great pain.

"*Jam berapa sekarang?*" she whispered in a voice as faint as a gauze scarf blowing in the evening wind.

"*Malam,*" Michael told her. She had wanted to know

what time of day it was and he had explained that it was night.

Again he asked her name. *"Siapa nama saudara?"*

But gradually she began to move away from him as if she were being blown by an unfelt breeze. Other families began to move away too, to vanish behind the shrines. One young man remained, however, looking at Michael as if he recognized him. He was thin and frighteningly pale but quite handsome, with the thin-featured appearance of a man from the north, from Bukit Jambul.

"He envies you," the *pedanda* said, standing close by Michael's shoulder. "The dead always long to have their mortal bodies restored to them."

"They seem to be frightened," Michael remarked.

The priest pressed his left hand against his deaf left ear and listened keenly with his right. "They are. There must be leyaks close by. Leyaks prey on the dead as well as on the living. They capture their *antakaransariras* and drag them back to Rangda for torturing."

"Even the dead can be tortured?"

"Rangda is the Queen of the Dead. She can put them through far more terrible agonies than they have ever suffered during their lifetimes."

Michael turned and looked around the graveyard. He heard a rustling sound but it was only the creeper trailing against the shrines. Nonetheless, the *pedanda* clasped his wrist with fingers as bony as a hawk's and drew him back toward the graveyard gates.

"It is not wise to tempt the leyaks, especially since we are both in a death trance. Come, let us return to the temple."

They left the graveyard and stepped out into Jalan Mahabharata. The street was completely deserted, although some of the upstairs windows were lighted and there was the bonelike clacking of mah-jongg tiles, and laughter. The *pedanda* glanced around and then took Michael's sleeve. "Be quick. If the leyaks catch us in the open, they will kill us."

They began to walk along the street as fast as they could without alerting hostile eyes. They passed two or three tourists and a fruit seller, all of whom seemed to be moving on a different time plane, moving so slowly that Michael could have snatched the durian fruit from the market woman's upraised hand without her realizing who had taken it. One of the tourists turned and frowned as if sensing their passing, but before he could collect his wits, they were gone.

They were no more than three hundred yards from the temple gates when the *pedanda* said, ''There. On the other side of the street.''

Michael glanced sideways and caught sight of a gray-faced man in a gray suit, with eyes that shone carnivorously orange. He looked like a zombie out of a horror movie, but he walked swiftly and athletically, keeping pace with them on the opposite sidewalk; as he reached the small side street called Jalan Suling, the Street of Flutes, he was joined by another gray-faced man. Their cheeks could have been smeared with human ashes; their eyes could have been glowing lamps from the night market.

''Faster,'' the *pedanda* insisted. Now they made no pretense of walking but ran toward the gates of the Puri Dalem as fast as they could. The priest held up his robes, and his sandals slapped on the bricks. Michael could have run much faster but he did not want to leave the old man behind. There were three or four leyaks following them now, and Michael glimpsed their glistening teeth.

They had almost reached the temple gates when three leyaks appeared in front of them. They were larger than Michael had ever imagined and their faces were like funeral masks. The *pedanda* gasped, ''Michael, the gates! Open the gates!''

Michael tried to dodge around the leyaks and reach the gates. One of the creatures snatched at his arm with a hand that felt like a steel claw. The nails dug into his skin but somehow he managed to twist away and cling to the heavy ring handle that would open up the temple. The leyak snatched at him again, viciously scratching his legs, but then Michael heaved the gate inward and tumbled into the temple's outer courtyard.

The *pedanda* was not so lucky. The leyaks had jumped on him now; one of them had seized his left forearm in his jaws and was trying to pry the flesh from the bone. The other leyaks were ripping at his robes with their claws and already the simple white cotton was splashed with blood.

Michael screamed, "No! No! Let him go!" but the leyaks snarled and bit at the old *pedanda* like wild dogs, their eyes flaring orange. Blood flew everywhere in a shower of hot droplets. The noise was horrendous: snarling and screeching and tearing. Michael heard muscles shred, sinews snap, bones break like dry branches. For a moment the *pedanda* was completely buried under the gray, hulking leyaks and Michael thought he would never see the old priest again.

But then, like a drowning man reaching for air, the *pedanda* extended one hand toward the temple. Michael desperately tried to grasp it, missed the first time but then managed to seize the *pedanda*'s wrist.

"Barong Keket!" he shouted, although it was more of a war cry than an appeal to the sovereign of the forests, the archenemy of Rangda. "Barong Keket!"

At the sound of the deity's name, the snarling leyaks raised their heads and glared at Michael with burning eyes. And as they raised their heads, Michael tugged at the *pedanda*'s arm and managed to drag the old man into the safety of the temple courtyard. There were screams of rage and frustration from the leyaks, but none of them could walk on sacred ground. Their nails grated against the bronze doorway and they howled like wolves at bay, but they could come no further. Michael slammed the door and stood with his back to it, panting. The *pedanda* lay on the courtyard floor, his robes crimson with blood, gasping and shivering.

"We must leave this trance if we wish to survive," he gasped. "Quickly, Michael. Take me back to the inner courtyard."

Michael helped the priest to his feet. He could feel the sticky wetness of blood, the sliminess of torn muscle. The *pedanda* felt no pain because he was still deeply entranced, but there was no doubt that he was close to death. If Michael could not bring him out of the trance and take him to the hospital, the old priest would die within an hour. Breathing as deeply and as calmly as he could, Michael dragged the *pedanda* through the inner gate, the *paduraksa*, and back to the silken mats. The mask of Rangda was still there, covered by its cloth; the incense still smoked.

"You must recite . . . the *sanghyang* . . ." whispered the *pedanda*. "You are a priest now . . . your word has all the influence of mine."

Michael helped the priest to sit on his mat. The old man had once told him that these mats were the last remnants of the robes of the monkey general Hanuman. They had been brilliant turquoise-green once; now they were brown and faded with damp.

"O Sanghyang Widi, we ask your indulgence to leave this realm," intoned Michael, trying to remember the words the *pedanda* had taught him. "We ask to return to our mortal selves, three in one joined together, *suksmasarira* and *stulasarira* and *antakaransarira*. O Sanghyang Widi, guide us."

There was silence in the temple. The incense smoke drifted and turned ceaselessly. Michael repeated the incantation and then added the special sacred blessing: "Fragrant is the smoke of incense, the smoke that coils and coils upward, toward the home of the three divine ones."

Then he closed his eyes, praying for the trance to end. But when he opened his eyes, he knew that he was still inside the world within worlds, that the leyaks were still scratching furiously against the doors of the temple and that he could still see the dead if they were to walk here.

The *pedanda* looked across at Michael with bloodshot eyes. His face was the color of parchment. "Something is wrong," he whispered. "There is great magic here, great evil."

Michael pressed his hands together intently and prayed for Sanghyang Widi to guide them out of their death trance and back to the mortal world.

The *pedanda* whispered, "It won't work, it isn't working. Something is wrong." The little priest's blood was running across the stones of the inner courtyard, following the crevices between them like an Oriental puzzle.

Michael leaned forward intently. "I am a priest now? You're sure of that?"

"You are a priest now."

"Then why won't my words take us back?"

"Because there is a greater influence here than yours, some influence that is preventing you from taking us back."

Michael looked around at the temple's neglected shrines, at the rustling leaves on the courtyard floor. The shrines were silent and dark, their *meru* roofs curved against the night sky. There was no malevolence in the shrines; they were no longer visited by the spirits for whom they had been built.

Then he turned to the mask of Rangda, covered by its cloth. He looked up at the *pedanda* and said, "The mask. Do you think it is the mask?"

"The mask is very *sakti*," the *pedanda* whispered. "But it should not prevent us from going back. Not unless . . ."

"Not unless what, *Pak*?"

"Not unless your spiritual abilities are posing a threat to Rangda. Not unless she believes that you may someday do her harm. In which case, she will not let us go."

Michael hesitated for a moment. Then he reached forward and grasped the edge of the cloth that covered the face of Rangda. "It's only a mask," he said. "You said that yourself when you took me to my first Barong play. It is evil and it gives off evil feelings, but it is only a mask."

The *pedanda* said, "No, Michael, do not remove the cloth."

"It is Rangda, the Witch Widow, nobody else! The contemptible Rangda!"

He was about to whip the cloth away when the *pedanda* lurched forward and snatched it out of his hand. Michael, caught off balance, fell back. But the cloth was dragged off the top of the mask all the same, just as the *pedanda* dropped before it.

Michael gasped. The hideous mask was alive. Its eyes swiveled and its ferocious teeth snapped; it let out a coarse roar of fury that made Michael's hair prickle with fear. The *pedanda* screamed: it was the first time Michael had ever heard a grown man scream. And then the mask stretched

open its painted jaws and tore off the priest's head, expos-
ing for one terrible, naked second the bloody tube of his
trachea.

Michael turned and ran. He burst through the *paduraksa*
gate, sped across the outer courtyard and back to the bronze
doorway where the leyaks were waiting. His lungs shrieked
for air; his mind was bursting with terror. But he dragged
back the gate and ran out into the street, and there were no
leyaks there now, only gas lamps and fruit stalls and boys
on mopeds. And then he was running more slowly, and then
he was walking, and as he reached the corner by the night
market, he realized that he was out of the death trance and
that, suddenly, it was all over.

He walked for a long time beside the river, where the
market lights were reflected. He passed fortune-telling stands,
where mynah birds would pick out magic sticks to predict a
customer's future. He passed *warong* stands, where sweating men were stirring up *nasi goreng*, rice with chili and
beef slices. And in his mind's eye the mask of Rangda still
swiveled her eyes and roared and bit at the high priest's
head, and still the leyaks followed him, their eyes glowing.

Tears ran down Michael's cheeks. He called for his father, but of course his father did not answer. Michael was a
priest now, but what did that mean? What was he supposed
to do? His only guide and teacher had been supernaturally
savaged to death by Rangda; and Rangda's acolytes would
probably pursue him day and night to take their revenge on
him too.

He prayed as he walked, but his prayers sounded futile in
his mind. They were drowned by rock 'n' roll and the
blurting of mopeds. It was only when he reached the corner
of Jalan Gajahmada that he realized he had left his precious
bicycle behind.

ONE

Memphis, Tennessee, 1984

"Well, I believe that Elvis is still alive, that's my opinion. I believe that Elvis was sick right up to here with all those fans; sick right up to here of havin' no privacy; sick right up to here of all those middle-aged broads with the upswept eyeglasses shriekin' and droolin' and high-flyin' they step-ins at him; sick right up to here of belongin' to the public instead of his own self and bein' constantly razzed for growin' himself a good-sized belly when tell me what man of forty-two don't, it's a man's right. So he fakes his death, you got me? and sneaks out of Graceland in the back of a laundry truck or whatever."

The sweat-crowned cab driver turned around in his seat and regarded Randolph at considerable length, one hairy wrist dangling on top of the steering wheel. "You just remember where you heard it, my friend, when this white-bearded old man rolls back into Memphis one day, fat and happy, and says, 'You all recollect who I am? My name's Elvis the Pelvis Presley, and while you been showerin' my tomb with tears, I been fishin' and drinkin' and havin' an excellent time and thinkin' what suckers you all are."

Randolph pointed toward the road ahead with a flat-handed chopping gesture. "Do you mind keeping your eyes on the road? Elvis may have cheated death but you and I may not be quite so lucky."

The cab driver turned back just in time to swerve his cab

22

away from a huge tractor trailer that had suddenly decided to change lanes without making a signal. As the cabbie swerved, he was given a peremptory two-tone blast on the horn from a Lincoln limousine crowded with Baptist priests.

"Forgive me, forgive me," the cab driver begged the Lincoln's occupants sarcastically as the limousine swept by. "I done seen the wrongness of my ways. Or at least I done seen the ass end of that truck before we got totaled." He turned around to Randolph again and said comfortably, "That's a fair amount of potential forgiveness in one vehicle, wouldn't you say? But what do you think of the way I missed that truck? That's sixth sense, that is. Kind of a built-in alarm system. Not everybody has that, sixth sense."

"I'd honestly prefer it if you'd use your first sense and look where the hell you're going," Randolph told him testily.

"All right, my friend, no need to get sore," the driver replied. He turned around again, his sweaty shirt skidding on the textured vinyl seat, and switched on the radio. It was Anne Murray, singing "You Needed Me." He turned the volume up, surmising correctly that Randolph would find it irritating.

Randolph was a heavily built man, tall and big boned, and in accord with his appearance, he was usually placid. He made an ideal president of Clare Cottonseed Products, Incorporated, a business in which Southern tempers invariably ran hot to high. If he hadn't inherited the presidency from his father, the board would probably have chosen him anyway. He never raised his voice above an educated mumble. He played golf, and fished, and loved his family. He had gray hair and reminded his junior secretaries of Fred MacMurray.

He enjoyed being nice. He enjoyed settling arguments and making even the least of his two thousand employees feel wanted. His nickname at every one of Clare Cottonseed's seven processing plants was "Handy Randy." He usually smelled slightly of Benson & Hedges pipe tobacco. He had a degree in law, two daughters, one son, and a wife called Marmie, whom he adored.

But today he was more than irritated. He was upset, more

than upset. His phone had rung at 4:30 that morning and he had been called back from his vacation cabin on Lac aux Ecorces in the Laurentide forests of Quebec, where only two days earlier he and his family had started their three-week summer vacation. It was their first family vacation in three years and Randolph's only time off in a year and a half. But late yesterday evening fire had broken out at his No.2 cottonseed-processing plant out at Raleigh, in the northeast suburbs of Memphis. One process worker had been incinerated. Two other men, including the plant's deputy manager, had been asphyxiated by fumes. And the damage to the factory itself had so far been estimated at over two million dollars.

It would have been unthinkable for the company president to remain on vacation in Canada, fishing and swimming and buzzing his seaplane around the lakes, no matter how much he deserved it.

To complete Randolph's irritation, his company limousine had failed to show up at the Memphis airport. He had tried calling the office from an airport pay phone smelling of disinfectant, but it was 7:45 P.M., and there was no response. Eventually—hot, tired and disheveled—he had hailed himself a cab and asked to be driven to Front Street.

Now they drove west along Adams Avenue. The radio was playing the "59th Street Bridge Song." Randolph hated it. He sat back in his seat, drumming his fingertips against his Samsonite briefcase. "Slow down, you move too fast . . . got to make the morning last. . . ." The business district was illuminated by that hazy acacia-honey glow special to Memphis on summer evenings. The Wolf and the Mississippi rivers, which join at Memphis, were turning to liquid ore. The twin arches of the Hernando de Soto Bridge glittered brightly, as if offering a pathway to a promised land instead of to nowhere but West Memphis.

The day's humidity began to ease and surreptitious drafts wavered around the corners of office buildings. The breeze that came in through the open taxi window smelled of flowers and sweat, and that unmistakable coolness of river.

They drove along Front Street, known to the citizens of

Memphis as Cotton Row. Randolph said, "Here. This is the one."

"Clare Cottonseed?" the driver frowned. He wiped the sweat from his furrowed forehead with the back of his hand.

"That's me," said Randolph.

"You mean . . . *you're* Clare Cottonseed?"

"Handy Randy Clare in person," Randolph smiled.

The cab driver reached behind with one meaty arm and opened the door for him. "Maybe I ought to apologize," he said.

"Why?"

"Well, for sounding off, for driving like an idiot."

Randolph gave him twenty-five dollars in new bills and waved away the change. "It's hot," he said. "We're all acting like idiots."

The cab driver counted the money and said, "Thanks." Then, "Didn't one of your factories burn last night? Out at Raleigh?"

"That's right."

"Is that why you're here?"

"That's right," Randolph said again. "I'm supposed to be fishing in Canada."

The driver paused for a moment, wiped his forehead again and sniffed. "You think it was deliberate?"

"Do I think what was deliberate?"

"The fire. Do you think somebody torched that factory?"

Randolph stayed where he was, half in and half out of the taxi. "What did you say that for?"

"I don't know. It's just that some of the people I pick up, they work for other cottonseed companies, like Grayson's, or Towery's, and none of them seem to think that Clare's going to be staying in business too long."

"Clare is the number-two cottonseed processor after Brooks. Saying that Clare is going out of business is like saying that the Ford Motor Company is going out of business."

"Sure, but you know how things are."

"I'm not so sure I do," Randolph replied cautiously, although he had a pretty fair idea of what the man was trying to suggest. It was no secret in Memphis that Clare Cottonseed was a political and economic maverick. All the other big cottonseed processors in the area were members of a price-fixing cartel that called itself the Cottonseed Association but which Randolph unflatteringly referred to as the Margarine Mafia. Randolph's father, Ned Clare, had rarely upset the Association, even though he had always insisted on remaining independent. Ned Clare had kept his salad-oil and cattle-cake prices well up in line with the Association's, but when Randolph had taken over the company, he had wanted to expand and economize and he had introduced a policy of keeping his prices as low as possible. The members of the Association—especially Brooks—had made their displeasure quite clear. So far, however, their hostility had been expressed politically rather than violently, but Randolph had recently begun to wonder when political push might escalate into violent shove.

"Listen," the cab driver told him, "I believe in what you're doin', right? I believe in free enterprise, free trade. Every man for himself. That's the American Way as far as I'm concerned. I mean . . . I'm not sayin' it's a fact that somebody set light to your factory. Maybe I'm talkin' out of my ass. But, well, given the circumstances, it ain't totally beyond the bounds of possibility, is it?"

"I don't think I ought to comment on that," Randolph replied.

The driver said, "How would you like it if I kept my ears open? I'm always drivin' them other cottonseed people around. Junior veeps, mostly. They're the ones who talk a lot."

Randolph considered the offer for a moment and then said, "All right, you've got it, you're on." He reached into his pocket for his money clip and handed the man fifty dollars. The driver snapped the bill between his fingers and said, "Grant, my favorite president. After Franklin, of course." When Randolph handed him another fifty, he grinned and said, "Basic math. Two Grants equal one Franklin." He reached across to the window, shook Randolph's hand and handed him a business card. "See there? My name's Stanley Vergo. No relation to the barbecued-ribs Vergo. It's an honor to do business with you. You'll be hearin' from me just as soon as I got somethin' to tell you."

"Okay, Stanley," Randolph said patiently.

Stanley swung out into the evening traffic while Randolph, clutching his Vuitton overnight case, mounted the polished marble steps of the Clare Cottonseed building. Most of the cartel companies had moved into high-rise blocks but Randolph had preferred to stay in the ten-story, brick-faced building that his grandfather had erected in 1910. He liked the heavy, banklike style of the place, with its carved stone gargoyles and decorative cornices. He liked the mahogany and the marble and the dim, amber Tiffany lamps. They reminded him of deep-rooted Southern prosperity, of scrupulous manners and unscrupulous wheeler-dealing. Besides, it took only three minutes to get from his tenth-story office to the doors of the Cotton Exchange and only another three to reach Erika's German restaurant on South Second Street.

He unlocked the huge front door and the night security guard came to greet him.

"You should have rung the bell, Mr. Clare. I'd of let you in."

"That's all right, Marshall. Is Mr. Sleaman upstairs?"

"He came back just about twenty minutes ago, sir. I want to say that I'm awfully sorry about the fire, sir. I knew Mr. Douglas real well."

Randolph crossed the echoing marble-clad lobby and pressed the button to summon the old-fashioned, wrought-iron elevator. It clanked its way slowly upward until it reached the tenth floor, where Randolph got out and walked quickly along to the end of the corridor. Two massive oak doors led into his office, which was almost fifty feet square, with windows facing north toward the Cotton Exchange and west toward the gleaming confluence of the Mississippi and the Wolf.

The sky was already the color of blueberry jelly, and two or three lighted riverboats drew herringbone patterns across the surface of the Mississippi.

Randolph dropped his overnight case on the big hide-covered Chesterfield beside his desk and stripped off his coat. His Tiffany desk lamp was already alight and his secretary, Wanda, had laid out a file for him on Raleigh's production statistics together with Telex reports on the severity of the damage and an interim report on the fire by Neil Sleaman, his executive vice-president in charge of the No.2 processing plant.

He quickly leafed through the reports and then pressed his intercom to see if Wanda was there.

"Mr. Clare, you're back!" she exclaimed.

"Would you come in, please?" Randolph asked.

Wanda bustled through the door with her shorthand pad. She was a dark-haired, dark-eyed girl, very pretty in a way that reminded Randolph of Priscilla Presley, and with an exceptional figure. Randolph had not hired her for her looks, however. She was bright and she was creative, and she was also the daughter of one of the most productive cotton farmers in Mississippi, Colonel Henry Burford of Burford's Delight Plantation. Randolph was still buying cottonseed from Colonel Burford at 1980 prices: one hundred twenty-nine dollars the ton.

"What happened to the limo?" Randolph wanted to know.

"Herbert called in about ten minutes ago. He said he'd had some kind of a brake failure out on Lamar. The way he told it, he was lucky he didn't get himself killed. He called the airport as soon as the tow truck arrived and he had them try to page you, but you must have left by then."

"Well, as it happened, I hailed myself a cab," Randolph said. "But is Herbert okay?"

"He says so. A little shaken up, I guess. The car's okay too, apart from a dented fender."

"You can replace a dented fender. You could never replace Herbert."

"Well, that's for sure," said Wanda. "Would you care for a drink? Or some coffee maybe?"

"Canadian Club on the rocks, plenty of soda. And would you ask Mr. Sleaman to come on up?"

Wanda hesitated and then said, "We're all real upset

about the accident, Mr. Clare. Those people out at Raleigh, Mr. Douglas and all, they were like family.''

"Yes," Randolph said, "they were." He ran his hand tiredly through his hair. "I called their wives this morning from Quebec. I'll be going around to see them in the morning. Perhaps you can arrange for some flowers."

He paused for a moment and then said, "It was very tragic," even though "tragic" seemed hopelessly inadequate.

Wanda went across to the rosewood side table to pour Randolph a drink in a heavy crystal glass. Randolph sat behind his desk and rocked back and forth in the high-backed leather chair, sipping at his whiskey and rereading Neil Sleaman's reports. On the wall behind the side table hung a large oil painting of Randolph's father, a magnificently white-maned man in a cream-linen suit with a huge flowering orchid in his lapel. Randolph was not so sentimental that he ever stood in front of his father's portrait when he was in trouble and asked him what he should do. That was strictly for old Dick Powell movies. But all the same, the old man's deeply engraved face gave him reassurance that sometimes things had gone just as badly in the past and that from time to time, they would probably go just as badly in the future. Tragedies have to be faced, wounds have to be bound.

Neil Sleaman came into the office without knocking, one hand extended in sympathetic greeting for the whole time it took him to cross the thirty feet of pale-gold carpet between the door and Randolph's desk. When the handshake finally arrived, it was dry and far too forceful, as if Neil had wiped his sweating palm on the seat of his pants before he stepped in and psyched himself up to be earnest and direct.

Neil was thin, black-haired and heavily tanned from his recent vacation in Bermuda; a sharp-faced young man who fancied himself a snappy dresser, and by Memphis standards he was. Pale locknit suits, high-collared shirts and the inescapable bolus necktie. Randolph had employed him from Chickasaw Cotton, one of the smaller processors. Personally he did not care for the way that Neil tried too hard, but Neil was aggressive and efficient and he could get things done.

"I don't know what to say to you," Neil told Randolph, shaking his head. "I simply don't know what to say to you."

Randolph set down his drink. "Medicinal," he said. "Do you want one?"

Neil shook his head even more vigorously.

"Who's out at Raleigh now?" Randolph asked.

"Tim Shelby's in charge just for the moment. He's kept about twenty men on the night shift just to keep things running, but he's had to send most of the rest of them home. We can't function until we get the boilers repaired."

"How long is that going to take?"

"Week, week and a half."

"Make it a week."

"Well, we're doing our darndest, sir, believe me."

"You estimate the final damage at over three million and production losses at over one million, correct?"

"That kind of depends on whether we lose the Sun-Taste margarine contract as a consequence. We were on full capacity, just keeping up with the delivery schedule. By the end of the week, we'll be eight hundred fifty tons behind, and I don't see any chance of catching up."

Randolph thought for a long time, tapping the rim of his glass against his teeth. Sun-Taste was America's fastest-expanding new margarine company and the Clare Cottonseed board had been jubilant when the firm had landed the contract late last year to supply all of Sun-Taste's hydrogenated oil. To Randolph personally, it had been a vindication of his cost-cutting policies, and to the company as a whole, it had represented a solid new foundation for expansion and profit. There had been talk of "substantial" pay hikes, and the junior executives' offices had suddenly been discreetly littered with Cadillac brochures.

"Have you talked to anyone at Sun-Taste?" Randolph asked.

"They called this afternoon. Obviously they wanted to

know if we were going to have any difficulties in delivering the full quota.''

''And of course you told them there would be no difficulties at all.''

''Of course.''

''Have you tried shopping around to see if we can make up the difference by buying from somebody else?''

Neil shook his head again. ''Whoever we go to, sir, is bound to charge us a pretty hefty premium, quite apart from the fact that their prices are higher than ours to begin with. I thought I'd better wait and discuss it with you.''

Randolph finished his drink, rattled the ice cubes around for a moment and then abruptly stood up. ''Let's go take a look at that factory,'' he said. ''Do you have your car here?''

They went down in the elevator to the basement parking level. Neil adjusted his necktie in the elevator mirror and slicked back his hair. He never once took his eyes off himself, even when he was talking.

''I was on the point of falling asleep when they called me this morning,'' he said, tilting his chin slightly to improve his three-quarter profile. ''I took out that girl who works behind the salad bar at the Pirate's Cove.''

''I'm not sure I know her,'' Randolph replied. He hated stories of sexual conquest.

''You must have seen her. Very long blonde hair, all the way down to her fanny. Terrific body. And do you know what her name is? Can you guess what her name is?''

''I have no idea, really,'' Randolph said. He tried to be charitable and put down Neil's chattering to nervousness. All the same, three men had died and the short-term future of the company was at serious risk; he didn't honestly want to discuss Neil's latest bed partner, however devastating she was.

''Her name is Jeff, can you believe that? A girl who looks like that, called Jeff?''

''Well, I wouldn't go out with her if I were you,'' Randolph said. ''Not with a girl with a name like that.''

''Oh, really?'' frowned Neil. ''I thought it was pretty

cute. Her mother called her Jeff because she always wanted a boy.''

As the elevator arrived at the basement, Randolph said, ''There were two famous comic-book characters, one of whom was called Jeff. You wouldn't want to be called what the other one was called, would you? Because that's what would happen if you dated her.''

Neil did not quite know how to take that remark. He followed Randolph awkwardly out of the elevator and then hurried to catch up so he could show him the way to his car. ''It's right over there, the silver MK-Seven.''

Night had fallen out on Cotton Row as Neil's car reared out of the basement rampway and into the street, but Memphis glittered with life. They drove past Beale Street, where W.C. Handy had made the blues famous, now renovated and brightly alive. They drove as far as Union Street and then headed east, past Overton Square, and took Interstate 40 toward Raleigh.

''I'm sorry,'' Neil said. ''I shouldn't have said anything about Jeff. That was bad taste.''

''Forget it,'' Randolph told him, staring out at the Tennessee night and wondering how Marmie was coping. The boys would take care of her, he was pretty sure of that. John was fifteen now and Mark was eleven. And even though Issa was always arguing with her mother now that she was thirteen and on the very edge of womanhood, he knew that she was kind enough and courteous enough to make sure that the remaining days of their vacation would go well. He ached to be back in Canada, beside Marmie, but he knew where his responsibilities lay.

Neil said, ''The fire department won't commit itself.''

''What about the police?''

''Same story. There was an explosion in the wintering plant but no particular reason to suspect that it was caused deliberately.''

''No particular reason to suspect that it wasn't either.''

Neil glanced at him, his sharp profile illuminated green by the lights on the dash. ''You don't really think that somebody tried to bomb us out of business?''

Randolph grasped his knee and made a face. "Don't ask me. That just happened to be the considered opinion of the cab driver who brought me from the airport."

"The cab driver?" Neil laughed. "What would he know?"

"I don't know. Cab drivers listen and learn, don't they?"

"And this particular cab driver thought that this fire was started on purpose?" asked Neil. The diamond ring on his right pinkie suddenly sparkled as he turned the wheel.

"Well, who knows? In any case, he promised to keep his ears open in case he heard any gossip from any of his fares. Apparently he picks up Brooks executives quite regularly."

"And you overtipped him for that favor?"

"I guess you could say that. A hundred bucks."

"A hundred bucks? What's the guy's name? We ought to employ him in our accounts department."

Randolph shrugged. "I don't know. Stanley somebody. Wait a minute . . . he said no relation to the barbecued-ribs restaurant."

"Vergo," said Neil smartly.

"That's right. Stanley Vergo. And what a philosopher. His pet theory seems to be that Elvis never died, that he was only pretending in order to avoid his fans."

"I've heard that theory before," Neil said. "Some people have the same theory about Adolf Hitler."

They arrived at the processing plant. The buildings and the surrounding storage tanks covered over eighty-eight acres that were surrounded by miles of chain-link fence. The driveway was landscaped with mature magnolias blossoming like soft curds of cream, and the offices were set in a picturesque Victorian mansion with a white-pillared portico and fan-shaped skylights. But behind the stately facade there was one of the most modern and functional cottonseed-processing factories in the whole of the South, with a highly advanced solvent-extraction facility for extracting the crude oil out of the seeds, and a special research department for exploring ways in which the seed hulls that were left over could be converted into lacquers and resins and other profitable products.

The parking lot was still crowded with rescue vehicles

and demolition trucks. Randolph said nothing as they approached but Neil remarked, "It was pretty bad. I tried to tell you on the phone, but I think you'd better be ready for a shock."

They drew up outside. The plant manager, Tim Shelby, was there in a crumpled cotton suit, looking drawn and tired and sweaty. He came over, opened Randolph's door and shook his hand.

"I'm sorry about the vacation," he said. Randolph dismissed his condolences with a wave of the hand.

"I'm sorry you lost Bill Douglas."

They were joined by the technical manager and the wintering-plant supervisor, and then they walked in silence around the side of the Victorian offices until they reached the factory itself. Randolph had dramatically expanded the No.2 plant over the past three years and the wintering plant was shiny and gleaming and modern, with chilling equipment that looked as if it were part of a spaceship.

At least it had looked like that, before the fire. Now, under a battery of arc lights, there was nothing but a cavernous ruin of twisted girders, tangled wires, pipes distorted beyond recognition and scorched stainless-steel vats. Neil Sleaman had been right: it was far worse than he had been able to describe over the telephone, and Randolph stepped into the ruins with a profound sense of shock. As he looked around, he felt as if he were standing in the ruins of a bombed-out city. There was a sharp stench of smoke as well as that distinctly nutty odor of burned cottonseed oil.

"The man who was burned?" Randolph asked.

"He was standing right over there by the refrigeration controls, according to his buddies," Tim Shelby said. "There was a terrific explosion. The wintering tank burst apart and three hundred gallons of purified oil came bursting out and caught fire. He didn't stand a chance. They saw him struggling, they said, but he was just like a burning scarecrow."

"How about the others?"

"They were trapped in the corridor outside. They weren't burned but the door wouldn't open because it was buckled, and nobody could get in to save them because the fire was so fierce.''

Randolph bent down and picked up a workman's safety helmet. It was blackened and bubbled but he could still make out the name "Clare" on the front of it. He set it down again and said, "Goddam it." He rarely profaned but there was no other way to describe how he felt now.

"Have the police been here?" he asked after a while.

"They took a look. Chief Moyne came up in person."

"What did he say?"

Tim Shelby wiped the sweat from his face. "He commiserated."

Randolph nodded. "That sounds like Chief Moyne. Did his forensic people find anything?"

"If they did, they didn't tell us. They took away one or two pieces of piping and part of the tank casing, but that's all."

"Well, I'll talk to Chief Moyne in the morning," Randolph said.

He was just about to leave the ruins when a small group of five or six men appeared and stood outside the shattered factory, inspecting it with obvious interest. Randolph recognized them at once. Nobody could mistake the bulky, three-hundred-pound figure in the flapping white double-breasted suit and the wide-brimmed cotton-plantation hat. It was Orbus Greene, president of Brooks Cottonseed and chairman of the Cottonseed Association. Orbus had been a mayor of Memphis in the days before urban renewal, and plenty of local politicians still privately held the opinion that Memphis would not have needed half so much urban renewal had it not been for him and his friends.

The men who accompanied him were his minders: men who opened doors for him and reorganized restaurant tables so he could squeeze into his seat. They had the look of dressed-up yokels: gold rings, gold teeth, greasy kids' stuff on their hair.

Randolph picked his way out of the ruins. Orbus was standing so that his swollen, sallow face was half hidden by the brim of his hat.

"It pains me to see this, Randolph," he said. His voice was as high and as clear as a young boy's. Somebody had once told Randolph that Orbus could sing soprano solos from Verdi's operas capable of bringing tears to your eyes provided you were not required to look at him while he sang.

"Still," Orbus continued, "there's always insurance, isn't there? Insurance is better than ointment."

"I lost three good men here, Orbus," Randolph retorted. "Neither insurance nor ointment will bring any of them back. Now, if you'll forgive me, I have work to do."

Orbus thrust his pig's-trotter hands into his sagging coat pockets and raised his head so he was squinting at Randolph from underneath the brim of his hat, one-eyed.

"You're not the man your daddy was, you know," he remarked provocatively.

"I know that," Randolph replied equably.

"Your daddy was always an independent kind of man. Free-thinking, free-spirited. But he respected the cottonseed business, and he respected the people who make their living at it."

"I hope this isn't yet another invitation to join the Cottonseed Association," Randolph told him. "Believe me, I have enough clubs to go to. Useful, interesting clubs, where I do useful, interesting things, like playing squash. I have no interest at all in spending my evenings in smoke-filled rooms manipulating people and prices."

"Well, you sure paint a lurid picture of us," smiled Orbus. "Maybe you should remember the kidney machines the Cottonseed Association bought last year for the Medical Center and the vacations we gave to those crippled kids."

"I'm sure you didn't forget to enter those charitable donations on your tax returns," Randolph said. "Now, please, I just came back from Canada and I'm very pushed for time."

"You just wait up one minute," said Orbus. "What you've been doing these past three years, playing the market, selling *what* you choose to *whom* you choose at whatever *price* you choose, well, that was understandable to begin with.

Your daddy had been letting Clare Cottonseed stagnate, hadn't he? for quite a long spell. Me and my fellow members of the Association, we were prepared to some extent to let you re-energize your business, reinvest, build it up again to what it was. That's why—even though we expressed our disapproval—we didn't lean on you too hard. If Clare flourished, we thought it would be good for all of us."

Orbus licked his lips and then, as slowly and menacingly as a waking lizard, opened his other eye.

"Point is *now*," he said, "that you've gone way beyond re-energizing, way beyond rebuilding. Point is *now* that you're undercutting the rest of us on major contracts and that you've built up the processing capacity to handle them, the last straw that broke the camel's back being Sun-Taste."

Neil Sleaman broke in. "You listen here, Mr. Greene. Clare Cottonseed has every legal right to sell cottonseed oil to whomever it likes and at whatever price it likes. So kindly butt out. Mr. Clare has urgent business to attend to."

Randolph raised his hand. "Hold on a moment, Neil. Don't let Orbus get under your skin. I want to hear what he's got to say."

Orbus smiled fatly. His minders smiled too, in vacant imitation of their boss's smugness. Orbus said, "You're going to be pushed to the limit to meet your contractual obligations to Sun-Taste after this fire, aren't you? Don't deny it. Well, just let me tell you this: no member of the Cottonseed Association is going to help you out. You won't even get one single cupful of oil out of any of us, not at any price. You wanted to stand on your own. You were prepared to steal our profits from under our noses. Now you're going to have to learn what standing on your own really means."

Randolph laid his hand on Orbus's shoulder. Orbus did not like to be touched; his body chafed him enough as it was, and one of his minders stepped forward warningly. But Orbus, with an odd kind of whinny, instructed the man to stay back and he tolerated Randolph's hand with his eyes closed and his teeth clenched.

"Orbus," Randolph said, "I've *always* understood what standing on my own means. My father made me stand on my own from the day I could first stand up. There's only one thing I'm going to say to you in reply, and that is if any more of my factories happen to meet with explosions or fires or unprecedented accidents, that's when I'm going to stop believing that they *are* accidents and I'm going to come looking for the person or persons who caused them."

Orbus kept smiling in spite of the hand on his shoulder. "You know something, Randolph?" he said. "You would have made a fine cowboy actor. *High Noon in Memphis*, how about that? And who knows, you might even have wound up President."

"Get off my land, Orbus," Randolph told him quietly and firmly.

"I'm not the kind to outstay my welcome," Orbus replied and then turned to his minders and uttered another one of his whinnies. This one evidently meant "Let's go."

Randolph and Neil stood watching them walk back to Orbus's black limousine, OGRE 1, where one of the men opened the specially widened passenger door while the others heaved Orbus onto the backseat. The suspension dipped and bucked.

"What do you think?" Randolph asked as the limousine disappeared down the magnolia-strewn driveway.

Neil said, "He wasn't responsible for this. Leastways I don't think so. Even Orbus Greene wouldn't have the nerve to visit the scene of the crime so soon after it happened."

"Don't underestimate his capacity to gloat," Randolph remarked. "Orbus is one of the world's great gloaters. I think he's glad it happened even if he didn't actually set it."

"Maybe we ought to rethink our policy a little," Neil suggested.

"What do you mean?"

"Well . . . I'm not saying that we should think of giving up our independence. But maybe we've been acting a bit too aggressive for our own good. Men like Orbus Greene don't take very kindly to being outsmarted, especially when it comes to big money."

"That's business," Randolph replied firmly. "Besides, I wouldn't change my policies for any fat toad like Orbus."

"Don't underestimate him," Neil warned.

"Underestimate him? I'm not even thinking about him. I've got dead to bury and a factory to rebuild. That's all that worries me."

Neil said, "You're one-hundred-percent determined, aren't you, sir?"

Randolph nodded, although for some reason he felt that Neil was asking him a far more fateful question and that this single nod of agreement somehow set into motion some kind of dark and secret roller-coaster ride that he would never be able to stop.

TWO

Lac aux Ecorces, Quebec

They were sitting on the veranda overlooking the lake, with the moths stitching patterns around the lamp, talking quietly and eating potato chips, when they heard the first noise. It was an extraordinary crackle, seemingly close but so unexpected they could not believe they had actually heard it.

"Now *that* was something," John said.

"Moose probably," said Mark, who was afraid of few things.

"Are mooses dangerous?" asked Issa.

"What's the plural of moose?" their mother wanted to know. "It can't be mooses, can it?"

"Well, it isn't mice and it isn't moosen, so it must be mooses."

They sat quietly, listening. Mark crunched on a potato chip and they shushed him. But for a long time there was no sound other than the cool summer wind, blowing southwesterly across the silver surface of the lake and sighing in the trees like the saddest of abandoned women. The moon had only just disappeared behind the saw-toothed pine trees on the horizon, but it had left behind an unnatural glow in the sky, as if there were an alien city somewhere beyond the hills.

Marmie Clare held out her glass and said to John, "Pour me some more wine, would you, darling?" She watched with a smile as John carefully picked up the bottle of

Pouilly-Fuissé and attended to her glass with the same slow care his father would have taken.

At the age of forty-three, Marmie felt that she was beginning to blossom again, just like the magnolias down in Memphis. She was a tall, well-boned woman with deep-set brown eyes, a straight nose and a strong jawline. Her chestnut-colored hair was streaked with gray now, but whereas three years ago that used to horrify and depress her, she took it today as a mark of her newfound maturity and poise.

When she reached thirty-seven, Marmie had been frightened. The fear had started with the sudden realization that she was no longer young and that what she had then considered to be the best part of her life was behind her. She had stared hard at herself in the mirror, knowing that the tiny wrinkles beginning to appear around her eyes would never disappear. Then she had wondered what her life had been for, this brief, bright life that seemed now to be nearly ended before it had even reached its stride. It had hardly seemed worth the effort to make herself look attractive when the only man she had been trying to arouse was her husband of seventeen years. And why should she try to excel at anything else—at tennis, or music or swimming—when she was already too old to be the very best?

It was the death of Randolph's father that had changed her attitude toward herself. When Ned died and Randolph took over Clare Cottonseed, Randolph had been rejuvenated; it was a powerful and responsible job and a hair-raising challenge. Over the previous six or seven years, his father had allowed the Clare processing plants to collapse in a welter of lax discipline and obsolescent equipment, and he had relied for his dwindling income on long-standing "gentlemen's agreements" with cotton-plantation owners as conservative and decrepit as himself. Randolph had shaken the company like a dusty rag, from boardroom to loading bay, and during that time, he had relied on Marmie to be everything he had married her for: charming, elegant, patient, beautiful, tireless, cooperative, opinionated, warm and supportive.

Marmie had reached her forty-third year knowing that she

was someone special. She was looking to the years ahead, not to the years behind. And her children were just on the verge of proving what an accomplished mother she had been. She had emerged from self-doubt and dissatisfaction like someone newly born, someone who realizes that every human life consists of several different lives and that the arrival of each new one is an event to be welcomed.

Issa said, "Dad hasn't called." Issa resembled her mother except that her hair reached halfway down her back and she had inherited her paternal grandmother's extravagant bosom. Randolph always said there wasn't a boy in Memphis who wouldn't swim the Mississippi for Issa, although she was only thirteen; and Marmie always said that he was jealous, which was probably true. Tonight Issa wore a yellow- and white-striped T-shirt and white jeans, and with her pink-painted toenails and brushed-back hair and summer suntan, she could have been Miss Young America herself.

John said, "He's probably busy, for Christ's sake." John was his father all over again: the same profile, the same mannerisms, the same gentleness mixed with insanely stubborn ethics, the same sudden flares of incandescent, wildly unreasonable temper. And the same deep capacity to love. In fact, he was so much like his father that it was amazing that they got on together. By rights they should have been head-butting, but they rarely did. Most of the time they supported each other, made excuses for each other and were comfortable in each other's company.

Mark, on the other hand, was quiet and introspective. He loved both of his parents but he had his own way of looking at things, his own quirky sense of humor, his own ambitions. In appearance he was more like his mother than his father but he had inherited his father's well-meaning clumsiness. His taste in clothes had always been eccentric; tonight he was wearing a bright-green shirt and a pair of indigo-colored denim shorts.

John said, "We could take the kayak out tomorrow morning and catch some fish."

"If you want to," Marmie told him.

"Oh, I don't want to fish," Mark retorted. "Fishing's so goddam boring."

"Mark!" his mother admonished him.

"Well, it is," he grumbled. "And we never catch anything without Daddy being there."

Issa said, "I don't know why we didn't go home with Daddy. We could be back in Memphis now, watching TV."

"It's beautiful here," Marmie replied. "It's beautiful and we're going to stay, and if Daddy manages to finish his work in time, he'll come back and join us. Come on, I think you're all tired. It's time you went to bed."

"Sleep, eat, fish, sleep, eat, fish," protested Mark in a monotone.

It was then that they heard another crackle. They paused in silence, their heads lifted like caribou.

"Now that was definitely something," John said.

"It was probably only a porcupine," Marmie reassured him. "Your father said there are dozens of them around here."

"What if it's a bear?" asked Issa.

"Of course it's not a bear. Don't be ridiculous," John scoffed. "Besides, even if it is, we've got the gun."

There was another crackle, closer this time. Marmie frowned and set down her glass of wine on the wicker table. "I think we'd better go inside," she said. "You never know."

"This wouldn't be happening if we were back in Memphis," Issa complained.

All the same, Issa gathered up the magazines she had been reading, and John helped Mark drag the chaises back to the side of the veranda, against the cabin wall, and Marmie brushed down her dress and picked up her wine glass and the bowl of potato chips.

They were about to go inside when something dropped to the veranda steps from the roof of the porch with a quick, scrabbling sound and then scurried away. They jumped with fright and Issa screamed. Then they burst out laughing.

"A squirrel, after all that!" said Marmie.

"My heart's bumping!" Issa cried out. "Oh, my God, my heart's bumping!"

"Well, I think it's time we went inside anyway," Marmie told them. "It's getting kind of chilly to sit out here."

They went into the cabin's spacious living room and closed the door. Randolph's father had discovered the cabin about twenty years earlier, one day when he was fishing. In those days it had been dilapidated and abandoned, a home for martens and squirrels and occasional minks. Ned Clare had bought it from its owners, repaired it and extended it, and now it was a luxurious lakeside cottage which—to Randolph and Marmie, if not to their children—was heaven. The children's principal complaint, of course, was that there was no television, although Randolph had promised on his honor to install a VCR so that at least they could watch old movies.

"Could you stack the fire, please, John?" Marmie asked, walking across the wide, brown-carpeted living room and through to the kitchen. John went over to the old-fashioned brick fireplace and poked the spruce logs crackling in the grate. Mark followed his mother into the kitchen, obviously on the lookout for something more to eat. Issa sprawled on the tan-leather sofa and continued reading her magazines.

"Do you know what it says here, Mommy? It says you should always massage your moisturizer into your cheeks with your knuckles. Can you show me how to do that?"

"If I knew how, I'd tell you," Marmie called back with a chuckle.

"I wonder if Daddy's seen the factory yet," John said. "I can't believe that Bill Douglas got killed."

"Well, he said he would call before midnight," Marmie told him.

"Can I have one of these lemon Danishes?" Mark wanted to know.

"They were supposed to be for breakfast," Marmie said. "But, well, okay, if you're that hungry."

She came back to the living room. John had stacked more logs on the fire and for the moment, it was subdued and smoky.

"Why don't you use the bellows?" she suggested.

It was then that they heard three distinct clumping noises outside the front door, as if someone had stepped up onto the veranda. They froze and stared at each other.

"Don't tell me *that's* a squirrel," Issa said.

"A squirrel in hiking boots?" Mark asked.

"John, did you lock the door?" Unconsciously Marmie laid her hand across Mark's shoulders and tugged at his green shirt to draw him closer.

John said nothing but stepped cautiously toward the door, listened for a moment and then turned the key to lock it.

"Do you think there's anybody out there?" Marmie asked.

John shook his head slowly. "Probably one of the chaises fell over."

"All the same," Marmie instructed him, "go to your father's closet and get the gun and the box of shells."

John went through to the bedroom and Marmie heard him rattling around among the hiking shoes and tennis rackets and other equipment that always seemed to accumulate at the bottom of Randolph's closet. She had been trying for the whole of their married life to organize Randolph. Tonight she would have given anything to have him here, as disorganized and untidy as he wanted to be.

There was another bump. John came back into the living room carrying the .22 rifle over his arm, the way his father had taught him to carry it when they were out hunting. He looked at his mother with a serious face and put the box of shells on the table.

"Do you know how to load it?" Marmie asked.

"Sure, Daddy showed me."

Mark came over and watched as John carefully took the shells out of the carton, one by one, and slid them into the rifle's magazine. "John's a rotten shot," he said with sudden cheerfulness.

"I am not," John retorted.

"You are too. You couldn't even hit that duck when it was practically sitting on the end of the barrel."

"Will you stop arguing?" Marmie demanded. "There

could be somebody prowling around out there and this could be serious."

"Maybe we ought to call the ranger station," Issa said. There was no telephone of course, but in Randolph's study there was a radio transmitter with which they could summon either the forest rangers or the company that took care of Randolph's seaplane.

"Well, we don't know for sure that it's a prowler," Marmie said. "After all, we're a long way out from anywhere. We haven't heard a helicopter, have we? Or a seaplane? And it's nearly twenty miles to route one sixty-nine. I think maybe we're just letting ourselves get a little jumpy because Daddy isn't here."

"I think it's spooky," Issa said. "I vote we go back to Memphis tomorrow."

"I'll make some hot chocolate," Marmie volunteered.

She had nearly reached the kitchen when there was a sharp, earsplitting crack and the blade of an ax penetrated the outside door close to the lock. Issa screamed and jumped off the sofa. John picked up the rifle and chambered a round with a quick, flustered jerk. Mark stepped back and stared at his mother wide-eyed.

Marmie tried to shout out, "Who's that? What do you think you're doing?" but somehow her vocal cords failed to work. The ax blade cracked into the door a second time, then a third.

"John, shoot!" Marmie gasped. John aimed the rifle at the door and pulled the trigger but nothing happened.

"It's jammed," he said desperately. "It's all jammed up."

The ax chopped into the door with regular, powerful strokes, as if it were being wielded by a woodsman. Marmie thought wildly of going into the kitchen for a carving knife but a tiny voice of logic and self-protection asked what good that would be against a man carrying an ax and with the strength to chop down a heavy wooden door.

With a hideous, splintering groan, the door was forced open. Four bulky men in white ice-hockey masks and black track suits pushed their way into the living room. One of them was swinging a long-handled ax; the others were carrying sawed-off shotguns. Marmie screeched at them, "Get out! What do you want? Get out!" and gathered the children close, but the men took no notice and strutted into the room, systematically kicking over tables, tugging down pictures and overturning chairs. They were faceless and menacing, like malevolent puppets.

"What do you want?" Marmie breathed, her voice choked with fear.

The man with the ax came up and regarded them with expressionless eyes.

"Who are you?" Marmie demanded. "What right do you have to come bursting into our house?"

The man said nothing, although Marmie could hear him breathing harshly behind his mask. The other three men circled around behind them and stood with their feet apart, arrogant and stiff, holding up their short-barreled shotguns as if they were symbols of authority. Marmie glanced nervously over her shoulder at them and then back at the man with the ax.

"There's no money here," she said, her voice trembling but firm. "You can have my credit cards if you want them. There's a gun there; it's jammed but you can have it. Just take what you want and leave us alone. Please. We're on vacation, that's all."

The man with the ax beckoned to one of his associates and pointed to Mark. With his finger he made a throat-cutting gesture across his own neck.

Marmie screamed, "No!" but another man stepped up behind her and gripped her arm, so tightly that the sleeve of her dress tore. He pressed the muzzle of his shotgun to the side of Marmie's head; its roughly filed-off edges dug into her temple, and it was then she suddenly realized that these men in their bland ice-hockey masks had come not for money, nor for shelter, nor for anything else she could possibly offer them. They had come to kill, and that was all. Because who would travel twenty miles through the forests of the Laurentide Provincial Park, to a cabin that

stood by itself, armed with sawed-off shotguns and disguised with masks, but killers?

Marmie said, "I beg mercy of you." Her voice was
proud and clear. Issa whimpered and covered her face with
her hands, but John stared at Marmie as if amazed that she
was not able to protect him from these intruders. Mark
looked up at the man standing over him and with a strangely
hypnotized sense of obedience, stood up and followed him
to the other side of the room.

The man with the ax pointed to the arm of the sofa; his
colleague forced Mark to kneel so that his head was resting
on top of the arm, like an executioner's block.

Marmie half rose and said falteringly, "You can't do
that. Listen, that's my son. He's only eleven. Please, if you
have to kill somebody, kill me. But not my children. Please."

The man with the ax stared at her. Then he looked around
at his colleagues, but it was clear that he was in charge and
that the others had no say in what he was about to do. None
of them spoke. They could have been deaf and dumb for all
Marmie could tell.

"Listen," she insisted, "my husband is a very rich man.
If you leave us alone, if you save our lives, I will personally
guarantee that he pays you very well. Just leave my children
alone and I will personally guarantee you a million dollars. I
mean that. A million dollars. And you can take me as
hostage to make sure the money is paid."

The man with the ax said nothing but grunted when Mark
tried to raise his tousled head from the arm of the sofa. His
associate forced Mark down again.

"A million dollars," Marmie repeated. "No tricks, no
police tip-offs, nothing; I guarantee it with my own life."

The man with the ax lifted the ax head up, licked the ball
of his thumb and ran it down the edge of the blade to test its
sharpness. Blood mingled with saliva; the ax must have
been as sharp as broken glass. It was impossible for Marmie
to tell whether the man was smiling or scowling, but she
had the uncanny feeling that he was actually amused and
that he was going to kill them and enjoy it.

She felt that she had to go on talking. The longer she

talked, the longer her children would live. Tears streamed down her cheeks and she could barely speak, but she knew that her children's survival depended on her. Randolph wasn't here—Randolph was way off in Memphis—and she cursed him for having left them in this isolated cabin on Lac aux Ecorces when they could have been safe and sound at home, eating barbecued ribs, watching television and worrying about nothing more important than what they were going to wear for the Cotton Carnival.

"You could be wealthy men, all of you," she said, hoping to appeal to their sense of greed. After all, why had they come to kill her except for money? "I could make each of you a millionaire; four million dollars, to be split four ways. I know the company could stand it, and I know my husband would be only too happy to pay it. Please, think about it, one million dollars, in cash, for each of you. No questions asked."

With terrible disinterest, the man with the ax raised his weapon high above his head. For one split second, Marmie thought: *This is a nightmare, I'm dreaming this, it can't be real. If I hit myself, I'll wake up and we'll be back in Memphis, opening our eyes at dawn at Clare Castle, nestling up to designer sheets, with the fragrance of flowering azaleas drifting in through the shutters and the maids singing as they mop up the tiled patios outside, preparing for us to come out to breakfast.*

But then the nightmare became real and the ax whistled down. Mark screamed like an animal when the ax blade cut only a third of the way into his neck. Most of the force of the blow had been cushioned by the arm of the sofa. All the same, his carotid artery had been severed and bright-red blood came spurting. The man with the ax had to hit him again, and yet again, and then suddenly his head dropped off his shoulders and tumbled onto the carpet with a noise like a falling salad bowl. Marmie stared down in horror as Mark—her precious eleven-year-old son—stared back at her from under the table with a face anguished and white, and utterly dead.

She tried to drop to her knees, to collapse, to crawl across the carpet to save her son. That couldn't be Mark, that couldn't be real. Even though it must be a trick, he needed her. He was hurt, he was killed, and he needed her. But the man behind her pushed the muzzle of his gun even more fiercely into the side of her head so that she cried out in pain, and she knew beyond any doubt that he would kill her if she moved again.

Somewhere on the edge of her consciousness she was aware that Issa was screaming: a long, drawn-out scream that seemed to stretch like a band-saw blade, cutting through all sanity and sense. One of the men stalked stiffly across the room toward Issa, twisted her arm behind her back and thrust his gun up underneath her chin. But she was hysterical now, and all she could do was to scream.

"Leave her alone! Leave her alone!" John yelled in a shrill voice. He pushed over one of the armchairs and leaped over the coffee table to protect Issa as if he were jumping hurdles in a track meet.

The man holding Marmie did not hesitate. He was so deliberate and calculating about what he did that Marmie did not even feel his muscles tense. He lifted his gun from her temple for a moment and fired one barrel straight into John's stomach. The shot was earsplitting. John doubled up in midair and tumbled heavily against the edge of the sofa.

Sour blue smoke hung in the room like a hideous omen. John lay flat on his back, his face shocked and desperate, his legs shivering catatonically, his stomach torn into a tangle of T-shirt and glistening blue intestines. Marmie stared at him and couldn't think of anything except *How am I going to explain this to Randolph? What am I going to say?*

"Mom . . ." John whispered. He was looking at her and his lips were shuddering. "Mom . . . help me . . . my stomach hurts . . . Mom. . . ."

Marmie tried in a disconnected way to stand up, but the man turned his shotgun around and pointed it straight at her right eye so that she could see the engulfing darkness inside the barrel and smell the powder that had killed her firstborn son.

"The police will come," she said with a dry throat.

The men said nothing. Marmie looked from one to the other and repeated, "The police will come. Then you'll be arrested. You've . . . killed people. We're ordinary people. What have we ever done to you? Why do you want to kill us? We don't even have anything worth stealing! Oh, God, Mark. What did you do to Mark? Where is he? Mark!"

She sank heavily into a chair, her fingernails clawing distractedly at the upholstery, her mind blindly seeking ways in which she and Issa might escape. Perhaps they could run for the door. Perhaps she hadn't offered them enough money. Perhaps Randolph would call, realize that something was wrong and send for the rangers. After all, the men hadn't spoken, had they? And since they hadn't spoken, it could only mean that they didn't want her to recognize their voices, and that meant that they intended to spare her life.

"If you let me call my husband," she said in a faint, off-key tone, "I'll see if we can't raise the money to eight million dollars. That's two million dollars each, in unmarked bills or banker's drafts."

Issa had stopped screaming and was quietly sobbing, her free hand held across her face. The man with the ax walked across to her and carefully but forcibly pulled her fingers from her face so he could look at her. He inspected her for almost half a minute through the menacing slits of his mask, breathing slowly and heavily. Marmie could see his chest rise and fall. Issa did not look back at him. Her eyes wandered wildly as if she were drugged. Her cheeks were streaked with tears.

After a while the man lifted his hand and ran his fingers through Issa's long, tangly hair. She tried to twist her head away but he savagely gripped her hair and tugged it upward, so fiercely that he lifted her feet off the floor and Marmie heard the skin of her scalp crackle. Issa shrieked piercingly and thrashed her legs.

"She's only thirteen!" Marmie screamed. "Leave her alone, she's only thirteen! For God's sake, what kind of people are you? Leave her alone! If you want to hurt anyone, hurt me, but for God's sake, leave her alone!''

Almost casually, the man who was guarding Marmie punched her in the mouth with his gloved fist. One of Marmie's front teeth was knocked down her throat and the bridge on the right-hand side of her jaw was snapped in half. As her mouth filled with blood, she began to choke and gag.

Without even turning to see what had happened, the man with the ax hefted the weapon so that he held it close to the blade. Then, with three crunching slices, he cut through Issa's hair. Issa moaned, staggered and almost fell but the man holding her arm behind her back hoisted her to her feet again.

Now the man with the ax slid his right hand into the front of Issa's yellow- and white-striped T-shirt. He cupped Issa's breasts for a moment, his chest rising and falling heavily. Then he lifted the ax blade again, sticky with blood and hair, and used it to slice the T-shirt open from neckline to hem.

Marmie, weeping, her mouth running with blood, tried to protest. But the man turned and came over to her, indicating with an upward jerk of the ax that she should get to her feet. She did so unsteadily, almost to the point of collapse.

The man ripped open Marmie's blouse too, with rough, sawing tugs. Although Marmie closed her eyes, she could hear the irregular harshness of his breathing behind his mask. She felt the roughness of his gloved hand tugging at her bra and then the coldness of the ax blade against her skin. She kept her eyes closed as the ax sawed into the waistband of her jeans and cut the elastic of her panties.

She could scarcely move her feet as the men half-pushed, half-carried her into the bedroom. She could see the nightmare for herself in the full-length mirrors in the closet doors, the masked intruders as faceless and frightening as characters in a Japanese No play, her own white, nude body held between them. She cried, "Dear God, don't kill me!"

Issa was dragged into the bedroom too. Then both of them were forced onto the bed, guns pressed so hard against their foreheads that they imprinted scarlet circles in their skin. One of the men disappeared briefly and then returned with a length of nylon cord snatched from the clothesline outside. They tied Marmie and Issa face-to-face, their arms clutched around each other, and their necks, arms and ankles ferociously and painfully lashed with cord.

"Issa, don't cry, my darling. They're not going to kill us," Marmie promised. Issa's naked body felt so cold as it pressed against her, she was so close that all Marmie could see of Issa's face was one madly staring eye, red-rimmed with tears. Her shorn hair was in clumps, sticky with her brother's blood.

"Don't cry, darling. Whatever happens, they're not going to kill us."

She felt the weight of the first man press down the springs of the bed behind her. She strained her neck against the binding cords and saw a second man climb onto the bed behind Issa. She could see that he had taken off his track-suit pants and that he was brandishing himself in his fist as if he were holding a cudgel.

She cried aloud as the first man penetrated her but the silent cry she uttered inside herself when the other man penetrated Issa was by far more painful. For a few minutes there was a terrible, intense quietness in the room, interrupted only by the grunting of the men and the jostling sound of the bedclothes. Issa held her mother tight, every muscle in her body as rigid as high-tension wire, and Marmie prayed that the girl was too deep in shock to understand what was happening to her.

The men finished their ritual with shuddering climaxes and climbed off the bed but Marmie knew it was no use to hope that the defilement was over. She seemed to be falling down some echoing corridor into complete darkness, where there was nothing but humiliation and fear and terrible agony. Yet for Issa's sake, Marmie knew that she had to remain conscious and had to stay sane. The grappling, heaving, terrifying foulness of it went on and on, so that she came to believe that it would never end.

At last, however, there was silence. It must have been

almost dawn because the bedroom was illuminated in a ghostly blue light. Issa seemed to be either asleep or unconscious, but Marmie could feel the girl's heart beating and feel her breath on her shoulder, so she knew that at least Issa was alive.

Marmie tried to lift her head. It seemed as if the bedroom were empty and that the men had gone. She listened but there was no sound, only the early morning sapsuckers tapping at the trees outside, only the thin whistle of the wind across the lake. She thought about her ordeal but her mind refused to organize it for her. Instead, it told her with protective logic that she had suffered terribly and that it would take many years before she would be able to come to terms with what had happened. She knew that John and Mark were dead, but her tear ducts refused to indulge her grief. She knew that she and Issa had been grotesquely bound and raped, but she could think of nothing other than *How are we going to cut outselves free?*

"Issa," she whispered. "Issa, darling."

Issa opened the one eye that Marmie could see.

"Momma." That simple word bore all her suffering and sadness. In one night, Issa's family had gone, her innocence was lost, everything the world had given her had been stripped away.

"Issa, listen to me. Everything's going to be fine. All we have to do is untie ourselves. Then we can call the rangers and have the plane sent out."

"Momma, they killed John."

"Yes, my darling. They killed Mark too. But don't think about it. Everything's going to be fine, just as long as we take it easy and don't panic."

"Momma," wept Issa, close to hysteria.

Marmie shushed her, hugged her tight and called her all the pet names she could remember. "Come on, baby, it's over. It was terrible, but now it's over. Come on, baby, don't cry."

It was then, however, that the bedroom door abruptly opened and Marmie froze. From where she was lying, with her neck tied to Issa's, she could not see who had stepped into the room. But after a tense pause, the man with the ax came into sight and bent over them, his eyes glinting inside his mask. Marmie said nothing; she felt too vulnerable and too frightened. Besides, the man was unpredictable. He did not speak even now but only stared at her as if relishing her predicament. He lifted the ax blade and held it close to Marmie's face, and although it was impossible for her to see his face, she found it easy to believe that he was smiling.

"What are you going to do?" she asked, her voice a gasp.

The man stood up and beckoned one of the others from the doorway. This man came forward with a coil of barbed wire, one end of which had been fashioned into a noose.

"Momma, what is it?" begged Issa. "What is it? What are they doing?"

Marmie knew then that she would not be able to bear what the men were going to do to them. "Shoot us," she said hoarsely.

The man with the ax slowly and deliberately shook his head.

"Shoot us!" screamed Marmie. "Shoot us, for the love of God! Shoot us!"

THREE

Memphis, Tennessee

Randolph called Marmie as soon as he awakened at six-thirty that morning, but there was no reply. He sat at the small white cast-iron table on the bedroom balcony, over-looking the walled garden that Marmie had planted with roses and magnolias, drinking strong black coffee, eating buttered toast and reading the early morning edition of the *Memphis Press-Scimitar*, which announced, "Clare Blaze 'Not Arson' Opines Police Chief."

He picked up the white cordless telephone beside the silver coffee pot and asked for a second time to be put through to the cottage on Lac aux Ecorces. There was a radio-telephone link from Hebertville, although that was nearly thirty-five miles to the north of the lake and reception was sometimes fuzzy and erratic. After ten minutes the operator called back to say that she could rouse no response from Lac aux Ecorces but that she would keep trying at regular fifteen-minute intervals and let him know when she had managed to get through.

Randolph finished his toast, swallowed the last of his coffee and brushed off his white summer trousers. A Tennessee warbler, green-backed and white-fronted, perched on the balcony railing, cocked its head to one side and sang *chip chip chip* before suddenly flying away.

Randolph's valet, Charles, came in, a gray-haired black man who had served Randolph's father for almost thirty years. Charles, as far as Randolph was concerned, was part of the family, even though Charles himself liked to live in the past and distanced himself from his employers with petty courtesies and unsolicited attentions. Randolph often teased Charles by saying that he would have been the despair of Martin Luther King, Jr., but Charles in return would make a show of not thinking that this was a funny joke at all, particularly since the civil-rights leader had died in Memphis, at the Lorraine Motel on Mulberry Street.

"Are you going out now, sir?" Charles asked. He rarely smiled. He reminded Randolph of Dred Scott, or at least of the history-book picture of Dred Scott. Charles, however, would never have such an influence on American life. As far as Charles was concerned, there was a way things should be done: the old way, prior to freedom marches and school bussing and James Meredith.

"I'm going down to Cotton Row for beginners," Randolph said as Charles helped him into his coat. "Then I'm lunching at Grisanti's. As far as the afternoon is concerned, well, that's open-ended. But you can call Wanda if you need to know where I am."

Charles fussily brushed Randolph's shoulders with a leather-backed brush.

"Listen, Charles, dandruff doesn't show up on a white jacket."

"Sir, you don't have dandruff."

"Then why are you brushing me?"

"A gentleman's valet *always* brush a gentleman before a gentleman go out. That's the rule," said Charles.

"Who makes the rules around here? Me or you?"

"Those are the kind of rules that *nobody* make. Those are ettykett."

Herbert, the chauffeur, was waiting in the semicircular asphalt driveway outside Clare Castle in a silver-gray Chrysler New Yorker. Herbert was another of Clare Cottonseed's old retainers. He had a face grizzled up like a red cabbage, white hair that was always firmly greased back and a voice as deep and smooth as the silt that poured down the Mississippi. He opened the car door for Randolph and handed him

The Wall Street Journal. "Sorry about the car, sir. The Cadillac won't take longer to repair than two or three days."

Randolph settled into his seat. "You must tell me about that."

"Well, sir," said Herbert as they started off, "I couldn't really explain it. I was heading toward the airport on Lamar, all ready to pick you up, with chilled cocktails sitting in the cabinet, and then just when I was turning on to Airways, the brakes failed and I couldn't stop her, two and a half tons of limousine. I ended up halfway down the bank, lucky not to turn over."

Randoph said, "Brake failure. That's not common, is it?"

"In a Cadillac limousine, sir? They have dual hydraulic master cylinders, tandem vacuum power boosters, ventilated discs in the front, duo servo drums in the back, four hundred twenty-five square inches swept area, believe me."

"What did the mechanic have to say?"

Herbert glanced up at Randolph in the rearview mirror. "The mechanic laughed, sir, to my chagrin."

"But he couldn't say why the brakes failed?"

"No, sir. Not unless there was tampering."

Randolph shook out his *Journal* but did not read the headlines. "Tampering?" he asked sharply.

"Well, sir, it could have been deliberate."

Randolph looked up. "I think I'm missing something," he said. "Why should anybody have wanted to tamper with my limousine?"

"I don't like to sound pessimistic, sir, but they do say that Clare Cottonseed has become something of an irritation, especially to Mr. Greene and the Cottonseed Association. Whether they're trying to tell you something, sir, by way of practical action . . . well, I don't know about that. But it may be worth bearing in mind."

"You don't seriously think that somebody from the Margarine Mafia fixed the brakes on my car, do you?"

"It's not beyond the bounds of possibility, sir." Again those cornflower-blue eyes floating in the rearview mirror.

Were they stupid or wise? Was Herbert trying to overdramatize his accident in order to excuse some piece of negligent driving, or had the brakes really failed because Orbus Greene had wanted them to? Could Orbus really have worked himself up to such a pitch of resentment that he was prepared to sabotage factories and kill workers in order to keep total control of the cottonseed market? The newspapers had reported Chief Moyne's opinion that yesterday morning's explosion at Raleigh had been "unquestionably accidental." But then Chief Moyne was a long-standing drinking buddy of Orbus Greene's from the bad old days when Memphis had been nothing more than a jumble of wharves, warehouses and run-down tenements and the city had been controlled by men who could be distinguished from alligators only by the way they laughed. Whatever Chief Moyne decided about a crime, his forensic department took serious note. So no matter how fair and true the *Memphis Press-Scimitar* might endeavor to be, it could report only the information the police department had given it.

Randolph said thoughtfully, "You're the second person in two days to suggest to me that the Margarine Mafia is starting to put pressure on us."

"Well, sir, that's the feeling among some of the workers and some of the staff. Maybe it's nothing but rumor. Maybe it's nothing but the summer heat. You know what happens to Memphians in the summer, they always go a little daffy. But somebody's been passing the word, mainly through the union locals. Nothing o-*vert*, if you know what I mean, but with the implication that it might not be too healthy for anyone to work for Clare Cottonseed. Bad moon rising, if you understand me."

"Has anybody said that to you?" Randolph asked.

"Not in so many words, sir."

"Then how?"

"Well, sir, I was talking to Mr. Graceworthy's driver two or three days back, just after you left for Canada, and he said something that started me thinking. He said, 'Have you ever wondered where you might be, Herbert, a year from now?' and I said, 'What kind of a question is that?' I mean, we've known each other five or six years, me and Mr. Graceworthy's driver, why is he all of a sudden asking me that? But he only says, 'Think about it, that's all.' And believe me, sir, I did think about it when the Cadillac went off of the road. A year from now, I thought to myself, I could have been doing nothing at all. I could have been dead meat in a box.''

Randolph sat back on the deep cushioned velour seat. There seemed no question but that the Cottonseed Association was trying to make clear to him its displeasure, although for the past six months he had been so preoccupied with his own building and business-investment plans, and so isolated from the daily turmoil of Cotton Row, up in his tenth-story office or out at Clare Castle, that he had completely failed to sense the increasing hostility that must have been building up against him.

All the same, hostility or not, he still found it hard to believe that anybody from the Cottonseed Association could have been crude enough or violent enough to burn down his factory or to tamper with the brakes of his limousine—not even Orbus Greene for all his grossness, both physical and mental; and certainly not Waverley Graceworthy, the "Grand Old Man" of Cotton Row.

Yet, apart from Orbus's rancorous remarks last night up at Raleigh, neither Orbus nor Waverley had deigned to speak to Randolph since the Sun-Taste contract had been signed; and Randolph could well believe that the whole cottonseed industry would breathe a mighty sigh of relief if he were to go out of business, or even if he were to end up embedded in one of the reinforced concrete uprights on Interstate 55.

He decided to be cautious and for the time being at least, to *assume* that the Margarine Mafia would much prefer it if he were eliminated. He had seen in the past how quickly a preference could become a reality, especially in a high-keyed city like Memphis. The town had not produced W.C. Handy and Elvis Presley for nothing.

Randolph reached his desk at one minute past eight and

immediately pressed the buzzer for Wanda. Behind him, the Mississippi lazed into the morning studded with steamers and necklaced with chains of cotton barges. Wanda came in with a cup of steaming coffee on a silver tray.

"I've been trying to contact Marmie at Lac aux Ecorces," he told her. "The operator is going to keep on trying, but I would appreciate it if you would advise her that I'm here and that I want to speak to Marmie as soon as possible."

"Of course," Wanda replied. She looked crisp and efficient in a white-silk blouse and a tight gray skirt, with a fresh camellia pinned to her lapel. "There's something else," she said. "I had a call about five minutes ago from Mr. Graceworthy's secretary. She said that Mr. Graceworthy intends to pay you a visit around eight-thirty."

"And what did you say to that?"

"I said that you wouldn't be here, that you had to visit the families of the men who had been killed up at Raleigh."

"And?"

"She said that Mr. Graceworthy was coming anyway and that he really would prefer it if you could wait up for him."

Randolph picked up his coffee and sipped it. "Brasilia," he murmured. He enjoyed being able to identify coffee; it was a knack his father had taught him. Then he said, "All right. But I'll wait until eight forty-five, no later."

"Yes, sir. And, sir? These reports came in . . . from the chief of police, the fire chief and city hall. They all relate to the accident."

"The accident, hmm?" Randolph asked, putting a slightly sarcastic emphasis on the word "accident."

Wanda frowned at him. "You don't think it *was* an accident?"

"Everybody I meet seems to be nudging me and winking and telling me different. I'm beginning to feel like I'm the only person in town who doesn't know he's got something unpleasant on his shoe."

"The fire chief said it was an accident." Wanda picked

up the report and leafed through it. "Here it is. 'Volatile fumes were apparently escaping from a leaking pressure valve in the wintering plant and spontaneously ignited.' "

"And what does Chief Moyne have to say for himself?"

" 'No suspicious circumstances,' " Wanda quoted.

Randolph sipped his coffee. "No suspicious circumstances. I see. Where are my cookies?"

"You told me not to bring you cookies anymore. You said they were fattening."

"Those little Swiss cookies? I told you that?"

Wanda nodded and smiled. "You said that it was an irrevocable order and that no matter what you said, no matter how much you pleaded, I was never to bring you those cookies again."

"Well, I irrevocably reverse that irrevocable order. Bring me some cookies."

Wanda thought for a moment and then said, "All right, two. And that's your limit."

"Three."

"Two, and that's not negotiable."

"Okay, two . . . and try calling the cabin for me, will you, please? Marmie must be back there by now, wherever she went."

At that moment Neil Sleaman came in. He was wearing a powder-blue nylon suit, a yellow shirt and a gold-tipped bolo tie.

"Good morning, Mr. Clare. I just heard that Waverley Graceworthy has invited himself over."

"So it seems."

Neil sat down uninvited. "Do you have any idea of what he wants?"

"Do *you?*" asked Randolph. He began to read through the fire chief's report on the blaze out at Raleigh.

"I guess it has something to do with what Orbus Greene was talking about yesterday, out at the plant."

"You mean he's going to threaten me, only more politely?"

"You can see the Association's point of view, Mr. Clare."

"Can I?" queried Randolph, looking up. He smacked the

fire chief's report dismissively with the back of his fingers. "This whole thing is one weasel word after another. Listen to this: 'Although there is no evidence to suggest that safety regulations at the Clare processing plant were not adhered to, there is room for speculation that the valves in the wintering plant were not up to the standards required or had not been maintained up to the standards required.' What this actually means is that he has no evidence whatever about what happened out there and he's guessing . . . only he's making damn sure that we sound as if we've been negligent."

Neil inclined his head and nodded as if to say, "Well, that could be so, but it isn't really the main point."

Randolph stood up and thrust his hands into his pockets. "Why should I harbor any sympathy for the Association's point of view when it does nothing but slow down expansion and reduce quality? We've built ourselves into the second-biggest cottonseed processor in Memphis because our prices are low and our product is good, and I'm not interested in anybody's point of view if it compromises either of those criteria. And I'm particularly not interested in *anybody*'s point of view if I'm being made to accept it by violent means."

"Sir . . . surely that couldn't have been sabotage," Neil protested.

"Well, I'm glad *you're* sure because *I'm* not."

"Whatever you think of the Association, Mr. Clare . . . they're all honorable men."

"What are you, their public-relations officer? Orbus Greene is the tackiest, most devious, most self-serving mountain of human flesh that ever disgraced this city, and as for Waverley Graceworthy—"

"As for Waverley Graceworthy," put in a clear, husky, patrician voice. "Waverley Graceworthy is here to pay you his respects."

Randolph turned around. Petite, white-haired, dressed immaculately in a gray Cerruti suit that could have been made for a ten-year-old boy, the Grand Old Man of Cotton Row walked into the office, his glasses flashing for a moment in the reflected light from the window, his tiny shoes twinkling. He held out his hand to Randolph almost as if he expected it to be kissed.

"Your dear secretary was nowhere to be found," Waverley said. He had been brought up in Corinth, Mississippi, and his accent was as high-stepping and as steel-sprung as the arches of the Hernando de Soto bridge. "You won't object if I sit down?"

"How can I help you?" Randolph asked. "Would you care for some coffee?"

Waverley perched on the edge of the sofa, supported his withered chin on his liver-spotted fist and regarded Randolph with an expression bordering on amusement. Behind his rimless glasses, his eyes were rheumy and bloodshot, but they were acute nonetheless.

"I have come to pay my respects, as I said. I was very distressed to learn of what happened to Bill Douglas and those two workers of yours. Also, to that fine new factory. A considerable tragedy."

"Well, thank you for your condolences," Randolph acknowledged, trying not to sound churlish. Neil Sleaman shifted uncomfortably in his chair, as if he would have preferred not to be there at all.

"I gather that Orbus had a few words to say to you out at the plant," Waverley went on. "You know something? You mustn't take too much notice of Orbus. He has a way of expressing himself that tends to put people's backs up. Remember that he was brought up the hard way, when a man had to be sly, uncompromising and even unprincipled if he was going to survive. Even your father, may his soul rest in peace, was not the paragon of virtue that *you* can have the luxury of being now that times have changed."

"Do you want to get to the point?" Randolph asked.

Waverley was silent for a while, watching Randolph carefully with those swimming, pallid eyes. Then he sat back, neatly folded his arms and said, "You're causing us considerable grief, you know. Far more grief than your father ever did. Your father could at least be accommodating. Your father understood that in the cottonseed business, the interests of each processing company are intertwined. You, for instance, you may *think* that you're an independent, but there's no such thing. Your prices wouldn't be low if ours were lower. Your delivery dates wouldn't be quick if ours were quicker.''

"Then why don't you cut your prices and speed up your delivery dates?'' asked Randolph. "I'm not afraid of competition.''

"Well, I'm afraid that things don't work that way,'' Waverley replied. "Some members of the Association are strong, but the strong are far outnumbered by the weak. Most of the processors around here could not stay in business if the Association didn't fix prices, and that would mean that many of the cotton plantations would go out of business too. We're talking about the wider picture here, you see. We're talking about what would happen to this whole district, to Shelby County and DeSoto County, if the Association didn't take care of its members' interests.''

"I'm afraid you don't impress me,'' Randolph growled. "You're thinking about your profits and little else. What's more, Orbus is sore because he didn't get the Sun-Taste contract.''

"Orbus has a right to be sore. Brooks is the biggest processor around here and Sun-Taste should have gone to him as a matter of sheer practicality. He could have subcontracted at least two-thirds of the supply to some of the smaller members of the Association.''

"At rock-bottom rates, no doubt,'' said Randolph dryly. "And besides, Sun-Taste specifically insisted that there should be no subcontracting whatever.''

"You're always making things difficult, aren't you?'' Waverley asked mildly. His fingernails picked at a stray thread on the arm of the sofa.

"I don't have to make things difficult. Things are difficult enough already.''

"Randolph, there isn't any need for us to argue. I came here today with a proposition. I know that the unfortunate fire out at Raleigh has somewhat reduced your ability to meet the demands Sun-Taste has been placing on you. Might I suggest that the Association assist you to meet your requirements . . . in return for a more cooperative policy on your part in the future?''

"You can suggest what you like. I think I'd rather cooperate with the Ku Klux Klan.''

"Randolph!'' Waverley said sharply. "This is not being wise.''

"Well, apparently not,'' Randolph agreed sarcastically. "It seems to be common knowledge in Memphis that the Association is going to start squeezing me out. If not by negotiation, then by vandalism and threats. For all I know, with that fire out at Raleigh and my company limousine going off the road, you've started already.''

Waverley stood up. It was impossible for Randolph to see his eyes because of the silver reflection on the man's glasses. "I resent that,'' Waverley said, his voice gently admonitory rather than resentful.

"You can resent it as much as you like,'' Randolph told him. "That's your privilege.''

Waverley stood unmoving for a moment, as if he were about to say something. But he apparently changed his mind, nodded first to Randolph and then to Neil Sleaman, and buttoned up his coat.

"You're causing us grief, Randolph,'' he repeated.

"I know.''

"You know what you'll get in return.''

"Tell me,'' Randolph challenged.

"You'll get grief of your own, that's what you'll get.''

Randolph eased himself off the edge of his desk, clapped his hand on Waverley's shoulder and escorted him to the door. Wanda stood there, looking anxious.

"Wanda,'' said Randolph with false magnanimity, "Mr. Graceworthy is leaving. I just want you to know that if he ever turns up here again without an appointment, you are to refuse him admission and redirect him to the Memphis Zoological Gardens, where he can join the other reptiles.''

"Well, cheap shot,'' said Waverley, taking his gray fedora from the hatpeg and opening the door. "I can see myself out, thank you," he assured them.

Once he had closed the door behind him, Randolph turned to Wanda and said, "I mean that. This office is off limits to anybody from the Cottonseed Association, and especially to *him*."

"I don't know," put in Neil. "I still think Waverley has great dignity."

"A boa constrictor has great dignity," Randolph retorted. "Just because those men managed to squeeze all but the very last ounce of independence out of my father, it doesn't mean they're going to do it to me."

"Mr. Clare," Wanda appealed to him.

"Did you get my cookies?" Randolph asked.

"Mr. Clare," Wanda repeated, and Randolph looked at her and suddenly realized that her eyes were filled with tears.

"Wanda? Are you okay? What's the matter?"

Wanda went suddenly white and sat down behind her desk.

"Wanda?" Randolph repeated and came around the desk and laid his hand on her shoulder. He looked up at Neil and mouthed the question, "What's wrong?" but Neil could only shrug.

At last Wanda managed to collect herself enough to say, "I had a phone call only a minute ago."

"You had a phone call? From whom?"

"It was the ranger station at the Laurentide National Park. They spoke mostly French, so I couldn't really understand them at first."

A freezing-cold feeling of dread began to clutch at Randolph's heart, even before Wanda could begin to tell him what the rangers had said. Marmie had not answered her calls this morning, had she? And why? She rarely woke up early. She always stayed in bed, even after he had left for Cotton Row in the morning, lingering over her breakfast. Even when they were on vacation, she rarely got up before half-past eight.

Why hadn't it occurred to him that something was wrong?

"Wanda," he said; his voice seeming oddly dispersed, like raindrops on a polished car. "Calm down, Wanda. Just tell me what they said."

Wanda looked up at him, tears streaming from her eyes. "They said that somebody had called them from the fishing club. One of their anglers had gone out early this morning and—" she paused, breathing deeply to collect herself— "and his outboard motor had broken down, and he had managed to row to the shore where the cabin is, and he had gone to the cabin to ask for help."

"And what?" asked Randolph. "*What*, Wanda? What else did they say?"

Wanda could scarcely speak through her grief but somehow she managed to go on, and when she had finished, time seemed to stand completely still, as if it would always be 8:47 in the morning, in early May; as if Randolph and Wanda and Neil would never move again; as if the world outside would hold its breath forever after, the traffic motionless, the flags frozen, the steamboats marooned in the middle of a gelid river.

But then Randolph lifted his head and turned around, and time started up again, slowly at first, as if he were wading across the office toward his desk, and then faster and faster, like a blurt of broken film, until he toppled and fell, hitting the side of his head against the corner of a chair and lying sprawled on the floor on his back, unconscious.

"Ambulance," Neil ordered.

Wanda, her face splotched with tears, dialed Emergency. Meanwhile, Neil knelt down beside Randolph and loosened his necktie. Randolph was pale and breathing harshly but the cut on his head appeared to be superficial and there was very little blood. Neil tugged his neatly three-cornered handkerchief out of his breast pocket and dabbed at the wound as gently as he could.

"The medics said four minutes," Wanda said, coming across the office. She stopped and looked down at Randolph. "Is he unconscious?"

"Shock or concussion, maybe both. Whichever it is, he's probably better off."

"I still can't believe it," Wanda pressed her hand against her mouth. "How could all of them be dead?"

"The rangers didn't say?"

Wanda shook her head. "They kept repeating 'serious accident,' that's all. Perhaps there was a fire."

Neil said, "Hand me that cushion, would you? He'd be better with his feet raised."

Wanda did as she was told and then turned away, her face covered by her hands and sobbing in silence as if she would never stop.

FOUR

He woke up and the afternoon sunlight was spread across the ceiling in fanlike stripes. His head no longer seemed to belong to his body and there was a steely taste in his mouth, but he felt peculiarly serene and wondered if he had been involved in a serious traffic accident.

After all, hadn't someone been talking about the brakes on his car only a few minutes before, describing how they had failed?

He tried to raise his head off the pillow. It was an effort and it hurt his neck, but he managed to see that he was in a large, plain room decorated in the palest of greens. There was a modernistic print on the wall, not very distinguished; a sickly yucca stood in a woven planter on the opposite side of the room, its leaves tipped with brown as if it badly needed watering. The light was filtering through a parchment-colored venetian blind that had three broken slats.

He let his head fall back on the pillow. It had not occurred to him yet to wonder who he was or what he was doing here. It seemed enough that he was alive.

He slept for a while and then woke up again. The stripes on the ceiling had faded, and he had the feeling that some-one had been in the room to look at him as he slept. The bedside table had been moved.

He began to try to piece together the recent events of his life. For a brief flicker of an instant he thought he could

70

remember tires squealing and metal crunching, that terrible smash-bang sound of serious accidents. Yet he was sure that somebody had told him about that and that he hadn't experienced it for himself. His brain must be making excuses, trying to divert his attention from what had really happened.

It began to enter his mind then that something truly terrible had taken place, not simply an automobile accident. But what was it? He kept trying to form a coherent picture of it in his mind's eye, but it always seemed to refract and break up, like the shadow of a huge shark deep underwater. He frowned and concentrated, but the shadow slipped away.

Twenty minutes passed. From somewhere in the distance he could hear the sound of shoes scuffling, and amplified voices. He slept, and then he awoke. It was growing dark now and the blinds had turned to blue. He groped around beside him and found a trailing light switch, which he clicked on. A bright bedside light shone into his eyes and he turned his face away.

After a while he slowly lifted his right hand so he could examine it. He was wearing a wide-sleeved gown of pale-yellow cotton, obviously industrially laundered to judge by the inaccurate but well-starched creases in it, and there was a plastic band on his wrist. When he twisted the band around, he could see that it was carrying somebody's name, written in ball-point pen. He squinted hard at the writing, trying to decipher it, but after two or three minutes he decided that he must have lost the ability to read. The squiggles of the pen refused to coagulate into letters and the letters themselves refused to assemble into comprehensible words.

He thought: *I can't read. I must have suffered brain damage. There was an automobile accident and I suffered brain damage.* He even believed that he could remember his forehead striking the walnut cocktail cabinet in front of him. Howling tires. Splintering decanters.

But that shadowy shark was rising out of the depths, bearing that shadowy, threatening truth that his mind was desperately trying to keep submerged. He had half an idea of what it was, more than half of an idea. And he knew that when it broke surface, he was going to be faced with the absolute reality of what had happened, and why, and what he was doing here lying in this bed. The shark was rising swiftly now. At any moment he was going to have to accept the truth it brought, and he knew that he would not be able to bear it. His brain would not let him articulate what it was even though his mouth was struggling to form the words that would describe it. Suddenly his hands flew up before him as if he were trying to protect himself from a blizzard.

He shouted, "*Marmie!*" But at that very moment a dark-faced man in a pale-blue overall walked into the room and abruptly called out, "Mr. Clare!"

Randolph opened his eyes and saw that his hands were lifted up. Slowly, dazedly, he lowered them and turned his head to stare at the intruder who had interrupted his nightmare. A dark-faced man, but not black; an Oriental with a flat-featured face and peculiarly glittering eyes. Randolph thought that perhaps he was still hallucinating and that this man was not real. Perhaps his brain damage had gone far beyond affecting his ability to read and write; perhaps he was clinically mad.

"Mr. Clare," the man repeated, his voice more gentle this time.

"Mr. Clare?" Randolph queried, his mouth dry.

The man approached the bed. "I am Dr. Ambara." He stood looking down at Randolph and then, without warning, he bent forward, peeled back each of Randolph's eyelids in turn and peered into them with a lighted opthalmoscope. Randolph saw crisscrosses of white light dancing amid patches of scarlet.

"Well, well," said Dr. Ambara. "How do you feel?"

Randolph did not know what to say. He stared back at the doctor and tried to mouth the word "Fine," but somehow his brain refused to pass on the order.

Randolph could see that Dr. Ambara was a young man, only twenty-six or twenty-seven, and that he had a silky black mustache and a chocolate-colored mole on his left cheek in the shape of a diving bird. He didn't know what had made him think of a diving bird, but he articulated thickly, "Something's happened." He hesitated and then added, "Something bad."

Dr. Ambara said briskly, "Yes, Mr. Clare. Something's happened. Do you know where you are?"

"Mo," replied Randolph. His lip were too dry and swollen to say "No."

"This is the Mount Moriah Memorial Clinic," Dr. Ambara told him. "You were brought here this morning suffering from shock and a mild concussion. I gave you a sedative when you were admitted and since then, you have been sleeping."

"What's the time now?" Randolph asked. The shark was still rising but any kind of conversation would keep his mind from having to turn around and face it when it surfaced.

"The time now is seven-seventeen," said Dr. Ambara, consulting his large gold digital wristwatch.

"Almost the whole day," Randolph murmured.

"Yes," said Dr. Ambara.

Randolph licked his lips and said, "I keep thinking it was an automobile accident, but it wasn't, was it?"

"No," Dr. Ambara replied. He drew up a chair and sat down beside the bed. His face was half-hidden by the bedside light, although Randolph could still see his mouth as he spoke and the gleam of his silky mustache.

"You know, the mind often plays us unusual tricks," Dr. Ambara went on. "It understands our limitations, our restricted ability to cope with some of the things that happen to us. Sometimes when we have suffered a terrible crisis, the mind simply will not accept that the crisis has taken place, at least not until our emotions are sufficiently calm to deal with it."

Randolph said, "You're trying to tell me that a terrible crisis has taken place in my life, is that it? That that's why I'm here?"

Dr. Ambara nodded and then without any embarrassment, he took Randolph's hand and held it.

"Something's happened to Marmie. Is Marmie hurt?"

Dr. Ambara nodded again, and Randolph was intrigued to

see that there were tears running down his cheeks. "I have to tell you that your wife is dead. Also that all your children are dead."

The shark fumed to the surface and Randolph was face-to-face with its rows of snarling teeth. He felt fear, desperation, desolation, panic and—most of all—unutterable grief. He was unable to speak.

In a quiet voice, Dr. Ambara went on. "They were found in your cabin in Quebec. There was no chance of saving them. They were beyond help."

Tears poured from Randolph's eyes in a hot, unquenchable stream and he clutched Dr. Ambara's hand.

The doctor said, "I am sorry to tell you that they were murdered. Somebody broke into the cabin and killed them. It was a very bad event."

Randolph swallowed and managed to ask, "Did they suffer? Did any of them suffer?"

"I would be lying to you if I said not," Dr. Ambara replied.

Randolph crumpled and sobbed uncontrollably. Nonetheless he managed to say, "You must tell me what happened."

"I can tell you only what the police have explained," Dr. Ambara said.

"All the same, tell me."

"I have to warn you that it was a very unpleasant scene."

"Tell me. I'm going to have to find out sometime."

Dr. Ambara released Randolph's hand and went over to the window. He parted the blinds and looked southwest toward the distant lights of the Stroh Brewery and Memphis International Airport. Planes circled in the night like fireflies. Dr. Ambara watched them for a while and Randolph waited with patience. Apart from the fact that he was still sedated and therefore calmer than he normally would have been, he was prepared to believe that Dr. Ambara himself was deeply upset by what had happened and that for this reason, the man could share in his grief.

At last, without looking from the window, Dr. Ambara said, "It was late last night as far as the police can tell.

Three or four men broke into the cabin. One of them broke down the door with an ax and then used that same ax to kill your younger son, Mark.''

"Mark," Randolph whispered, hoping to God he wasn't going mad.

"After that," Dr. Ambara went on, "they shot and killed your older son, John, with a shotgun."

Randolph was too grief-stricken to even pronounce John's name. Tears began to slide out of his eyes again and he had to clench his teeth to prevent himself from crying out loud.

Dr. Ambara turned away from the window at last and said, "I am telling you this because you have to know and the sooner you know, the better it is going to be. Your mind will have enough to cope with without constantly wondering what has happened and why everybody is being so solicitous to you."

Randolph wept and nodded. He had not cried like this since his mother had died. He couldn't speak anymore. He lay back on the pillow and waited for Dr. Ambara to tell him the worst.

"Your wife and your daughter were tied up. The police say that they were raped several times. Then they were hung with barbed wire from a beam in the living room. The police said they must have suffered but not for very long."

Dr. Ambara bent over Randolph and wiped the tears from his eyes with a tissue. His face was sympathetic and infinitely understanding. He studied Randolph for a moment and then explained to him with great gentleness, "I have told you because you have to know. It was a terrible tragedy, and everybody in the clinic feels for you deeply. They have pain in their hearts for you that they cannot express."

He sat down and added, "You must understand that I am your doctor, that I am here to make you better and to overcome your misery. Whatever you want to know, I will tell you. Whenever you want to talk, I will talk with you. This is a shattering event that you will have to think about and talk about over and over again. You will always ask yourself many questions, beginning with why. Why did I leave my family in Canada and not bring them back home with me? Why is fate so cruel? Why did it have to be them? Perhaps the greatest difficulty you will have to face is that none of these questions have answers.''

Randolph said, ''They were so beautiful, all of them.''

''Yes,'' said Dr. Ambara.

There was a pause and then Randolph said, ''I'm trying to think of the very last second I saw them. They came out to the jetty to see me onto the plane. I hugged the boys, Mark first, then John. Then I kissed Issa. Last of all, I kissed Marmie. Do you know . . . I can almost feel them in my arms.''

''That feeling will never leave you,'' Dr. Ambara assured him.

''What do I do now?'' asked Randolph. ''I'm alone.''

''Well, you must stay here for a day or two under observation. You lost consciousness when they gave you the news that your family was dead and you hit your head when you fell. We have to make sure there is no damage to your brain.''

''Is that likely?''

Dr. Ambara shook his head. ''No, it isn't. But I think you should also take the opportunity to rely on somebody else for a little while; on me, and on the nursing staff. Your own doctor—Dr. Linklater—will be coming to see you later and if you wish, you can see your priest. Usually, however, I find that people who have been suddenly bereaved prefer to ask questions about the religious implications later, when the sense of shock has subsided.''

''What do you believe?'' Randolph asked.

Dr. Ambara looked surprised. ''What do I believe? Well, I am Indonesian and my religion is Hindu, so what I believe may be rather mystifying to you.''

''Tell me,'' Randolph persisted hoarsely.

Dr. Ambara sensed that Randolph was clinging to any thread that would begin to weave itself into some kind of explanation that he could accept even tentatively. He thoughtfully rubbed his chin for a moment and then said, ''I believe that death is not a separation but simply a journey of the soul to the next resting place, which is heaven. In heaven there is peace, and freedom from worry and pain.''

"Do you really believe that? Do you really believe that my family is still there somewhere, that their souls are still there?''

Dr. Ambara smiled. ''It depends on what you mean by 'there,' Mr. Clare. Heaven exists both inside and outside the human mind. But, yes, I believe that your family still exists, and as a Hindu, I also believe that one day they will each be reborn, reincarnated, as we all will, probably as the grandsons and granddaughters of distant relatives.''

Randolph said, ''Thank you.''

"Why do you thank me? As far as I am concerned, this is what actually occurs.''

"I wish I had your faith.''

"Well, what we believe is for each of us to decide,'' said Dr. Ambara. ''But all faith is based on fact, and there are many stories in Indonesia that substantiate our belief.''

"What do you mean?''

"I mean simply that people who have lost their sons and daughters have sometimes spoken to their grandchildren and discovered that these grandchildren have possessed a knowledge of people and events that only their dead children could possibly have known. It is so common, this faculty, that it is not even remarked upon in the town I come from. I am sure that American children have the same faculty but their parents are not aware of it, and would not believe it even if they were. And so the children rapidly forget the memories they brought out of the womb with them from their previous lives.''

Dr. Ambara was silent for a moment and then added, ''There are those who claim to have met and spoken to the dead—mystics usually—but the high priests do not ordinarily approve of such things.''

He picked up the progress chart hanging at the foot of Randolph's bed, unscrewed the cap of his fountain pen and jotted a few notes. Then he said, ''Whatever you need, do not hesitate to ask for it. I know you are an active man; I know that you are the president of a very important company and that there are great pressures on you. But for your own sake, give yourself a few days in order to absorb and understand what has happened to you. Feel free to talk about it as much as you want. It is vital for your health—even for your survival—that you do not suppress your grief."

He left Randolph alone then, and for almost an hour Randolph lay by himself, the light switched off, and wept. At about eight o'clock, however, a young nurse came in carrying a tray. She drew the drapes, switched on the bedside lights and helped Randolph sit up, his back propped by pillows.

"My name is Suzie," she smiled. She was red-haired and freckle-faced. She could have stepped straight out of a Norman Rockwell picture: the bouncy young American nurse. She swung a tray around in front of Randolph and set his food on it: chicken soup, fresh-baked rolls and a glass of fruit juice.

"This isn't a Jewish hospital, is it?" Randolph asked. It was a deliberate attempt to say something light and amusing. Unfortunately, his voice was strained from sobbing and the young nurse did not understand him.

"I'm sorry?" she blinked.

"The chicken soup," Randolph told her. "Chicken soup is what Jewish mothers give their families for all conceivable ailments."

"Oh," said Suzie and tugged his bedcovers straight.

Randolph looked down at his supper and knew that he could not eat it. "You'd better just take this away," he said. "I can't even swallow."

"Dr. Ambara said that you have to eat something."

"I'm sorry, I can't."

Suzie parked her well-rounded bottom on the bed and picked up the spoon. "If you can't eat for yourself, I'm going to have to feed you."

"Please," said Randolph. "I'm really not hungry at all."

But she ladled out a spoonful of soup and offered it up to his lips. "Come on," she urged. "You don't want to upset Dr. Ambara."

Randolph allowed her to pour the soup into his mouth.

But he felt so childish and vulnerable when she did that his grief came rising up and he burst out sobbing. The soup splattered all over the tray and his gown.

"Oh, God," he wept. "I'm sorry."

Suzie took away the tray and swung the table back against the wall. She dried him with a towel and then sat on the bed again and held him in her arms. "Sssh," she soothed him, stroking his hair. When he felt the softness of her nylon-covered breast against his cheek and smelled the perfume of her femininity, he could scarcely stop himself from screaming out in agony. It was as though every nerve in his body was being wound tighter and tighter and his brain was going to implode like a smashed television screen, leaving only fragments of his identity.

"Sssh," she whispered again and kept on stroking his hair.

Later during the night, they gave him another sedative. He heard the door swing open and close several times, and voices. Somebody was saying something about Dr. Linklater. Every time the door opened, light shone into his eyes and he could hear the bustle of the clinic outside his room.

He slept at last and dreamed that he was frantically trying to run back to Quebec. He had to reach Marmie and the children. It was crucial. A dark wave of panic was rolling in behind him while a snarl of brambles was clinging to his trouser legs, making it impossible for him to hurry. He saw Marmie and the children in the distance, running from him across a stormy wheat field; clouds were building over their heads in inky castles. He tried to free his legs so he could catch up with them and warn them, but the brambles had grown into his skin now and he couldn't take another step.

He shouted "Marmie!" but the wind was rising and his voice was carried away.

He shouted "Marmie!" again and this time she turned around; he could see that her face was as white as wax. She was staring at him with such frightening accusation that he stopped shouting, dropped his arms by his sides and looked back at her in guilt and terror. Then the children turned around—John and Mark and Issa—and their faces too were as white as wax and there was no love in them, only condemnation.

"I didn't know," he told Marmie. He raised his hands toward her, begging her to forgive him and to come back and embrace him. "Marmie, I swear it. I didn't know."

Marmie stared at him for a moment longer and then she turned away, and the children turned away too, and they began to glide through the deserted street that had taken the place of the wheat field until they reached the banks of the Mississippi.

"You'll drown!" he desperately tried to warn them. But they continued to glide away across the surface of the river, and at last the dark clouds descended to the opposite shore and they were gone.

He woke up, found himself staring at his pillow in horror . . . and knew with absolute finality that they were dead.

Slowly he turned and looked toward the window. The drapes had been drawn back and sunlight was illuminating the blind. His head ached and his limbs felt stiff, but he managed to raise himself up on one elbow.

Just then the door opened and Suzie came in. Behind her, sleek and tanned, his gray-winged hair neatly combed, his eyes shining, came Dr. Linklater.

"Randolph," the doctor said, coming over and taking his hand.

"Hallo, Miles," Randolph said. "How are you doing? Didn't expect to be seeing you for a while."

Suzie asked, "How about some breakfast?"

"Coffee," Randolph told her.

"Oh, come on now, you have to have more than coffee," Dr. Linklater chided him. He turned to Suzie and said, "Bring the man a bowl of Rice Krispies and some fruit."

"Miles, I never eat Rice Krispies," Randolph protested.

"Quiet, or you'll get Count Chokula instead."

Randolph eased himself into a sitting position. "Were you here last night?" he asked.

"Sure was. Looked in at nine, and then again at eleven."

"I guess I'll see it on my bill."

Dr. Linklater tugged his chair closer. "This has been a terrible business, Randolph. I want you to know that Marjorie and I, well, we're so stunned that we don't even know what to say. But you have our heartfelt sympathies, and you know that you can count on us for anything you need."

Randolph said, "Will I have to go to Canada?"

The doctor shook his head. "There was some suggestion of it from the Canadian police, but I vetoed it on health grounds. They'll be sending two of their detectives down to talk to you tomorrow, if you can stand it."

Randolph nodded. He felt disassembled this morning, and nothing seemed to make much sense. But he acquiesced because he knew that time had refused to stand still, even at eight forty-seven yesterday morning, and that in one way or another, he was going to have to start living again, walking around and talking to people, and running his business.

"Will I have to . . . look at them?" Randolph asked.

"You mean will you have to identify the remains? No, that's already been done. Your Cousin Ella flew up to Quebec yesterday afternoon and did everything necessary. She'll be getting in touch with you later, but she'll fly the remains back just as soon as the police have released them, and she'll help you make the funeral arrangements."

"Funeral arrangements," Randolph mouthed as if they were words in an alien vocabulary.

Dr. Linklater reached out and held his hand. "I called your office too. Your Mr. Sleaman said that everything was fine and that you shouldn't concern yourself about getting back to work until you are really ready. He said the Raleigh factory should be back on line within four days now."

"Funeral arrangements," Randolph repeated.

Dr. Linklater gave him a tight, professional smile. "All you have to think about now, Randy, is number one. Getting yourself back into shape, learning to come to terms with what happened. Your family is tragically dead, but you're still alive, and you know as well as I do that Marmie and the kids would never wish anything harmful to happen to you, not ever."

Randolph frowned at him with unfocused eyes. "Miles," he said, "do you believe in spirits? I mean souls?"

"Sure."

"No, no, I don't think I'm making myself clear. Do you believe in them, do you believe they're real? I mean really real?"

"I'm not too sure of what you're driving at," Dr. Linklater confessed, sitting upright and taking his hand away from Randolph's.

Randolph rubbed his forehead with the heel of his hand. "It's not too easy to explain," he said, "but Dr.—whatever-his-name-is—he was talking about it. The Indonesian guy."

"Oh, you mean Dr. Ambara. Yes, excellent doctor. One of the best. Came from Djakarta originally and graduated from University Hospital in Baltimore. What did he say?"

"He said that in the Hindu religion, when you die, your soul doesn't vanish forever, like the Christians think it does. It goes to heaven and waits to be reborn."

"Well, yes, that's what Hindus believe, sure. Reincarnation, coming back to earth as a sacred cow, that kind of thing."

"No, no, it's much more than that," Randolph said. "There are mystics, he said, who can actually talk to the dead, actually meet them."

Dr. Linklater looked uncomfortable. He cleared his throat, wrung his hands and inspected the floor. "What you have to understand, Randy, is that what Dr. Ambara was saying to you was probably just his way of trying to console you, of trying to make you feel that you hadn't lost Marmie and the kids forever. I think he may have slightly miscalculated the effect that his words were likely to have on you at this crucial stage in the grieving process."

"You mean you don't believe that Marmie and the children are anywhere at all? You think they're just gone, forever?"

"Randy, I didn't say that I didn't believe in heaven. I'm a Christian, goddam it, and I believe what the Good Book has to say on the subject. But Dr. Ambara has no right to suggest to you in any way that your family is still alive in a human sense and that they're hovering around in some kind of celestial anteroom. I believe in life everlasting, Randy, but I also know for a fact that once you've shaken off this mortal coil, you don't come back. Your family is sitting on the right hand of God, Randy, but once you're sitting on the right hand of God, I'm sorry but you're beyond recall.''

Randolph nodded slowly and attempted a smile. ''I'm sorry I made you struggle with religious philosophy so early in the morning,'' he said.

Suzie came in with Randolph's coffee and Rice Krispies. She poured out the milk for him while the doctor continued to talk.

''I'm sure that Dr. Ambara was well-intentioned. He wanted to give you hope for the future and reassurance about your family, and of course he related their deaths to his own religion. Well, that's perfectly legitimate. There is no discrimination in Tennessee hospitals on religious grounds. But, Randy, you're not a Hindu. You're going to have to come to terms with this according to your own religion and your own upbringing.''

Randolph ate his cereal slowly and carefully. He was just beginning to realize how hungry he was. ''Suppose I converted?'' he asked.

''That wouldn't solve anything. You have to understand that Marmie and the kids are gone from this world, and no matter where they are—and I believe that wherever they are, they're happy—you won't see them again.''

''You don't think a spiritualist might be able to get in touch with them?''

Dr. Linklater shook his head. ''They're gone, Randy.''

Tears suddenly began to pour down Randolph's cheeks and he choked on the Rice Krispies.

''There was so much I didn't have a chance to tell them,'' he said. ''There was so much I wanted to say.''

''I understand,'' Dr. Linklater told him in a confiding voice. ''Believe me, Randy, I know how you feel.''

Suzie came bustling in again and Dr. Linklater said uneasily, ''I'd better go. I'll come back later, after I'm through with evening surgery.''

Randolph said, "Okay. Thank you."

"Listen," said Dr. Linklater, glancing meaningfully at Suzie to make sure she understood what the problem was, "don't start getting ideas about spiritualists or mediums or any of that kind of stuff. Believe me, Randy, it will only confuse you, give you false hopes and delay your recovery."

"All right," Randolph agreed. He wiped his eyes with his napkin.

"That's fine," smiled Dr. Linklater. "Now finish your breakfast and I'll catch you later."

FIVE

Randolph was attended to that evening by a different doctor, a crew-cut M.D. with a stiff, peremptory manner who assured him that his scalp wound was going to heal like new within three days and that most illnesses were all in the mind. When Randolph asked him where Dr. Ambara was, the doctor pushed one hand deep into the pocket of his overall, gave a crooked smile and said, "We're pretty damn busy here, believe me."

But the next morning the crew-cut doctor returned. He sat on the end of the bed uninvited, leafed through Randolph's chart and muttered to himself, "Whole damn family, huh?"

Randolph said, "I want to see Dr. Ambara."

"I'm sorry, Mr. Clare. Dr. Ambara had to take some time off."

"I insist on seeing him."

"I can pass your message on. Unfortunately, I can't guarantee that Dr. Ambara will respond to it."

That afternoon when Dr. Linklater stopped by, Randolph demanded, "What happened to Dr. Ambara? They took him off my case."

Dr. Linklater puffed out his cheeks and looked uncomfortable. "I'm afraid to say that they did it on my instructions."

"But why? What right did you have to do that? I liked

85

him, he helped me. What he was saying to me was reassuring, for God's sake. It gave me confidence."

"Confidence in what, Randy? Confidence that you would somehow talk to Marmie and the kids again, tell them everything you never had time to tell them when they were alive? Come on, Randy, I'm your friend. You've been through a terrible, traumatic experience. Right now your mind is vulnerable and suggestible, and while people like Dr. Ambara may mean well, they won't do your recovery process any good."

Randolph pulled back the bedcovers and swung his legs out of bed.

"What the hell are you doing?" Dr. Linklater wanted to know.

"What the hell do you think I'm doing? I'm discharging myself. I'm not going to lie here for the next five days and be treated like a rutabaga."

"You can't do that. You're sick. You're under sedation. You had a concussion, clinical shock and psychological trauma."

"Maybe I did. But now I'm better and I'm going home."

"The Canadian police are coming here this afternoon to talk to you."

"I'm sure the hospital can redirect them."

Randolph untied his gown, went to the closet and took out his clothes.

"How do you think you're going to get home?" Dr. Linklater demanded.

"I'm sure I can prevail on you to drive me."

"I'm not driving you anywhere. My medical advice to you is to stay put until you're well enough to go home; even then, you should have a private nurse in attendance."

"If you won't drive me home, Miles, I'll just have to call Herbert."

"Herbert doesn't happen to be there today. I know that because I called Charles about arrangements for private medical care and Charles said that Herbert had gone to the body shop to pick up your limousine."

Randolph stuffed his shirttails into his pants and zipped

up his fly. "I'm discharging myself, Miles, and that's all there is to it." He knotted his necktie and went across to the side-table drawer where Suzie had put his wallet. He took out the card that Stanley Vergo had given him, lifted the telephone receiver and punched out the number.

"You're making a serious mistake here, Randolph," Dr. Linklater said.

"Let me be the judge of that," Randolph told him.

Stanley Vergo's yellow cab drew up in front of the Mount Moriah Clinic less than ten minutes later.

"How are you doing, Mr. Clare?" Stanley asked, getting out and opening the back door of the cab with one hand and wiping the sweat from his forehead with the other. Randolph had not seen the man out of the driver's seat before and was suitably impressed by his girth and the size of his belly. When Stanley got back behind the wheel, he sniffed, smiled at Randolph in the rearview mirror and said, "They didn't send your limo?"

"It's being repaired. That was the reason it didn't show up on Tuesday. It was involved in an accident."

"You ought to fire your driver. Hey, you want a new driver? I've always wanted to drive a limo."

"It wasn't my driver's fault."

"Oh, well . . . if it ever *is* his fault, you know my number."

They drove in silence for a while. Then Stanley said, "That was too bad about your family. That really shocked me when I heard about it. I guess that's why you was in that clinic, huh?"

"You know about it?" asked Randolph defensively.

"Tell me who don't. It was on the TV, it was in the paper. Front-page news. Cottonseed tycoon's wife, children, in brutal slaying."

"You're the first person who's talked to me about it. I mean the first person who's talked to me about it and hasn't treated me like a freak or an invalid."

Stanley took a left onto Old Getwell Road. "I lost my younger brother in an auto smash. He died right in front of me, staring at me. Death don't hold no mysteries as far as

I'm concerned. It's a part of life. I couldn't stand the way folks whispered about it then and I can't stand the way folks whisper about it now. What can you do? It's a part of life, death.''

They said nothing while they drove past the airport but then Stanley added, "Do the cops know who might have done it? And why?"

"Not as far as I know. The Canadian police are coming to see me this afternoon."

"That was just one of the thoughts that kind of crossed my mind," Stanley said. He reached across to the front-passenger seat and picked up a Mars bar. He tugged off the wrapper with his teeth and began to devour the candy with audible relish. "What I thought to myself was, one day Mr. Clare has this factory fire, the next day his family gets totaled. I mean to say, could there be some kind of a connection? Take your law of averages. How often do two things as bad as that happen to one person in one week?"

Randolph stared at the back of Stanley's neck. Blond bristles and crimson spots, seasoned with a few freckles and basted with sweat. A similar thought had occurred to him, too, in the depths of the night when he had been all cried out and his mind had been racing over the fire and the murder and the limousine wreck . . . over and over again. "You haven't heard anything that might substantiate what you're thinking, have you?" he asked.

"It's only what you might call a theory," Stanley said with his mouth full, driving one-handedly. "But I heard one young executive type from Brooks talking about it; he was saying that you would probably take the loss of your family pretty hard and that you may decide that staying independent would be too much of a strain. He said you may decide to quit altogether, that was the feeling at Brooks."

Randolph said, "Do me a favor, would you, Stanley? Keep your ears open really wide. If there's even the slightest suggestion that what happened to my family might have had anything to do with Brooks or Graceworthy or any other Association company, you let me know. I'll make it worth your while."

"Will you let me drive your limo?"

"I might even do that."

"Okay, Mr. Clare, you're on."

The taxi swept into the gates of Clare Castle and along the graveled driveway until it reached the pillared porch, where one of the maintenance men was up on a stepladder, painting the carriage lamp in black and gold enamel.

Stanley opened the taxi door and Randolph wearily climbed out. The maintenance man set down his brushes and hurried down the ladder.

"Mr. Clare! Nobody said that you were coming!"

"It's all right, Michael. I'm fine. Is Charles at home?"

"Yes, sir. And Mrs. Wallace."

Randolph waved a farewell salute to Stanley and went in the house. The entrance hall was cool and gloomy because the blinds had been drawn. There were vases of flowers everywhere—roses and irises and gladioli—and almost all of them were tagged with black-edged cards. The fragrance was overwhelming: the sweet fragrance of sympathy.

Mrs. Wallace appeared at the top of the curving marble staircase. She was the Castle's housekeeper: a middle-aged Memphis widow who had once had an elegant home of her own, before her husband lost all his money in a wild real-estate speculation and drowned himself in the Mississippi. She was small, plain and fussy, with color-rinsed hair curled up like chrysanthemum petals and a way of tweaking at her earrings and talking archly about "people of *our* background."

This morning, however, she came down the stairs distraught. She took Randolph's hands between hers and trembled with sorrow. "Oh, Mr. Clare, your poor family! Oh, Mr. Clare, I'm devastated!"

Randolph put his arm around her shoulders and held her until she stopped sobbing. "It's going to take us a long time to get used to an empty house," he told her, "but I guess we'll manage it somehow, won't we? What do you think?"

His own heart was breaking as he stood in the house he had redecorated and refurbished entirely for Marmie, but he knew that if he did not appear to be strong in the presence of those who depended on him, their lives would fall to pieces, as well as his.

"I'll tell you what you can do for me, Mrs. Wallace," he said. "You can empty all of Mrs. Clare's closets and pack her clothes in trunks. Take away all of her cosmetics before I go upstairs, everything personal. Tomorrow perhaps you can start on the children's rooms."

"Oh, Mr. Clare," wept Mrs. Wallace, her eyes blind with grief.

Randolph hugged her. She felt as fragile as a small bird. "I know, Mrs. Wallace, I know. But if you can do that one thing for me, you'll save me a great deal of unnecessary pain."

"Yes, Mr. Clare," she whispered.

Randolph walked through to the library. This was his sanctuary, the one room in the house that contained nothing to remind him of Marmie and the children. There were rows and rows of leather-bound books, most of them scientific and historical, framed eighteenth-century prints of cotton plants on the walls. High windows looked out across the gardens, the curving lawns and the flowering azaleas.

Randolph picked out his favorite pipe, a meerschaum that Marmie had given him two years ago for Christmas, and then lifted the lid of the red-and-white porcelain tobacco jar. He filled his pipe simply and ritualistically and then lit it. Sitting back in his favorite leather-upholstered chair, he idly watched the clouds of smoke rise and fall.

He was still sitting there, his eyes closed and thinking about Marmie, when the telephone rang. He let it ring for a while before reaching over and picking it up.

"Mr. Clare? I'm sorry to trouble you. It's Suzie."

He took his pipe out of his mouth. "Suzie?"

"Your nurse from Mount Moriah Clinic."

"Ah, yes, Suzie. I'm sorry. I'm still a little erratic, I'm afraid. How can I help you?"

"I hope that *I* can help *you*. I heard you talking to Dr. Linklater and I know you wanted to get in touch with Dr. Ambara."

"That's right. Dr. Linklater asked that he be taken off my case. That was the reason I discharged myself."

"I heard all about it. Dr. Ambara was very upset. He tried to talk to you about it, but you were already gone."

"As far as I'm concerned," Randolph told her, "Dr. Ambara is the only doctor at Mount Moriah who has any idea of what people go through when they lose somebody close. I know that his ideas about souls and spirits are—well, what could you call them?—kind of unorthodox. Very mystical, very Oriental. But he made me feel better. He made me believe that Marmie and the kids hadn't been just wiped out as if they'd never even lived."

Suddenly, without warning, grief began to surge up within him again and he found his throat so tight that he was unable to speak. He sat up straight and put down his pipe, pressing his hand hard against his mouth and hoping that Suzie would understand why he was silent.

"Mr. Clare," she said after a moment, "I can give you Dr. Ambara's home telephone number. He's too reserved to call you himself, and besides, it wouldn't be ethical. He lives in Germantown, so he isn't very far from you."

Randolph managed to say, "Thank you," as he jotted down the number on his desk blotter in bright blue ink.

"I hope you find what you're looking for," Suzie said.

"I hope so too," Randolph replied. "I appreciate your calling me."

Suzie said simply, "You've just lost everything, haven't you? Your wife, your children, your whole life. Nobody seemed to understand that except Dr. Ambara."

"And you," Randolph told her. "*You* understand, don't you?"

"A little," she said and hung up.

Randolph picked up his pipe again but did not relight it. Instead, he went to the window and stared out over the gardens. After a while Charles came in and sadly and respectfully stood by the door. He was wearing a black armband and his face was wet with tears.

"Hello, Charles," Randolph said.

"Welcome back home, Mr. Clare."

"It's not a very happy time, Charles."

"No, sir. We're all real sorry for what happened. We don't even have the words."

"I know."

"Would you care for a little luncheon, sir? You really ought to eat something."

"Yes, I'll have something light," Randolph answered. Suzie's telephone call had made him feel optimistic again, raised his spirits in the same way that Dr. Ambara's explanation of death and reincarnation had. There was a rational part of Randolph's mind that told him that Dr. Ambara's beliefs about souls and spirits might be utter nonsense and that even if they were not, they might not apply to Western people. Did the Hindu gods answer Christian prayers? Dr. Ambara could well be nothing more than a religious eccentric, a mischievous charlatan or an out-and-out fanatic. But Randolph's wife and children had been snatched away from him so abruptly and so violently that he was prepared to accept any means of getting in touch with them, if only to bid them good-bye.

Dr. Ambara had assured him that spirits pass out of the body and into heaven, in preparation for being born again. Dr. Ambara had said that it was possible to contact these spirits, even possible to see them and talk to them; and because Randolph could not bring himself to believe that Marmie and the children had been totally eliminated, he had to believe—wanted to believe—in Dr. Ambara.

He ate his lunch on the patio outside the library where a warm May breeze played with the fringes of the awnings. A little smoked chicken cut into thin, appetizing slices, a little green salad, a glass of dry white wine.

Charles came out to pour him some more wine and said, "Whatever you want, Mr. Clare, all you have to do is ask."

Randolph smiled and said, "Thank you, Charles, that's appreciated." Had Charles been less reserved, Randolph would have taken his hand. But Charles believed in formality and the proper observance of social distances, and Randolph knew he would have only succeeded in embarrassing him.

At two o'clock that afternoon, two officers from the Royal Canadian Mounted Police arrived at Clare Castle in a rented Ford Granada. Charles showed them through to the garden and they came out onto the patio shading their eyes against the sun, awkwardly holding their hats and their briefcases. Charles said to Randolph, "Police officers, Mr. Clare, from Quebec."

The older of the two policemen came forward and held out his hand. "Inspector Dulac, sir. We were told by the Mount Moriah Clinic that you were here. The clinical director explained that you had decided to discharge yourself. This is my colleague, Sergeant Allinson."

"Please sit down," Randolph said, aware that he sounded vague.

The two policemen sat uncomfortably in the striped canvas chairs Randolph offered them. Inspector Dulac was well into his fifties, with silver hair that was short and severely cut and a heavy, square face, very French. Sergeant Allinson had a narrow head, wavy brown hair and a large Roman nose beaded with perspiration. Both men wore gray suits, long-sleeved shirts, and neckties. Neither had come dressed for a humid Mississippi summer.

"You will forgive us for calling on you without a proper appointment," said Inspector Dulac with a strong Quebecois accent. "We had expected you to be lying in your hospital bed, you see, a captive audience."

Sergeant Allinson nodded in agreement, lifted his brown-leather briefcase to his knees and began to poke around inside it.

"First of all, it is my duty to offer you the condolences of the Royal Canadian Mounted Police," Inspector Dulac said. "What happened to your wife and children was terrible and tragic, and I want to reassure you that we are making extraordinary efforts to capture the perpetrators. You will understand, I hope, the painful necessity for this visit. We need all the information we can possibly procure."

"I understand," Randolph said hoarsely. Then, noticing

Charles standing on the other side of the patio, he asked, "Would you care for a drink? Fruit punch maybe, or lemonade? It's pretty damned hot."

"I think a lemonade would be welcome," said Inspector Dulac. Sergeant Allinson nodded. "Yes, a lemonade."

Inspector Dulac held out his left hand and Sergeant Allinson passed him a thick sheaf of papers. "From experience," he said, "I am anticipating that you will wish to know in considerable detail how your family died. If you do not, please tell me, but usually the process of healing the mind cannot begin until the event is fully understood."

"Yes," Randolph said. He picked up his sunglasses from the wicker table beside him and put them on.

Inspector Dulac said, "What I will tell you about it will be most painful to you because the crime was very brutal and apparently without motive. It is always easier to accept brutality when one knows why it was used; if it was out of rage, perhaps, or for robbery, or for lust, or for revenge. But so far it appears that this was a multiple homicide that was perpetrated for no coherent reason whatever. I will upset you, I have no doubt of that. But you seem to me to be the kind of man who has to know everything before he can come to terms with his distress. It is always the unanswered questions that cause the most pain."

He picked up the top sheet of paper and began to recite to Randolph the plain facts of the tragedy as if he were reading his evidence in court. Randolph listened, and as he did, he grew colder and colder; it was as if the sun had died out, the wind had swung around to the northeast and the world had rolled over on its axis.

"On the morning of May tenth, nineteen eighty-four, at approximately six twenty-five, Mr. Leonard Dolan was fishing in his boat off the southeast shore of Lac aux Ecorces when his outboard motor failed. He decided to row to shore and seek assistance at the lodging known as Clare Cabin. On reaching the structure, he discovered that the front door had been smashed off its hinges; upon approaching more closely, he found that the living room was in violent disarray and that the walls and the rugs were heavily blood-stained. Entering the living room, he saw the dead bodies of the Clare family: John Clare, fifteen years old, who had been shot in the abdomen at close range with a twelve-gauge shotgun; Mark Clare, eleven years old, who had been decapitated by a woodsman's ax; Mrs. Marmie Clare, forty-three, and her daughter Melissa Clare, thirteen, who were bound together with cords and hanging by their necks from the ceiling beams with nooses fashioned of barbed wire. Mr. Dolan found that the cabin's radio telephone had been deliberately put out of action, and so he rowed with some difficulty back to his fishing camp and called the police. Upon examination of the scene of the incident, it appeared that whoever had committed the homicides had forcefully gained access to the cabin with the same woodsman's ax later employed in the killing of Mark Clare. The perpetrators had killed the boys first; the coroner later established that their deaths had occurred between nine and ten o'clock on the evening of May ninth. The two females, however, had been taken to the main bedroom, where they had been bound together in the manner in which they were eventually discovered by Mr. Dolan, and sexually assaulted. Both of them were raped repeatedly, and later examination of the semen ejaculated by their attackers established that there were four different men involved in the rape. The females had been hung and strangulated early the following morning, probably less than an hour before Mr. Dolan approached the cabin. A twenty-two rifle was found in the living room with a jammed magazine, indicating that the members of the Clare family had attempted to protect themselves against assault. Fingerprints and shoe prints, as well as hair, skin, fiber and semen samples, are being forensically examined at the headquarters of the RCMP in Ottawa, and preliminary results have already been forwarded to the FBI in Washington.''

Inspector Dulac lowered the hand that had been shielding his eyes from the sun. He watched Randolph carefully, as if Randolph might be a young son of his who had just learned to ride a bicycle.

"Do you want any more?" he asked. "That's just the résumé."

"I think, for the time being, that's sufficient," Randolph told him, with intense self-control.

"Do you wish to ask any questions?"

Randolph swallowed and thought for a moment. Then he asked, "Did nobody see them? The men who did it?"

"There were no witnesses. The footprints suggest that the men landed by boat or dinghy just out of sight of the cabin, around the headland, and then made their way up to the cabin by walking through the woods."

Sergeant Allinson put in, "This of course suggests that the attack was not spontaneous. The men knew where the cabin was and they approached it with the deliberate intention of breaking in. They were not just passing fishermen who took it into their heads to butcher your family."

Inspector Dulac straightened his papers and said to Randolph, "You might care to make out a list of all those people you can think of who might dislike you sufficiently to have contemplated such an act."

"Nobody dislikes me like that," Randolph said in a hollow voice. "Not like that."

Inspector Dulac said, "I have the official police photographs. If you wish to see them, you may. I must warn you that they are very distressing. But they will be produced in court when these men are eventually brought to justice and it is probably better that you see them now rather than later, if you are going to see them at all."

Randolph said, "Very well."

Sergeant Allinson passed him a brown cardboard-backed envelope marked with the crest of the Royal Canadian Mounted Police. Randolph waited for a moment or two, then took off his sunglasses and tugged out a dozen eight-by-ten color prints. For some reason he had been expecting the photographs to be in black and white. Maybe it was all those old gangster movies he had watched when he was a kid, blood spattered blackly on light-gray suits, flashbulbs flaring white. It seemed to him as if only fairgrounds and

pretty girls and favorite pets should be photographed in
color. Dead bodies should be monochromatic, like nightmares.

He could hardly recognize John. The whole of John's
stomach looked as if it had been ground up like dark-red
hamburger meat, and his face was puffy and swollen. Mark
looked more normal and natural until Randolph realized
that what he had taken for Mark's chest and shoulders were
two discarded cushions and that what he was actually looking at was Mark's severed head. It was so shocking that it
was almost ridiculous. *How could that be my son? How
could either of these corpses be my sons?* But when he
reached the photographs of Marmie and Issa, he began to
weep because suddenly the picture was complete; suddenly
the full extent of Mr. Dolan's terrible discovery became
clear to him; suddenly he could imagine what it must have
been like. Bruised, naked bodies. Chins jerked upward by
tangled barbed wire. Blood, tousled hair and eyes like the
eyes of unfeathered birds that have fallen from their nest.

"Are you all right, Mr. Clare?" Inspector Dulac asked,
leaning forward and taking the photographs.

Randolph swallowed, wiped his eyes and said, "I'll get
over it in time. I just couldn't imagine how terrible it was,
that's all. I'm glad you showed me."

"It is not my invariable policy," Inspector Dulac said,
"but I believed that you could cope with it, and I think it is
important for you to understand."

"What can I tell you?" Randolph asked.

"Is there anything you *wish* to tell me?"

Randolph said, "They're dead, aren't they, all of them?"

Inspector Dulac knew that this question was not absurd. It
sometimes took the relatives of murder victims months,
even years, to come to terms with the idea that their loved
ones were actually dead and not simply missing, or hiding.

He said, "Yes, Mr. Clare, they're dead."

"Do you believe in reincarnation, Inspector?"

"Reincarnation? No, sir, I regret that I don't. I have to be
truthful with you. Perhaps we would feel better about our
grief if indeed we did believe in reincarnation, if we had

some indisputable proof that death is not really the end. But, unfortunately, nobody can say that it is true."

Randolph sat in silence, his head bowed, for almost a minute. Inspector Dulac did not attempt to intrude on his thoughts. Eventually, however, Randolph raised his head and said, "Will you catch them, do you think, the men who did it?"

"I believe so, given time," said Inspector Dulac.

"And how will they be punished?"

"Not in the way you would like to see them punished, perhaps. There is no death penalty in Quebec. But according to the law, yes, they will be punished very severely."

Randolph stood up and looked out over the garden, his arms clutched around himself as if he were cold. "Marmie would have loved a day like this," he said as though talking to himself. "May, the Cotton Carnival, the Beale Street Music Festival, the barbecue contest. She loved it all. And especially the garden."

He turned around to face Inspector Dulac and said bluntly, "You didn't come around here because you thought *I* had anything to do with killing her, did you?"

Inspector Dulac smiled and shook his head. "No, Mr. Clare, I didn't. The husband is often a prime suspect, of course, in cases of domestic homicide. But this is only because crime statistics tell us that seventy-five percent of homicides are committed by people who are known to the victim and that of this seventy-five percent, nearly eighty percent are committed by spouses or lovers or close relatives. I am obliged to interview you, not because I believe for one single second that it was you who killed your family, but because statistics say that you are more likely than anybody else to have killed them."

Randolph said, "Sure," and then, "sure."

Sergeant Allinson put in, "We have to take a statement if you can manage to give it to us, sir. Simply describe what happened when you went on vacation, how you left your family, and why."

"Of course," Randolph agreed. Then he rubbed his forehead abstractedly as if he were thinking about something else altogether, which he was. He could almost see her, Marmie, walking across the sunlit lawns toward him, wearing her wide-brimmed summer hat, the one she always wore when she was gardening, and carrying her basket filled with blue flags, the state flower of Tennessee. He could almost hear her voice calling him. But her voice was not quite audible, and then the sky was scratched by the sound of a 727 landing at Memphis International and the moment was over. Marmie was gone. Inspector Dulac said, "It won't take long, Mr. Clare. We can do it inside if you wish."

"Are you too hot out here?" Randolph asked. "I'm sorry, I should have thought."

They were walking back into the house when Charles came out and said, "There's a telephone call for you, Mr. Clare. The caller says it's urgent."

"Do you know who it is?"

"He said Stanley. He said you'd know which Stanley."

Randolph said, "Excuse me one moment," to Inspector Dulac and went through to the library and picked up the phone.

"Mr. Clare?" said Stanley.

"That's right. Have you heard something? The Canadian police are here."

"Listen, Mr. Clare, don't involve no police, not yet. There's a rumor been goin' around and so far I ain't been able to substantiate it. I didn't pick it up from no cottonseed executives, nothin' like that. Come right out of the gutter, if you get my meanin'. There's somebody who may want to talk about your family, but he's shy and he's nervous, and he wants to see you in person and discuss the pecuniary side of it too."

"Who is he?"

"He asked me not to say, but his name's Jimmy the Rib. Can you come downtown and meet him? Say, nine o'clock at the Walker Rooms on Beale Street?"

"Stanley," Randolph insisted before Stanley could hang up. "Stanley, does he know who did it?"

"He wouldn't say, not direct. But I think he might."

"All right," said Randolph. "I'll see you later, at nine."

"Take a regular cab," Stanley suggested. "You don't want to make this no circus by showing up in a limo. And I think it's better if too many people don't see that Randolph Clare keeps on ridin' in Stanley Vergo's cab, if you get my drift."

"What sort of people?" Randolph wanted to know. "What's going on here?"

"I gotta go," said Stanley and hung up. Randolph slowly put down the phone and saw Inspector Dulac and Sergeant Allinson waiting for him in the dark-paneled hallway.

"Whenever you're ready, Mr. Clare," said Inspector Dulac.

SIX

After the two policemen left at three-thirty in the afternoon, Randolph went back to the library with a glass of chilled Chablis to write a few personal letters. He spent most of the time, however, with his pen poised two inches above the paper, staring out the window and thinking about Marmie and the children. "Dear Sophie . . ." his first letter began, and he tried to think of all the sad and elegant ways in which he could express his distress at his family's deaths. But he could see only those bruised and swollen eyes, those bloody and strangulated necks, those arms viciously tied with cords.

At five o'clock Neil Sleaman arrived, leaving his new white Corvette parked under the pergola in front of the garage. He sat confidently cross-legged in the green-leather armchair on the other side of the room and gave Randolph a lengthy report on the emergency repair work at Raleigh and on general production figures. Then, with a directness he had obviously been practicing all afternoon, he said, "You're going to kill me for bringing this up at this particular moment, Mr. Clare. Perhaps it's insensitive of me, but life has to go on."

Randolph's glass was empty and his pipe had just gone out. He blinked at Neil and said, "What do you mean, life has to go on?"

"Well, sir, the unavoidable fact of the matter is that

unless we can get substantial assistance from the Association, we will be totally unable to meet our promised quota to Sun-Taste.''

''What will the shortfall be?''

''Twenty-two percent by week's end, Mr. Clare. Maybe as much as thirty-three percent by the time we get the Raleigh factory back on line. And we have no capacity to make the shortfall good, even by working treble shifts.''

''So what is your suggested solution?''

''I know that joining the Association has always been anathema to you—''

''You're damned right it has,'' Randolph interrupted.

''But, Mr. Clare, there really isn't any other way. If we lose Sun-Taste, we won't be able to support our investment program and the next thing we know, we'll have to start closing plants.''

''Neil,'' said Randolph, ''this company was founded on the philosophy of independence and free competition and as long as I'm in charge of it, it's going to stay true to that philosophy.''

''I'm sorry, Mr. Clare, but right now I believe that the philosophy of independence and free competition—at least in the case of Clare Cottonseed—is pretty well bankrupt. And so will the company be if we don't wake up to the fact that times have changed and that we're part of an interdependent industry.''

''The strong helping the weak, is that it?'' Randolph asked, sarcastically quoting Waverley Graceworthy.

''Well, if you like,'' Neil agreed, oblivious to the bitterness in Randolph's voice. ''The business community pulling together for the greater good of every participating member—''

''Neil, you're beginning to sound like an after-dinner speech at the Memphis Chamber of Commerce.''

''But there isn't any *future* in remaining independent, Mr. Clare,'' Neil protested, sitting forward in his chair. ''And after everything that's happened—your family, the fire out at Raleigh—''

Randolph leaped to his feet with such violence that he knocked his chair over. He could feel the fury roaring up inside of him, so hot and spontaneous that he was almost blinded by it. He was not furious with Neil alone. He was furious with everything and everybody. With Marmie's murder most of all; with the killing of his children; with the factory fire that had forced him to abandon his family and destroyed years of skillful and patient work; with Orbus Greene and Waverley Graceworthy; with the heat; with the wine that had gone to his head; and with the whole damned world in which he had suddenly found himself alone. With God.

"Do you think for one moment that losing my family and losing the most important business contract we've had in seventeen years is going to do anything—*anything!*—but make me ten times more determined?" he shouted.

Neil edged back on the seat of his chair and dropped his gaze to the floor. "I'm sorry, Mr. Clare. I should have realized that you weren't ready to discuss this yet."

Randolph was picking up his chair. "Neil, you listen. I'm not ready today, and I won't be ready tomorrow, and I won't be ready the day after that, nor ever. This company stays independent and that's all there is to it."

Neil said nothing but fiddled with the binding of the file he was holding on his lap.

"I simply won't discuss it," Randolph shouted.

"And what if the other plants catch fire? The Frank C. Pidgeon plant? The Harbor Plant? What then?"

Randolph slowly sat down again. The sun was beginning to sink westward toward the city skyline and to make sparkling patterns in the leaves of the tulip trees. A strange time of day, he thought: gentle and regretful. He watched Neil sharply, feeling oddly suspicious of him now, and in a way, almost frightened.

"You'll have to make yourself clearer," he said.

"How clear does anything have to be?" Neil demanded. "It was clear from the moment you undercut the Association's prices that they were going to want to put you out of business. I told you that myself, sir, when you recruited me from Chickasaw. All you could say was, 'There's room for everybody to make a buck,' the same thing your father used to say. Well, I have news for you, Mr. Clare. The cottonseed business has changed since your father's day. There just aren't enough bucks to go around.''

Randolph said, ''You don't have to give me a grade-school lesson in modern commodities, thank you, Neil. When I asked you to make yourself clearer, I was asking you if you thought the Association was really behind that fire at Raleigh.''

''You seemed to be pretty convinced yourself that it was when you talked to Orbus Greene out at the factory.''

''Having an opinion is not the same as having legal evidence, Neil. Besides, Orbus Greene always provokes me.''

''Well, I don't have any legal evidence, Mr. Clare, and Orbus Greene didn't necessarily set that fire or have anything to do with it. Almost all of the smaller processors feel aggrieved by the tactics you've been using: undercutting their prices, headhunting their staff. Every ounce of cottonseed that we process at rock-bottom prices means one ounce less of business for Chickasaw Cotton, or DeWitt Mills, or Mississippi Natural Fibers, or any of those medium- to small-sized plants.''

''That's still no justification for arson.''

''No, sir, it isn't. But it's an explanation.''

Randolph was silent for a moment. Then he said, ''It's no justification for homicide either.''

''Sir?'' asked Neil, frowning.

''Why are you so surprised?'' Randolph asked. He felt as if he were swimming through dangerous waters now, untried currents, but he had plunged in and there was no choice left to him but to continue. ''If anyone from one of those medium- to small-sized plants felt sufficiently aggrieved to set fire to my wintering plant at Raleigh and sacrifice the lives of three of my process workers, why shouldn't that same individual feel that a very effective way of warning me off in person would be multiple homicide? Murdering my family while I was busy taking care of the fire. I mean, has that thought ever occurred to you, Neil? That the fire was not only set to disrupt our production of processed cottonseed oil, but to make it imperative for me to leave my family all alone in an isolated cabin in a remote part of the Laurentide forest? Or maybe that was the *sole* purpose of the fire at Raleigh: a diversion to bring me rushing back to Memphis.''

"Mr. Clare, I think you've been suffering quite a lot of stress,'' Neil said in a gentle and whispery voice. "Maybe we'd better finish this discussion tomorrow.''

"Well, Neil, that may not be such a bad idea,'' Randolph told him. "The fact is, I'm going to go meet my taxi-driver friend tonight. He called me earlier this afternoon and said he had some interesting information about the men who killed Marmie and my children.''

Neil tilted his head to one side as if he found this news of only minimal interest. "You should be careful of people like that, Mr. Clare,'' he advised solemnly. "After all, what can he know, a Memphis taxi driver, about a homicide that happened all the way up in Quebec?''

"That's what I hope to find out,'' Randolph said. "Will you have a glass of wine?''

"Well, no, I don't think so,'' Neil replied. "I have to have a clear head this evening. We're running through the distillation figures.''

Randolph said, "I'm sorry I'm not much use right now, but I'll be back at my desk by Monday.''

"You would have been away on vacation anyway,'' Neil reminded him. "All the arrangements you made for three weeks of delegated management are still in force.''

"Neil—'' Randolph began but then waved his hand as if he were erasing Neil's name from a blackboard.

"I know things are difficult for you, sir,'' Neil told him, "but I would like you to apply your mind to how we're going to cope with the Sun-Taste supply crisis.''

Randolph sat back in his chair and made a face. "We could of course put our pride in our pockets and join the Association.''

"Do you mean that?'' Neil asked, half-believing him.

"Oh, sure,'' said Randolph. "Pride never counted for

much in this company, did it? Pride in product, pride in efficiency, pride in freedom and independence?''

''Mr. Clare—'' Neil began.

''Mr. Clare nothing,'' Randolph retorted. ''I've listened to your recommendations to join the Association because it's your duty and your job to make recommendations. But let me make it one hundred and one percent clear to you here and now that the only way Clare Cottonseed is going to affiliate itself with the Association is over my dead body. Not my family's dead bodies, and not those of my managers and my workers either. Mine.''

Neil closed his file and tucked his gold Gucci pencil back in his pocket. The late-afternoon sun slanted through the library window and partly dazzled him, making his eyes water. He looked like a young cave animal emerging into the light for the first time.

''Yes, sir,'' he said. ''I understand.''

Randolph sat thinking for a long time after Neil left. He knew that technically Neil was right and that the sooner they came to terms with the Association, the better their chances of financial survival. But how could he possibly stomach the prospect of working and socializing with Orbus Greene, Waverley Graceworthy and all those small-time processors who had long ago surrendered their pride and independence in favor of continuously smoking chimneys?

On the other hand, was his own personal pride worth more than the jobs of the seventeen hundred men and women who worked for him? Was his own personal pride worth more than the prosperity of Memphis and the cotton plantations that supplied him with seed?

Thoughtfully he bit at his lip. Then he flicked his telephone switch and called Wanda at the office downtown.

''Wanda? This is Randolph Clare.''

''Oh, Mr. Clare. How are you feeling? Did Mr. Sleaman come out to see you?''

''Yes, he did. He just left. Listen, Wanda, I should be back in the office on Monday. But do you think you could connect me through to Orbus Greene at Brooks?''

"Yes, sir, no problem. Could you hold the line for just a moment?"

While Randolph waited, Charles came in to see if there was anything he wanted and he gestured that he would not object to another glass of wine. "Is Herbert back yet?" he asked.

"Yes, sir."

"Well, tell Herbert to call the Yellow Cab Company for me and arrange for a taxi to call at eight forty-five."

"Yes, sir."

Just then Orbus Greene came on the phone. There was a lot of background noise on the line—talking, sirens, typing—which indicated to Randolph that Orbus was using his desk amplifier. Orbus found that keeping his arms lifted to hold up a telephone receiver was too strenuous.

"Randolph," breathed Orbus, "I heard the tragic news. I want to tell you how grieved we all are here at Brooks. Marmie was such a honey."

"Thank you," Randolph said, trying not to sound offended at Orbus's oleaginous pronunciation of Marmie's name. "It was quite a shock, I can tell you."

"Is there anything I can do to help you?"

"Well, I wanted to talk over some business possibilities more than anything else."

"I'm open to suggestions," Orbus replied.

Randolph said cautiously, "I think you probably know as well as I do that Tuesday's fire out at Raleigh has seriously affected our capacity."

Orbus cleared his throat. "That's the intelligence *I* received, yes. One estimate I had was that you could be as much as a third down on production."

"Well, Orbus, it's possible that it may be worse than that, but a third is the chalked-up figure I'm working to."

Orbus said with obviously deliberate blandness, "I suppose it's too much to hope that you might have changed your mind about joining our select little band at the Cottonseed Association."

"Joining you? No." Randolph watched as Charles poured him another glass of wine. "I'm afraid there isn't any chance of that, Orbus. But I'm willing to make a practical suggestion. If the Association can help me overcome this temporary shortfall, I won't bid against you when the Western Cattle contract comes up for renewal in September, and I'll buy in an equivalent amount of unprocessed oil from Association members to make up on other contracts.''

Orbus grunted. ''I was wondering when this day would come, when you would have to turn around to the Association and beg for help.''

''I'm suggesting a deal, Orbus. I'm not begging.''

''Your father at least had the wit to realize when he was licked.''

''Listen, Orbus, are you interested in the arrangement or not?''

Orbus understood that he had pushed Randolph too far. ''I'll have to talk to Waverley about it, as well as to some of the other members.''

''Call me back in twenty-four hours.''

''Do you realize that you don't hold any cards? Sun-Taste has already called us to talk about a possible backup if you can't meet their quotas.''

''Right now, Orbus, I'm holding a legal contract with Sun-Taste that contains provisions that allow me seven days to make up any shortfall in production. If you don't know that, your intelligence network isn't as good as I always imagined it to be.''

''My dear Randolph, I have a copy of your contract in my files.''

''Get it out then and read it because I promise you this: if the Association isn't interested in helping, I'm going to do everything I can to make sure that one day I split it right down the middle. You want to talk about antitrust laws? You want to talk about price fixing? You want to talk about bond washing, coercion and insurance fraud?''

''Strong words, Randy, for a man so recently struck by tragedy,'' Orbus said complacently.

''Well, you get back to me, Orbus, because I wouldn't like to think that this was the day when one tragedy began to breed another.''

"You're a difficult man, Randy. I'll be talking to you soon again."

Randolph switched off the phone. He was breathing hard. He should not have called Orbus, he supposed, after drinking so many glasses of wine. Orbus always brought out the worst in him: his obstinacy, his hotheadedness, his blustering streak. It also occurred to him that if the Association had somehow been involved in the Raleigh fire and, God forbid, Marmie's murder, extending a direct challenge to Orbus may not have been the wisest thing for him to do.

Herbert knocked at the library door and came in. "Mr. Clare? You wanted a taxi this evening? You don't have to, you know. The limo's back."

"No, no, I want to take a taxi. I have some business downtown and I prefer to go as discreetly as possible."

"Whatever you say, Mr. Clare. Do you want me to come with you?"

Randolph shook his head. "There are one or two things I have to do on my own," he said, "and what I have to do tonight is one of them."

SEVEN

Downtown, Stanley Vergo was driving west on Pontotoc Avenue toward Front Street when he was hailed by two men in business suits standing on the sidewalk outside the headquarters of the Church of God in Christ.

It was humid and sweaty but Stanley had been trying to keep as close to Beale Street as possible so he could keep his appointment with Randolph Clare at nine o'clock. This was probably going to be the last fare he would have time to pick up before heading over to the Walker Rooms, or maybe the second-to-last, depending on how far these two button-down specimens wanted to go.

Stanley drew into the curb and leaned across the passenger seat. "Where's it to be, gents?"

"Your name Stanley Vergo?" one of the men asked.

"That's right," Stanley said, then, "Hey, what goes on here?" as the other man immediately snatched open the back door of the cab and scrambled across the backseat close behind Stanley. The man was big-faced and pale and smelled of Vaseline. His eyes were two tiny black pinpricks, with lashes as blond as a pig's.

"What goes on here?" Stanley demanded. "I have a right to refuse a fare, you know, if anybody starts getting funny."

"You don't have no right to do nothing except to shut your facial entrance and drive where we tell you," the big-faced man told him.

110

The other man climbed into the taxi beside his companion and slammed the door. He was Italian-looking, with thick, crimson lips and a flattened nose. "Better do like my friend here suggests," he remarked almost sweetly.

"I ain't drivin' you bimbos nowhere," Stanley said. He picked up his radio-telephone mike and called, "Victor One, Victor One."

The second man reached over the seat and Stanley felt a sharp, cold sensation across his knuckles. He dropped the microphone and stared down at his hand, streaked with blood. He looked up at the Italian in fright and outrage.

"The next time you try anything like that, it's the whole hand," the man informed him. "Now why don't we stop fussing and get going."

"President's Island," the first man instructed him. "Take the Jack Carley Causeway as far as Jetty Street."

"I'm supposed to be meetin' somebody," Stanley said. "When I don't show up, he's goin' to start worryin' about me."

"That's the general idea," said the big-faced man.

Stanley shifted the taxi into gear and headed out into the busy Friday-evening downtown traffic. He was sweating like a horse, and the back of his right hand, where the Italian had cut it, was stinging viciously. The blood had run down to his elbow and was slowly drying and tightening his skin.

He headed west toward Main Street, where he would turn off south, away from the center of Memphis, and go down to E.H. Crump Boulevard and out to President's Island. The city was bright and noisy and normal. The restaurants were open, the sidewalks were crowded with shoppers and sight-seers and there was that happy, dissonant mixture of jazz and automobile horns. He could smell pepperoni pizzas and as he sat in his cab and tussled his way through the traffic, he wondered if he would ever have the chance to eat another pepperoni pizza. He sniffed and wiped the sweat from his forehead with the back of his hand.

"What's this all about?" he asked in a cracked voice.

The big-faced man was staring out the window. "You don't know what this is all about? Nobody told you?"

"Why should they? I ain't done nothin'."

"Well, we don't know what you're supposed to have done. Nobody tells us nothing. All they say is, find this taxi driver called Stanley Vergo."

"And then what?" asked Stanley, glancing up at the man's reflection in the rearview mirror.

"What do you mean, 'And then what?' "

"Exactly what I said, 'And then what?' You're supposed to take me someplace or what? You're supposed to kill me or somethin'?"

The man glanced across at his companion as if he were totally baffled. "What's he talking about?" he asked.

"Don't ask me," the Italian-looking man replied. "I don't know what he's talking about."

"What, you're goin' to take me out someplace and kill me?" Stanley demanded, almost hysterical.

"Did we say anything about killing?" asked the man. He leaned forward, close behind Stanley's left ear, and said, "Nobody said nothing about killing, you got me? All we want you to do is to take us out to President's Island, down the Jack Carley Causeway as far as Jetty Street, which in any case is about as far as you can go."

Stanley took a left on Main, waiting for a moment while a flock of nuns crossed the street in front of him. Then he drove slowly toward E.H. Crump Boulevard, looking nervously from side to side and checking every few seconds the implacable faces he could see in the mirror. A black family in a Ford station wagon drew up beside him at the next traffic signal and the wife put down her window and said, "We're looking for Central Station."

Stanley turned around. "What do I tell them?" he asked.

"Tell them how to get there, you meathead," the big-faced man ordered.

But the traffic signal changed to green and Stanley jerked away from the line with a squeal of tires and a bucking of the rear suspension, leaving the black family staring and amazed.

"What the hell's gotten into you? You're driving like an ape," the big-faced man shouted at him.

"Well, what do you expect, for Christ's sake? I'm scared," Stanley retorted.

"I'll kill you right here and now unless you do as you're told," the man threatened. "You want to check out right now?"

"Will you give me a break?" Stanley appealed. "I never did nothin' to nobody. All I do is drive cabs around all day, I swear to God."

"Sorry, friend, it's not up to us," said the Italian-looking man. "All we was told to do was to find this taxi driver called Stanley Vergo. Same name as Vergo's Barbecued Ribs, that's what they said."

"Mother of God," Stanley prayed but kept on driving south until they crossed the dark neck of land between the Mississippi and Lake McKellar, a muddy isthmus over which the Jack Carley Causeway carried them to President's Island and Memphis Industrial Harbor.

The glittering lights of downtown Memphis were behind them now, wavering slightly in the eighty-degree heat of the evening. Ahead, random lights dipped and glimmered in the broad curve of the river, the navigation markers of cotton and oil and chemical barges. They drove the whole length of the causeway, jouncing over potholes in the blacktop where the industrial fill had deteriorated. Across Lake McKellar to the left, the floodlights of the T. H. Allen generating plant glared in the darkness, bright and heartless and remote.

Eventually the first man said, "Turn off here," and Stanley drove off the causeway onto a wide, flat area of ash and clinker, half-overgrown with strangely vivid green grass. In the bouncing beams of the headlights, Stanley saw a dark limousine parked about twenty yards away and five or six extraordinarily white-faced men standing about, but then the man said, "Kill the lights. Now stop," and Stanley had to obey.

"All right," said the big-faced man. "We're all going to

get out of the cab and we're all going to do it real slow and easy and not make any sudden moves. You got that?''

Stanley shivered and nodded. He switched off the engine, jingled the keys sharply in the palm of his hand and then opened the door and eased himself out. He stood beside the cab feeling desolate and miserable while the two men stood on either side of him, not too close but obviously prepared to stop him should he try anything.

"I could use a leak," Stanley said. "I been drivin' all afternoon. I was about to go to the john when you stopped me."

"Will you shut your facial entrance?" the big-faced man fumed irritably.

"I'm scared, for Christ's sake," Stanley muttered.

There was a noisy crunching of ash and then the white-faced men who had been standing by the limousine approached them through the darkness, all of them wearing ice-hockey masks. They were dressed in black-nylon running suits and two of them were carrying sawed-off shotguns.

"Now this ain't no joke," Stanley stammered. "Will you tell me what goes on here?"

The masked men said nothing. Somewhere out on the Mississippi a barge hooted mournfully, and nearby, birds rustled in the grass as if the hooting had disturbed their sleep. It was then that two more men appeared out of the darkness, one of them small and delicate, with white hair and glasses; the other burly, with a heavy, iron-gray mustache, three bulging layers of coarsely shaved chin and wearing the kind of short-sleeved khaki shirt common to bush rangers or police officers.

It was the little man with the white hair who spoke first.

"Are you Stanley Vergo?" he asked. His accent was neat and precise, and very Southern.

"I want to know what goes on here before I start answerin' any questions," Stanley replied, trying to appear confident and challenging.

"Are you Stanley Vergo?" the little man repeated as if he hadn't heard Stanley.

"What if I am? What if I ain't?"

"Well, if you're not, these two gentlemen are not going to be paid for bringing you here. In fact, they're going to be punished. And if I punish *them* . . . well, you can imagine what they're going to do to *you*."

"So I don't win whether I'm Stanley Vergo or not?"

"But you *are* Stanley Vergo, aren't you?"

"If you know, why're you askin'?"

"I suppose it helps to break the ice," the little man smiled. He rubbed his hands together as if contemplating a gourmet feast. "And besides, I do like to be sure. It would be such a waste of time if I were to ask you lots of complicated questions when you didn't have a clue to the answers because you were somebody else."

"What questions?" asked Stanley.

"Well, all manner of questions. But mainly questions about the work you've been doing. I suppose you could call it investigative work."

"I ain't been doin' no investigative work. I've been drivin' my taxi."

"Oh, come now," the little man smiled. "We're none of us here as dumb as we might appear. You have been doing some investigative work, for money, for Mr. Randolph Clare."

"I don't know what you're talkin' about. You mean Mr. Randolph Clare of Clare Cottonseed? Handy Randy?"

"The very man. He paid you money to keep your ears open for him, didn't he? He wanted to find out everything he could about that fire out at Raleigh, isn't that right?"

Stanley remained silent. He looked around at the men in the masks, at the heavily built man with the iron-gray mustache, at the Italian with the flat nose and the big-faced man.

The man with the iron-gray mustache said, "Do you know me, Stanley? Do you know who I am?"

"It seems like you're kind of familiar," Stanley replied. "Darned if I could put a name to you though."

"Well, the reason I seem familiar is because my name is Dennis T. Moyne and I'm the chief of police. It just happens that Mr. Graceworthy here called me to assist him when I was off duty. No uniform, you see; that's why you couldn't place me.''

"You're Chief Moyne and this is Mr. Graceworthy?" Stanley repeated in amazement. "Then what's this all about, you two draggin' me all the way out here and threatenin' me, and these fellers here with guns and all? And that Eye-talian feller cut my hand bad, for nothin' at all, no comprehensible reason whatever.''

"We just wanted to ask you some questions, that's all," said Mr. Graceworthy. He walked around Stanley in a slow circle; Stanley felt almost as if a tarantula were crawling up his bare back.

"And you had better think about answering, and answering truthful," Chief Moyne added. "Anyone who undertakes investigative work for money without a state-approved private investigator's license, well, he's liable for quite a long spell behind bars.''

"You got nothin' on me," Stanley told him. "Else why would you bring me all the way out here where nobody can see us? And who are these guys with the masks? This isn't legal, sir, whether you happen to be the chief of police or not.''

Waverley Graceworthy came around and stood in front of Stanley. "Let me be straight with you, Stanley. Things happen in even the best-run cities that require swift and effective action, even though they may not be strictly against the law. Now, Mr. Randolph Clare has been causing considerable financial and social distress in Memphis, especially in the cottonseed industry, and while his actions have not been *illegal*—you can't arrest a man, after all, for cutting his prices—they have caused sufficient harm to warrant some positive retaliation. Are you a native-born Memphian?''

"Yes, sir," said Stanley suspiciously.

"Then you will know that the name Memphis means 'the city of good abode.' And in the city of good abode, we expect all our fellow citizens to abide with each other in peace and harmony. Unfortunately, Mr. Clare does not seem to want to do that. For the sake of his own personal wealth, he is destroying all the careful and caring work the Cottonseed Association has contributed to the cottonseed business in particular and to the city of Memphis in general. And you—*you*, Stanley—you took his money and agreed to help him.''

"What if I did?" asked Stanley. "You said yourself that he ain't doin' nothin' against the law. It's free trade, that's all. And free trade's guaranteed under the Constitution of the United States, both in particular and in general."

Waverley Graceworthy stepped forward and jabbed his finger at Stanley. "You better listen to me. You don't even know the meaning of the words 'free trade.' You were planning to meet Mr. Clare tonight, weren't you? And you were going to give him certain information regarding the killing of his family. Isn't that true?"

"Ah, bullshit," Stanley retorted. "You guys, you're all wind. You don't even got the guts to show your faces, half of you. If I was planning to talk to Mr. Clare tonight, that's my business."

He turned around, sorted out his ignition key and climbed back into the taxi. Just as he was about to insert the key, he felt a sharp prick against the side of his neck. The Italian was leaning over him, his knife leveled at Stanley's jugular vein.

Waverley Graceworthy came around to the side of the car and ordered, "Get out. I haven't finished with you yet. I want to know what it was that you were intending to tell Mr. Clare tonight. In full, no omissions."

Stanley hesitated but then the Italian dug the knife into his neck a fraction deeper and called, "Say the word, Mr. Graceworthy."

Stanley climbed out of the cab again. "Give me the keys," Waverley Graceworthy ordered, and when Stanley failed to hand them over as quickly as the little man would have liked, "The keys, damn it!"

"Now, just one question," Waverley Graceworthy said quietly once he was clasping the keys in the palm of his hand. "Who do you think killed the Clare family, and why, and who told you?"

"I ain't sayin' nothin'," Stanley replied. He turned to Chief Moyne and called in a harsh voice, "You're a police officer, Chief, isn't that so? You know that nobody has to say nothin', not unless they got theirselves an attorney."

Chief Moyne gave a bland smile, the smile of a man for whom everything in life is direct and easily solved. "These gentlemen here will act as your attorneys," he said, nodding toward the four men in masks.

"Are you going to answer my question?" Waverley Graceworthy asked. "Otherwise, I promise you, you are going to suffer."

Stanley's pores suddenly sprang out with a welter of fresh sweat. It was the only indication he had of how frightened he actually was since his mind had already closed down its more sensitive circuits and the challenging voice coming from his mouth seemed to belong to somebody else altogether. He felt as if he were two Stanleys: one who was almost terrified into insensibility, the other who was bragging and foolhardy and loud-mouthed and kept pulling the terrified Stanley deeper and deeper into trouble.

"Do you know who killed the Clare family?" Waverley Graceworthy demanded.

"I don't have to say nothin', and even if I knew, I wouldn't tell you."

"Who does know if you don't know?"

"Oh, plenty of people know, and by the end of tonight, plenty more people are going to know, so what are you so worried about? Don't tell me that it was you and this gang of pie-dish faces over here."

Instantly Chief Moyne snapped his fingers. The masked men stepped forward and seized Stanley by the arms. He was too fat and too slow to resist. They folded his hands forward and then pressed them relentlessly against the joints of his wrists until he roared out loud.

"Now then," said Waverley Graceworthy, "do you happen to know who killed the Clare family?"

"No, sir," Stanley said, sweating and sobered. "I promise you, sir, I was never made a party to that information, sir."

"But you were supposed to be meeting Mr. Clare this evening to discuss the matter."

"All I was going to do, sir, was to introduce him to an individual who told me he knew who done it. And that's the truth, so help me dear Lord, that's the one-hundred-percent absolute truth."

Waverley Graceworthy nodded and rubbed his hands again. Then he said, "This . . . other individual . . . can you tell me his name?"

"No, sir." Stanley could hear his captors breathing roughly behind their masks. "I swore by Almighty God that I would never tell his name."

"But you do know his name, even though you have sworn never to tell it?"

Stanley did not reply but tried to struggle against the men who were holding him. They pressed his hands again, more forcibly this time, and he gritted his teeth and grunted in pain, "*Duh!*" and stopped struggling.

"You know his name?" Waverley Graceworthy repeated.

Stanley nodded.

"Well," said Waverley Graceworthy, "in spite of your pledge, I need to know this individual's name. It's very important for everybody concerned, for the good of the city and the welfare of those who labor in the cottonseed business."

"I swore," said Stanley desperately. "If he ever finds out it was me, Jesus, he'll kill me."

"Then you are caught between Scylla and Charybdis," Waverley Graceworthy smiled.

"What in hell does that mean?"

"It means that you have two equally unpalatable options. Your friend will kill you if you tell and *we* will kill you if you don't."

Stanley thrashed and kicked and finally collapsed to his knees on the cinders, the masked men still holding him. "Chief Moyne!" he shouted. "Did you hear that, Chief Moyne? That was a threat against my life! You can't tell me that threatenin' anybody's life is legal!"

Chief Moyne thrust his thumbs into his wide brown belt

and looked the other way, out across Lake McKellar toward the generating plant.

Then one of the masked men hooked his forearm under Stanley's chin and slowly forced him backward until he was lying on the cinders, spread-eagled. Another man held Stanley's hands above his head, while another held his legs. The fourth disappeared from view for a moment and returned hefting a gleaming machete that looked as if it had been bought from a discount sports store just half an hour earlier.

"What in the name of Christ are you doing?" Stanley screamed. He wrestled and writhed, but the three masked men held him firmly to the ground.

Waverley Graceworthy appeared in Stanley's line of sight. One of the spotlights from the generating plant was momentarily reflected in his glasses and his hair shone white against the starry sky.

"Now, Stanley," he said, "you must listen to this. None of us are violent men. We abhor physical coercion, isn't that right, Chief Moyne? But it is our duty to make sure that the cottonseed industry thrives, and the cottonseed industry is more important than individual lives. Yours, my friend, included."

"What are you goin' to do?" Stanley gasped hoarsely. "Are you goin' to kill me or what? For Christ's sake, have mercy! I didn't do nothin'."

"Ah, but you did. You agreed to betray the sacred trust of your passengers, those who believe that they can sit in the back of a taxi and talk about anything and everything without their conversations being passed on, and you betrayed that sacred trust for money. In fact, I believe that I can quite rightly call you a Judas."

"What, Judas? What the hell are you talkin' about? You're crazy. Do you know that? You're right out of your fuckin' tree!"

Waverley Graceworthy stood up straight as if he were about to sing in church. In his impeccable Southern accent, he said, "You have a choice now, Stanley. Either you tell me who you intended to introduce tonight to Randolph Clare or I will have to ask this gentleman to hurt you. He will hurt you so badly that within a half-hour you will require emergency medical treatment. We will not summon this treatment, however, unless you agree to give us this individual's name.''

Stanley tried to lick his lips with a tongue that was dry like tweed. He looked up at the shining machete, so new that every thumbprint showed on its blade, and he looked at the faceless man holding it. Then he thought of Jimmy the Rib: black, wild-eyed, skeletally thin, with a heroin habit that could have bought him a brand-new Cadillac every week. Jimmy the Rib would stick a two-foot-long Bowie knife up your backside when you were least expecting it, and he never forgot, and he never forgave. Stanley had thought he was being smart and brave when he had persuaded Jimmy to talk to Randolph Clare. He had not counted on Waverley Graceworthy and the forces of law and order.

Jimmy the Rib would kill him without any hesitation whatever. But these people, what would they do? They must be bluffing. How could the Chief of Police stand around here and witness murder? That just didn't make sense. And Waverley Graceworthy was a one-time councillor and a distinguished county commissioner. Men of this social standing were not going to murder a perfectly innocent taxi driver in the middle of the night just because he wouldn't tell them somebody's name. Or would they?

"Believe me," said Stanley, "I just can't tell you who he is."

"You have five seconds," Waverley Graceworthy said quietly.

"I *can't* tell you! Do you know what he does to people who let him down? He's a crazy man. He killed his best friend and his girlfriend all in the same night, and both the same way. A Bowie knife, two feet long, straight up between the legs."

"Two seconds," said Waverley Graceworthy. "One." Then, "None."

The man with the machete leaned forward and tugged open the buttons of Stanley's shirt as swiftly as if he were tugging weeds from a garden. He pulled back Stanley's shirttails to reveal Stanley's soft, protuberant stomach.

"What are you goin' to—" Stanley began, but he did not even have time to think about it. The masked man swung the machete diagonally across Stanley's stomach, slashing it with crimson, and then suddenly Stanley's intestines bulged out of the cut and poured onto the ground beside him with a plop like thick paint from a bucket. Stanley was too shocked to even scream. The masked men who had been holding his arms released him and he jerked up his head and stared down at his stomach in horror. Then, gasping, he grabbed handfuls of the slippery red-and-white tubes and tried to push them back inside his body.

Waverley Graceworthy watched him placidly.

"You ki . . . you killed me," Stanley panted. "You killed me, for Christ's sake."

Waverley Graceworthy removed his glasses and idly polished them with his pocket handkerchief.

"It is possible that you will survive if medical emergency units reach you soon enough," he said. "They have excellent facilities at the Memphis Medical Center, so they tell me. We don't mind paying for your medical expenses." He paused and then added, "*If* you give us the name."

"Name?" Stanley asked in desperation. He let go of his guts; they were covered with grit now and he knew that he should not try to put them back until they were washed. Better to let them lie there until the medics arrived. His head sank back onto the ash and he stared up at the stars, wondering where on earth he was and what was happening to him. His heart seemed to be beating like a man walking through a forest and hitting each tree trunk with a baseball bat. Bang, bang, bang, bang, regular and slow.

"The name," somebody repeated.

The name? he thought. What name? He couldn't even think of his own name, let alone anybody else's. His stomach felt cold and strange, and every time he breathed in and out, he gurgled. It occurred to him that he had been hurt very badly and that he was going to die. The fringes of the sky seemed to be darkening and in the outer circle of his vision, the stars appeared to be winking out. When the very last star was gone, he would be dead, and what a release that would be. He would never have to drive that goddam taxi, never again; he would be happy.

He had never known happiness, not real happiness. Now he was quite sure that he was going to find out what it was.

"The name," the voice kept insisting. "Tell us the name."

He licked his lips again and coughed. His mouth was filled with something salty and sticky.

"The name," the voice urged. The voice was close now, as if somebody were bending over him.

"I'm . . . dying," he said, and the thought gave him a peculiar sense of satisfaction, as if he were doing something pleasant and exciting that none of the people standing around him could do.

"Stanley," the voice demanded. "This is your last chance. Tell us the name."

Stanley opened his eyes and focused blurrily on Waverley Graceworthy, who was kneeling in the cinders next to him in his thousand-dollar suit. He had forgotten who Waverley Graceworthy was or what he was doing here, but he seemed to remember that they had been talking about death. Well, there was one person for sure who wasn't dead, no matter what everybody said about him. There was one person who was hidin' away someplace for sure, fishin' and meditatin' and havin' one whale of a time.

With one blood-streaked hand, Stanley managed to beckon Waverley Graceworthy even closer. Then he clutched at the lapel of the old man's suit, bubbled blood at him and cried out harshly, "Elvis Presley!"

EIGHT

At six minutes of nine, Randolph's taxi drew up outside the Walker Rooms on Beale Street and Randolph paid the driver and climbed out. The night was hot and sticky and there was music in the air, although the Beale Street of nineteen eighty-four was nothing like the Beale Street that W. C. Handy and B. B. King and Rufus Thomas had known. This was the Beale Street National Historic Preservation District, a sanitized version of the Beale Street that had once been, the Beale Street of blues clubs and whores and tangled trolley-car cables. The black high-steppers had long since gone, in their shiny top hats and tails and their ladies on their arms. So had the farmers in their straw hats and bibs. Hulbert's Lo-Down Hounds had not been heard here since the Forties, and even the Old Daisy Theater had become an "historic, interpretative center."

Still, the Walker Rooms retained something of their post-war sleaze. There was a red-flashing neon sign outside saying "Blues, Food," and Randolph had to climb a narrow, worn-out staircase to the second floor, where an air-conditioning unit was rattling asthmatically and a black girl with dreadlocks and a tight white sleeveless T-shirt was sitting at a plywood desk silently bopping to a Walkman stereo. On the wall there was a Michael Jackson calendar with torn edges and a sign saying "Occupancy By More Than 123 Persons Forbidden By Law."

Randolph stood awkward and tall and white-faced in his buff-colored Bijan suit and told the girl, "I'm looking for Stanley Vergo."

"Ain't never heard of him," the girl replied laconically.

The sound of blues came leaking out through a beaded curtain next to the girl's desk.

> If Beale Street could talk, if Beale Street could talk,
> Married men would have to take up their beds and walk,
> Except one or two, who never drink booze,
> And the blind man on the corner who sings the Beale Street Blues.

Randolph said, "Jimmy the Rib?"

"Jimmy the Rib? What you want with Jimmy the Rib?"

"Stanley Vergo's a cab driver. He said he was going to introduce me to Jimmy the Rib."

The black girl took the stereo headphones out of her ears and stared at Randolph seriously. "You ain't the man?"

"Do I look like the man?"

The girl shrugged. "Nobody never can tell these days. There was a time the man always had the decency to look his part, or at least to smell like what he was. But you, what could you be? Rich or poor, honest or crooked? Who knows?"

"Is Jimmy here?" Randolph asked.

The girl said, "Wait up, will you?" and pranced her way through the beaded curtain. Randolph heard laughter and smelled the split-pea aroma of marijuana; he wished he had brought his pipe with him, although he was conscious that it would have made him look more like Fred MacMurray than ever. He remembered Marmie's telling him not to look so staid. "Your joints are all rusted up," she used to say, laughing. "Relax, for goodness' sake, and enjoy yourself."

If only Marmie were alive now, he thought, instead of cold and blind and dead in a coffin in Quebec.

The black girl took a long time in returning. When she did, she went straight to her desk without even looking at Randolph, hooked in her earphones and went on bopping.

Randolph waited patiently for three or four minutes and then the bead curtain rattled and a tall, skeletally thin black man emerged, wearing a dusty black suit with wide lapels and a black Derby hat. His fingers were covered in silver rings, most of them in the form of skulls, and he carried a cane with a silver-skull knob on top of it.

He looked Randolph up and down in the way any black man had the right to look any white man up and down when he ventured into Beale Street. Then he rapped his cane on the floor seven or eight times and said, "This ain't right."

"Are you Jimmy the Rib?" Randolph asked.

"What if I am?"

"My name's Randolph Clare. I was supposed to meet Stanley Vergo here."

"Well, Stanley Vergo ain't here."

Randolph anxiously rubbed the side of his neck. "Could we still talk? Stanley said you had some information I might be interested in."

"I don't know. What proof you got that you are who you say you are?"

Randolph took out his wallet and showed Jimmy the Rib his credit cards and his driver's license. Jimmy the Rib examined them with exaggerated intensity and then turned the plastic leaf in the center of the wallet, where he discovered the photograph of Marmie and the children that Randolph always carried with him.

"This your family?" he asked. "The family they wasted?"

Randolph nodded without speaking.

Jimmy the Rib returned Randolph's wallet and said, "Come on through. I don't want nobody to see us talking out here."

Randolph followed him through the bead curtain, past the entrance to a dimly lit bar where men and women were sitting on bar stools drinking and listening to a blues sextet in shiny mohair suits. Then Jimmy the Rib opened a door at the end of the corridor and showed Randolph into an untidy office. There were tattered posters on the walls showing blues concerts and riverboat parties and jazz festivals. On the desk there was an ashtray crammed with cigar butts, and a minstrel money box.

Jimmy the Rib closed the door with the point of his cane. "I hope you come here prepared to pay," he said.

"I brought five hundred dollars in cash, all unmarked bills," Randolph said. "If the information turns out to be worth more, I'll pay more."

"These are dangerous people we're discussing here," said Jimmy the Rib. He sniffed, the dry, thumping sniff of the regular cocaine user. "These are people who don't take kindly to no fooling around. The only generosity I ever knowed these people to demonstrate is when they feed the fish. And I don't have to clarify to you what with."

Randolph took out an envelope and handed it to Jimmy the Rib without a word. Jimmy lifted the flap, moistened the edge of his thumb and riffled through the bills with cautious satisfaction.

"There's a gang of real hard men working in town," he said, keeping his eyes fixed on the opposite wall as if that would somehow absolve him from the guilt of snitching. "They don't bother with the street scene; they don't have their hand in dope or hookers or shakedowns or anything like that. They're not Eye-talians either. They work for big business, and all they do is make sure that anybody who don't agree with what their bosses want gets to change their mind."

"Do you know who they are?" Randolph asked softly.

"There's four or five of them, not always the same guys. The only name I heard is Reece, and he's supposed to be some spaced-out veteran from Cambodia or someplace like that, a frightening man from what I hear tell. I don't know any of the others, and as you can guess, they don't actually advertise themselves on WMKW."

"What evidence do you have that these are the men who killed my family?" asked Randolph.

"Nothing you could tell to a judge," Jimmy the Rib replied. "But your taxi-driving friend, Stanley Vergo, put the word out all around town that he was listening for who wasted your family up in Canada, and a friend of mine from the airport called me last night and said he's seen something of interest and since he didn't trust no whites, maybe *I* could pass it on for him in exchange for a piece of the money Stanley Vergo said you was prepared to pay for such news. My friend works as a skycap, and on Monday afternoon he saw four men take an American Airlines flight to Quebec, and the reason he noticed them was that, number A, they was very hard-looking dudes indeed, definitely not your Memphis Theological Seminary boys' choir, and, number B, he recognized one of their faces from six or seven years back in the Shelby County Penal Farm, when he himself was serving a small amount of time for rescuing Cadillacs from their unappreciative owners. He couldn't recall this dude's name but he remembered that he was tough as all shit and that it was not considered wise to irritate him in any way.''

Randolph said, ''Your friend is very observant. If I can check the passenger list for the flight they took, I might be close to finding out who the murderers are.''

''Listen to this,'' Jimmy the Rib said solemnly. ''These characters are absolutely no fun whatsoever. You don't know the streets and you don't know who's who. Take my advice and let the police do the work for you. And that's the first and only recommendation I'm ever going to give the pigs in my whole natural life.''

''Well, I'm supposed to be talking to Chief Moyne tomorrow,'' Randolph said.

''I guess nobody gets all the breaks,'' Jimmy the Rib commiserated.

Randolph held out his hand. ''Thank you anyway for telling me what you know.''

''Thanks for the lettuce,'' Jimmy the Rib replied, holding up the money. Then he showed Randolph out to the staircase. ''If I should hear of anything more,'' he said, ''could you still be interested?''

''All you have to do is call me at Clare Cottonseed. I'll make it worth your while.''

''Take care, Mr. Clare.''

"I will. And if you *do* see Stanley Vergo, tell him I've been here."

"You have my assurance."

Randolph caught a taxi on the corner of Beale and Danny Thomas Boulevard. The taxi driver was a silent black with hair shaved flat on top and an earring made out of tigers' teeth. Randolph leaned forward and asked him, "Are you on the radio?"

The driver turned his head and stared at him.

"I said, are you on the radio?" Randolph repeated.

The driver lifted his microphone. "What this look like? Electric toothbrush?"

"You can do me a favor," Randolph said. "Call your base and ask them if they can contact a driver named Stanley Vergo. Can you do that?"

"Stanley whut?"

"Stanley Vergo. Will you do that, please? I just want to know where he is."

"Okay, man." The driver switched on his microphone and called, "Victor One, Victor One."

After a while a crackly voice said, "Victor One."

"Victor One, this is Zebra Three. Fare wants to know where a hackie name of Stanley Vertigo is at. Can you assist?"

"You mean Stanley Vergo?"

"Vertigo, Vergo, whatever."

There was a lengthy silence while the cab driver turned onto Linden Boulevard, heading east, and approached the busy intersection with the Dr. Martin Luther King Expressway. Traffic streamed through the night like red-and-white corpuscles flowing through the darkness of the human body.

After a few minutes, the cab company's controller came back on the air. "Zebra Three, I've been calling Stanley Vergo for you. Can't raise him. He's supposed to be working tonight but maybe he's taking his break. Last word I heard from him was round about eight o'clock on Monroe, when he finished a delivery for the Medical Center."

"Long coffee break," the cab driver remarked laconically, clipping the microphone back onto the instrument panel.

"Yes," Randolph agreed. He sat back, feeling his sticky shirt cling to his skin. He was worried now. If Reece and his men were really as vicious as Jimmy the Rib had suggested, if they were the men who had killed and tortured Marmie and the children, there was no question but that they would deal equally violently with anyone they believed to be a threat. And who could be more of a threat than somebody like Stanley, driving around town dropping the word everywhere he went that he was interested in knowing who the Clare-family killers might have been?

"You say something?" the cab driver asked.

"No, I think I was praying out loud."

"For money?"

"For somebody's health."

With sudden and unexpected good humor, the cab driver said, "I heard a joke about that the other day. There was these two black brothers, you know, and they bought guns and they went out to assassinate Ronald Reagan. Well, they was waiting in ambush outside his hotel but a whole day went by and Reagan didn't appear. So one of the brothers turns to the other and says, 'Hey, I hope nothing's happened to him.' "

Randolph managed a faint smile.

"That's some joke, huh?" the cab driver asked. " 'I hope nothing's happened to him.' Isn't that something?"

As soon as he reached home, Randolph called for Charles to bring him a drink and then went through to the library. He switched on the desk lamp, took out his black-leather telephone book and looked up Chief Moyne's private number at police headquarters on Poplar. Chief Moyne answered almost immediately, sounding as if his mouth was full of food.

"Dennis? This is Randolph Clare. I'm sorry if I disturbed you."

"Not at all, Randolph. I was snatching myself a little late supper, that's all. Some of Obleo's wieners, to go."

"Dennis, I think I need your help."

"You name it," Chief Moyne replied. "We're going to be meeting tomorrow in any case, aren't we, when they fly your poor family back from Quebec?"

"Yes," Randolph said. "And this is connected with what happened up there. I've just been given some information that the killings may possibly have been connected with four men from Memphis."

"From Memphis?" Chief Moyne echoed. "What kind of information?"

"Well, I've heard that some of the big-business interests in this city keep a small army of what you might call hired persuaders. One of the men is supposed to be a Vietnam vet named Reece. At least one of the others has a criminal record. Apparently these men are employed to enforce whatever commercial policies their bosses consider to be to their best advantage, and anyone who argues with these business bigwigs is liable to find himself in more trouble than he can handle."

There was a pause and then Chief Moyne said, "Randolph, I'm chief of police here in Memphis and I've never heard of any hired army, not like you describe it. I mean, you're a businessman yourself. Have *you* ever heard of such a thing before?"

"I can't say that I have. But that doesn't mean it doesn't exist."

"You're right. It doesn't mean that at all. But it kind of makes it less likely, wouldn't you say? A hired army going around bullying people into keeping their prices fixed or whatever? That doesn't ring true, Randolph. Not in an orderly business community like Memphis. Who told you such a thing?"

"I'm sorry, I promised to keep his name confidential."

"Did you pay him money?"

"Well, yes, as a matter of fact, I did. Five hundred dollars."

"Then I'm afraid that for all your business acumen, Randolph, you've been taken. Somebody's taken advantage of your grief and stung you."

Randolph insisted, "All the same, Dennis, four men

killed my family, and four men were seen leaving Memphis airport on Monday afternoon before the killing with tickets for Quebec. One of these men was a known criminal and something of a head case, from what I can gather.''

"Randolph, I'm sorry, but scores of men left scores of airports all over the country on Monday afternoon and headed for Quebec, and there were plenty of men already in Quebec who might equally have carried out this crime. It's very important that you don't start playing Sherlock Holmes. You'll only wind up upsetting yourself, aggravating your grief, and quite apart from that, you could seriously jeopardize the official police investigation without even realizing it.''

Charles came in with a whiskey for Randolph on a silver tray. He set it down on the table, bowed in that old-fashioned way of his and then withdrew.

Chief Moyne said, "It would be a genuine help, Randolph, if you could tell me the name of your informant. I could check his story to see if any of it holds water, and if it does, well, we could pursue it in the proper way, with the full assistance of the FBI and the Royal Canadian Mounted Police.''

"I don't think he'd appreciate a visit from the police, especially if he knew I was the one who tipped you off.''

"Come on now, Randolph, your name doesn't even have to come into it. We can talk to him on any pretext we like. Out-of-date license plate, failure to have his automobile tested, anything.''

"Well . . .'' Randolph hesitated. "He did advise me himself to talk to the police.''

"In that case, I may have misjudged him,'' said Chief Moyne genially. "He may not be a rip-off artist after all. But it's essential for me to check out his story one way or another. I mean, if there *is* some kind of secret army working on behalf of some of our big businesses, I think it's time I knew about it, don't you?''

"I guess you're right,'' Randolph conceded. "The man's name is Jimmy the Rib. At least that's the name I was given. I met him at a blues club called the Walker Rooms on Beale Street.''

"So, Jimmy the Rib, huh?'' Chief Moyne repeated. "It's been a while since I've heard anything out of him.''

"You know him?'' Randolph asked.

"Everybody downtown knows Jimmy the Rib. He's an unpredictable man. You were lucky you didn't upset him in any way.''

"He seemed quite affable to me.''

"Well, you must have caught him in a good mood. When he's roused, he has an unpleasant habit of thrusting knives up between people's legs.''

Randolph said, "In that case, you just make damn sure he doesn't know it was me who tipped you off.'' He was only half-joking.

Chief Moyne laughed, his mouth crowded with wiener. "Believe me, Randolph, from this moment on, you don't have anything to worry about.''

Randolph exchanged a few more pleasantries with Chief Moyne and then hung up. He eased back in his chair and swirled his whiskey around in its glass. He was beginning to feel tired but the prospect of going upstairs to bed was bleaker than he could bear. He could tolerate his newly imposed loneliness during the day, when there were matters to occupy his attention, but the past two nights had been almost intolerably silent and sad. Last night he had awakened just after the moon had set, when the house was at its stillest and darkest, and the reflection in Marmie's dressing-table mirror had gleamed like a silvery window through to another world, where shadows moved like living people. He had listened and listened, and the most overwhelming thing of all had been the silence. No breathing next to him, no breathing in the children's rooms. A house of silence and empty beds. A house in which death had pressed its finger against the lips of memory and whispered, "Sssh!''

He had just raised his glass of whiskey to his lips when the telephone rang.

"Who is it?'' he asked.

"Mr. Clare? This is Dr. Ambara of the Mount Moriah

Clinic. I understand from Suzie that you were interested in getting in touch with me.''

Randolph sat up straight and put down his glass. ''As a matter of fact, Dr. Ambara, I was. In fact, I was thinking of calling you later this evening. Suzie said you didn't usually get home until late.''

''How are you, Mr. Clare?''

''Coping, just about. I'm fortunate that my work keeps me pretty busy.''

Dr. Ambara said, ''That is not always fortunate. You must not forget to be sad for your lost family, you know.''

''That was one of the things I wanted to talk to you about.''

''Your grief?'' asked Dr. Ambara. It was clear from the evasive tone in his voice that he was trying to divert the conversation from the subject of reincarnation and of talking to the dead.

''I wanted to discuss the possibility of seeing my family again.''

''Well, yes, I thought as much,'' said Dr. Ambara. ''But would it be possible for me to dissuade you from following this course? I have to warn you that there are very great dangers involved, not only to yourself but to others. Possibly to your loved ones as well.''

''But it can be done? There is a chance I might see them?''

Dr. Ambara was silent. Then he said, ''We will have to meet to talk about this properly. Are you free tomorrow? Meet me at the Dixon Gardens at eleven.'' He hesitated again and then said, ''Should you change your mind between now and tomorrow when we meet, please believe me when I say that it will be better for everybody concerned. When you explore the regions of death, Mr. Clare, you open a two-way door, a door that can let things in but that can also let things out.''

NINE

They met beside a cascade of scarlet azaleas, azaleas as scarlet as freshly splashed blood, in a silvery morning fog the sun had not yet dissipated. The formal gardens covered nearly seventeen acres. Along every path there were flowering magnolias as white as wax, and willows that sadly trailed their branches through the fog like the hair of drowning brides.

Randolph thought, as he watched the tourists moving through the gardens, *Last Year at Marienbad*, a stylized film from a 1960s art-house movie. He felt dislocated, not only by the fog but by tiredness and grief, and by the memories that crowded around him every waking minute of the day. He had dreamed of Marmie and the children again last night, a dream in which they had been beckoning him to join them at a table set with white plates. They had been singing, or chanting, and their voices had been echoing and high-pitched, like the voices of children heard at the far end of a tunnel. He had approached the table and looked down at the plates, and on each of them there had been human organs: a heart, a lung, a liver, all of them garnished with herbs and flowers as if part of a gruesome, ritual meal. An unhallowed Seder, with the bitterest of bitter herbs and the sourest of wines.

He had awakened sweating and shaking, with his sheets twisted around his legs like a rope.

Dr. Ambara arrived precisely on time, walking out of the fog in a gray mohair suit that looked as if it had been tailored for him in six hours flat in Okinawa. Under his jacket he wore a white turtleneck sweater. His eyes were tinted by orange sunglasses and under his arm he carried a copy of *The Commercial Appeal.* His silky mustache had been clipped since the last time Randolph had seen him.

"Well, Mr. Clare," he said, extending his hand, "I was afraid that you might be here."

Randolph solemnly shook his hand, which was limp and damp, the hand of a man who was making no attempt to prove anything about his masculinity or his sincerity. Dr. Ambara had no need to establish credentials of any kind. Randolph had sought him out, and Randolph would either believe what he had to say about contacting the dead, or not.

"I was very annoyed when I heard that Dr. Linklater had asked to have you taken off my case," Randolph said. "Quite frankly, he had no right to do that."

"I hope you will not allow such a small matter to cause any lasting bad feeling between you," Dr. Ambara remarked. "I am quite sure that Dr. Linklater was only doing what he considered best for you. He is a careful and considerate man in my experience. Perhaps too careful and too considerate, but all doctors are concerned about malpractice suits these days of course, and in a general practitioner, these apparent failings can sometimes be a virtue."

"He still had no right. I pay his bills, after all."

"Ah, Mr. Clare, paying a doctor's bills does not always give you the authority to question his professional judgment. Part of what you are paying him for is the fact that he knows a great deal more about your body than you do. And about your mind, too."

They started to walk as if an off-stage film director had suddenly instructed them to stroll side by side through the gardens, remembering their lines as they went. Randolph found Dr. Ambara's conversation peculiarly stilted, as if he were deeply reluctant to tell Randolph anything and yet felt that fate had already dictated that he must.

There was a sense of inevitability about this walk through the Dixon Gardens and about the course of their conversation, as if destiny had required them to come together at last, mismatched partners in what would prove to be an arcane game of Oriental checkers in which the white counters represented the living and the black counters represented the dead.

Dr. Ambara spoke quietly and with considerable formality. As they walked, he held his hands pressed together like a closed book that he was unwilling to open.

"As I believe I explained to you at the clinic, Mr. Clare, it is believed in my religion that the souls of the dead are not extinguished forever but that they pass through heaven in preparation for their eventual rebirth."

"But you said that they could actually be reached when they were in heaven . . . that they could actually be spoken to."

"I said this more to give you solace in your time of grief than to suggest it as a practical proposition. That, I regret to say, was my misjudgment."

"But it can be done? There is a way in which I could talk to my family again?"

Dr. Ambara looked at Randolph sharply. "Are you really sure you want to?"

Randolph said, "Perhaps I could judge that better if you were to tell me something about it, how it's done, what the dangers are."

"Well, Mr. Clare, as I mentioned on the telephone, the dangers are considerable, not only to those who attempt to contact the dead, but to the dead themselves."

They reached a long, dark yew hedge, immaculately clipped. It was still so foggy that Randolph could see only twenty or thirty feet in any direction, and the temperature had risen well up into the mid-eighties. A solitary man walked past them, regarding them with some suspicion through rimless glasses, his windbreaker rustling like brown paper that has grown soft from repeated folding.

Dr. Ambara waited until the man had passed and then said, "An essential part of our religious activity is the *sanghyang*, or trance. Anybody who is religiously devout and wishes to experience the spiritual ecstasies of closeness to the gods is capable of entering such a trance. And a measure of how powerful a trance can be is that those who enter it are often capable of extraordinary feats such as walking barefoot on fire, or of dancing complicated dances that nobody has ever taught them, often in unison with other entranced persons and in perfect step.''

''I think I've heard something about the *sanghyang*,'' Randolph told him. ''Can't people in such a state dig knives into themselves, something like that, and put skewers through their cheeks?''

''Well, perhaps you are getting a little mixed up with the penitents' rituals at Thaipusam,'' said Dr. Ambara. ''But essentially you have the idea.''

Randolph started walking again, thoughtfully. ''And it's this trance that enables people to meet their dead relatives?''

''A highly developed form of it, yes. It is popularly known as the death trance. It involves fasting and religious training of an intensive nature, and the chants and the rituals used are very complex and very *sakti*, which means magically powerful.''

''If you haven't had any religious training, is it still possible to enter one of these death trances?'' Randolph asked. ''I mean, could *I* do it? Is there any chance at all?''

Dr. Ambara took off his sunglasses and carefully polished them with his handkerchief. ''I suppose that for your own safety I should not really tell you any of this. But in my estimation, you are a man who is capable of taking a hand in his own destiny, as long as you understand that I am not *recommending* that you follow this course of action. On the contrary, for reasons which I will explain to you, you would be far better off if you were to forget that I had ever spoken to you about it.''

He held up his glasses to the foggy sunlight to make sure they were clean and then went on. ''There are only ten or maybe a dozen adepts capable of entering the death trance. Many try, many fail. The risks of entering the death trance, you see, are similar to the risks of fire-walking. During a trance it is possible for men and women to walk, even to dance, across a glowing pit of coconut husks. Their feet are quite bare, the coconut husks are white-hot, yet they do not even suffer from blisters. Some people do it regularly all of their lives and are never hurt. But sometimes a fire-walker's concentration is faulty, sometimes his faith is weak, sometimes his trance is not sufficiently complete. Who can say why? When that happens, the fire-walker falters both spiritually and physically and the fire burns him. I was at a temple blessing in Djakarta when my cousin lost both of his feet while performing a *Sanghyang Jaran*, which is a trance dance on a wooden hobbyhorse. In the time that it took him to dance from one end of the fiery pit to the other, his feet were burned down to the stumps of his shinbones, yet all the time he kept on dancing and did not cry out.''

The sun was at last beginning to penetrate the fog, and the gardens were transformed to misty gold. Randolph could feel the sweat glueing his shirt to the middle of his back.

Dr. Ambara continued. ''The risks involved in the death trance are similar but much greater. If the fire-walk goes wrong, you may lose your feet. If the death trance goes wrong, you will certainly lose your life. Of those ten or twelve adepts capable of entering the death trance, perhaps fewer than four have survived its dangers often enough to be capable of guiding a less-trained person into the realms beyond the veil. Out of those four, perhaps two could be persuaded to actually do it, although it is impossible to say whether they could be found and what they would charge for such a service. Needless to say, it is illegal in Indonesia for a death-trance adept to sell his services for money, and the government does everything it can to discourage such practices. I have heard, however, that several wealthy American families have paid death-trance adepts to contact their deceased relatives, families whose names you would recognize; and I know for certain that attempts were made to hire an adept to contact Howard Hughes in order to ascertain where his will might be. Nobody knows if Hughes was actually contacted or whether the adept failed to find him.

Perhaps he was found and had something to say that did not please the parties who had been trying to get in touch with him. You must understand, Mr. Clare, that meetings with the dead can be deeply distressing and frequently terrifying.''

Randolph said tightly, ''You mentioned dangers.''

''Yes, although I have tried not to be too specific. You have little or no knowledge of our religion, Mr. Clare, and so far I have not wished to sound patronizing. Perhaps you could compare me with a Western mechanic who is trying to discourage an Indonesian villager from driving a car by frightening him with the mystifying details of what happens when you strip the gears.''

Randolph smiled. ''You can be as mystifying and as detailed as you like, Doctor. I've listened to you so far, haven't I, without any outward signs of skepticism? I think I'm prepared to accept your basic premise that the dead are not irrevocably dead, that they've simply been removed for a while from the physical world that the rest of us inhabit. So, whatever else you have to say, it can hardly be any more difficult to swallow than that.''

''Very well,'' Dr. Ambara agreed. ''What you have to know is that when you enter the world of the dead, you are also entering the world of what I can only describe to you as demons. Well, you raise your eyebrows. I expected you would. But in their own realm, they are as real as the spirits of your loved ones are real.''

''And these . . . demons . . . they're dangerous?'' Randolph asked. The word ''demons'' felt as awkward in his mouth as an obscenity. He was a cottonseed processor, a businessman, a churchgoer and a pragmatist; for all his urgent need to believe that Marmie and the children were still reachable, could he really bring himself to believe in demons? Could all those childhood legends and all those dungeons-and-dragons fantasies really have some foundation in fact?

It was bizarre. And yet here was a highly qualified doctor telling him quite calmly that they did, in Dixon Gardens, in Memphis, on the most ordinary of days.

Dr. Ambara said, ''Of course I do not expect you to be

able to immediately accept what I am saying. For those brought up in the ways of Christianity and in the ways of modern Western education, the notion of demons must seem fanciful, even ludicrous. But whether you care to believe in them or not, they do exist, and if you choose to enter the realms of the dead, you will risk encountering them.''

"What exactly do they do? If that's the right question?''

"They are the acolytes of a goddess we call Rangda,'' Dr. Ambara explained. "They are a form of what, in popular terms, you might call zombies, the living dead. They are the wandering spirits of those whose souls were not separated from their mortal bodies by cremation and over whose remains the proper religious rites were never spoken. The Goddess Rangda promises them freedom from their misery if they snare fresh spirits for her, and that is what they do. They capture the dead and, whenever they can, the living, in order to feed their mistress. But she, of course, never keeps her promise to them and never releases them.''

Dr. Ambara paused for a moment, uncertain of how to explain the dangers of disturbing the Goddess Rangda to a man whose belief in Jehovah was far from unquestioning. Yet Randolph waited, eager to understand, anxious to hear the words that would convince him of Dr. Ambara's truths.

"You see,'' Dr. Ambara explained at last, "when a living being manages in a death trance to enter the realm of the dead, his physical presence alerts the demons. He sets up ripples, twitches, in the same way that a fly alerts a spider when it lands on its web. The demons will at once pursue the intruder and drag him back, if they can, to Rangda. A living being, for Rangda, is a rare prize, and she may richly reward the demons who brought him to her. She is the Witch Widow, the queen of all those evil spirits and ghouls who haunt the graveyards at night. Usually she has to be content with dead flesh and faded spirits. A living being is a feast.''

"You said on the telephone that there could also be danger to the dead relatives, to the people the living person is trying to get in touch with,'' Randolph said.

"Indeed," Dr. Ambara nodded. "In spite of her. voracious appetite for the living, Rangda does not of course completely eschew the dead. And any feast of souls is given greater relish if there is emotional agony to season it. She would no doubt delight in devouring the spirits of the dead loved ones in front of their living relative before she devours him too."

Randolph said with a hint of acidity, "You speak very eloquently, Dr. Ambara."

"All Indonesians know the stories and legends of Rangda. Besides, my uncle was a high priest, what we call a *pedanda*, and my father was the cultural attaché at the Indonesian office in Washington, D.C., for many years. I myself have given several lectures on Indonesian custom and religion since I have been here in the United States."

"These demons," Randolph said. "Do they have a name? Can you describe them? I'd like to know what I'm up against."

"They are called leyaks, Mr. Clare. It is difficult to say what they look like for few of those adepts who have encountered them have survived for long. But many talk of gray-faced creatures with eyes that are alight like coals."

"Presumably, though, if I were to try to get in touch with Marmie and the children, I'd have to do it here in Memphis, where they are going to be buried."

"That is correct."

"But surely there are no leyaks in the United States?"

"There is nothing that exists in Indonesia that does not exist in the rest of the world, Mr. Clare. Perhaps in a different guise, perhaps with a different mask, but still the same. There are leyaks in Memphis, my dear sir, grave-ghouls who remain invisible to everybody except those who are trained in the spiritual disciplines of Yama. The great Goddess Rangda is here too, the Witch Widow, although she may be seen in a different form. The world of gods and demons is not the same as ours, Mr. Clare. It is possible for them to be everywhere and nowhere; it is possible for them to alter their location in time and space as easily as opening a door. This is one of the first things we learn when we are young. Some of the lesser demons, perhaps, are not as versatile in their movements, but they find their own way of spreading their influence . . . the butas, for example, who breathe foul diseases into the mouths of their sleeping victims. As a doctor, I suppose I should not be telling you this, but an Indonesian specialist of very high repute is convinced that AIDS was first propagated by a buta breathing into the mouth of an American cardiologist called Lindstrom, who happened to be attending a medical convention in Djakarta in nineteen seventy-six. Dr. Lindstrom had apparently been something of an enthusiast for Zen and yoga and other Oriental disciplines and had put himself into a trance. It was while he was in this trance that the buta infected him. The unfortunate part about it was that apart from being a practicing heart specialist, Dr. Lindstrom was also a practicing homosexual.''

It appeared now that Dr. Ambara had little more to say. His waxy forehead shone with sweat. They had almost reached the gates leading out of Dixon Gardens to Park Avenue, but Randolph had the feeling that the doctor did not yet consider their conversation finished, and the way in which he had tried to dissuade Randolph from seeking out his murdered family had seemed peculiarly inconclusive.

It was almost as if Dr. Ambara had advertised the death trance like a cigarette commercial and then added a warning that "entering the realm of the dead is dangerous to your health.''

Randolph said bluntly, "If I were to pay all your expenses, would you find an adept for me, someone who could take me into a death trance?''

Dr. Ambara unfolded a clean white handkerchief and dabbed at his forehead. "Do you really believe any of what I have told you?''

"Is there a reason I shouldn't? You believe it, don't you, in spite of the fact that you've been educated and trained here in America?''

"Mr. Clare," said Dr. Ambara, "it is hardly your place to question or to define my beliefs. You have asked me how it is possible for a man to meet his dead relatives. Somewhat against my better discretion, I have told you. That is all I can do. That is all you can fairly ask me to do.''

"Dr. Ambara, I don't think you understand how much this means to me.''

"Well, I believe I do.''

Randolph said, "I'm sorry. I appreciate your taking the time to come down here and talk to me. I appreciate everything you've done. I didn't mean to be disrespectful.''

"Disrespectful?'' Dr. Ambara queried and then brushed at his cheek like a man who has been unexpectedly bitten by a mosquito. "I suppose it depends on your definition of respect. To my mind, you are trying to take me up on an offer I have not made.''

Randolph persisted, "Will you help me find an adept?''

Dr. Ambara gazed down the pathway.

"I can pay you anything you want,'' Randolph said, fully aware of how melodramatic his words sounded. "Maybe there's some clinical equipment you need. A new X-ray unit, something like that. Goddam, Doctor, maybe you want a new Cadillac.''

Dr. Ambara pursed his lips, turned away, thought for a while and then turned back again. "This cannot be undertaken frivolously,'' he said.

"Did anybody mention anything remotely frivolous?'' Randolph demanded. "I'm talking about my wife and children.''

"I suppose I could try,'' said Dr. Ambara.

His tone was too guarded. Randolph, as an experienced business negotiator, suddenly recognized the personal need that Dr. Ambara had been trying to conceal behind carefully selected words, behind tightly controlled sentences. He suddenly identified the real reason for Dr. Ambara's lack of conviction.

"There could be some mutual benefit here,'' he remarked.

Dr. Ambara glanced at him. He looked as if he were about to deny it, but then he quickly nodded his head and said, "I can make some preliminary inquiries. I have friends at the Indonesian Embassy, people who knew my father.''

"You know that I'll pay," Randolph told him.

"Well," said Dr. Ambara, "perhaps money is not the prime consideration in this matter."

They reached the gates and Dr. Ambara extended his hand. "I will call you, Mr. Clare, just as soon as I have anything to tell you."

Randolph said, "You're not a bad judge of character, are you, Doctor?"

Dr. Ambara blinked. "I'm not sure I understand you."

"What I mean is, when you first mentioned the possibility of my reaching my family, you had a fair idea that I would want to try to, didn't you?"

Dr. Ambara shrugged and looked away.

Randolph did not know whether he ought to go on questioning Dr. Ambara or not, but when the doctor made no move to go, he said at last, "You have your own reasons for wanting me to meet my family, haven't you?"

Dr. Ambara said, "I shall do my best to find you an adept. That is sufficient."

"Well, it will have to do for now," Randolph replied. "But I won't be able to see my way clear to paying out any money, not unless I know what you really want out of this."

Dr. Ambara suddenly turned and challenged Randolph with tear-filled eyes. "My wife, Mr. Clare. That is what I want."

"Your wife?"

Dr. Ambara nodded vehemently. "Her name was Muda. She died three years ago in an automobile accident on Poplar. I kissed her good-bye in the morning and then halfway through the afternoon, the Memphis police called me to say that she was dead."

Randolph said, "I'm sorry. You should have told me."

"You have quite enough grief of your own, Mr. Clare."

Randolph slowly rubbed his cheek. "So you want to get in touch with your wife just as much as I want to get in touch with mine?"

"Yes," said Dr. Ambara.

"Then why didn't you? Three years is a long time.

You had the contacts. Couldn't you find an adept before this?''

"Mr. Clare, I simply couldn't afford it. I contacted one man and he wanted half a million dollars. Another wanted less but had insufficient experience. I do not mind the risk to my own life, you understand, but I do not wish to die without seeing Muda again, and I do not wish to put her existence at risk.''

He blew his nose and then said, "When you came to the clinic, Mr. Clare, you came to me as a possible hope in spite of your tragedy. If you perhaps could put up the money to hire a skillful adept, then I too could benefit. But I had to be cautious in my approaches to you. I did not want you to think I was soliciting money from you, or favors, or that this was some kind of elaborate confidence trick to take advantage of your grief. Also, I could not deceive you about the dangers involved, which are quite real.''

Randolph said, "I'm going to have to go home and think this over.''

"I am not begging you," Dr. Ambara told him.

"No, I know that," Randolph said. "But what you've told me today . . . that's a lot to digest. I lost my entire family this week, and yet in the same week I've been told that I can speak to them again even though they're dead. I've also been warned about demons and witches and creatures with gray faces, like zombies. You have to admit, that's a lot to swallow. It takes most people most of their lives just to accept that their loved ones have been taken from them, let alone any of this other business.''

Dr. Ambara said, "Perhaps I have made a mistake.''

"No," Randolph reassured him. "No mistake. But maybe a little more honesty would have helped.''

"You are an American," Dr. Ambara remarked, and there was more to this reply than was apparent.

They shook hands and then the doctor walked away, stiff-legged, through the mid-morning haze. Randolph watched him briefly, then crossed the parking lot to his gold-colored Mercedes, opened the door and climbed in. As the buckle-up signal sounded, he was sure he heard someone speak his name but the voice was almost exactly at the same high pitch as the signal so that it was impossible for him to tell who it was, or even if he had really heard it at all.

He sat frowning, the ignition key poised in his hand, his ears straining, but he heard nothing more. He shook his head to clear it. Miles Linklater had warned him that he might experience hallucinations about Marmie and the children for a long time to come; he might hear their voices, glimpse them at crowded airports, feel their touch when he was half-asleep.

But nonetheless he had the distinct feeling that whatever the voice had said, however much of an hallucination it might have been, it was a warning, a message from Marmie to take care of himself.

He looked around. Tourists passed by, gaudy and solemn like saltimbanques from a disbanded carnival. A small boy skateboarded deftly between the parked cars. The tulip trees nodded and shivered in the fog, as if they were excited. There was something, somebody, around . . . some feeling that made Randolph hesitate for one more moment before starting the car.

Then he saw what it was. A motorcycle policeman in a khaki shirt and domed helmet, his eyes concealed behind mirrored sunglasses, watching him intently from the opposite side of the parking lot.

At first Randolph thought he must be mistaken. Why should a cop be watching him? But as he started up the Mercedes and pulled out of the parking space, he saw the man turn his head to follow him. There was no question about it, Randolph was under observation. As he drove west along Park Avenue toward Lamar between trees that leaned over the highway like attenuated ghosts, he checked the rearview mirror and he could see that the cop had mounted his motorcycle and was riding attentively twenty yards behind.

Randolph deliberately gave no indication that he had spotted the policeman but drove straight back to Clare Castle by the quickest route. As he turned into the gateway, he saw the policeman draw up outside for a moment, then engage his clutch and speed off, back toward the city.

Charles opened the door for him, serious-faced, dressed in black. "Mr. Clare?" he asked, as if he could sense that something unusual had happened.

But Randolph simply stepped into the house, walked briskly across the hallway and asked, "Did you lay out my black suit? We have to be at the airport by two o'clock to meet the plane."

"Yes, sir," Charles answered, his voice constricted by sorrow. "I laid out your black suit."

TEN

Orbus Greene sat like an emperor at his accustomed table at the Four Flames restaurant, steadily gorging his way through the house specialty of Chateaubriand Bouquetière for two. Waiters hurried back and forth, bringing him fresh baskets of muffins, refilled gravy boats, dishes of sweet potatoes and buttered asparagus. Apart from his ever-present bodyguards, who ate nothing, Orbus was lunching alone, and that was the way he preferred it. So did most of those Memphis businessmen who had ever had the misfortune to join him for a meal. Even Waverley Graceworthy had once admitted that watching Orbus eat was "not a pretty sight."

Dancing and ducking like a worried welterweight boxer, the maitre d' approached from the other side of the restaurant. "Mr. Greene, is everything satisfactory?"

Orbus nodded with his mouth full and his lips glistening with butter.

"I am sorry to have to interrupt your meal, Mr. Greene, but . . ."

Orbus lifted the large white-linen napkin that was tucked into his collar and dabbed at his mouth. His attendants raised their cold, empty eyes and stared at the maitre d' as if it would take only one word out of place to precipitate instant death.

"Well?" asked Orbus.

"I have been asked to direct your attention, Mr. Greene, to the fact that Mr. Graceworthy is waiting outside in his limousine. He would very much appreciate it if you could leave your table for just a moment and speak to him."

Orbus shifted his enormous white-suited bulk in the over-sized oak chair the management of the Four Flames had provided for him. His pouchy eyes rolled down toward his plate where his half-finished chateaubriand lay waiting for him, bloody and rare, and then across to the restaurant window through which the front grille of Waverley's Cadillac could be glimpsed, parked on the other side of Poplar Street.

Without a word, Orbus cut himself another slice of steak and chewed it with deliberation. Only when he had swallowed it and wiped his mouth again did he beckon to his boys and say, "Mr. Graceworthy desires to have words. Let's humor him, shall we?"

Nobody was fooled, of course. Not the maitre d', who knew from crucifying experience what happened to anybody who tried to disturb Orbus Greene during the sacred piggery of lunchtime; nor the boys either, who were regularly called upon to exercise some of their least-engaging skills on those who interrupted Orbus while he was eating. In uncharacteristic self-mockery, or in the sheer delight of insatiable greed, Orbus often referred to Memphis and its many restaurants as his "rooting-ground" because it was only in Memphis that he could find the dry-barbecued pork ribs, the smoked duckling, the blackened redfish and the oysters Bienville that he considered the fundamentals not just of civilized life, but of life itself.

The bodyguards assisted Orbus heave and sweat his way out of his chair. Then, covertly watched by the other diners, they escorted him with slitty-eyed overprotectiveness out the door and across Poplar, a procession that could have been painted by Brueghel. It was midday now, the haze had been burned away by the sun and the concrete pavement glared like desert sand. Waverley Graceworthy's Cadillac, perfectly waxed, was close to the curb, its body-work a galaxy of reflected stars. Its engine whistled softly to sustain the air conditioning inside. All of its darkly tinted windows were closed tight.

One of Orbus's men insolently rapped on the rear window with his knuckle even though he knew that he could be clearly observed from inside the limousine. Orbus stood on the sidewalk sweating until the Cadillac's door swung open, a breath of chilled air rippled out and Waverley Graceworthy said in an elegant whisper, "Take a seat, Orbus. It must be hot out there."

With his attendants clutching at his sides and his elbows to help him lower himself, Orbus struggled into the car. The suspension dipped and bounced. When at last Orbus's right leg had been forced inside, the door was closed with a subdued click, like the door of a safe. The bodyguards assembled themselves untidily against a nearby wall, where they combed their hair and picked at their fingernails with knives.

Waverley Graceworthy looked a little peaked. He was dressed in the palest of dove grays and he was sipping orange-flavored Perrier water from a tall, frosted highball glass.

"I'm so sorry to have interrupted your devotions," he said, and the word "devotions" utterly sterilized any apology he might have been attempting to make.

"Is it so urgent?" Orbus asked, dragging out his huge green handkerchief and burying his face in it. He suppressed a belch and the entire limousine shuddered. Waverley looked the other way in thinly disguised disgust.

"Randolph Clare is behaving unpredictably," Waverley began. "I don't know what he's up to but he's been downtown to see some black character called Jimmy the Rib, and apparently Jimmy the Rib has told him about Reece."

"Has he connected Reece with you?" Orbus asked, tucking away his handkerchief.

"Not so far, but Reece is making absolutely sure that he doesn't."

"Well, I don't know," said Orbus, "I think Reece has gone way over the top. I don't disagree with the principle of having a little tame muscle around to make sure business runs smooth, but Reece is a homicidal maniac. I mean, look at what he did to Randolph's family. He was supposed to scare them, for God's sake, not massacre them. Marmie Clare was a pretty woman, a fine woman. If I had been a different kind of man, I would have appreciated a woman like that myself.''

"What are you saying?" Waverley asked testily. "That we should allow Clare Cottonseed to expand uncontrolled, let them snatch all the choice contracts right out from under our noses? You needed that Sun-Taste contract, Orbus. What are your half-year figures going to look like unless you get it? Before we know it, Clare will be bigger and more profitable than the rest of us put together and the Cottonseed Association is going to look like the sick man of Memphis.''

"I still don't know why you have to take such extreme measures," Orbus told him. "A few fires, fine and dandy. A couple of cockroaches introduced surreptitiously into the product. That's all you need. That's the way you dealt with Shem Owen when he started to act up. Brought him to heel in days.''

"Randolph Clare is no Shem Owen, not by a long shot," Waverley retorted.

"But we've got him begging for assistance already," Orbus reminded him. "When he called me yesterday asking the Association to help him out, he wasn't playacting, he was serious. You could maybe make it a condition that we continue to supply him permanently, even after he's made up the shortfall.''

"He won't agree to that," Waverley snapped.

"In that case, he's probably going to lose Sun-Taste anyway, so what are you so fired up about?''

Waverley stared at Orbus venomously. "What the hell do you think? Supposing he *does* lose Sun-Taste, he'll still be alive, won't he? He'll still be in business and before we know it, he'll be back up behind us again, breathing down our necks.''

Orbus frowned. He had never seen Waverley so agitated. He had certainly never heard him speak so openly and so emphatically about destroying one of his competitors.

"You're talking about murder here, Waverley," he said soberly.

"I'm talking about survival," Waverley said, his cheeks beginning to mottle.

"Is there something personal in this? I know you and Randolph don't get along too good, but . . . but this is beginning to sound like something different."

Waverley touched his face with his fingertips as if to make sure it was still on straight, as if it were a mask rather than a real face. "Chief Moyne is keeping tabs on Randolph. If he shows any signs of poking his nose in too far . . . well, Chief Moyne is keeping in touch."

"And what about this black man? The one who told Randolph about Reece."

"I told you," Waverley said. "Reece will make sure he doesn't go spreading stories like that anywhere else."

Orbus shifted his weight from one huge buttock to the other. "Does that mean I'm going to be reading about him in the *Press-Scimitar* tomorrow morning? 'Black Man Found Dismembered With Chain Saw in the Meeman-Shelby Forest'? I have to tell you, Waverley, this is getting distinctly out of hand."

"Orbus," said Waverley coldly, "it's Randolph's life or yours, believe me."

Orbus was silent. At last he asked, "What am I going to tell him about his Sun-Taste proposal?"

Orbus was tempted to say he would like to pass the message on to Randolph not to bother about making any deals because Waverley would have him killed before they could sign the papers, but he wisely surmised that Waverley had taken about as much sarcasm as he could stand for one day. He had always suspected that Waverley was a dangerous man; now he was beginning to see how utterly ruthless he could be.

Waverley said, "Stall him. Make some encouraging noises,

as if we're really considering it seriously. He has only seven days to make up his shortfall; the more time we waste, the less chance he'll have to do any deals with anybody else.''

''How's the repair work shaping up out at Raleigh?'' Orbus asked.

Waverley smiled. ''Slow, thanks to our friend. With any luck, they shouldn't be back on line for another three days, maybe four.''

Orbus said, ''All right then. What are you going to do?''

''I'm going to allow a decent period of time to pass after Randolph buries his family and then I'm going to reassess the business situation. That's when I'm going to make my final decision. Our friend says that the half-year picture is even stronger than it looked last week, mainly because they sold off some of their docking interests and got rid of those warehouses up at Woodstock Industrial Park. Even if they do lose Sun-Taste, they could still be back up to ninety percent of today's production levels by August of next year, that's the prediction.''

Orbus began to tug out his handkerchief again. Even with its air conditioning down to sixty degrees, the interior of the Cadillac was warm enough to make him sweat. ''He's a good manager, Randolph, you have to give him that.''

Waverley did not rise to that. Instead, he said, ''Reece may be violent but he knows what he's doing. He can make it look like suicide. 'Grief-stricken Cottonseed Tycoon Decides to End It All.' You can read about *that* in the *Press-Scimitar*, my friend.''

Orbus wiped his face thoughtfully. He did not care for Randolph Clare. He disliked Randolph's self-confidence, which he perceived as smugness, and he particularly disliked Randolph's continuing refusal to become a member of the Cottonseed Association, which he perceived as arrogance. All the same, he was a less-than-enthusiastic supporter of Waverley's strong-arm techniques, and even if he didn't believe that other people's lives were quite as sacred as his own, he still thought that they were reasonably sacred. There was nothing in the cottonseed-processing business, in Orbus's opinion, actually worth killing for, although woe betide anybody who was stranded alone on a desert island with Orbus Greene and with nothing for either of them to eat.

He hooked one fat pinkie into the Cadillac's door handle and opened the door. Immediately one of his bodyguards leaped across and took his arm. "Everything okay, Mr. Greene?"

"Thank you, Vinnie, everything's fine," puffed Orbus. "I think we can get ourselves back to that chateaubriand now."

"Hey, I tell you what, Mr. Greene, on account of you had to leave it midway and on account of it getting cold, I told them to knock up a fresh one for you."

Orbus pinched Vinnie's narrow, foxlike cheekbone. "You're a good boy, Vinnie, you're going to go far. Good afternoon, Waverley. It was a pleasure to talk to you. Perhaps you'll be kind enough to keep me informed."

"You can count on that, Orbus," Waverley said, drumming his delicate fingers on the Cadillac's armrest and wondering how long it would take for the smell of garlic and perspiration to filter away through the air-conditioning system.

Waverley Graceworthy disliked Orbus Greene so poisonously, and he was so obsessed with his own physical fragility and with the wrongs that he obsessively believed had been done to him, that he lived in a perpetual state of rancor. And lately his ire had increased, his bitterness had deepened. Two of his secretaries had resigned, one after the other, because of his caustic remarks. He was like a vituperative marionette, a vicious Charlie McCarthy. But no one had noticed that his ill temper had increased in direct and exact proportion to the rising success of Clare Cottonseed and the burgeoning wealth of Randolph Clare.

As his chauffeur piloted him back downtown to Cotton Row, he looked out of the Cadillac's opera window and thought of the old times before Kennedy and Johnson, the real Southern Democratic times, and of all those humid Memphis summers when blacks had been paid what they deserved and nothing more and when there had been parties and festivals and the ladies had worn their white dresses and he and all those cotton-wealthy friends of his had danced and drunk and flirted with the prettiest girls. They had played real blues on Beale Street in those days, real dirty blues, not the homogenized honky-tonk they played now at the Old Daisy theater. There had been no Mud Island recreational center then, no shopping malls, no Swiss monorails, no bistros. Elvis Presley had been a young trucker and Waverley Graceworthy had been the prince of Memphis.

Hot, dirty, squalid, exciting days, long gone by. Just as Ilona had long gone by and left him, and eventually died.

He never spoke her name these days, although he had promised himself he would, every single morning when he first awoke. It hurt too much, and that was the extraordinary and distressing part about it: that instead of forgetting her gently as the years went by, the pain of losing her had become increasingly acute, until some days it was almost intolerable. He knew why, of course, although he would not always admit it to himself. He understood his own psychology very clearly but he preferred not to face up to it. If he faced up to it, he would have to question the intensity of his anger and the veracity of his vengefulness, and the truth was that he actually enjoyed feeling vengeful, he derived pleasure from his rage. He was a man of exceptional cruelty because he understood his cruelty, what caused it and what could cure it.

He and Richard Reece were perfect partners because Richard Reece was cruel without knowing or caring why. They could admire each other's heartlessness while admiring each other's extraordinary mentality. Richard Reece was awed that Waverley could instruct him to do what he did. Waverley was awed that Richard Reece could actually go out and obey him.

Jimmy the Rib was about to discover the perfection of their partnership, for just as Waverley's limousine was turning into Linden Street, Jimmy was awakened in an apartment on Tutwiler Street, where he had inadvertently spent the night, by a furious knocking on the bedroom door.

"Who that?" he called out. He sat up in bed, dragging the rumpled sheets around himself. "That you, Linda?"

The knocking was repeated, more violently than before. Jimmy the Rib shuffled across the bed and reached down to the floor for his shirt and pants. He was worried now. He had spent the night with Linda because she had invited him to and because she had wanted to share the fresh white snow he was carrying; nothing immoral had happened apart from Linda's dancing around the room to the heavy thumpings of Z. Z. Top, flopping her bare breasts up and down in her hands and giggling sweet and high. But Linda's lover, Earle Gentry, might not see the situation that way, even though Linda had gone to work hours ago and Jimmy the Rib had been left here snoozing the day away in gloriously fetid isolation.

"Who that?" Jimmy the Rib repeated, struggling into his pants and hopping across to the brown-painted dresser where he had left his long-bladed knife. "That you, Earle? Why you knocking like that?"

The knocking abruptly stopped. Jimmy the Rib stopped too, halfway across the floor. Linda's apartment was on the wrong side of the building to catch the sun but a bright, cheeselike slice of reflected light hovered on the floral wallpaper and touched the tip of Stevie Wonder's nose on the poster opposite. Linda thought that after "I Just Called to Say I Love You," they should have stopped writing songs altogether. As far as she was concerned, that was the definitive song. "Makes me shuddah," she claimed.

Jimmy the Rib stepped nearer to the door. "Anybody there?" he wanted to know. Sweat glistened on his jet-black forehead and in the concave dip of his breastbone. Around his neck he wore a crucifix, an ankh and good-luck talismans from almost every religion known to man. He ran his tongue around his big yellow teeth and gave his dry, thumping sniff.

"I said, is anybody there?"

The reply was earshattering and spectacular. With three systematic kicks, the door was smashed off its hinges and it crashed inward, flat on the floor. Jimmy the Rib danced

backward and reached for his knife, hissing between his
teeth, *Okay you mothers, you wait until you see what you up
against here, Jimmy the Rib, okay, only the fastest, mean-
est, least-kindly knife artist east of anyplace at all.* But that
first confident surge of aggression and power died away like
a run-down gramophone when three tall, broad-shouldered
men stepped into the room, their faces covered with ice-
hockey masks. One of them was carrying a sawed-off shotgun. The second was carrying a bale of wire. The third was
twanging a coarse-toothed logging saw against the open
palm of his hand.

"What you dudes want?" Jimmy the Rib demanded
fearfully.

The men said nothing but surrounded him. The shortest
of them was almost four inches taller than he was, and all of
them were far more heavily built. Jimmy the Rib could hear
their harsh breathing behind their masks.

"What you want?" Jimmy the Rib repeated. "Who sent
you here? This is some kind of a mistake, huh? Is that it?
Some kind of a error? Maybe somebody got their lines
crossed. I mean, what is this, breaking the door down and
all? This ain't even my *place*, man. Hey, this some kind of
a telegram maybe? A Scare-U-Gram or something?"

The man with the sawed-off shotgun nudged Jimmy in his
bare belly with the muzzle and directed him toward the bed.
Jimmy retreated step by step until at last he was forced to sit
down.

"You touch me, you guys, and I warn you, I've got
friends. I've even got friends in the police department."

But the men took no notice. They put down the saw and
the bale of wire and then they forced Jimmy's arms over his
head and wired his wrists to the head of the bed. Jimmy
sweated and grunted and wriggled, but the men were too
powerful for him and he was too afraid to mouth off anymore. The man with the sawed-off shotgun kept the muzzle
so close to Jimmy's nose that he could smell the oil. Besides, these men did not look like humorists. The wire cut
into Jimmy's skin and the harder he struggled, the more

painfully it bit. He gritted his teeth and grunted, but the men remained silent.

"You guys making some kind of mistake here," Jimmy protested. "Believe me, I didn't even touch that woman. We was snorting coke, that's all. And maybe we danced a little, but I didn't even touch her."

Still there was no reply. Jimmy found the lack of response unnerving. He was a hard man himself; he had stabbed both men and women without any compunction. But he had never met anyone as cold and as uncommunicative as these masked men. You killed because you were angry, right? You killed because somebody had done you wrong, insulted your woman, stolen your money, totaled your car. But you always let your victim know what you were doing, and why. At least Jimmy the Rib did. And that was why these silent, faceless men terrified him. They were going to do something bad, there was no question of it, but he didn't know what, or why, or even who they were.

"I got some money, all right? You understand that? I can pay you off. How much is it going to take? A couple of thousand each? I can manage that. Maybe two thousand, how does that sound?"

It was then that two of the men seized Jimmy's ankles while the third man, the biggest, picked up the coarse-toothed saw. He stared down at Jimmy through the slits in his mask and shook his wrist so the blade of the saw rumbled and sang.

With a dry mouth, Jimmy asked him, "What you going to do to me? What you going to do with that saw?"

Without any further taunting, the man grabbed Jimmy's right thigh and drew the teeth of the saw across it, tearing through the black cotton of his pants, through black skin and scarlet flesh. Jimmy shrieked and yanked against the wires that held his wrists.

"My legs, man! Not my legs! For Christ's sake, man, not my legs!"

He screamed and screamed, but the people in that building on Tutwiler Street were the kind of residents who kept themselves to themselves, and even if a husband was stran-

gling his wife in the next-door apartment, they would not
come out, except later to see the body as it was wheeled
along the hallway. Yelling as hideous as Jimmy the Rib's
meant real trouble and so they turned up their televisions,
double-locked their doors and wondered how serious it was
going to be.

Because, Jesus, that man was screaming like you never
heard *anybody* scream before.

Jimmy the Rib was blind with pain, deafened with fear.
Every now and then he jerked his head up to see what the
big man was doing to him. The teeth of the saw were
rust-red with blood, and there was blood splattered all over
the bed, and when the teeth had at last torn their way
through fat and muscle and cut right down to the bone, there
was a hideous ripping vibration that went all the way through
Jimmy the Rib's pelvis, up his backbone and into his brain
. . . and he went on screaming and screaming and praying
for the sawing to stop.

But he did manage at last to say through ash-gray lips,
"Not the other one, man. Leave me with one. Please, not
the other one."

But the man with the saw walked around to the other
side of the bed so he could take hold of Jimmy the Rib's
other leg.

Jimmy was beyond screaming now. He lay back and his
eyes filmed over like a sleeping crow's. All he could think
of was agony and of how he wasn't here at all; he was back
home with his mother in days gone by, his sister Juliette's
birthday, that must have been the nicest day he ever had, all
those years ago, before he started running with the teenage
gangs. He could see the candles shining on his sister's
birthday cake, shining and wavering in the draft that blew in
through the screen door. *Momma, dear Momma, why did I
let you down so bad? Me and that skunk of a father of mine.*

"Not the other one, man," he hissed between bloodied
lips, his tongue bitten through. But he could hear the saw
rasping even if he couldn't feel it now, and he could hear
the sound of sirens somewhere outside, and birds singing,
those birds that always nested in Linda's roof.

If Beale Street could talk, if Beale Street could talk,
Married men would have to take up their beds and
    walk,
Except one or two, who never drink booze,
And the blind man on the corner who sings the Beale
    Street Blues.

The man lifted up Jimmy's second severed leg. Jimmy stared at it and then said dully, "You done crippled me, man."

The man shook his head.

"You done took my legs off, man," Jimmy insisted.

But he had missed the point. The man had done more than cripple him. The bed was already dark with blood as both femoral arteries flooded onto the sheets. Within ten minutes Jimmy the Rib would bleed to death.

The three men left the apartment. He heard their feet on the stairs. He lay back, his wrists still wired to the head of the bed, and tried to think of what he could do. He knew his legs were gone but he could not really believe it. He could still feel them, and they hurt. Maybe, if he could work himself free, he could limp down the hall to the telephone and call his friend Morris. He knew Morris would drive over and help him, even if nobody else would. Morris was cool.

Time went by. He opened his eyes and tried to figure out whether he had been sleeping or not. He thought he heard voices but he could not be sure. Then he heard someone shouting, and a woman calling her children, again and again, so repetitively that it began to irritate him. The cheese-shaped slice of sunlight gradually grew thinner and then faded altogether. Linda had always complained of how dark her apartment was, you had to switch the light on at four o'clock.

A white face appeared above him like a Hallowe'en lantern. A blurry voice said, "Is he dayud, what jawl thayunk?"

Jimmy the Rib opened his eyes wide and said, "I ain't

dead, man. I'm only resting,'' and the white face let out a horrified yell and disappeared.

Jimmy smiled, just a little, but he was lying again. The last minute of his misspent life ticked away and he was gone. The white face came back and after a long pause said, ''He's dayud oright. You cain't fewl me. That's one dayud nigrah.''

ELEVEN

They stood in a close, silent group at the far end of the
United Airlines freight hangar, watching with sad attention
as the hearses drew away from the cargo hold of the recently arrived 767 outside: four hearses, black and gleaming
with wax, with silver crests and black-feathered plumes
fluttering on their tops, a solemn procession to carry home
the martyred family of Randolph Clare.

They said nothing to each other as the hearses approached
and drew up beside them, and the vice-president of Arjemian
& Prowda, Morticians, tall and serious in his black suit and
his black fedora hat, stepped out of the leading hearse and
approached Randolph with five or six different expressions
of sympathy: the lowered head, the raised chin, the eyes
dropped sadly to one side, the brave but understanding
frown.

"We shall take the remains directly to the home of rest,"
he said. "I gather from your personal assistant that you
have no desire to view them."

Randolph glanced at Wanda, who was dressed in a black
tailored suit and a black veiled hat. Wanda, who had been
talking to Dr. Linklater, had gently tried to persuade Randolph that he ought to view the bodies. The morticians,
after all, would have carefully disguised most of the traces
of what had happened to them. The most important point,
though, was that if Randolph were to view the bodies, he

would at last be forced to come to terms with the fact that his family was actually dead. At the moment, Dr. Linklater was concerned that this reality had not properly sunk in and that sooner or later Randolph was going to suffer a damaging psychological crisis.

Neither Dr. Linklater nor Wanda could possibly have understood that Randolph had declined to view the bodies for the simple reason that he expected to see Marmie and John and Mark and Issa *alive*, or at least spiritually alive. These four black caskets with their silver handles contained nothing more than the physical likenesses of the family who had left him, nothing more than their earthly shells. It was easier for him to believe in Dr. Ambara's philosophy of reincarnation if he did not see them. It was easier to believe that they were still breathing, talking, living, laughing. Not here of course, but somewhere, and not too far away.

Wanda said, "You're sure? It might be a way of saying good-bye."

"You're beginning to sound like Dr. Linklater," Randolph replied, although not accusingly.

The mortician raised his eyebrows interrogatively at Wanda, who shook her head.

"Very well," he said, bowing in reluctant acceptance. "But I can assure you, Mr. Clare, that your loved ones received the very finest attention."

"I'm sure," Randolph said, although he thought to himself with a sudden, agonizing spasm of grief: *Marmie, my darling*.

The four hearses were driven out of the hangar into the sunshine. Randolph watched them go and then beckoned to Herbert to bring the limousine around and drive him to the funeral home. Neil Sleaman, who had made a point of staying in the background, stepped forward and said, "Would you like me to come with you, sir?"

Randolph shook his head. "I'd rather you went back to Front Street and took care of that consignment from Levee Cotton. And could you see what progress they're making out at Raleigh? They seem to be dragging their feet."

"They had some trouble with the refrigeration system,"

Neil explained. His forehead was beaded with perspiration and there was a dark sweat stain on the front of his white shirt. The temperature was ninety degrees in the sun and the humidity was eighty-seven percent.

Randolph said almost offhandedly, "I may be taking some time off. Not too long, nothing more than a week. But we're going through crucial times here, Neil, and I want you to understand that if you can hold things together for me, if you can get us back on line . . . well, you'll reap the rewards of whatever you've done."

Neil smiled tightly and said, "Thank you, sir. I appreciate that."

"There's just one more thing," Randolph told him. "I'm expecting a call from Orbus Greene in reply to my suggestion that we might be able to work out a deal with the Cottonseed Association and keep the Sun-Taste contract supplied. Do you think you can handle that?"

Neil said, "Surely, no problem. But if it looks like it's getting complicated, I'll refer him to you." Then he hesitated for a moment and finally said, "Are you thinking of going away, Mr. Clare? I mean, are you thinking of leaving town for a while?"

Randolph said, "I'm not too sure yet. I won't know until after the funeral. But you know this has all been pretty much of a shock. I think I would be doing a disservice to everybody at Clare Cottonseed if I went on working and pretending that I hadn't been affected. Of course I've been affected. My wife and my children were just driven out of here in funeral cars. So the best thing I can do is to give myself some time off . . . not too long, but long enough to come to terms with what's happened."

Neil took Randolph's elbow and gripped it uncomfortably tight. "Sure," he said with overeffusive familiarity. "Sure, I understand. And you just leave Orbus Greene to me. No problem. If he was as smart as he was fat, huh? That would be something."

"Yes," Randolph agreed. "That would be something."

Wanda was silent during most of the drive along Elvis Presley Boulevard as they headed toward the funeral home.

Randolph sat back in his seat, half-closed his eyes and tried to think of Marmie and the children, but somehow the reality of downtown Memphis kept intruding—the streets and the buildings and the traffic—and he was more aware of Wanda's perfume than he was of his memories. As they drew up before the traffic signals at Linden, Wanda said, "You didn't tell me you were thinking of going away. Did you decide that this morning?"

"More or less. Let's just say that a very good friend made it sound like an attractive idea."

"Have you decided where you're going to go?"

Randolph hesitated and then nodded. "Yes, I have. To Indonesia."

"Indonesia?" Wanda echoed in bewilderment. "Is there any particular reason?"

"Yes," he told her, "there is."

"I didn't know you had friends in Indonesia."

"I don't."

"So you're just going off on your own?"

Randolph leaned his head on the back of the seat and stared out the window. "I'm taking a friend. Well . . . more of a guide than a friend."

Wanda said, "You worry me."

Randolph turned and looked at her and smiled. "There's nothing to worry about, I promise you. Really, there's nothing. Besides, I didn't know you cared."

"Of course I care," Wanda retorted. "You don't think that a secretary can work for a man from nine o'clock in the morning until seven o'clock at night, day after day for three years, and not get to care about him?"

"Well, that's flattering," Randolph said. "But I promise you, I'll be okay."

Wanda said, with a flush in her cheeks, "Take me with you."

Randolph looked at her carefully for a long moment. Then he said, "How should I react to that suggestion?"

"You can react to it in any way you like. But the way I see it, you've suddenly found yourself abandoned, cut loose with no stability and no ties, and if you're not two-hundred-percent careful, you're going to find yourself drifting off right away from reality, right away from everything you know."

"You *do* sound like Dr. Linklater," Randolph said.

"Well, what if I do? Dr. Linklater called me a couple of times after you left the Mount Moriah Clinic and he's just as worried about you as I am. I happen to agree with everything he says, if you must know. You need taking care of, someone to keep your feet on the ground. I flattered myself that maybe it could be me. I know you well enough, after all. Maybe you forget some of the time that I exist. But I was hired to take care of you and after a while it stopped being a job and started being a vocation instead."

Randolph looked at her and for almost the first time, he realized how pretty she was with her dark, wavy hair; her wide-apart, bright-blue eyes; her fully curved, vivid-pink lips. He knew that since she had been working at Clare Cottonseed, she had broken off a longstanding engagement to a naval officer from the U.S. Navy air station at Millington and that immediately afterward she had briefly dated a musician and then a devastatingly handsome young executive from the Baptist Memorial Health Care System, Inc. But Randolph had never realized how much she cared about *him*; not romantically of course, but as a man who counted on her loyalty, her undemanding friendship and her continued daily devotion.

"You've embarrassed me," he said.

"I'm sorry," she replied, flustered.

"No, no. The fault is all mine. You've embarrassed me because I never realized until now how well you look after me. I've been taking you for granted ever since you've worked for me. Expecting everything and giving nothing."

"That's not true, Mr. Clare. You've always been appreciative, and you pay me well. I can't ask for anything more than that."

"You're wrong, Wanda. You can, and you just have."

"I don't understand."

"Well . . . let's just say that you may be right. I may need somebody to keep me anchored. It isn't easy, losing a

family. It's strange rather than sad. Your whole world
suddenly ends up as ashes in your hands . . . all your plans,
all your schemes, everything you ever took for granted. It's
nothing but ash that blows right through your fingers. And
do you know what? You suddenly find yourself free when
you never expected to be. You suddenly find that you have
nobody else to worry about, nobody else to take care of.
You can get up in the middle of the night and play jazz and
nobody says, 'Come back to bed, for God's sake, I'm trying
to sleep!' You can lie in the tub for three hours, until the
water's cold and your fingers get crinkly, and nobody says,
'Come on out and here's a towel to wrap around yourself.'
That's the strange part. That's what hurts. And maybe that's
where you and Dr. Linklater are especially understanding
and right. Maybe I do need somebody to stop me from
floating away.''

Randolph thought to himself as he watched the sunlight
flicker through the passing trees and dapple Wanda's face:
*You're hedging your bets, Mr. Handy Randy, the way you
always do. You're just making sure that if Dr. Ambara's
theories of reincarnation are untrue, you have someone to
protect you, someone to salvage your vanity and your
confusion.*

"You really want to come with me?" he asked redun-
dantly but magnanimously, as if he were asking a starving
peasant woman if she wanted anything to eat.

Wanda nodded. "To Indonesia? You mean it?"

Randolph gave her a smile that meant yes. "I don't think
I deserve you," he said in a congested voice.

Wanda took his hand and clasped it carefully between
hers. She had long, perfectly manicured nails painted shell
pink. A small gold band on the third finger of her right
hand. No wedding band, no engagement ring. She said softly,
"You deserve more than you think. You've always been
kind and understanding to everybody around you. Your
friends, your family, people in the office. I've heard you.
I've seen you. Why should it be so hard for you to accept
that those same people want to show *you* some kindness
now that you need it?''

They reached the funeral home on Madison. The four hearses were already lined up along the curb and the caskets had been carried inside. The front window of the funeral home reflected the jostling afternoon traffic, the shoppers and the tourists and the street musicians, the ragged clouds and the shining windows and the dark-blue sky. The living, hurrying past the dead. There were gilded letters on the window in an old-fashioned script that read "Arjemian & Prowda, Funeral Services."

Randolph spent only ten minutes in the chapel there. Wanda waited outside. She was afraid to see him cry, and afraid that she might cry herself. The four Clare caskets were laid side by side on a long purple-covered plinth, and candles burned, and the sun gradually died behind a stained-glass window showing Jesus Christ with his arms outstretched in sympathy. "And He shall wipe away every tear from their eyes; and there shall be no longer any death; there shall be no longer any mourning, or crying, or pain."

Randolph, kneeling, with the trousers of his black suit hitched up so that the knees wouldn't crease, with his starched white collar cutting into his neck, thought to himself: *Why does the life everlasting have to be won at such terrible cost? If the life everlasting is true, why can it be achieved only through death, through grief, and through agony? What kind of God is it who gives us the world and everything in it, and the capability of loving so fiercely, and then takes it all away?*

When he had first fallen in love with Marmie, his love had been jumpy and light and erratic. But the love of middle age was something else altogether. It burned inside of him like the greatest fire ever lit. It was overwhelming, so strong that it was almost an obsession. In middle age he had begun to understand for the first time the marriage vows that he had taken. *With my body, I thee worship.* And worship had not been a word too strong for the way he had felt about Marmie, nor for the way she had felt about him.

He tried to say a prayer over the caskets in which his family now lay but all he could manage was, "Good-bye. I love you."

But when he reached the door of the chapel, he turned around, looked at the caskets and the dipping candles and whispered, "I'll see you again. I'll do my best. I promise."

Wanda stood in the polished-marble reception area, her hands clasped in front of her, staring out the window at the passing traffic. Randolph touched her arm and she looked up at him to see if he had been crying.

"It's all right," he told her. "I'm fine."

The vice-president of the funeral home came forward and said, "Thank you, Mr. Clare. Monday morning at Forest Hill?"

Randolph nodded dumbly. He found it impossible to describe the way he felt. One part of himself was sure that Marmie and the children were gone forever, but another part of himself was clinging desperately to the belief that Dr. Ambara was right. He was a doctor, wasn't he, an educated man, and if he said that Marmie and the children were still alive in heaven or wherever they were, then they *must* be, surely.

I mean, how could they possibly have vanished without a trace, like the blown-out flames of the chapel candles? Vanished, like blown-away smoke?

Randolph said to Wanda, "Would you have dinner with me tonight? At Clare Castle?"

"Can Herbert take me home to change?" she asked.

"Is that the only condition?"

"You must promise to talk about your family if you feel like it."

Randolph lowered his head. "Yes," he said. "I think I can promise you that."

Herbert opened the limousine door for them and they climbed inside. Wanda said, "There's just one thing. I don't want you to think that I'm taking advantage of you because of what happened to your family. I don't want anything out of this except to know that you're feeling better."

Randolph touched her arm. "I hope you'll accept it as a compliment if I tell you that I knew that already."

"That's a compliment," she agreed.

They had dinner in the sun room because it was more informal than the dining room. The walls were cluttered with watercolors: scenes of European beaches, mountains in New Mexico, girls with fluttering parasols. The oil lamp on the table shed a gentle, diffused light and sparkled on the silver cutlery. Randolph ate sparingly. His stomach seemed to have become permanently knotted since Marmie's death and it was all he could do to chew his way through two small filets of red snapper with a little broccoli. Wanda said that she was on a never-ending diet but he persuaded her to have some of Mrs. Wallace's glacé chestnuts. Mrs. Wallace waited on them kindly and discreetly, although she occasionally joined in their conversation with a remark or two. She had always done this and so Randolph was used to it. She still believed that she was "quality."

After dinner they sat in the large living room, with its polished floors and green-and-white floral drapes, and looked out over the gardens. It was so humid that all the French doors were open and the bushes glowed with fireflies. Randolph put on a record of Brahms' Symphony No. 4 and poured them each a glass of sauvignon from the Cakebread Winery.

"Was this one of Marmie's favorites?" Wanda asked, listening to the music. She had changed into a flowing chiffon dress with wide sleeves and a striking pattern of crimsons, blacks and yellows. Her hair was brushed into wild curls, and for the first time, Randolph saw her as a girl and nothing else. The businesslike secretary had been left behind in the office.

"No," he told her. "Marmie hated Brahms."

"Exorcizing ghosts?" asked Wanda.

Randolph reached across to a side table for his lighter. "No. I don't believe in ghosts. Not in that way."

"What do you believe in?"

"I'm not sure. Some sort of life everlasting, I suppose. But I've never had to think about it except when my parents died, and in those days I guess I was too busy to try and work it out."

"Dr. Linklater said he was concerned that you were too calm."

Randolph lit his pipe. "Just because I'm calm, it doesn't mean I'm not grieving. I've taken his advice and I've tried not to bottle my feelings up." He paused for a moment, studying the flame of his lighter. "I do cry, you know," he said in a level voice.

Wanda said, "I'm sorry. I didn't mean to intrude."

"You're not intruding."

She stood up and walked across to the open window. Moths flitted against the coach lamps on the patio and there was a constant sawing of cicadas. She sipped her wine in silence for a while and then said, "What made you choose Indonesia?"

"Do you really want to know?"

"If you're serious about taking me along, then yes."

Randolph crossed his legs and puffed at his pipe. He looked at Wanda with an expression she had never before seen on his face: strangely introspective and unfocused, as if he were talking to someone inside his mind rather than to her. "They have an interesting view of death in Indonesia," he said. "The Hindus see it as a purely temporary condition and they believe that even after people have died, they are still with us, quite close by."

Wanda looked at Randolph anxiously. "You haven't been reading any crazy books, have you?"

Randolph shook his head. "I've just been talking to someone very knowledgeable and very sincere. Someone who went through the same experience as mine and came out the other side of it with the sure and certain knowledge of life everlasting. Isn't that what they say at funerals?"

"Something like that," Wanda said in a whisper. "But what are you trying to tell me? That Marmie and the children aren't really dead at all? I mean, is that why you're going to Indonesia . . . to try to make some sort of contact with them through some kind of Hindu religious ceremony?"

"Marmie and the children are dead in the sense that they no longer inhabit their physical bodies. But their spirits, their personalities, what they *actually* are . . . that hasn't died. At least that's what the Indonesians believe, and I'd like to believe it too. In fact, I think I do believe it.''

"But how can going to Indonesia help you?" Wanda asked. She came over and sat down next to him. He laid aside his pipe in the heavy onyx ashtray.

"I'm not asking for judgment here, Wanda," he told her gently. "I'm not asking for your opinion on whether I'm screwy or not, or whether spirits really do exist. My wife and my family were suddenly killed and I didn't even have the chance to protect them, or hold their hands, or tell them good-bye. That's why when someone said he believed the dead could still be reached, even after they were cremated . . . well, that's why I was prepared to give him some time.''

He paused and then went on. "It seems to be possible for certain Indonesian religious adepts to get in touch with spirits, to talk to them, to actually see them sometimes. That's why I'm going to Indonesia, to try to find one of these adepts and see if he can't pull off the same trick for me.''

Wanda whispered, "Randolph . . . Randolph, believe me, it can't possibly work.''

"Who says it can't possibly work? You? The Pope? Cardinal Baum? The Smithsonian Institution? The man I've been talking to says different. Maybe it doesn't work. Maybe it *does* work but needs a greater act of faith than I could ever give it. I'm prepared to come back home with nothing more than a suntan and a three-thousand-dollar bill from the Djakarta Hilton, but at least I won't spend the rest of my life wondering if it might have been possible, even for a second, to talk to Marmie again, and to the children, and to tell them how much I love them.''

Wanda touched his shoulder, a gesture more guarded than she would have made to a man who was not her employer. There were no tears in Randolph's eyes but his throat was strung tight with emotion and she could tell that he was suffering, although she could only half-guess just how much. To Randolph, the pain was worse than knives, worse than fire, worse than anything he could ever have imagined.

"And you really want me to come with you?" Wanda asked.

He shrugged. "If you can put up with me. I'm not forcing you to come, not by any means."

They listened to more music and talked very little. At ten o'clock Charles came around and closed the French doors because the insects were flying in. Wanda checked her watch and said, "I must go."

"I'm sorry I wasn't particularly inspiring company," Randolph apologized.

She took his hand. "No, you were very interesting, believe me. I always thought you were so practical, so pragmatic. It's fascinating to see you taking a chance on something extraordinary."

"Well, maybe I'm cracking up," he said wryly, guiding her through to the front door where Charles was waiting with her wrap.

"You won't know until you try it," Wanda said. She reached up and kissed his cheek. She was soft and warm and smelled of Chanel Cristalle. He recognized it because Marmie had always liked it but had never been able to wear it. He was suddenly grateful that Wanda had come and spent the evening with him, particularly since his fretting about Marmie and the children had torn away at the evening's conversation like the teeth of a nutmeg grater.

In the library, the telephone rang. Randolph said, "That may be Neil. I'd better answer it."

Wanda said, "I'll see you tomorrow. Are you coming in to the office?"

"For a while probably. Good night."

Wanda gave him a small wave that was unexpectedly shy. Then she went quickly down the steps to the driveway, where Herbert was waiting for her with the limousine.

Randolph went through to the library and picked up the phone. It was Neil and he sounded tired. "They've had another complication out at Raleigh. It seems like they can't get hold of the right valves. Anyway, I'm going to see what I can do in the morning. We may be able to fly them in from Germany."

"Any news from Orbus Greene?" Randolph asked.

"A kind of a holding message from one of his assistants. Apparently the Association is talking to its lawyers, in case the deal you suggested has any legal ramifications. But the general view seems to be that they could very well be interested."

"They don't have too damned long," Randolph said. "If we can't make up our shortfall by the middle of the week, Sun-Taste is going to start pushing us real hard."

"I don't see that we have any alternative but to wait for them," said Neil. "After all, where else are we going to get cottonseed oil?"

"I'll get it from Egypt if I have to. I might even talk to Don Prescott at Gamble's."

"I'm afraid you'll be lucky if Don Prescott agrees to even speak to you, Mr. Clare. He was almost as sore over the cattlecake contract as the Cottonseed Association was over Sun-Taste."

Randolph wearily rubbed his cheek. "The high cost of independence, huh? Very well. Thanks for calling, but keep on top of Orbus Greene, won't you? I don't want him stringing us along until the Sun-Taste contract goes into default."

"No, sir. You bet, sir."

Randolph was still sitting in the library when Charles came in with a whiskey for him.

"Everything all right, Mr. Clare?"

"Yes, Charles, everything's fine."

"Have you decided when you're going to Indonesia, Mr. Clare?"

"Directly after the funeral Tuesday afternoon. That's if Dr. Ambara can get away. I shall be calling him tomorrow to find out if he's managed to arrange his schedule."

"All right, sir. I'll start to pack just as soon as I know for sure."

Randolph sipped his whiskey, then looked up at Charles and said, "Give me your honest opinion about something."

"If I can, sir."

"Tell me, do you think I'm going crazy? Do I act like I'm going crazy?"

Charles smiled and shook his head. "No more crazy than anybody would expect, Mr. Clare, given what you had and given what you lost."

Randolph thought about that and nodded. "I guess craziness is relative, like everything else."

"That's for sure, Mr. Clare. Even life and death, they're relative too."

Randolph looked at Charles acutely and wondered if the valet knew more about his plans than he was letting on. Maybe Charles had already guessed that on Tuesday afternoon he was going to bury his dead and then go in search of their immortal souls. *For an hour is coming in which all who are in the tombs shall hear His voice, and shall come forth.*

TWELVE

The funeral was held in ninety-degree heat under a heavy, clouded sky. The bodies were laid to rest in the Clare family plot at Forest Hill Cemetery next to the white-marble angels who for four years had kept sad and sightless watch over the graves of Randolph's father and mother.

Randolph stayed close to Ella, the only Clare daughter who now remained single. Ella worked for Century Realty and was always smart, brisk and very well organized. She had arrived in Memphis the day after the caskets arrived, having closed up the cabin on Lac aux Ecorces and made sure that it was properly protected against casual vandals and ghoulish sightseers. One of the popular scandal sheets had offered her twenty thousand dollars for permission to photograph the inside of the cabin, complete with models to simulate the bodies of Randolph's slaughtered family.

Ella had spent the weekend completing the funeral arrangements but today she devoted her energy to taking care of Randolph. He was more grateful than he could have explained. He had expected the funeral to be melancholy. He had not realized how agonizingly final it would be—for all that he was trying to believe that their spirits were still alive—to watch the shining black caskets containing his family as they were lowered into the earth. He cast a handful of soil on each of them, tears running freely down his cheeks. Then Ella helped him away, her gloved hand tightly holding his.

The funeral guests left Clare Castle at two o'clock: cars scrunching away across the gravel one after the other; black-veiled sisters and black-suited brothers kissing and shaking hands and promising not to make it so long until they met again; all of them stunned by the violence of what had happened and uncomfortably conscious of their own mortality.

Randolph's suitcases were packed and standing in the hallway. He was flying from Memphis to Los Angeles and from there on to Djakarta, stopping at Honolulu and Manila. Dr. Ambara had arranged to meet him at the airport, and Randolph had arranged to collect Wanda along the way.

Ella came out into the garden where Randolph was having a last whiskey and looking out over the flower beds. The heavy clouds were beginning to break a little toward the west and the evening promised to be fine.

Ella said, "You're sure you're doing the right thing, flying off like this?"

"I don't know," he told her, and he really didn't.

She took his hand. "You know that you have people who love you, people who want to look after you."

"Yes, and I appreciate it. I don't know what I would have done today without you."

"You've done enough for me in the past. Besides, we all loved your family. We loved Marmie and we loved the children. Nothing can ever replace them."

Randolph nodded. A bee swung past, heading toward the hibiscus. Somewhere off to the south, thunder rumbled like God's anger.

Charles came out into the garden accompanied by Mrs. Wallace. "I believe it's time that you left now, Mr. Clare. Your airplane leaves at three-thirty."

Mrs. Wallace was weeping unashamedly. Every now and then she took out her balled-up handkerchief and loudly blew her nose. "You will take care of yourself, Mr. Clare?"

"Don't worry," Randolph smiled, touching her shoulder. "I won't do anything rash."

Herbert brought the limousine around to the door and

Randolph kissed Ella good-bye. Then he was driven off to collect Wanda and he did not look back at the house nor did he look out the windows at the streets of Memphis passing by. His attention now was focused exclusively on the future, on finding his family again. This was a time for hope and faith, not for reminiscences and grief.

Wanda was ready for him, waiting outside her apartment building on Kyle Street. She wore a crisp white-linen suit and a white straw skimmer. Herbert stored her bags in the limousine's trunk and then they drove off toward the airport.

"You look as if you're going on safari," Randolph smiled.

"On this trip, I think I'd better be prepared for almost anything," she told him, smiling.

Dr. Ambara was waiting for them by the American Airlines counter. He was wearing a disheveled seersucker sports coat in pastel plaid and carrying two cameras, a carry-on suit bag and a huge, untidy folder crammed with magazines and newspapers. Randolph introduced him to Wanda and they checked their baggage and walked through to the departure gate.

Herbert said, "This time I'll make sure that I'm waiting for you when you get back."

Randolph lifted a hand in acknowledgment. "Look after yourself, Herbert."

Dr. Ambara said in a matter-of-fact way, "I was speaking this morning to an old friend of mine who works in the Indonesian economic department. I called him two days ago but he did not reply until today. He said that if we are truly serious about locating a death-trance adept and if we have enough money to pay the necessary bribes, it would be worth our while to meet a man in Djakarta called I.M. Wartawa. Apparently I.M. Wartawa is the man who arranged for the death trance in which they were searching for the will of Howard Hughes, and also for a death trance to talk to Jimmy Hoffa."

Randolph tried not to look skeptical but he glanced at Wanda, who in turn glanced away. Dr. Ambara said, "Miss Wanda here . . . you have told her the purpose of this expedition, I presume?"

"Yes," Wanda interjected. "She's not sure that she approves. She's not sure that she understands. But she's willing to come along to give moral support and any emotional Curads that might be required."

Dr. Ambara seemed to find Wanda's presence discomfiting. However, he nodded acceptance of her words and inclined his head courteously to the airport security guard as she took his suit bag and laid it out flat on the endless belt that would take it through the X-ray machine. Randolph found the hint of anatagonism between Wanda and Dr. Ambara somewhat amusing. He had always found that his staff worked better when its members were in competition with each other, and he had no doubt but that Wanda and Dr. Ambara would outdo themselves to look after him. Without being patronizing and without being weak, he had accepted that he needed looking after, at least for a while.

During the flight to Los Angeles, Wanda gradually began to break down Dr. Ambara's reserve until she was talking to him about his career in America, about his beliefs in reincarnation and, most sensitive of all, about his dead wife and his hope of seeing her again.

"I still don't understand why the Indonesian government is so down on death trances," she said. "Surely they could make a fortune in foreign currency if they allowed adepts to offer their services freely. I mean, if it really works, who wouldn't want to talk to his dead mother and father, even to his grandparents?"

Dr. Ambara stirred his vodka and tonic with a plastic airlines swizzle stick. "It is dangerous, that is why the government forbids it. Many adepts have been killed in the death trance, even though they were experienced priests. Perhaps other people have been killed as well but the government does what it can to keep the statistics quiet. They won't even officially admit that there *is* such a thing as a death trance."

Wanda said gently, "Your wife, if you were to see her again . . . what would you say to her?"

Dr. Ambara looked thoughtful. Then he said, "I would

tell her that I loved her and that I will always love her. And then I would ask her to forgive me.''

"You didn't kill her. Why should you ask her to forgive you?''

"No, but I am still alive and she is dead, and I have always felt that it is the responsibility of every human being to do everything he can to protect his loved ones. I know that what happened was an accident. There was nothing I could have done to save her. And yet I still feel responsible. I still feel that it was my fault. If I can hear her say that she forgives me, perhaps I will be able to continue my life without the burden of guilt I have been carrying.''

Wanda put her hand on Dr. Ambara's wrist. They were approaching Los Angeles now and the seat-belt warning had chimed. Below, in the sunny haze of mid-afternoon, traffic sparkled along the freeways, and turquoise swimming pools dotted the suburbs like unstrung necklaces. Wanda said, ''If you do ever get to see her, do you know what I think she will say? I think she will tell you that she always loved you and that she never blamed you for one single minute.''

Dr. Ambara stared at her and then mumbled, ''I hope so, Miss Wanda. I hope your intuition is proven to be right. In fact, I pray so.''

The flight from Los Angeles to Djakarta was delayed for two hours. They sat in the airport lounge drinking cocktails and talking desultorily. There was little need for them to talk. This journey was beyond their experience, beyond the experience of human life itself. There was nothing they could say about it until they had lived through it. Passengers jostled and pushed their way around them, en route to London, Chicago, New York, St. Louis, keeping their appointments with the living. Only Randolph and Wanda and Dr. Ambara knew that they, by contrast, were keeping an appointment with the dead.

At last they were called to the gate. Standing behind them in the line to board were four tall, hard-faced men. One of them, who looked to be the leader of the group, impressed Randolph by his withdrawn silence, stonily maintained even when the other three were talking. His head looked as if it had been sculptured in granite: angular, uncompromising and scarred. One ear had been crumpled, either by fire or by a punishing beating, and there was a white mark running upward from his left jaw into his close-cropped hairline. His eyes were as gray and cold as the ocean on a cloudy day. He chewed gum incessantly and seemed disinterested in what went on around him. More than disinterested, contemptuous.

"Veterans, I should think," Dr. Ambara remarked as the men walked past. "Probably traveling to Vietnam to commemorate the fall of Saigon. It is interesting to compare their pilgrimage with ours. It seems as if human beings have a burning urge to revisit the past, to try to understand its meaning. We are hopeless revisionists, I suppose. We forget that the future is unfolding with every minute that goes by and that in time we shall want to correct what we are doing today."

They flew out from Los Angeles into the grainy orange of a Pacific sunset. They would stop over at Honolulu, then at Manila, where they would change to the Indonesian airline, Merpati, for the last leg to Djakarta. Randolph did his best to sleep although every time he did, he had vivid dreams of Marmie's casket as it was lowered into the ground. Once he woke up to find Wanda holding his hand tightly and saying, "Sssh, sssh, it's all right. It's all over."

"Was I talking in my sleep?" he asked. He touched his eyes and discovered they were wet with tears.

"You were calling out, that's all. Don't worry about it. You can't keep it bottled up inside you all the time."

He wiped his eyes. "I'm sorry. Maybe I should take some sleeping pills."

"It's all right," Wanda reassured him. "Don't worry."

The flight attendant came up and asked him if he wanted a drink. "A large whiskey," he told her. Wanda signaled her disapproval with her eyes but Randolph said, "I buried my family today. I think I qualify for a drink."

Randolph and Wanda and Dr. Ambara were flying first class. It was only when Randolph went to the rest room that he saw the four men who had been standing behind them in

the line at the Los Angeles airport. They were sitting in
business class, smoking cigarettes and playing cards. As
Randolph waited for a vacant toilet, the man with the
scarred face uncoiled himself from his seat and came up to
stand close beside him. The man wore army fatigues with a
khaki canvas belt and a badge from the First Airborne Cavalry with the name tag "Ecker."

Randolph nodded an acknowledgment to him but the man
remained impassive, unsmiling, unmoving, although he kept
his eyes steadily fixed on Randolph. Randolph turned away
but every time he glanced back, the man was still staring at
him. After a while, irritated by this constant attention, Randolph said, "Was there something you wanted? I mean, can
I help you with something?"

The man smiled to himself and turned away without
answering. Randolph concluded that he was probably shell-
shocked, one of those Vietnam veterans who had brought
back his body but not his mind. When Randolph had spoken, the other three men had raised their heads from the
card game and stared at him with equal coldness, but Randolph ignored them. It was no good reading anything into
their apparent hostility. If Randolph had served in Vietnam,
he would probably have finished up just as gratuitously
hostile as they.

After he had used the rest room and combed his hair, he
returned to his seat. Wanda was asleep, a blanket drawn up
to her neck. Dr. Ambara was reading *Cardiology Today* and
studiously ignoring the in-flight movie, which starred Elliott
Gould and Joanne Woodward, one of those movies that
seemed to have been specially made for showing on long-
distance flights. Randolph finished his whiskey and stared at
his reflection in the darkened window. The film flickered
silently: Elliott Gould running, Elliott Gould standing still, a
car driving through a cold street.

Randolph plugged in his earphones and as he was changing channels, he was sure that he caught a woman's voice
saying,"—*dolph, please, Ran*—" He flicked the control
back through seven, eight and nine but the voice was gone.
There was folk music now, and canned laughter, both of

them half-drowned by the endless roaring of the plane's engines.

The flight attendant came up, smiled and said, "Would you care for another cocktail, Mr. Clare?"

Randolph shook his head. "No, thanks, no. I think I'll try to get some sleep."

He reclined his seat and tried to relax, but the steady thundering of the 747's progress across the Pacific kept him awake, apart from the fact that he was afraid of the nightmarish visions that sleep might bring: Marmie and the children running away from him, always running away, through cities and corridors and winding mazes; glimpsed but never caught. And then the sudden strangulation of barbed wire twisted tightly around the neck. Eyes distended, tongue protruding, lacerated fingers clawing at the barbs in a hopeless struggle to breathe. He had seen the fingernail scratches on Marmie's neck in the photographs Inspector Dulac had shown him. Her own fingernail scratches, inflicted as she had helplessly torn at the wire.

He lowered his head to his chest. He could not imagine the pain that Marmie must have suffered. He could only hope that those who died in pain were beatified, that their agony bought them eternal peace. Where and how, he was not sure. By believing in Dr. Ambara and by flying to Indonesia, he had denied his own religion, such as it was, and Marmie's religion too. He hoped that Dr. Ambara's heaven was the same as Marmie's heaven and that Dr. Ambara's god was the same God in whom Marmie had always believed.

They stayed for four hours in Honolulu and ate breakfast as Wednesday morning gradually lightened the eastern horizon. The flight for Manila left at seven-fifteen and they walked to their plane under a sky that was pale and high and streaked with cirrus clouds. Randolph saw the man called Ecker shuffling down the aisle toward his seat, and for a second their eyes made curious and antagonistic contact. As soon as he had settled in his own seat, Randolph beckoned the flight director over and said, "I hope this isn't the kind of question a fellow passenger shouldn't ask, but do you have any idea of who those four men in combat fatigues might be?''

The flight director smiled and shook his head. "I'm sorry, Mr. Clare. I really don't.''

On a sudden impulse, Randolph reached clumsily into his wallet and dislodged a hundred-dollar bill. He folded it and offered it to the man between two stiffened fingers. "Do you think that *now* you might be able to remember?''

The flight director stared at the bill impassively. "I'm sorry, Mr. Clare, they're nothing more than names on the passenger roster. I haven't had any special advisories on them. You know, sometimes—between you and me—I do if there's a recently bailed felon on board, or a woman of particular wealth, or even somebody quite innocent who didn't do anything more than attract the attention of the security guards back at the airport. Some people act very strange when they fly. It's mostly fear.''

Randolph tucked away the bill. "Okay," he said. "At least you're honest. On another airline, they might have taken the money and spun me ten minutes of hooey. But . . . let me put it this way . . . if you *do* happen to catch anything that gives you a clue as to who they are and what they're doing here . . . well, it's a long way to Manila and I don't have any place to spend this hundred dollars except on this plane. I might as well try to get my money's worth.''

He felt more than a little embarrassed, particularly since the flight director had rebuffed him so politely, but Wanda seemed to be impressed. "I never thought I'd ever catch you trying to *bribe* somebody," she smiled. Then she turned around to see if she could catch a glimpse of the four men in fatigues. "And anyway, why did you ask him who those men are?''

"I don't know. It's the way they've been looking at me, I guess. I have this peculiar feeling that they've been following us.''

Dr. Ambara looked up from his magazine. "The East always seems more mysterious than the West. You are beginning to see conspiracies where none exist. Those men are not following you. They simply happen to be traveling to Manila on the same flight."

However, the next time Randolph went to the rest room, the flight director lifted a finger and beckoned to him as he passed the galley. Randolph stepped into the niche and the flight director drew the curtain behind him. One of the stewardesses was perched on a fold-down seat and eating a belated breakfast but she ignored them. The flight director fixed his attention on Randolph's right shoulder and said between almost immobile lips, "From Manila, they are flying on to Djakarta."

"That's what I'm doing. Are they traveling by Merpati?"

"They don't have any choice. That's the only airline available."

"Do you know when they booked their flight?"

The flight director picked up his clipboard and checked through the passenger roster. "Monday morning. The seats were booked through from Memphis."

Randolph resisted the temptation to peer over the top of the clipboard. "Does it say who booked the tickets?" he asked.

"I shouldn't tell you that," the flight director said flatly. He kept his eyes on Randolph's shoulder.

"What if I double the previous arrangement?" Randolph suggested.

The flight director thought for a moment and then turned his clipboard around so that Randolph could read it. There were four names, each booked at the same time. *Ecker*, Richard. *Heacox*, James T. *Louv*, Frank. *Stroup*, Robert Patrick. Their seats had been booked through MidAmerica Travel of Monroe Street, Memphis, and the billing address was the Brooks Cottonseed Corporation.

Without a word Randolph handed the flight director two hundred-dollar bills, noting that the man accepted them with that extraordinary sleight-of-hand at which many who serve the public become skilled.

"They haven't been talking very much," the flight director added, turning his clipboard around again. "The one called Ecker doesn't speak at all. Mute possibly, or deaf-mute. His friends order his drinks and his meals for him. They're not on vacation though, I can tell you that much. They're working, and they're traveling on expenses. I heard one of them complaining that they would have to stay at the Hotel Keborayan in Djakarta. He said the Hotel Keborayan stunk and that they never would have stayed there if he'd had anything to do with it.''

Randolph nodded and then passed the flight director another hundred. The flight director said with undisguised surprise, ''Do they mean *that* much to you?''

Randolph said, ''I'm not sure. It's possible. But let's just say that I like to know who I'm flying with.''

''Well, any time,'' said the flight director. ''How about a drink?''

When Randolph returned to his seat, Wanda was listening to music. He signaled that she should remove her earphones and then he leaned over and said, ''Those four men . . . I think I was right. Their tickets were booked by Brooks Cottonseed.''

''You mean that they've been sent to follow us to Indonesia?''

''It seems like it. Maybe Orbus Greene thinks I've discovered a new source of cottonseed oil and wants to keep tabs on it. Maybe he just wants to know what I'm doing. I always did make him nervous.''

Dr. Ambara, who had overheard this, said with a frown, ''You would have thought that if they were doing nothing more than keeping an eye on us, they would have sent somebody less conspicuous. They look more like mercenary soldiers than private detectives.''

''Perhaps that's the whole point. Perhaps Orbus *wanted* us to find out who they are. Perhaps he was deliberately trying to intimidate us.''

''Are you intimidated?'' Wanda asked.

''Of course not,'' Randolph told her.

''Well, then,'' put in Dr. Ambara, ''if it really was his intention to intimidate you, he has failed. Is it conceivable that he had something else in mind? Something more positive? After all, it could not have been inexpensive to send four men executive-class to Djakarta. It is not the sort of excursion anyone would pay for unless he was expecting to reap some tangible benefits from it."

"I'm not sure of what you're getting at," Randolph said.

"Neither am I," Dr. Ambara replied. "But—since we are obviously being kept under close surveillance—I suggest that we conduct ourselves with extreme caution."

Randolph had been thinking the same thought ever since he had first seen Richard Ecker staring at him so intently. What had Jimmy the Rib told him? "There's four or five of them, not always the same guys. The only name I heard is Reece, and he's supposed to be some spaced-out veteran from Cambodia or someplace like that, a frightening man from what I hear tell."

Was it possible that the man calling himself Ecker was really the man whom Jimmy the Rib had called Reece? There were distinct similarities. Reece was supposed to be a veteran and Ecker certainly dressed like one. Reece was supposed to be employed by the Cottonseed Association and Ecker's tickets had been bought through Brooks. Yet Randolph was reluctant to make the final assumption that would have made his guesswork complete. Reluctant because it was too neat. And reluctant because the implications of it were too frightening to think about. He felt almost paranoid, as if he were beginning to suffer delusions that he was at the center of a dark and complicated conspiracy. But it seemed to be too much of a coincidence that Ecker-Reece was flying on the same plane on the way to Djakarta with three henchmen in combat fatigues.

Jimmy the Rib had actually suggested that Reece might have been responsible for killing Marmie and the children. The thought that the same man was sitting here now, within thirty feet of him, made Randolph feel tight and cold all over, as if he had been suddenly plunged into icy water. But it made terrible sense of Ecker's presence here if Ecker were really Reece. Ecker-Reece had slaughtered the wife and the children. Now he was after the father.

There was no proof of course. Ecker might have been doing nothing more sinister than flying to Djakarta on one of Orbus's overseas engineering programs. He might have caught the same plane as a matter of coincidence. But Ecker had been booked on this flight *after* Randolph had made his travel arrangements, and there was no doubt in Randolph's mind that he and his men were showing more than a passing interest in him.

Randolph scribbled a note on one of the back pages of his diary, tore it out and passed it over to Dr. Ambara, who read: "I believe these men may have been sent to kill us. I have no cast-iron evidence but it will probably be safer if we can manage to shake them off our tail. Perhaps we can manage it when we reach Manila?"

Dr. Ambara studied the note carefully, then passed it back. Wanda read it, too, and looked at Randolph with alarm.

"I can't understand why anybody at the Cottonseed Association should want to get rid of you so badly," she hissed. "Surely you couldn't have upset Orbus Greene that much, that he should want to kill you?"

"I don't know," Randolph replied soberly, tearing the note into confetti and cramming it into the ashtray beside him. "I don't understand it either. Maybe we've been hurting them more than we've realized. After all, Brooks lost six percent of the market share last quarter while we gained eight and a half percent."

"But to kill you—to kill your family—that's just insane!"

"I agree with you. But ever since that fire out at Raleigh, people have been telling me that Orbus Greene and Waverley Graceworthy and all the rest of the good old boys have been determined to finish me off. I never thought they could be capable of murder . . . but, well, maybe I've been too naive. Maybe I've failed to realize what a dog-eat-dog world it is out there."

Wanda touched his arm. "I'm frightened," she said.

Randolph took her hand. "Don't you worry. We know a lot more about what's going on than the Cottonseed Association seems to think we do. If they had known what Jimmy the Rib told me . . . well, they wouldn't have sent Ecker or Reece or whatever his name is to follow us."

"Randolph," Wanda said, "you ought to tell the police."

"Tell the police what? That the highly respected chairman of the Memphis Cottonseed Association has sent a team of veteran killers to rub me out all over a couple of cottonseed-processing contracts?"

"You're friends with Chief Moyne. Perhaps you could call him."

"Maybe. But I'm going to need something a little more substantial before I start bothering Chief Moyne."

"He's a friend of yours."

"He's also a friend of Orbus Greene's."

For the remainder of the flight to Manila, they said little. But they kept their eyes on the man called Ecker and his companions, and there was no doubt that whenever Ecker passed Randolph in the aisle or at the galley, he stared at him as coldly as a striking snake. In a strange way, Randolph found it fascinating that this man might have been paid to kill him, fascinating and frightening. But Dr. Ambara had assured him that once they reached Manila, they would be able to lose their entourage for sure. They would have to rearrange their flight schedule to Djakarta, but that would present no difficulties. Oddly, Dr. Ambara seemed to find the idea of being pursued from Memphis to Djakarta quite unsurprising. Perhaps it was his philosophical Oriental mind. But Randolph found it unreal, and his sense of unreality was heightened by the twelve-hour time difference between Manila and Memphis as well as by the change in climate and culture.

They landed in Manila early in the afternoon, right after a rainstorm. The humidity was even more oppressive than it was in Memphis and Randolph was soaked in sweat by the time he claimed their baggage for the flight to Djakarta. Wanda was feeling jet-lagged and groggy, mainly because she had been dozing for the last two hours of the flight. Dr. Ambara, however, now that he was nearing his native Indonesia, was almost ebullient and kept telling wry jokes. Randolph did not understand any of them but was polite enough to grunt and smile.

They asked the porter to take them across to the Air

Merpati desk. Randolph, glancing around, saw Ecker and his three associates still waiting for their baggage by the carousel. Ecker was wiping the back of his neck with a handkerchief but he kept his eyes fixed on Randolph, who had no doubt by this time that the man was Reece and that he had been sent by the Cottonseed Association to either keep a close watch on him or to make sure that he never returned from Indonesia alive.

Dr. Ambara said to the Indonesian girl behind the Air Merpati desk, "Hold these bags for now. We have business here in Manila. We may not get back to the airport in time to make today's flight. But make sure nobody knows that we haven't checked in. If anybody asks about Mr. Clare and his party, say they will certainly be leaving for Djakarta this afternoon. Do you understand that? It is a business matter, very confidential."

"Yes, sir," the girl assured him. "We thank you for choosing Air Merpati."

Randolph went to the Pan Am courtesy lounge and while Wanda and Dr. Ambara sat at the bar and drank cocktails, he called Neil Sleaman in Memphis.

"Neil? This is Randolph Clare. I'm calling from Manila. No, the flight for Djakarta doesn't leave for two hours yet. Listen, Neil, can you hear me? Good, because it seems like we have a difficulty here. There are four guys traveling on the same flight with us, all of them dressed in combat gear, very hard-looking characters indeed. Their names are Ecker, Heacox, Stroup and . . . I forget the fourth one. But the point is that their tickets were booked by Brooks and they almost exactly fit the descriptions Jimmy the Rib gave me. They've been keeping a close watch on us, too close. Well, of course I'm concerned. If there was only half a grain of truth in what Jimmy the Rib had to say, they could be the men who killed Marmie and the children, which would mean that Orbus Greene and Waverley Graceworthy are prepared to do just about anything to put me out of business, including homicide."

Neil said, "Perhaps I should talk to Chief Moyne. He could do some investigating. You know, check to see if any known criminals have left the city in the past twenty-four hours.''

"I think you ought to leave Chief Moyne out of this for the moment. All I want you to do is make sure that security at the plants is double-tight, and keep pushing Orbus Greene for an answer on Sun-Taste. He makes optimistic noises but I have a strong feeling he's going to say no. Maybe he's stringing us along until his hired maniacs can dispose of me altogether. Maybe I'm misjudging him badly and he doesn't mean to do me any harm at all. But keep an open mind. And, please, do whatever you can to get Raleigh back into production as soon as possible.''

Neil said calmly, "Okay. Everything's under control. We should be back up to seventy-five-percent production by the end of the week.''

"Well, try for more," Randolph urged.

"I'll do my best, sir. Have a good flight.''

"I'll call you from Djakarta, although we may be leaving here tomorrow instead of today. I'd very much like to get those four hired gorillas off our backs.''

Neil said disparagingly, "I shouldn't think they're anything but wartime veterans, sir, making a pilgrimage. It's the tenth anniversary of the fall of Saigon, remember.''

Randolph hung up the phone and went out to join Wanda and Dr. Ambara at the bar. "What's the plan?" he asked Dr. Ambara.

"Well," the doctor said, "I personally believe it would be wiser to wait here in Manila for one night. There is another Air Merpati flight tomorrow, straight to Djakarta. If these men really are pursuing us, as you say, they will be obliged to return to Djakarta airport tomorrow and wait for us and by doing so, they will show their hand.''

They took a taxi out into the clamorous streets. The sky was dark red, like freshly spilled blood, and the high-rise buildings of Manila stood black and skeletal on either side. There was a strong smell of tropical mustiness, exhaust fumes, charcoal-broiled pork and sewage. Taxis hooted, bicycle bells jangled and lights streamed along the city streets. The taxi driver leaned back on his worn-out vinyl seat and asked, "Hotel Pasay?"

"That's right," said Dr. Ambara firmly.

"Hotel Pasay is not for American," the taxi driver remarked.

"Just go there," Dr. Ambara insisted.

"Maybe you make a mistake. Maybe you want to go to Manila Hilton. Also Hotel Bakati is first class."

"Either you take us to the Hotel Pasay or I call a policeman," Dr. Ambara told him.

"All right, buddy," the taxi driver told him in an odd Filipino-American accent. "Your funeral."

The center of Manila, as they drove through, was noisy and crowded and jammed with traffic. Although, after Dresden, Manila had been the second-most-devastated city of the Second World War, it had not been rebuilt on utopian lines. Instead, it had become an architectural portrait of the desperate social divisions between its rich inhabitants and its poor. Behind the guarded walls of Forbes Park and Makati stood some of the most opulent mansions in the East. Around the walls, within sight of the mansions' balconies, clustered derelict tenements, squatters' shacks and some of the most squalid slums Randolph had ever seen. Even in its worst days, Beale Street had been nothing like this. And over the whole city, reflecting the scarlet neon and the glaring street lights and the dangling lanterns, hung the haze of air pollution—the exhaust fumes of thousands of taxis, buses, Datsuns and worn-out Chevrolets—mingling with the foggy pall that rose from the South China Sea.

They drove past rows of modern stores advertising Sony televisions, hot dogs, "authentic" souvenirs. Then they were jouncing into a run-down suburb with stalls lining the streets, and peeling buildings, and lanterns hanging on every corner. Eventually they reached a narrow-fronted building painted in vivid pink and with a hand-painted sign reading "Hotel Pasay, All Welcome, Icey Drinks."

They climbed out of the taxi and Dr. Ambara paid the driver. Randolph looked up at the hotel dubiously. Wanda discreetly made a face. The night was hot and smelly and they were tired. Three small children were teasing a mangy dog on the hotel steps. A blind man with eyes as white as ping-pong balls was sitting on a nearby wall whistling monotonously. Two sexy little Filipino girls in red-satin miniskirts and ruffled white blouses were bouncing up and down on the saddle of a parked motorcycle.

"Nice neighborhood," Wanda remarked. "Did I hear that it was on the way up?"

Dr. Ambara took her arm. "You will be safe here, that is the important thing. This is not a rich neighborhood but the people here are friends. Come up and meet one of my cousins."

"You really think we're safe here?" Randolph asked.

"For now," replied Dr. Ambara.

THIRTEEN

Manila

Dr. Ambara's "cousin" turned out to be a handsome, motherly Javanese woman who had fled from Djakarta when General Suharto came to power. Her husband had been arrested and shot for his pro-Soekarno politics. Apparently Dr. Ambara's father had helped her escape to Manila and had lent her enough money to buy the Hotel Pasay, where she catered to whores, schoolteachers and a motley assembly of Indonesian refugees.

Dr. Ambara called her Flora, which of course was not her real name, but most of those Javanese who had escaped from Djakarta in 1966 had forgotten their real names and left their old identities behind. Flora wore a bright scarlet sari and a yellow-silk head scarf, and her neck was decorated with twenty or thirty necklaces of shells and beads and Balinese silver. She led them into her own parlor at the back of the hotel; there was a low table, cushions were spread over the floor and a portable television constantly played. A red scarf draped over the light bulb gave the room an unhallowed dimness, and when he first entered, Randolph failed to see the two small children sitting in the far corner watching television, and the girl in the cheap satin teddy who was painting her toenails with long-drawn-out concentration.

"You look very well," Flora told Dr. Ambara. "How is life in the United States?"

"Sometimes I miss Djakarta," Dr. Ambara replied. He knew that he spoke for both of them.

"Well," said Flora, "if you have come all this way to see me, I must feed you. Ana, bring the whiskey."

"I think I'd prefer a beer, if it's all the same to you," put in Randolph.

"You have Anker Bier?" asked Dr. Ambara.

Flora nodded. Dr. Ambara said, "Three Anker Biers then." He touched Randolph's arm and explained, "Brewed in Djakarta."

The girl in the teddy screwed the cap back on her nail-polish bottle and clomped through to the kitchen on her heels so she would not smudge her toenail polish. She came back with three bottles of beer and three glasses and uncapped the bottles with disinterested dexterity, as quick as an oyster shucker. She stared at Randolph unblinkingly as she poured out his beer. She was flat-faced, remorselessly pretty, with pearly white teeth and a diamond stud in the left side of her nose. Her nipples peaked up under the satin in tiny cones. She could have been any age from fourteen to twenty-four. She was probably closer to fourteen.

Flora settled herself on a cushion and they sat around her. "It is many years now since I have seen this man," she said, "but he is always welcome here. His family saved my life."

"Those were bad times in Indonesia," Dr. Ambara commented. "Over one million people died when Suharto took power. Flora's poor husband was one of those who died for his political opinions. He was a considerable scholar, especially in Chinese matters."

A bald man in round glasses and a KLM T-shirt entered apologetically, bent forward and whispered into Flora's ear. Flora nodded, and nodded again, and then said, "*Ya, saya bisa tunggu. Tidak mengapa.*"

"One of my guests from Djakarta," she explained when he had gone. "He has lived with me now for twenty years, ever since I came here. He teaches mathematics at the local school and he asks every month if he could be late with his rent money. Of course I always say yes. To live here without harassment is a debt I owe to the people of my country, not them to me.''

They sat and talked and drank beer for nearly an hour. Then Ana came in with a huge bamboo tray crowded with porcelain bowls of fish soup, *adobong sugpo*—tiger prawns fried in butter with garlic and black pepper—and beef *tapa*. There were more chilled bottles of Anker Bier, and pots of jasmine tea.

Randolph had not realized how hungry he was. For the first time since he had heard that Marmie had died, he ate with an unrestrained appetite. Wanda had difficulty with her chopsticks but eventually Ana, smiling, brought her a porcelain spoon.

''I don't think I'm ever going to get the hang of those things,'' Wanda complained. ''It's like trying to write a letter with your pen between your toes.''

Later Randolph lit his pipe and sat back against the parlor wall as Wanda went upstairs to take a shower and Dr. Ambara chatted with Flora. He closed his eyes for a while but he did not sleep. He could hear the television chattering in Filipino, and the stairs creaking as guests climbed up and down, and the distant honking of traffic.

When he opened his eyes, Flora said to him with considerable interest, ''Ambara has been telling me why you have come here. It is not the usual reason for Americans to visit Indonesia. Usually they come for the beaches, and for the folk art.''

Randolph sat up straight. ''I suppose it is unusual for an American to believe that the spirits of his loved ones can still be contacted after their death.''

''Ambara has told you of the dangers?''

''I think he has made them pretty clear.''

Flora raised one finger to indicate that he should take serious note of what she was saying. ''You are not dealing with ghosts, my dear sir, or with mischievous demons. I hope Ambara has told you that. You are trespassing into the territory of the Goddess Rangda herself, the great terrible one, and into the country of the leyaks.''

Randolph said, "Do you know anyone who has actually been into a death trance?"

"Fatmawati, the wife of Soekarno, she attempted it once. I do not know if she was successful. But it has always been against the law in Indonesia. They say it is prohibited because it would encourage foreign tourists to abuse the sacred ceremonies of the Trisakti, but the real truth is that they are afraid of the leyaks."

"In what way? Surely the leyaks can harm you only if you put yourself into a trance."

Flora shook her head and her shell beads clattered. "This is not true. Did not Ambara tell you that the gateway to the region of Yama is two-way, both entrance and exit, and that there is always a risk that when you leave the world of the dead and return from your trance, you will be followed by leyaks, who can use your gateway to gain admission to the real world. That is why the government prohibits the death trance. It is not the life of the adept that concerns them. If an adept is foolish enough to take the chance of being devoured by the Goddess Rangda, that is his own concern. But the authorities are terrified that leyaks might escape into the community, for every time that has happened, there has been a wholesale slaughter of innocent people. The leyaks are quite merciless. They think of nothing but serving their goddess and of finding rest for their own tormented spirits."

Randolph said, "I have the distinct feeling that you are trying to discourage me from carrying this through."

"It is not for me to encourage you or to discourage you. It is not my place. Ambara's father saved my life and permitted me to survive. If Ambara believes that it is right for you to enter the world of Yama in search of your family, I cannot argue with him. I have a debt. But let me tell you this. I lost my husband and he was dearly beloved. There are two thousand thousand things I wanted to say to him and that had to remain unsaid after he was dead. But I would not attempt to enter into the death trance to say those things. It is against the teachings of the Trisakti. It is blasphemy. And—apart from that—it is far too dangerous."

Dr. Ambara smiled, trying to be lighthearted. "Flora was always the pessimist. Yes, Flora?"

But Randolph regarded her seriously and at length; he could tell by her expression that she was sincere. Her dark eyes glittered in the subdued scarlet light from the scarf-covered bulb and she exuded a perfume of musk and jasmine and civet oil.

"Tell me," Randolph said. "If a living person were to go into a death trance and if he were to be caught by the leyaks, what would happen?"

"No question, my dear sir. No question at all. He would be ripped to pieces in the way that a fox is ripped to pieces by hounds. Do you hunt in Tennessee? Is that a place where people hunt?"

"Yes, they do," Randolph said a little impatiently. "But what happens to their souls once the leyaks have them? Do their souls still go to heaven?"

Flora shook her head. "A person who is killed by leyaks becomes a leyak himself and is forever doomed to roam the world beyond the veil, seeking spirits for the Goddess Rangda."

"What about spirits that are dead already? Say, the spirits of my family? What would happen to them if the leyaks caught them?"

"They would cease to be, my dear sir. They would experience nothingness for time eternal. How can I put it? They would be like people in a coma. But this would be a coma from which they could never awaken."

"So they would never be reincarnated?"

"Indeed," Flora nodded. "It is the life essence of reincarnation upon which Rangda feeds. Without that life essence, the spirit is powerless. It remains in a gray dream, a dream without pictures, a dream without feelings, for ever and ever. To be reborn into a happier life than ever before . . . that is the reward every spirit seeks. But for those whom Rangda has devoured, there is no reward. Only oblivion."

Wanda had come down from her room and was standing in the doorway wearing a silk Filipino bathrobe, her wet hair wound in a towel. She had been listening to Flora with close attention and when Flora finished speaking, she asked quietly, "Is it really so dangerous to go into one of these death trances?"

Flora looked up. "If I could persuade anybody not to attempt it, my dear lady, I would. But Ida Bagus Ambara and Mr. Clare have journeyed many miles to fulfill their quest. Both of them knew the dangers before they set out. Who am I to try to convince them otherwise?"

"Randolph," Wanda said, "I didn't realize."

Randolph felt almost embarrassed. "I should have told you. But I'm prepared to take the risk."

Wanda was nonplussed. "You're prepared to take the risk? For what? Just to see your family again? You can never bring them back to life. Can't you let them alone? I mean, what *good* is it going to do even if you do see them?"

"I don't know," Randolph slowly said, "but I have to try."

"Suppose you get killed? Then what?" Wanda demanded.

Randolph lowered his head. Wanda could scarcely hear him over the chattering of the television. "I should have died along with Marmie. I should have been there. I won't be taking any risks that Marmie didn't take. And if they kill me . . . well, perhaps that's all I deserve."

Randolph looked up then, challenging Wanda to argue with him. He had not meant to sound morbid or self-indulgent. But the fact remained that he had taken care of Marmie for nearly twenty years, and he had taken care of his children from the moment of their conception, and he still felt responsible for all of them. If their spirits were alive, if their spirits were reachable, he was certainly not yet prepared to consign them to tearful memory and home movies. If he had seen them struggling in a stormy sea, beyond saving, he still would have leaped off the cliffs to try to rescue them, or else to die with them if nothing else. His love for Marmie and the children had been as intense as that, as intense as life itself.

As far as Randolph was concerned, it was worth risking

everything simply to tell Marmie that he loved her and always would and to wish her happiness in whatever new existences might lie ahead of her.

Wanda came over and sat down beside him. "These demons . . . what are they, leyaks? Supposing these leyaks escape?"

Flora shook a Marlboro out of a nearly empty pack and said offhandedly, "Supposing an airliner falls on this house? Supposing a plague sweeps through Manila and kills us all in our sleep? Supposing the world comes to an end tomorrow?"

She lit her cigarette and looked at Wanda slitty-eyed through the curling smoke.

Wanda said, "Airliners and plagues, they're accidents. But going into a death trance, that isn't an accident. That's something you do on purpose."

"Well, my dear lady," said Flora, "I am afraid that shows how little you understand it. For all that I disapprove of it, I can recognize that it is an irresistible need. Death overtakes the ones we love all too quickly. Have you ever been bereaved? If you have, you will know what I mean. To speak to the loved ones we have lost, if only for a minute! The dreadful attraction of it!"

Wanda unwound the towel from her head and raked her straggly wet hair with her fingers. "I understand how dangerous it is. You said yourself that it is dangerous."

"Of course. But crossing the street is just as dangerous. And what do we achieve by crossing the street?"

"We get to the other side," Wanda countered.

"Well, you are right," conceded Flora and beckoned to Ana to bring more beer.

Their conversation for the rest of the evening was scrappy and disjointed. Everybody was aware that Wanda and Randolph were going to have a serious argument, and everybody made sure that they spoke about anything but death trances and leyaks and visiting the recently deceased. They talked about politics, investments and the cost of living in Manila. They talked about the latest movies and Filipino food. Flora gave Randolph her recipe for *sinigang na sugpo*, prawns in vegetable soup.

But Wanda remained angry and restive and Randolph was acutely aware of her mood. She had imagined when Randolph had invited her to join him that they would be going on nothing more than a slightly spiritualistic vacation, doing a little sightseeing and a little swimming, indulging in a great deal of thinking and forgetting, spending an hour or two with Oriental mystics, then going back to Memphis and back to work, refreshed and restored. There had been no suggestion that what Randolph intended to do was dangerous, or that he might be meddling with evil and carnivorous spirits. It sounded like nonsense. In fact, it sounded totally ridiculous. But all the same, if even half of it were true. . . .

She thought of some of the horror movies she had seen, and for a split second her mind was tangled with images of throats torn out, of faces stretching into werewolf masks, of heads exploding and all the other special effects of horror-film technology. She was overtired. The night was desperately hot. She felt as if she were dreaming that she was here, as if she would turn over in her own bed and open her eyes and find herself back in her apartment in Memphis, with the sun shining through the window and that serene Japanese geisha looking down at her from the wall, safe among her own plants and her own books and her own security.

Randolph touched her shoulder and said, "You're tired. Why don't you get some sleep?"

Wanda said, "You and I have a bone to pick."

"I'm sure we do. I understand that now. But let's pick it in the morning."

Wanda nodded. She stood up and said good night to Flora and Dr. Ambara. Flora, smoking, smiled at her and said, "*Selamat malam!*"

Randolph said to Dr. Ambara, "I'll be down in a moment."

He followed Wanda up the narrow staircase to the second-floor landing. There were bamboo blinds over the windows and painted wicker horses hanging from the ceiling. Wanda's room was the first on the right, one of the rooms Flora reserved for special visitors. Upstairs there was a warren of rooms in which her old friends from Djakarta made their nests, accompanied by their photographs and religious effigies and incense burners. Behind each door there was a decorated screen that had to take the place of the *aling aling*, the wall Indonesian villagers build in front of their houses to prevent demons from entering at night. It is well known among Indonesians that demons have difficulty turning corners in the dark.

Randolph watched solicitously as Wanda sat down on the side of the bed.

"Are you all right?" he asked. "I don't want you to feel that you *have* to stay. You can fly home if you want to."

"If anybody ought to be flying home, it's you," she retorted.

Randolph said nothing but closed his eyes briefly to indicate that he had heard her and that he understood what she was trying to tell him.

"You don't know what's going to happen if you go into one of those death trances," Wanda went on. "I mean, I don't really believe in leykas. Is that what they're called?"

"Leyaks," Randolph corrected her. "And I don't really believe in them either."

"But what if they *are* true? You seem to be sure that you're going to see Marmie and the children. You think *that's* true. Why shouldn't the leyaks be true?"

Randolph puffed out his cheeks tiredly. "I don't know," he confessed. "This whole expedition is probably ridiculous. But it has to be done. Unless I attempt it, I can't go on. At least I can't go on living in the way I have been until now. That may sound crazy."

"No, it doesn't," Wanda said. "But you mustn't let your grief for Marmie dominate everything you do."

Randolph said, "I have to go back downstairs. You know, courtesy and all that. Why don't you get some sleep? You don't have to get up early tomorrow. The plane doesn't leave until two."

Wanda reached out a hand and Randolph took it and put his other hand on top of it.

"I do care about you," Wanda told him. "I wouldn't have come along if I didn't."

"I know," Randolph said. "And I care for you too."

He leaned forward and kissed her on the forehead. She stayed where she was and said nothing as he left the room, closing the door quietly behind him.

Downstairs, Dr. Ambara and Flora were talking about the old days in Djakarta. When Randolph came back, however, they nodded their greeting and Flora clapped.

"This Wanda is a very pretty girl," Flora said in appreciation.

"I'm afraid she's nothing more than my assistant," Randolph told her.

"Is that an obstacle?" asked Flora, suddenly cackling with laughter.

Dr. Ambara raised a cautioning hand. "Mr. Clare was unlucky enough to bury his wife and family only yesterday, Flora."

Flora stared at Randolph and then suddenly reached over to the small white Chinese vase beside the television and drew out a peach-colored orchid that she offered Randolph with an expression of almost agonized sympathy. "You must think the worst of me for speaking as I did. I had no idea that it had happened so recently. You must be very shocked, and I apologize."

Randolph took the flower and held it up to admire its delicacy. "You mustn't feel bad," he replied. And when Flora looked at him questioningly, he said, "I don't. I'm trying to look forward to the time when I can see them again."

They drank Anker Bier and ate *sapin sapin* until well after midnight. During the evening, the door chimes jangled incessantly, men came and went and girls scurried up and down the stairs. Between ten o'clock and one in the morning, Ana seemed to spend most of her time running through the parlor with trays of soup and noodles and bottles of *tapoy*, and Randolph was amazed at the volume of business the Hotel Pasay was doing at a time when most American hotels would be closed for the night.

"If you are ever interested in selling a share of this place, you can count me in," he told Flora.

Flora laughed. "A businessman like you? You could not own the Hotel Pasay or any part of it. What would your shareholders say if they found out that you owned part of a pleasure house?"

Randolph raised his glass to her and Flora bowed her head in return.

"We should drink this toast in *arak*," said Dr. Ambara. *Arak* was a colorless brandy distilled from palm wine.

Flora clapped her hands gleefully and when Ana appeared, she asked her for three glasses and a bottle of *arak*.

"I don't know what my head is going to feel like in the morning," Randolph said slurrily, but he didn't really care. His family was buried, he was sitting cross-legged on a cushion in Manila in the middle of the night, and what the hell did anything matter?

After they had poured out three glasses of palm brandy, Dr. Ambara raised his glass and said, "A compliment to the best home stay in Southeast Asia, the Hotel Pasay, and to its alluring proprietor."

Flora started laughing, a hissing laugh that went on and on and that Randolph found absurdly infectious. Soon they were all laughing, the tears streaming down their cheeks, and Flora clutched Randolph's arm and buried her face in his shirt.

Randolph at last went upstairs to bed. Flora had given him one of the larger rooms overlooking the backyard. There was a sagging double bed covered with nothing but a fawn-colored durry, a chest of drawers, a rattan chair and a faded photograph of Djakarta, cut from a magazine and pasted under glass. Randolph opened the loose catch on the balcony windows and stepped outside. The air was warm and smelled of cooking and gasoline fumes. The lights still glowed over downtown Manila as if the city were a carnival. Randolph lit his pipe and smoked for a while, thinking about nothing; he was so tired that his mind refused to function.

At two o'clock in the morning, while he was dozing, his

bedroom door opened. A moment later his mosquito net was lifted and a warm, perfumed body slid into the bed next to him.

"*Sssh*," said Wanda when he raised his head.

He said nothing. He lay back, glad that she was here, but hoping she would not expect anything from him but company.

"I feel strange," she whispered.

"Me too," he told her.

"I don't know whether it's day or night. My watch keeps telling me it's time to sleep, but my stomach keeps saying it's lunchtime."

"It'll take a while to get adjusted."

They lay together in silence for a minute or two. In the darkness Randolph could just make out the shine of her hair, the curve of her naked back. She was wearing only a thong but she lay facedown and made no move to touch him.

"I can't make love to you," he told her.

"I know," she said. "I didn't come here for that. I came only to keep you company."

"Well, thank you for that. Not many people seem to realize what it's like, going home to an empty bed."

"It was like that when my engagement was over," Wanda said. "I don't know what was worse. The hurt pride or the bed with nobody in it."

They slept for over an hour. The room was insufferably hot and mosquitoes buzzed around them persistently. Somewhere somebody was playing Beatles records on a worn-out hi-fi, over and over again. "She loves you, yeah, yeah, yeah." Outside, the traffic grumbled and honked until dawn began to smear itself over the sky and the tattered palm trees beyond Randolph's window were sharply silhouetted by the rising sun.

Wanda opened her eyes and stared at him. "I hope you haven't gotten the wrong idea," she said.

"What's the right idea?" he asked.

She propped herself on her elbows. Her breasts were full and rounded, suntanned on top, paler underneath, with a tracery of blue veins.

"The right idea is that I'm very fond of you and that I want to give you comfort."

Randolph smiled, leaned forward and kissed her shoulder. "I think the right idea is that you're a little more special than I ever gave you credit for. And you're very pretty, and I thank you for a sociable and celibate night."

Wanda did not take her gaze away. "It doesn't have to be celibate."

"I know," he replied gently. "But I would like it to be, for now at least."

"Yes," she said, and although it was clear that she wanted him, it was also clear that she understood.

They breakfasted on omelettes and *ukoy* and *bibinga* and then Dr. Ambara gave them a brief guided tour of Manila before they returned to the airport for the afternoon flight to Djakarta.

As they sat in the lounge drinking *basi* cocktails and waiting for their flight to be called, Randolph said to Dr. Ambara, "You wanted to stop over here, didn't you?"

"Perhaps 'wanted' is the wrong word," the doctor replied. He took off his glasses and studiously polished them. "There are times for all of us when we have to refer to other people's experience and other people's opinions."

"Well," Randolph asked, "what did you learn from Flora?"

Dr. Ambara replaced his glasses and said simply, "I learned that it is important to distinguish between danger and fear. I learned also that if one is truly dedicated to any particular belief, one must hold fast to one's dedication regardless of other people's warnings."

He paused and then said, "Even Flora's warnings."

Air Merpati's flight to Djakarta was called at three o'clock. They flew southwest over Brunei and Borneo, sometimes sleeping, sometimes sitting quietly and thinking. Wanda sat across the aisle from Randolph. For most of the flight she tried to read *Mistral's Daughter*, but in the end she tucked it into the pocket of the seat in front of her, folded her arms and closed her eyes.

Randolph asked, "You're not too tired?"

She shook her head without opening her eyes.

"You can still go back if you want to."

She shook her head again.

"You heard what Flora said. It could be very dangerous."

She opened her eyes and looked at him. "That's why I'm coming along. What do you think Marmie would have said if she thought I'd left you to do all this on your own?"

Randolph leaned back in his seat. "Maybe we can find out."

FOURTEEN

Djakarta

I. Made Wartawa sucked on his cigarette and then carefully propped it back on the edge of his Leica ashtray. He snorted noisily, cleared his throat and stood up and looked out the window, peering at the traffic on Jalan M.H. Thamrin as if he had never seen it before, as if it were the sudden and unexpected arrival of an alien spaceship fleet against which all of Djakarta would be powerless.

He was an ugly man, with horn-rimmed glasses, greased-back hair and a white short-sleeved shirt that had obviously been pressed by a commercial laundry. There was very little in his office but gray-steel filing cabinets, dust and airline posters.

"You are talking about something that is totally forbidden," he said with a strong Javanese accent. "Of course I cannot help you."

Dr. Ambara said, "You were recommended very highly."

I.M. Wartawa shrugged as if indifferent to recommendations.

Randolph looked across at Dr. Ambara interrogatively but the doctor gave him a secretive little wave of his hand to indicate that there was still plenty of room for negotiations.

"I was told that you were the only man in Java who knew where to find a death-trance adept. At least the only *reliable* man. We know there are many tricksters and thieves."

I.M. Wartawa came away from the window and retrieved

his cigarette. He drew on it deeply, his face taut with concentration, and then he said, "In the old days there were many adepts. But times have changed. We have television now, and videos. The young men are no longer interested in becoming priests and exploring the limits of the Hindu faith. You may complain, you Americans, but you have only yourselves to blame. Your benevolent materialism has destroyed our culture far more thoroughly than the Japanese could ever have done with their guns and their swords."

Randolph said, "If you were to help us, our materialism could be exceedingly benevolent indeed."

"You mean you would pay me very well? Of course. I would expect it for conspiring with you to break the law and also for arranging a supernatural feat unattainable anywhere else in the world."

He sat down and stared at Randolph through the thick magnifying lenses of his glasses. "There was a time when I would do almost anything for money. I was one of the greatest entrepreneurs in Djakarta, especially in the early days of Suharto. I could acquire anything that anybody wanted, whether it was narcotic, alcoholic, sexual or spiritual. But I am a little older now. I am not as interested in money as I used to be. Most of my friends are dead or vanished, and I suppose that I have learned to be more careful. I have a shadow on my lung. I want to live out the rest of my life in comparative peace."

Dr. Ambara said, "In exchange for your assistance, I could arrange to have you flown to America and treated by a specialist."

"America? Why should I want to go to America? No, my friend, there is nothing you can tempt me with." He reached into the pocket of his shirt and took out a crumpled pack of Lion cigarettes. "These days I manage to get by with whiskey money, a bowl of *nasi goreng*, a few *rupiah* for playing cards with my cronies. It is not an extravagant life but I manage."

Randolph sat forward on his chair, his hands clasped tight together, his face drawn and serious. "Dr. Ambara and I have flown a long way to talk to you today," he said gravely.

I.M. Wartawa made a sympathetic face. "I did not solicit your visit, I'm afraid. I cannot feel obliged to help you just because you have traveled so far."

Randolph said, "We were prepared to travel such a long distance because we each feel a deep and urgent need to get in touch with the people we lost. I lost my whole family, my wife and my three children. Dr. Ambara lost his wife. Both of us left so much unsaid, so much undone. I know that Indonesians set great store in making sure the human spirit is set free from its earthly body after death. But at the moment, Dr. Ambara and I are like spirits that can never be free. Our minds dwell constantly on the loved ones we lost, yet we have to remain here, inside our bodies. If you refuse to help us, you are condemning both of us to years of torment, to years of regret."

I.M. Wartawa listened to this unblinkingly. Then he lit his cigarette and said, "You speak very persuasively, sir. But why should it be my responsibility to save you from torment? I am simply a man who does a little business and drinks a little whiskey now and again."

Randolph said, "I will pay you fifty thousand dollars in cash. Half now and half later."

Wanda's eyes widened but she said nothing. Dr. Ambara glanced uneasily from Randolph to I.M. Wartawa and back again. I.M. Wartawa brushed cigarette ash across the surface of his desk with the side of his hand. He blew out smoke.

"Fifty thousand dollars is a considerable amount of money."

Randolph nodded. "If you invested it wisely, you could live off it very comfortably for the rest of your life."

"Well, that is true. You have surprised me. Up until now, my fees for arranging a death trance have not been much more than six or seven thousand dollars. I have to confess that fifty thousand dollars is extremely interesting."

"Do you want some time to think about it?" Randolph asked.

I.M. Wartawa twisted his wrist around and peered at his gleaming gold watch. "It is two o'clock now. Let me make some inquiries and call you later this evening. Where are you staying?"

"At the Hilton," said Dr. Ambara. "Ask for suite nine-oh-eight."

They shook hands with I.M. Wartawa and went noisily down the uncarpeted stairs to the street. It was an overcast, humid day and the palms rustled over the constant honking and grinding of traffic. Wanda asked, "Do you think he will do it?"

"For fifty thousand dollars, he would be a fool not to," replied Dr. Ambara.

"That's an awful lot of money," Wanda said. "Are you sure he deserves it? I mean even if he *does* find you one of these adepts?"

Randolph thrust his hands into the pockets of his lightweight summer trousers. "Marmie had stocks and investments totaling three or four million. I can't think of a better way to use those investments."

"Randolph . . ." Wanda said gently and took his hand.

"It's something I have to do."

"But fifty thousand dollars."

"It's only money. And personally I believe it's worth it."

They returned to the Hilton to shower and change. Wrapped in a towel, Randolph telephoned Ella, and then Neil Sleaman. There was a distracting echo on the satellite link but he managed to gather from Neil that the Raleigh plant had suffered another setback because of technical problems with the refrigeration unit and that Sun-Taste's chief marketing manager had been calling all day asking for reassurances that Clare Cottonseed would be able to make up its shortfall in less than a week.

"Any word from Orbus Greene?"

"Not a thing."

"I'll call him myself as soon as he's open for business."

"Don't worry, sir. I'm sure I can handle it."

Randolph put down the phone. He was convinced now

that Clare Cottonseed would get no help from the Margarine Mafia and that Orbus was deliberately delaying his response. Randolph was prepared to pay top prices for Orbus's cottonseed oil; he was prepared to make wide-ranging concessions on future contracts. He was not prepared, however, to join the Cottonseed Association, and he was deeply concerned that Sun-Taste might take its order elsewhere. It was not as much a question of profits as one of keeping his new factories and his newly hired staff in productive work. If Sun-Taste went, he would have to start devolving and dismantling and he would lose all the expansive impetus of the past three years, not to mention having to pay Federal taxes on last year's profits out of this year's sharply reduced income.

That afternoon Dr. Ambara took them around Djakarta, through the Chinese district and the old town, and as evening began to thicken, into the pungent street markets and the crowded shanty villages. They sat at a small roadside stall under a hissing pressure lamp and ate bowls of *nasi campur*, rice mixed with chopped meat and vegetables, and *betutu bebek*.

All the time, however, they were thinking about I.M. Wartawa, wondering whether he had called them. They had almost completely forgotten about Ecker-Reece and his companions. Randolph had seen no sign of them at Halim airport when they had arrived, and their taxi to the Hilton had certainly not been followed. Dr. Ambara had remarked, "They were probably nothing more than veterans after all. I think perhaps we were being too sensitive."

They returned to the Hilton just after nine o'clock. The message light was flashing on Randolph's telephone. He picked it up and the desk clerk told him that I. Nyoman Sutarja had called, on behalf of I. Made Wartawa. They were to meet I. Made Wartawa at eight o'clock on the following morning at a restaurant on Jalan Sultan Hasanuddin in Kebayoran Baru.

"Was that all?" Randolph asked, looking across the room at Dr. Ambara.

"He said to tell you that everything is dandy," the desk clerk told him.

Randolph put down the phone. "It seems like we're in business," he said. "Wartawa wants to meet us at eight o'clock tomorrow morning."

Randolph scarcely slept that night. He read an old copy of *Playboy* that he had found in the back of the closet. Then he mixed himself a whiskey and ginger out of the refrigerator and sat smoking his pipe until three o'clock had beeped on his traveler's alarm clock. He lay on his bed and dozed for two hours before getting up at five-fifteen and showering and shaving. He was beginning to understand how holy men experienced strange visions after days without sleep. The hotel floor kept swaying as if shaken by an earthquake and for the first time in years, Randolph realized that he was suffering from severe jet lag.

Wanda had not come into his room during the night, nor had he ventured into hers. There seemed to have developed an understanding between them that they were strongly attracted to each other and that at the right time and under the right circumstances, they might have become lovers. That right time and those right circumstances might very well coincide one day. But neither of them wanted to jeopardize the possibility of a future relationship by clumsily rushing into anything now. Tensions were too high; nerves were too raw; and the dead were too recently buried.

Nonetheless, when Randolph knocked on Wanda's door at seven o'clock and she called for him to come in, she was standing in front of the bathroom mirror brushing her hair and wearing nothing but white-lace panties. She dressed in front of him as openly as if they were already intimate and both of them knew what she was trying to say to him: *I'm yours, when you want me.*

Her openness did not upset or offend him. He took it in the way she meant it and was reassured and, in a strange way, comforted.

"It really looks as if Wartawa might have found us an adept," he said, clearing his throat.

"Are you scared?"

Randolph thought about it briefly and then nodded. "I think anybody would be."

"Do you actually believe you're going to see Marmie again?"

"I don't know. The nearer I get to it, the more impossible it seems. You know, when Dr. Ambara first talked about it in Mount Moriah Clinic, it all sounded so easy. You pay your money and you get to see the loved ones you've lost. But now, I don't know. Now I'm starting to think about how I'm going to feel if I really do see Marmie again, what I'm going to say. And what is *she* going to feel? Do spirits have the same kind of feelings as mortals? Suppose it upsets her to see me? And what's going to happen when the trance is over and I have to leave her behind?"

Wanda sat down beside him on the edge of the bed and took his hand. "You could always back out now. If nothing else, you could save yourself a lot of money. You could probably save yourself some heartache too."

She hesitated and then went on. "They're *dead*, Randolph. You have to let go some time."

Randolph did not answer. He recognized that she was probably right and that this expedition to Indonesia was nothing more than an irrational attempt to assuage his guilt. If only he had been there when the door of the cabin at Lac aux Ecorces had burst open and those men had invaded his family's lives with axes and wire and nothing in their hearts but murder. He found that he was clenching his teeth and that his fists were so tight that his knuckles showed as white spots.

Wanda lightly kissed his cheek. "All right. I know. You have to go through with it."

They took a taxi to Keborayan Baru, the spacious residential district to the south of Djakarta. Dr. Ambara had slept "like a rhinoceros," as he put it, and was nervous and excitable. Randolph found himself somewhat lethargic and couldn't stop yawning.

The restaurant on Jalan Sultan Hasanuddin was called "Wayang" after the Indonesian traveling theaters. It was elegant and looked expensive, with painted screens, and *ider-iders* draped from the ceiling, strips of cotton traditionally hung from shrines during festivals. A small, dapper man showed them through to the back of the restaurant, where I.M. Wartawa was sitting with a glass of beer and a cigarette.

"*Selamat pagi,*" he called as they walked across to join him. "Good morning. *Saudara mau minum apa?*"

"Coffee would do fine, thanks," said Dr. Ambara.

I.M. Wartawa lifted his hand to the dapper little man and said, "*Tolong, berikan saya tiga kopi.*"

"*Silakan duduk,*" he invited them. "Please sit down."

They sat around the table. I.M. Wartawa crushed out his cigarette, swallowed a large mouthful of whiskey and said, "I telephoned many of my friends yesterday afternoon. Some did not answer. Maybe they are gone away, or dead. I renewed some old acquaintances. But after some time, I managed to find the kind of person I believe you have been looking for."

"In Djakarta?" asked Dr. Ambara.

"He was here briefly, and also in Jogjakarta for a while. But now he lives on Bali, in Denpasar, the capital. He is not an easy man to locate and it may be difficult to persuade him to help you, but he is supposed to be one of the most skillful of death-trance adepts, even greater than Ida Bagus Darwiko, who died two years ago in Kintamani."

"Do you have his name?" Randolph asked.

"Yes, sir, I have his name. When you pay me, I shall give it to you. You must understand that I am not being unhelpful. I simply wish to protect my interests."

"You shall have your money by tomorrow," Randolph said. "But first of all—even if you don't want to give me his name now—tell me something about this man. I have to know whether he's genuine or not."

I.M. Wartawa slowly shook his head. "There is no question about his being genuine, sir. I have heard of him before, but he is very secretive and it is hard to say whether all the stories about him are true."

"What stories?" Randolph wanted to know.

"Well, sir, they say that he became adept at entering the death trance because he was seeking revenge against the Goddess Rangda. Apparently the very first time he was taught to enter the death trance, his religious tutor was killed by the Witch Widow and ever since that day, he has sought to destroy her. Few adepts enter the death trance unless they really have to, or unless they are seeking somebody special. But this man is said to have entered the death trance again and again, night after night, for the sole purpose of hunting down leyaks and killing them, and with the ultimate goal of meeting Rangda face-to-face and slaying her."

"That sounds like a dangerous obsession," Randolph commented.

"Passing beyond the veil is always dangerous," I.M. Wartawa remarked. He sat back in his seat while a pretty Javanese girl set out their cups of coffee. *"Tolong, berikan saya satu Johnny Walker?"* he asked her.

"Tentu," she said and took his glass.

"What other stories do they tell about this celebrated adept?" Randolph asked. He was about to part with twenty-five thousand dollars in cash; he felt entitled at the very least to a little background on what he was going to get for his money.

I.M. Wartawa sniffed. "They say he is the first and only adept who has ever managed to hunt leyaks and kill them. Of course there is no proof of this because you cannot kill a leyak in the land of the dead and then drag his body back to the real world to show what you have done. Leyaks are invisible in the real world. It is only when you go beyond the veil that you can see them."

"How does one actually go about hunting and killing a leyak?" asked Wanda.

"You will have to ask him that yourself," replied I.M. Wartawa. "I can only suppose that it is done by magic of a kind."

"Is there anything else you can tell us about this man?" Randolph asked. "Where he comes from? How old he is?"

"He is very young," said I.M. Wartawa. "In fact, he is

barely a man at all. He may be nineteen or twenty, no more than that. The other interesting thing about him is that he is part American."

"That's interesting," said Wanda.

"Well, of course there are thousands just the same all over Southeast Asia. The legacy that the United States left after the Vietnamese war was not just cultural. This man, however, has sought to train himself in the ways of his mother while at the same time using the superior physical strength and the Western sense of logic he inherited from his father. From everything I have been told about him, he sounds formidable."

Randolph sipped his coffee. It was Java coffee, hot and thick. "How would you like me to pay you?" he asked I.M. Wartawa quietly.

I.M. Wartawa produced a well-worn business card. "Have the money delivered here in a plain parcel, addressed to me. As soon as I receive it, I will telephone you at the Hilton and give you the name of the adept and where you might start looking for him."

Randolph said, "You realize what will happen if the money is delivered and you *don't* phone?"

I.M. Wartawa gave a small, tight, U-shaped smile. "You will have to trust me, I regret to say. It is against the law to procure death-trance adepts in Indonesia, but it is also against the law to seek to hire one. If I were to disappear with my twenty-five thousand dollars, you would have no recourse. But then, I am known as an honorable man, and I can promise you that I will keep my word. It would be foolish of me, after all, to escape with only half the money."

Randolph looked at Dr. Ambara for a sign of reassurance. Dr. Ambara said, "I. Made Wartawa was given the very best of references, Randolph. That is all I can say."

"Very well," said Randolph. He stood up and offered I.M. Wartawa his hand. I.M. Wartawa transferred his cigarette from his right hand to his left and solemnly shook on the deal. "It is a delight to do business with you, sir," he said.

The small, dapper man came up then and asked, "Will

you eat some breakfast before you go? You should try our steamed tomatoes with butter and garlic, or the Gado-Gado salad.''

"My brother-in-law," I.M. Wartawa explained with a laconic wave of his hand.

"Thanks all the same, but I think we'd better be getting back to the Hilton," said Randolph. "I have to arrange for your money to be wired over."

"A breakfast will delay you only half an hour," said Wartawa's brother-in-law.

"Don't delay them, Verra," I.M. Wartawa admonished him. "Not even for one minute. They can think about breakfast after they've dealt with their business affairs."

He smiled with exaggerated slyness and raised his glass. "Once one has decided to be trusting, one should go ahead full speed," he remarked. "Be quick! Trust, like drunkenness, always wears out in the end."

"Very philosophical," Randolph complimented him.

They stepped out into the sunlight. Most of the overcast had torn itself away now, and apart from a few cloud shadows moving across the ground, the morning was clear. Their taxi driver was still waiting for them, reading a Mickey Mouse comic book in Basaha Indonesian. He started up the engine as they appeared and tucked his comic into the elastic band around the sun vizor.

"*Tolong hantarkan saya ke Hilton-Hotel,*" Dr. Ambara told him.

They were turning around in the middle of the street when a bright flash caught Randolph's attention. It was nothing more than sunlight glancing off the windshield of another car, but it was the fact that the car had started moving at exactly the same time as their taxi that attracted Randolph's interest. He twisted around in his seat and frowned at it through his sunglasses.

"What's the matter?" Wanda asked.

"I don't know. That car started moving off as soon as we did, that's all, and now it has turned around to follow us."

Dr. Ambara turned around too. "Volkswagen," he remarked. "Looks like a rental."

"Four men in it," Randolph observed.

"Do you think it's them?" Wanda asked.

"It could be."

"But how did they find us? They weren't at the airport, were they, when we arrived?"

Randolph said, "If they knew which flight we were taking, they probably knew what hotel we were staying at. And if you're an American, you can't get much less imaginative than the Djakarta Hilton, can you? That would be the first place I would have started looking if I were them."

"What do we do?" Wanda asked. "Call the police?"

Randolph said, "No. Not yet anyway. Remember that what we're trying to arrange here is strictly illegal. And apart from that, they haven't actually done anything except to follow us, and that's supposing it's really them."

"It's difficult to see," said Dr. Ambara, shielding his eyes against the glare of the sun.

They turned to the center of Djakarta and to the Hilton Hotel. While Wanda ordered drinks, Randolph telephoned George Twyford, his accountant, who was not particularly pleased about being called at six-thirty in the evening, Memphis time, when he was just about to leave the office after a hard day. But he agreed to wire twenty-five thousand dollars to the Bank of Indonesia by the time Randolph woke up in the morning.

"Twenty-five thousand is going to buy you an awful lot of noodle suppers."

"I'm buying some Javanese sculpture."

"Are you sure Javanese sculpture is a good investment?"

"I'm doing the right thing, George, believe me."

The accountant sniffed. He sounded tinny and far away. "It's your money," he conceded.

Randolph put down the phone and settled back in his armchair. Dr. Ambara said, "It's all settled?" as if he could hardly believe it.

"The money will be wired here during the night."

Wanda was standing by the window, looking down nine stories to the street below. "That Volkswagen is still there," she reported. "They've parked it across the road."

Randolph joined her. "It certainly looks like the same one."

They waited and watched the Volkswagen for two or three minutes. Suddenly the passenger door opened and a tall man eased himself out. Randolph recognized him immediately, even at this distance.

"That's the one called Ecker. No doubt about it. And I'd bet you money that his real name is Reece."

"If he really is Reece, he's the man who killed Marmie and the children."

Randolph whispered, "Yes."

Wanda stared at him. "He might just as easily kill us too."

"No. The difference is that now we're ready for him."

FIFTEEN

Bali

The Fokker Fellowship of Garuda Airlines whistled smartly to a halt at the end of the runway and then taxied without hesitation toward the terminal. "Lady and gentleman, welcome to Bali International Airport Ngurah Rai. For your safeness, stay in your seat until we have completely arrested ourselves."

Randolph peered out of the plane's window at the white-painted buildings, at the dark clumps of palms alongside the perimeter fence, and at the ground-traffic controller in the sunglasses and the splashy orange-and-green shirt who was directing the jet up to the gate. The engines died away and they unbuckled their seat belts.

"I always wanted to visit Bali," Wanda said as she collected her bag from the overhead rack. "Not under these circumstances though."

They had arranged for a rented car to meet them outside the terminal. There was no further sign of Ecker and his companions but as a precaution, they had requested that their driver hold up a sign for "Mr. Berry" instead of for "Mr. Clare." When Wanda had asked Randolph why he had chosen the name Berry, he had shrugged and said, "You remember the song. 'Long-distance Information, Get Me Memphis, Tennessee.' That was Chuck Berry."

"Before my time," Wanda had reminded him.

A dusty black Volvo was waiting for them by the curb,

222

driven by a young Balinese in a chauffeur's cap, an immaculately pressed black jacket that he wore without a shirt underneath, tennis shorts and black knee-length socks.

"Your flight was good?" he asked as they drove away. "Sometimes that flight from Djakarta can be bumpy." He switched on a small electric fan attached to the top of the dashboard and searched up and down the radio dial for two or three minutes, past blurts of singing, Balinese music, Morse code and news in Basaha Indonesian, before he finally located the station he wanted: country-and-western.

"I am a personal fan of Tammy Wynette's," he announced as if that should make them feel at home.

It took them a half-hour to drive the twelve kilometers north to the Balinese capital of Denpasar. As they drove into the city center on Jalan Hasanudin, their car was brought to a crawl through the narrow streets by bicycles, Bemo buses, shoals of buzzing and crackling mopeds and the traditional *dokar*, horse-drawn buggies. The sidewalks teemed wih brightly dressed shoppers and every storefront was crowded with brilliant batik, gaudy souvenirs, masks, brassware and heaps of lurid plastic sandals. The noise and chattering were tremendous, like the noise of a never-ending fairground; in the early afternoon humidity, the smoke from *warong* cooking stands hung heavy with the smell of charcoal-broiled pork and *chop-chai*.

They had decided not to stay at the Hotel Bali, an elegant old building dating from Dutch times and the best hotel in Denpasar. Instead, they had found a cheaper *losmen* on Jalan Diponegoro, a shabby twelve-bedroomed building next door to the Very Delicious Restaurant and the offices of I.B. Padura Spice Export. The hotel lobby was decorated in a style that Randolph described as Oriental Bombastic, with gold-foil wallpaper, Balinese headdresses, soiled crimson carpets and a little palm-leaf thatch over the reception desk.

A shriveled old man with one gleaming gold tooth and a pretty, plump young girl showed them to their rooms. The driver brought up their suitcases and assured them that he would be available twenty-four hours a day. "Stand by your man,'' he smiled and left, touching his cap. He did not expect a tip; in Bali, tipping was still a rarity.

''Not exactly the Waldorf Astoria,'' Randolph remarked, parting the bamboo blind over a window and looking down at a cluttered courtyard where chickens pecked among rusted mopeds and empty oil drums. His room was dominated by a king-sized bed with a white-vinyl headboard, and a carved armoire that smelled of tropical mustiness and mothballs. There was no air conditioning but each of their rooms had a small and noisy refrigerator that had been well stocked with Coca-Cola, Anker Bier and a fruit drink called Air Jeruk.

''If Ecker and his friends are still following us, they will have great difficulty in locating us here,'' said Dr. Ambara.

Randolph sat down on the end of the bed and opened the folded note I.M. Wartawa had given him as soon as the $50,000 fee had been paid. He only hoped that the information it contained was worth the huge expense. It said simply, ''Michael Hunter, sometimes known as Michael Arjuna. Last verified address, Jalan Pudak 12a, Denpasar.''

''Do you want to start looking for him right away?'' asked Dr. Ambara.

''I want a shower first.''

Randolph soaped and washed himself under a rattling shower fixture and then dressed in clean white slacks and a blue short-sleeved shirt. While he was combing his wet hair in front of the mirror on the back of the closet door, Wanda came in wearing a low-waisted cotton minidress in yellow and a bright bead necklace.

''How's your room?'' he asked.

''Oh, it's fine,'' she said, not altogether enthusiastically. ''I can see the roof of some kind of temple.''

''This is quite a place, isn't it?''

Wanda went to the window. ''Do you really think you will find this man?''

''I'm going to want my money back if I don't,'' Randolph smiled.

''I don't know,'' Wanda mused. ''Now that we're here, it seems so farfetched, this death-trance business.''

Randolph finished combing his hair and closed the closet

door. "How about pouring us both a beer? Then maybe we can go find this character and see how real or unreal the death trance actually is."

They took a taxi through the center of Denpasar, past the statue of Guru, the demon giant, which stands at the intersection of the city's two main streets, Jalan Gajahmada and Jalan Udayana; then past Puputan Square, where the state temple of Pura Jagatnatha lifts its decorative roof to the afternoon sun. And everywhere around them there was music, and talking, and the ripping noise of mopeds.

The house where Michael Hunter was supposed to have lived was a smelly, derelict bungalow with a cramped garden overgrown with wild orchids. Half of its roof was sagging and the windows were covered with galvanized iron.

"So much for that pricey piece of information," Randolph said, his hands on his hips.

Their taxi driver remained parked by the curb, watching them with unabashed curiosity. "You look for somebody, Tuan?" he asked.

"An American, a young American. We were told that he lives here."

The driver climbed out of the ancient Volvo and walked on slap-slapping sandals across to the house next door where an old woman was sitting on the steps sorting through baskets of fresh-picked nutmegs. He had a lengthy conversation with her, nodding and pointing and occasionally smacking his hands together. Then he came back over to Randolph and announced proudly, "This American you look for, he was here for one year. Then he left, one or two months ago. The old woman doesn't know where he lives now. But she says he used to go to the Two Sisters restaurant because sometimes he brought her back Chinese food."

Dr. Ambara said, "It seems that we have no choice but to look for him there. Will you take us, please?"

"Bagus," agreed the driver. "Fine."

The Two Sisters restaurant was halfway along Jalan Tabalan in a run-down area northeast of the night market, populated by Chinese, Arabs and Indians. It was quieter here, more reclusive. None of the storefronts spilled out into the street in the way they did around Jalan Gajahmada and Jalan Veteran. Apart from small, hand-painted signs on the facades, usually in Chinese or Arabic characters, it was often impossible to tell whether one would find a general store behind them, or a restaurant, or a gambling parlor. A pack of mangy dogs yapped and tussled in the road.

The front of the Two Sisters was covered by a pierced iron grille and a sign reading, "Rumah Makan 2 Sisters." Randolph paid off the taxi driver and they pushed their way through a clattering beaded curtain to the restaurant itself. Inside, it was gloomy and smoky and hot. Running the length of the righthand wall, there was a bar behind which a small Chinese woman was mixing cocktails in a shaker. There were a dozen tables covered with green oilcloth; almost all of them were taken, mostly by elderly Chinese patrons. A young Balinese girl was carrying around trays of crab soup, frogs' legs and fried noodles. On the far wall there was a yellowed painting of mountains in China with cranes flying over them.

Five or six people were sitting at the bar, three of whom were Westerners: A handsome-looking girl of twenty-four or twenty-five in a turquoise-blue sarong and head scarf; a fat man of about fifty who looked rather like a down-and-out Orson Welles; and a boy of nineteen or twenty with short-cropped black hair who was wearing a faded T-shirt with an Ever-Ready Battery motif on the front, and washed-out jeans.

Everybody in the restaurant turned around and stared as Randolph, Wanda and Dr. Ambara walked in. There was one thing that Randolph could say for the Far East: nobody was embarrassed about showing how interested he was in anything that was going on around him.

Randolph walked to the bar. "*Selamat siang*," he said to the Chinese woman. Dr. Ambara had taught him how to say "Good afternoon" in Basaha Indonesian.

The Chinese woman finished shaking the cocktails and poured them into large glasses. She did not exactly ignore Randolph but neither did she exactly acknowledge him. There was only a slight, subtle half-closing of the eyes.

Randolph said, "I'm looking for an American. I was told that he used to come here to eat."

The Chinese woman said, "No American here."

Randolph looked along the bar at the young man with the black hair and the Ever-Ready T-shirt. "How about you?" he asked him. "Did you ever see any Americans in here? A young American boy I'm looking for, round about your age. Name of Michael Hunter, or Michael Arjuna."

The girl in the sarong stared at him. "Who wants to know?" she asked in a strong New England accent.

Randolph nodded toward the young man. "Is that him?"

"This isn't anybody. This is just a friend of mine."

Randolph walked around behind the other customers at the bar and approached the young man. The girl jumped down from her stool and stood protectively in front of him.

Randolph looked the boy straight in the face and asked, "Are you Michael Hunter?"

The boy returned his gaze with eyes that were dark and lifeless. His face was emaciated and yellowed by malaria and there were sores at the sides of his mouth and in his hairline. Close up, Randolph could see that his hair was actually blond and that he had dyed it. The ash-colored roots were beginning to show through.

The girl said defensively, "He just wants to be left alone, okay?"

Randolph did not take his eyes from the boy. "I've traveled all the way from Memphis, Tennessee, to talk to Michael Hunter."

"Well, Michael Hunter isn't talking," the girl retorted, "so you can just travel all the way back to Memphis, Tennessee."

Randolph stood still for a moment or two and then reached into his shirt pocket to take out his billfold. He noticed the way in which both the boy and the girl stared at his money and his credit cards with the unabashed hunger of the really poor.

"Maybe I can buy you folks a drink," he suggested. "Maybe something to eat. I've been looking for you all over. That's thirsty work. Hungry work too."

The girl said, "Mister, whoever you are, Michael is just not interested."

Randolph made a face. "Well, I'm sorry about that. I thought that maybe we could simply sit down and have a meal together, that maybe you could advise me on what I ought to be eating and then I could put my proposition to you and see whether you're interested or not. There doesn't have to be any pressure involved. You don't even have to talk if you don't want to. All I'm asking you to do is to listen."

The girl said, "Forget it," but the boy reached out and held her arm, keeping his eyes fixed on Randolph.

"You want to eat?" Randolph asked.

The boy nodded and then in a slightly hoarse voice, said, "Don't expect me to say yes to anything, that's all. I know why you've come here. I know what you want. You've got to understand that I don't do that kind of stuff anymore."

Randolph gave him a tight smile. "And what kind of stuff is that, the stuff you don't do anymore?"

"You know what I mean," the boy replied coldly.

Randolph said, "For sure, I know what you mean."

The girl said with ill-disguised fury, "If you try to get him involved in any of that trance business, so help me, I'll scream out rape."

"Rape?" Randolph inquired, trying hard not to sound amused.

"That's what you're trying to do, isn't it?" the girl asked defiantly. "Rape Michael's mind, the same as all the others did. Now he's caught between the devils in one world and the devils in the other, and believe me, there isn't much to choose between them."

"Do I look like a devil?" Randolph asked.

"Don't you know?" the girl demanded. "Devils always have smooth tongues. Devils are always tempting."

Michael Hunter shook her arm to show her that he understood what she was saying and that he appreciated the way she took care of him but that he wanted to eat. "Come on," he urged. "Let's go sit down. Let's see what the devil has to say for himself. Simply listening won't do any harm."

They sat down at one of the oilcloth-covered tables, close to the jukebox. It was an old 1960s Wurlitzer, although the records in it were modern: Chinese versions of "Thriller" and "Purple Rain" and "Ninety-Nine Red Balloons." Randolph introduced Wanda and Dr. Ambara, and Michael laid his arm on his companion's shoulder and said, "This is Jennifer Dunning, although I call her Mungkin Nanti."

Wanda asked, "What's that, some kind of a pet name?"

"I think it's a joke," said Dr. Ambara. "It means 'maybe later.' "

Michael propped his bony elbows on the table and took out a pack of Indonesian cigarettes, Monkey brand. He lit one without offering them around and blew smoke out his nostrils. "Did you learn of me in Memphis?" he asked, "or did somebody in Denpasar give you the nod?"

"A man called I. Made Wartawa in Djakarta," Randolph told him.

Michael nodded without taking the cigarette out of his mouth. "Oh, yes. Wartawa. Strange guy. Quite ethical for a crook. He sent somebody on to me before. A meat packer."

The Balinese waitress came over and Michael ordered *wulung tuzhu*, sea slugs and pigeon eggs; *jiachang shaozi niujin*, simmered beef tendon; and *caogu zhenji*, chicken with straw mushrooms. He looked at Randolph after he had ordered and said a little sarcastically, "Their specialty here is stir-fried cobra and fried rolls in the shape of Buddha's hand, but I guess you can wait until next time."

A large pot of jasmine tea was set on the table between them. While the girl called Maybe Later poured for everybody, Randolph watched Michael Hunter through the rising steam and tried to figure out what might tempt this extraordinary young man to take him into a death trance.

"You say you don't do 'this kind of stuff' anymore," Randolph remarked, sipping his tea.

Michael shook his head.

"Is there any particular reason for that? Wartawa seemed to think that going into a death trance was one of your major pursuits. He said you were the only person he had ever heard of who actually did it for sport."

"Sport? What did he mean by sport?" Michael asked sharply.

"He said you went hunting leyaks."

"Hunting leyaks is not sport. And besides, what do you know about leyaks?"

"My friend, Dr. Ambara here, is something of an expert on the Hindu religion as practiced in Indonesia."

"Your friend, Dr. Ambara, should be careful of what he says."

"Oh, yes?" asked Randolph. There was a faint challenge in his voice.

Michael said, "I gave up hunting leyaks because we nearly had an accident. Nanti could have been killed. I promised not to do it after that."

"So what have you been living on since then?"

Michael at last took out his cigarette and allowed the smoke to seethe around his discolored teeth. "I work at the Museum Bali some mornings. Sweeping up, cleaning the display cases, that kind of thing."

"How's the pay?" asked Randolph.

"How would you think it is?" Mungkin Nanti demanded aggressively. "But it's better than being torn to pieces."

The waitress brought a large dish of *hunsu pinpan*, cold meats—spiced lamb, breast of duck and marinated chicken—arranged in a fan shape. Michael and Mungkin Nanti immediately picked up their chopsticks and began to eat. Wanda frowned and studiously tried to arrange her chopsticks so they didn't tangle.

"Go ahead, use a spoon," Michael suggested. He chewed duck, then took another suck at his cigarette. "I guess you must be bereaved," he told Randolph. "Your mother? Your father?"

"Both long dead already," Randolph replied. He suddenly realized that this was the moment he had been thinking about, over and over again, ever since Dr. Ambara had told him it was possible to go beyond the gate of death. "I lost my wife and my three children. I buried them Tuesday." He found that his throat had constricted so tightly that he was unable to carry on.

Michael looked up, a piece of lamb in his chopsticks, unmoved by Randolph's emotion. "What was it, auto accident?"

"Homicide. They were up in Canada, alone in a cabin we used for vacations. Somebody—three or four men, maybe more—broke into the place and killed them."

Mungkin Nanti kept on eating, as undisturbed by the death of Randolph's family as was Michael. Randolph watched both of them for a while, wondering what it would take to provoke them into reacting to what had happened to him, but then he guessed that for somebody who had already been into the realm of death many times, hearing about somebody else's homicide must be pretty uninteresting. Death had been Michael's business, at least until Mungkin Nanti had persuaded him to give it up. He was no more impressed by death than a coroner was, or a mortician.

Randolph said, "My friend here—Dr. Ambara—lost his wife. That was an auto accident. He wants to make contact too."

"Well, I've told you," Michael said, deftly picking up a decoratively sliced radish with the tips of his chopsticks, "that I don't do that kind of stuff anymore. Besides, if I had to do it for you people, it would mean going back to Memphis with you, and believe me, of all the places in the world, I really don't feel like going to Memphis."

"Have you ever been to Memphis?" Randolph asked.

"No, and I don't intend to go."

They sat back for a while and after they finished the *hunsu pinpan*, the waitress brought them hot towels. Michael wiped his face all over and the back of his neck too, as if he were suffering from a fever.

"Tell me about yourself," Randolph urged Michael. "How did you get into this death-trance business?"

"Do you really want to know?" Michael asked.

"Yes," Randolph told him. "You're an American, aren't you? Well, at least fifty-percent American. What makes even a fifty-percent American want to get involved with Indonesian religion? Isn't there enough religion at home?"

"Home?" asked Michael. "You call it home? Well, I

guess you would. But my father could never call it home, not after he came out to the East. He was a junior adviser in the U.S. Military Mission in the days of President Diem. He argued so strongly with the Pentagon that the Vietnam War should never be fought and could never be won that in the end they sacked him. But he didn't go back to the United States. He felt betrayed, you know, and let down. And more important than that, he was beginning to develop some kind of an understanding of the Eastern mentality. He went to Java first and then wound up here. He said that Bali was the spiritual center of everything, of the whole darned world. In fact, the Balinese call Gunung Agung, the volcano, the navel of the world. That's a really fantastic way of putting it, don't you think?''

"Your father married a Balinese girl?" Wanda asked.

Michael smiled. "She was a village girl from Sangeh. My father met her when he was exploring the famous monkey jungle. Her father refused to let him marry her so in the end he followed the old Balinese tradition and kidnapped her. He took her away on his moped, would you believe?''

It was obvious that Mungkin Nanti resented Michael's speaking so freely, but she did not interrupt him. Not only was he halfway between the world of death and the world of life, he was halfway between East and West, and he was plainly enjoying the opportunity to speak to Americans for all that he scorned the idea of the United States as home.

The waitress began to set out the hot food in front of them. Randolph took one look at the sea slugs, lying gray and juicy in their sauce of peanut oil, and decided to stay with the chicken.

Michael said, "My father made friends with one of the local high priests and had himself trained in the mystic arts of the Trisakti, the holy Hindu trinity of Brahma, Vishnu and Siwa. But he was always a Westerner at heart. An least that's what he used to tell me. He could understand what the high priest was telling him . . . like, intellectually. He could glimpse the inner meanings of things. But when it came down to it, he couldn't actually *be* a Hindu.''

Michael picked up a sea slug with his chopsticks and bit one end of it. "You should try these, they're good. It's one of the best dishes they do here."

Wanda looked at Randolph and swallowed hard. "I don't think I'm all that hungry. Jet lag, you know. My stomach just doesn't know what time of day it is."

Michael said, "I was born on the day the Marines first landed at Da Nang. Nineteen sixty-five. My father said it was an omen. I don't know what it was. It was also Kuningan, the last day of the feast of Galungan, which celebrates the defeat of the demon king Mayadanawa. To me, that *was* an omen."

They ate for a little while in silence and then Michael said, "My father took me by the hand one day and walked me down to the Temple of the Dead. I was seven years old. He introduced me to the high priest, the *pedanda*, and told me that from now on, the *pedanda* was going to be my spiritual father, which, as it turned out, he was. And something of a real father too, because my own father died when I was ten."

"I'm sorry," Randolph said.

"Well, you needn't be," Michael told him. "I met my father again, in a death trance, and I know now that he's quite content."

"You actually met your father after he died?" Randolph asked.

Michael stared at him and put down his chopsticks. "I thought you *believed* in the death trance," he said. Dr. Ambara looked uneasy. Wanda sensed that something was going wrong and said, "Taste some of that beef, Randolph. It's absolutely delicious." But everybody ignored her.

"Of course I believe in the death trance," Randolph said evenly. "I wouldn't be here if I didn't."

"Ah, but you don't *really* believe. You're just another one of these curiosity hounds. A tourist. You wouldn't have sounded so surprised about my meeting my father if you weren't."

Dr. Ambara put in, "You're misjudging Mr. Clare, and you're misjudging him quite seriously."

"I can't take anyone into a death trance who doesn't believe in it totally. You know that. It's far too dangerous."

"Michael," Mungkin Nanti insisted, "you're not *doing* death trances anymore. Especially not with these people."

Dr. Ambara said, "Mr. Clare has come a long way toward understanding and believing in the ways of Yama. But just remember that to Western minds the concepts are difficult, not so easy to grasp, just as Western ways are often a mystery to us."

It was Dr. Ambara's use of the word "us" that salvaged the moment from complete breakdown. Dr. Ambara had shown that he counted Michael not as a half-caste, but as an Indonesian, and that he respected Michael's spiritual abilities. Besides, it was becoming evident that Michael was far more interested in doing business with Randolph than Mungkin Nanti was trying to make them believe. It was one thing to sweep up at the Museum Bali for ten *rupiah* an hour, it was quite another to go hunting for leyaks through the regions of the dead. The sheer terror of what lay beyond the gate of death was stimulating beyond human imagination. Michael's adrenalin level was rising even while he was trying to argue that he would never take anybody into a death trance again and that Randolph was an unbeliever. Dr. Ambara, in the subtlest of ways, had given Michael all the justification he needed to break his promise.

Michael picked up another sea slug and said, "My father killed himself."

Randolph said nothing but watched and waited.

Michael went on. "He went out one day into the yard when I was playing inside the house. He was wearing his temple sash, a loincloth and a long white band around his head. He sat on the stones in the middle of the yard and laid out all his copies of the *lontar* manuscripts around himself in a special arrangement. Then he poured gasoline over his shoulders and set himself on fire. I remember hearing a crackling noise. I went outside and there he was, blazing. There were flames streaming out of his face. He was completely quiet, completely impassive. I didn't know what to do but something told me that he would never forgive me if I tried to save him. He was seeking something, I understood that much. I saw him turn black. He collapsed on the ground after a while and was obviously dead."

"Did he leave a note? Any explanation?" Randolph asked.

"No," said Michael. "And as I found out later, he deliberately intended his death to be a mystery. When I eventually met him in a death trance, he explained that the only way that had been left to him to achieve spiritual understanding was to burn himself, to release his soul from his body, his *antakaranasarira*. It had been the happiest moment of his life, he said, and I should never grieve. He had left no explanation of why he had killed himself because he had wanted me to continue with my studies. Only by learning how to go into a death trance would I ever be able to find out why he had died."

Randolph ate a little beef. Then he asked, "Will you help me find my family?"

Michael pressed his hands together in front of his face as if he were thoughtfully praying. His eyes stared at Randolph like the eyes of a *sanghyang* dancer seen through the holes in a mask.

The girl called Mungkin Nanti very slowly shook her head. "He won't do it. He *can't*. You shouldn't ask him. The last time he nearly died."

"Don't you think he ought to be allowed to answer for himself?" Randolph suggested.

"He's not well. You can see how sick he has been."

"Yes," Randolph persisted, "but he's the only person in the world who can do this for me."

"Michael, you have to say no," Mungkin Nanti pleaded, taking his arm.

Michael shrugged. "I don't have to say anything, yes or no." He picked up another sea slug and ate it, washing it down with tea.

Dr. Ambara said, "All your expenses to Memphis would be paid for. This young lady could accompany you if you so wished it. And, believe me, Mr. Clare would be most generous in his appreciation."

"How generous?" Michael asked.

"How much do you charge?" Randolph responded.

Michael thought for a moment and then lowered his head. "No," he said, "I won't do it. I made a promise to Nanti, and that's a promise I have to keep."

Mungkin Nanti put her arms around him and hugged him. He looked up again and from long experience, Randolph knew that the flicker in his eyes was a little something called indecision.

He said the same words that he had spoken to I.M. Wartawa. "Fifty thousand dollars in cash. No questions asked. If you continue living here in Bali, you won't ever have to work again for the rest of your life."

Randolph knew that his offer was outrageous, almost absurd. But he had developed over the past few days the deepest aversion to inheriting any of Marmie's money. He felt that he would prefer to give it away rather than continue to use its interest, especially and most painfully because he no longer had any children to whom he could pass it on. He would far rather use the money to see Marmie again and tell her how much he still loved her.

Michael said, "How much? Fifty thousand? Are you serious?"

"How much were you paid before?"

"Five, ten thousand dollars. I think the most I ever got was ten."

"That was still quite a respectable fee. How come you're so broke?"

"Mah-jongg," put in Mungkin Nanti sharply. "The last time, after he was almost killed, he gambled away the whole fee in three hours flat. That's one of the reasons I made him promise to stop."

"Well, you can do whatever you like with your money," Randolph said. "I guess fifty thousand would last longer than ten, even if you lost it all at the gaming tables."

"You really mean that you'll pay me fifty thousand dollars if I take you into a death trance?"

Randolph nodded.

Mungkin Nanti said with undiluted bitterness, "I was right to call you a rapist, wasn't I, Mr. Clare? Rapists always attack the weak, and rapists always make sure they get what they want."

"Rapists usually take what they want by force, Miss Nanti. I'm offering money."

"So much money that it almost amounts to violence," Mungkin Nanti protested. "If you kill Michael, believe me, you'll be just as brutal as those men who killed your family."

"Michael has a choice. My family didn't."

"Who can possibly have a choice when he's offered fifty thousand dollars? The money or poverty. What kind of a choice is that?"

Michael raised his hand to silence them. "Mungkin Nanti's right," he said in his quiet, hoarse voice. "There isn't a choice. I'll do it."

"You promised!" Mungkin Nanti breathed at him fiercely. "Michael, you promised!"

"Nanti, in the face of fifty thousand dollars, not many promises stand much of a chance."

"So that's the price of your life, is it?" Mungkin Nanti snapped at him. "I've always wanted to know what kind of a value you place on yourself, and on me. Well, now I know, don't I? Down to the last cent."

She got up from the table, knocking her chair over backwards, and marched out of the restaurant. The Balinese waitress came over and picked up the chair. "Are you finished?" she asked hesitantly, looking at their dishes of uneaten food.

Michael took out a cigarette and lit it. "*Ya, terima kasih.*"

"*Berapa semuayana?*" asked Dr. Ambara. He seemed to have appointed himself to the position of Randolph's business manager.

"American dollar?" the waitress asked.

Dr. Ambara took out his wallet.

"Five dollar," the waitress told him.

"*Terlalu mahal,*" said Dr. Ambara flatly.

"Four dollar," the waitress suggested. Dr. Ambara thought it over and then made an acquiescent face and counted out four dollar bills.

"You people amaze me," Michael said. "One minute

you're offering me fifty thousand dollars to take you into a death trance and the next minute you're haggling about one lousy dollar for the price of a meal.''

Dr. Ambara said, ''I wanted to emphasize, Mr. Hunter, that we expect to have our money's worth. We expect to get as much value from every single one of those fifty thousand dollars as we did from every one of those four dollars we just spent on lunch.''

''I understand,'' Michael said. He glanced from Randolph to Wanda to Dr. Ambara and back again, his face veiled in cigarette smoke.

''What about your friend?'' asked Randolph.

''Oh, she'll be back. She always is.''

''She seemed pretty annoyed with you this time.''

Michael said, ''She saved my life. She's been keeping me together, in one reasonably cohesive piece, and I don't appreciate her half as much as I should. But sometimes, you know, you don't need people like that. Sometimes you have to throw yourself headfirst off the precipice, and it's better for everybody concerned, including yourself, if there's nobody there to grab your ankles. All of life is centered around commitments. My father was so committed to the Hindu ideal that he burned himself alive. When your father has done something like that, how can you spend the rest of your life sweeping floors and polishing windows? The leyaks are waiting for me. Rangda is waiting for me. I knew that right from the beginning. There are times when you can't rewrite your own destiny, no matter how much you may want to.''

Randolph drummed his fingertips on the table and then said quietly, ''How would you describe yourself if I asked you?''

Michael smiled. ''Mystic. Idiot. Religious zealot. Potential suicide.''

''But you've achieved what your father failed to achieve. You *are* Hindu. You understand the Trisakti from the inside . . . spiritually, not just intellectually.''

''Mr. Clare,'' Michael said. The circles under his eyes were as dark as plums. ''My suicide would be quite different from my father's. My father was trying to find total understanding. I *had* that understanding, right from the very moment I could understand anything. It is not the understanding I seek. It is the confrontation with the forces of evil. It is the challenge to Rangda. Sooner or later I am going to have to test myself against her. In one way or another, at one time or another, every man has to do it. Very few, of course, have the privilege of meeting her face-to-face. Few have the competence to be able to fight her, or the nerve. But . . . well, I think I've known all along that I'm going to have to come to grips with her sooner or later. Your money really hasn't made that much difference. It wasn't the deciding factor. It has simply helped me to make up my mind.''

Dr. Ambara said soberly, ''If you challenge Rangda, you will die.''

''Probably,'' Michael said, drawing tightly at his cigarette.

SIXTEEN

I.M. Wartawa was locking the door of his office when a tall man came quickly and quietly behind him, seized his left arm and touched the razor-sharp blade of a Bowie knife against his naked neck.

"Where did they go?" the man demanded hoarsely.

"Where did who go? I don't understand you," Wartawa protested.

"Mr. Randolph Clare, that's who. And his secretary. And that nigger doctor."

"I don't know what you're talking about," I.M. Wartawa winced. "I never heard of such people in my life."

"How would you like a free on-the-spot tracheotomy?" the man asked.

I.M. Wartawa licked his lips. "All right. I've heard of Mr. Randolph Clare."

"Where is he now?"

"How should I know? He came to talk to me about import-export. Then he went away."

"You're lying," the man told him, pressing the blade of the knife even more viciously against his Adam's apple. I.M. Wartawa felt blood slide warmly down the front of his neck and into his collar. Although he was frightened, he did not lose his self-control. He had been working for too long among the heavyweight gangsters who dominated Djakarta's crime; he had escaped too many times from sawed-off

240

shotguns and Molotov cocktails and splashes of concentrated sulphuric acid. There was always a get-out. There
was always a deal to be made. Everybody wanted something; everybody had his price. This man, whoever he might
be, would be no exception.

"Let's talk about this reasonably," he said.

"Let's talk about this now," the man retorted.

"All right, you want to talk about it now. Mr. Clare left
Djakarta this morning on Garuda Airlines."

"Where was he headed?"

"How should I know? We talked a little business, that's
all."

"If that's all you talked about, buddy, then believe me, I
don't need you anymore and I'm going to cut your throat.
Here and now, from ear to ear. Look around. You see this
hallway? This is where you're going to die."

I.M. Wartawa said, "He flew to Bali."

"Bali? Why'd he go there?"

"He went there because I suggested it."

"Oh, yes?" the man asked caustically. "And why did
you suggest that?"

"Listen," said I.M. Wartawa, "I can pay you twenty
thousand dollars. That's how much Mr. Clare gave me."

"Now why would you want to do a thing like that?" the
man asked with a sudden grin.

"To let me go. To take that knife away from my throat.
All of it, twenty thousand in cash. Right here and now."

The man said, "You still haven't told me why Mr.
Randolph Clare and his friends flew off to Bali."

"I don't know. They wouldn't discuss it."

"But you suggested it."

"Just for the scenery, that's all."

"The scenery? That's rich. You have twenty seconds left,
hairball, and then you're going to die."

"They were looking for somebody." I.M. Wartawa managed to choke out.

"Oh, yes? They were looking for somebody, were they?
Well, I hope you don't mind if I'm impertinent enough to
ask you who that somebody might be. I mean, that some-

body must've been somebody pretty special for a man like Mr. Randolph Clare to fly all the way from Memphis, Tennessee, to find him and, in addition, to pay off a scum-bag like you.''

"Mr. Clare was looking for a death-trance adept."

"Mr. Clare was looking for *whut*?''

"A death-trance adept. Somebody who can take you right through the spiritual barrier of death so you can meet friends and relatives who might have recently passed away.''

"Are you putting me on?'' The knife cut even more viciously into I.M. Wartawa's skin.

"It's true. That's the whole reason Mr. Clare came to Indonesia. He told me his family was recently killed. He wanted to talk to his wife and children again. The only way he can possibly do that is through a *pedanda*, a special high priest, somebody trained to go into a death trance and guide other people into the trance with him. That way Mr. Clare can go beyond death, into the world of the dead; don't you understand me? He can meet his family again, their spirits. He can talk to them, touch them as if they were real, as if they were still alive. It sounds crazy, I know, but it can be done; it *has* been done. It's all in a trance.''

The man said, "He goes into this trance and he meets his family again? He meets them for real?'' His voice crawled with suspicion.

"Do you think I would say such a thing with a knife at my throat if it wasn't the absolute truth?''

There was a long pause. The man kept the blade pressed hard against I.M. Wartawa's larynx. Although the blood had stopped flowing now, I.M. Wartawa could feel the stickiness around the collar of his shirt.

"They went to Bali, huh?'' the man asked at last. "What part of Bali? To Denpasar?''

"That's right. To Denpasar.''

"You got a name? Who was it they went to see? One of these death-trance guys? One of these addicts?''

"Adepts,'' I.M. Wartawa corrected him with a painful swallow.

"Well, who was it?"

"One of the best. Michael Hunter. He's half-American, but he was trained in Hindu mysticism from childhood. He has a special talent for the death trance."

"How about a location?" the man wanted to know.

"I was given an address on Jalan Pudak. Number 12a."

"You're not trying to fool me, are you?"

"Fool you? Why should I try to fool you?" I.M. Wartawa gasped.

Without another word, the man sliced the Bowie knife from one side of I.M. Wartawa's throat to the other, cutting through to his windpipe. I.M. Wartawa knew instantly that he had been killed, but as the blood fountained out of his neck, he found it impossible to speak, impossible to cry out. His legs buckled under him and he found himself staring at the linoleum on the floor, his body shivering and shaking as if he were cold. The man stood over him, watching him die. The dark blood formed a wide oval pool on the landing, with the glossiest and most reflective of surfaces. I.M. Wartawa suddenly thought of something his father had told him, something he had never understood. It seemed clear now, crystal clear, and he wondered why it had taken death to bring him realization.

His father had said one morning, close to the end of his life, "The good is one thing, the pleasant is another. It is well with him who clings to the good; he who chooses the pleasant misses his end."

I.M. Wartawa tried to turn his head, to explain to the man who was standing over him what he had at last understood. But there was nothing except darkness; the man seemed to have vanished. The world had turned into a black, hollow, echoing tunnel.

He died, feeling that he was falling.

The moment he died, Michael Hunter was arriving at Randolph's *losmen* on Jalan Diponegoro and paying off the taxi driver with some of the fifty *rupiahs* Dr. Ambara had given him. It was a brilliant, hot morning and the air was bright with dust and fragrant with the sweet aroma of flowers. Michael wore the same Ever-Ready T-shirt he had been wearing the day before and a pair of ragged shorts that had once been jeans. He was smoking a cigarette. His hair was wet, just washed, and combed straight back from his narrow forehead. When he asked the pretty, plump girl behind the desk for Mr. Clare, she pointed upstairs and said, "Number Five."

Michael knocked briskly at Randolph's door. "It's me," he called, and for some reason, he felt more American than he had in years, although he had never been to America. He pinched his cigarette out between his fingers and tucked it behind his ear.

Randolph opened the door. He was dressed in light-gray summer slacks and a white shirt, and he looked tired. Michael said, "Here I am, as promised."

"Good," Randolph said. "Do you want to come in?"

"We shouldn't be too long," Michael told him. "We have to start your studies right away. You didn't eat any breakfast, did you?"

"No, I didn't eat any breakfast."

Michael prowled around the room, prodding the bed, picking up the book Randolph was reading, *Iacocca*, peering out the window, running his fingertips down the bamboo blinds.

"This isn't much of a place, is it?" he asked. "A man like you, with fifty thousand dollars to spend, why doesn't he have a suite at the Hotel Denpasar?"

"I prefer someplace modest," Randolph said. "Maybe you could call it a fetish of mine."

"Well, this is modest all right," Michael agreed.

"Is the temple far?" Randolph asked.

"It's just beyond the market on Jalan Mahabharata. We can walk if you prefer. It's more calming to walk."

Michael had recommended that Randolph begin his training first, before Dr. Ambara, since the doctor was already acquainted with the Trisakti, and with the demons and gods who influenced the natural world. Michael had also insisted that the first week of training be undertaken here in Denpasar, the navel of the world, where the spiritual forces were strongest. In Memphis it would be far more difficult for Randolph to sense the subtle changes of atmosphere that preceded the death trance; it would be even more difficult for him to sense the closeness of the spirits, both benign and malevolent.

They walked together along Jalan Diponegoro. Michael seemed more settled than when Randolph had first met him, although he talked quite busily, waved in a friendly way to several stall-keepers he knew and kept his eyes flickering around as if he were always alert, always looking for the tiniest indication that the forces of the spiritual world might be making themselves felt in the everyday bustle of the streets.

"Did you make up with your girlfriend?" Randolph asked.

"We're still a little on edge," Michael confessed.

"What happened the last time you went into a death trance? Was it really as dangerous as she claims?"

Michael reached into his shirt pocket for a cigarette. "I was trying to trace the dead husband of a woman who lives in Sanur. She was pretty wealthy. Her husband had been a merchant and when he died, he left everything to her. At least he *said* he had. All of a sudden his former secretary started driving around in a new Mercedes. The woman wanted me to find her dead husband for her and straighten things out, to find out just how much he had given his secretary. I guess her actual intention was to challenge his will."

"That seems like a very mundane, materialistic reason for doing something incredibly spiritual," Randolph suggested.

"That's what people pay for," Michael said, shrugging. "You don't often see much in the way of sentiment, not in this business. If people have enough money to pay for a death trance, they're usually the kind of people who are looking for more money. You know what I mean? Their greed goes even beyond the grave."

He guided Randolph across Puputan Square. "Mind you," he said, "I was approached by a man once who wanted to see his dead mistress just so he could insult her. I refused to take him. You can't go into a death trance when you're angry or upset. Well, you *can,* but it's too dangerous. The leyaks have terrific sensitivity for negative emotions. They can pick up your anger almost instantly, and then they're on to you.''

He led the way across Jalan Durian and between a host of jangling bicycles. ''That's what happened the last time. The woman confronted her dead husband and he admitted that he had given his secretary something like two hundred thousand dollars. Before we went into the death trance, the woman had promised me faithfully that she would keep her cool no matter what her husband said to her. But when she heard him say that, she went crazy. She was absolutely hysterical. I couldn't get her out of the trance, she was so furious, and I couldn't very well leave her there. The leyaks were after us like wild dogs. I managed to keep them off, and in the end I managed to bring the stupid woman around, but it was pretty damned hair-raising at the time.'' He opened his shirt and showed Randolph an ugly tear-shaped scar that looked as if some vicious animal had tried to bite a lump of flesh from his chest. ''One of them got me just as I was coming through. I was lucky they didn't follow me; I would have been dead meat for sure.''

He took a deep drag at his cigarette and said, ''That's when Nanti made me promise not to do it again. Well, I don't blame her. She had to nurse me for nearly two months. I couldn't go to a doctor because he would have asked me how I got hurt, and the death trance is against the law. The bite went septic, septic like you wouldn't believe.''

They walked together along the narrow, shabby street where the Pura Dalem still stood, the Temple of the Dead. Randolph stood back, staring in silent apprehension at the carved effigies of Rangda and Barong Keket, thick with moss and wound around with creeper.

''That's Rangda, the Witch Widow,'' Michael explained. ''Take a look at that statue and pray you never meet her in the flesh.''

Randolph turned to Michael and attempted a smile, but Michael was not smiling.

They pushed open the green-copper gates and stepped

inside the outer courtyard. Although the sun was shining brightly, it hardly penetrated this courtyard and there was an unexpected chill in the air. They took off their shoes. Michael walked across the courtyard on silent feet and Randolph followed him.

"Doesn't anybody use this temple anymore?" Randolph asked in a hushed voice.

"Only me," Michael replied, looking back at him with dark Balinese eyes.

"I'm surprised the city administrators let the place stand."

"It's sacred ground. Inside these walls we are neither on earth nor in heaven. The general belief is that when this temple finally collapses, it will be sucked away into the world beyond the veil and there will be nothing left here at all."

"Do you believe that?"

"When *you* believe it, tell me," Michael replied.

They went through to the inner courtyard. Michael said, "Please take off your clothes and then sit on the floor. I must light the incense."

"Do we have to be naked?" Randolph asked.

Michael was already stepping out of his shorts. "To begin with, yes. It's very difficult for a novice to pass through the spiritual levels of death when he is carrying any physical reminders of the real world. Remember that we will be going out of this world, and we have to go out of this world in the same condition as we entered it."

Rather reluctantly Randolph undressed and folded his clothes neatly beside one of the shrines. He eased himself onto the stone floor and waited while Michael went to each of the incense burners and lit them. Thick, pungent clouds of spices and sandalwood began to drift across the courtyard, half-obscuring Michael's lean, bare figure.

When all the burners were lit, Michael came over and sat facing Randolph cross-legged, his hands spread out with the palms facing upward.

"Is your mind at peace?" he asked.

"I think so."

"Your mind must be completely at peace. It must be a bright blue lake whose surface is utterly tranquil. You must think of nothing; you must not even wonder if you are at peace or not. You must ask no questions, doubt no doubts."

Randolph sat still and tried to empty his mind. It was not as easy to do as Michael had made it sound. He could picture the bright blue lake but its surface was ruffled by fretful little questions. Was he really going to be able to see Marmie and the children? Was he making a fool of himself, sitting here bare-ass naked in a stone-floored courtyard in Bali? Would Sun-Taste allow him more time to make up the shortfall in supplies? Why was his back aching so much? How the hell had he managed to get himself into this? And for fifty thousand dollars too.

Michael said, "You're too agitated. Your mind is like alphabet soup. Calm down. Make a deliberate effort to calm down, a really strenuous effort. Then relax. After the second or third attempt, your mind should remain calm."

Randolph closed his eyes and tried to force all the jumbled questions and fragmented worries out of his head. At last darkness and emptiness began to supervene and he relaxed.

"That's better," Michael said. "You may have to do that again in a moment, when the thoughts start forcing their way back in again. But next time you will find it much easier to dismiss them."

Randolph opened his eyes. Michael was watching him expressionlessly.

"This morning we are not going to enter the region of the dead," Michael said, "but I am going to take you to the first spiritual plane so you will understand both the togetherness and the separateness of your body and your soul."

Randolph was aware of the doubts and the questions babbling back into his mind and he made another fierce effort to quiet them.

"Sit in the way that I am sitting," Michael instructed him. "Keep your eyes open, look straight ahead and try to picture your spirit as something that has its own freedom, a life force that is occupying your body simply as a way of manifesting itself in the physical world. It will help you if you repeat the mantra *Om*, the sacred word that embodies all the divine principles of Hindu theology.''

Randolph sat in the way that Michael was sitting, his hands outstretched, his back balanced and perfectly straight. Under normal circumstances he would have found this position desperately uncomfortable. He remembered sitting on the floor at a Japanese restaurant in San Francisco and ending up with a backache for a week afterward. But this morning, somehow the position seemed to be perfect. He did his best to keep his mind empty and he stared straight ahead, and when Michael prompted him, he began to hum the mantra. ''*Ommmmm*. . . .''

He hummed on and on, keeping his brain as calm as he could. It was strange but the humming of the mantra seemed to set up an extraordinary vibration within him, as if his bones were resonating. It was infinitely tedious, humming and humming like this, and yet he found it peculiarly difficult to stop. Somehow the idea of stopping seemed to be unpleasant, almost threatening.

''*Ommmm*. . . .''

He could not imagine what to expect. The temple courtyard appeared to remain the same as before, with its crumbled rows of shrines. Dried leaves still rustled across the flagstones and incense-smoke still wafted thickly in the air. The humming went on and on, overwhelming everything: the traffic, the sound of distant music, the roar of a plane above. Randolph felt as if his whole being were vibrating, as if he would shatter into dust if he tried to stop humming the mantra.

He stared at Michael. Then he stared at him again more closely. He wondered if the incense was making his eyes water or if he needed to wear his glasses more often. But Michael's outline appeared to be blurred; it was as if hot air were rising between them, or as if Michael were lying just below the surface of a clear but quickly running stream.

He wanted to say something, to ask Michael what was happening, but his mouth refused to do anything but hum the mantra. Then, right in front of his eyes, a liquid kind of creature slithered out of the top of Michael's head and spiraled off into the smoky air. Randolph followed it with his eyes as it spun and danced and hovered over the courtyard, and then as it slowly returned toward Michael, and he was stunned with fascination and fear. The liquid creature was actually Michael; it looked like Michael except that it was translucent and completely fluid. Randolph could distinguish Michael's features, he could recognize his face, and yet Michael's forehead kept rippling and stretching, his arms and legs flowed and twisted. Michael's real body remained where it was, sitting on the floor of the courtyard, its eyes open, still staring blankly at Randolph and humming the mantra.

Michael's spirit—for that was what the liquid creature actually was, his *antakaranasarira*—beckoned with both arms to Randolph and smiled a fleeting, watery smile. Randolph heard a slight deflection in the endless vibration of *Om* and it seemed to mean to him, "Rise, rise up, join me, rise out of your body and join me."

For an instant Randolph thought: *This is impossible, it can't be done.* But then the split second afterward, a huge and sudden realization rushed out at him with the darkness and power of a hurtling locomotive and he was yanked out of his body upside down and sent spinning end over end; he saw rooftops, clouds, walls, traffic and trees before sinking again, much more slowly now, sinking toward the courtyard floor; and there below him was *himself*, naked, cross-legged, humming his sacred mantra.

Michael's spirit flowed across to meet Randolph as he descended. All of Randolph's fear had left him now. He slowly approached his material body and drifted around himself to see what he looked like. He found the experience astonishing. He looked much older than he had imagined himself to be, and much more heavily built. His stomach could do with some exercise, he thought, and there was a wider bald patch at the back of his scalp than he had realized; but apart from that, he was not bad looking. Michael's spirit followed him, watching him, and then raised an arm to point upward, toward the sky.

Together they floated high over the temple, higher than the rooftops of the tallest shrines, higher than the trees, floating like two kites over the markets and the streets and the glittering river. They dived and dipped and soared and then at last began to sink back toward Jalan Mahabharata, and the Temple of the Dead, and their material bodies.

Sliding back into his body felt to Randolph like sliding under the bedclothes on a summer's night. For the first few moments he felt hot and stuffy and constricted, and he shook his arms again and again to relieve the feeling of heaviness. Michael laughed and stood up.

"Everybody does that. You're feeling the weight of your body after having had no weight at all."

Randolph stared up at him and then turned to look at the sky. "Were we really there? Did we really do that?"

"Our spirits were there."

"I never before understood what my spirit is. Why haven't I been doing that all my life, going out of myself? It is fantastic! Who needs to go by plane?"

Michael tugged on his shorts and zipped them up. "I don't think you understand just how much I was helping you. I practically pulled your *antakaranasarira* out of you by its roots. Besides, it's dangerous to do too much of that flying around; it can get to a point where your spirit is unable to get back into your body. Then all your spirit can do is hover around and watch your body die. That's what happens to people in comas. Their spirit leaves their body for so long that it can't get back in again. Just remember that when your spirit leaves your body, you're halfway dead."

Randolph eased himself to his feet. "Is that all we're going to do today?"

Michael said, "We can go back to your *losmen* now and I'll teach you the first of the chants you're going to need to know. I'll tell you what you're going to be allowed to eat too. From now on, until we enter the death trance, you have to stay with a special holy diet."

As they left the temple, Randolph said, "This all seems quite practical. I had the impression when Dr. Ambara first described it to me that it was going to be very mystical, very religious.''

"The ways of the Trisakti have always been practical,'' Michael said. "It's only through practical experience that you can achieve enlightenment. Of course there are many different kinds of enlightenment. Some kinds are completely theological, completely abstract. Other kinds can be much more ordinary, much more concerned with earthly things.''

Randolph walked back through the streets of Denpasar feeling as if he had just been born. He felt innocent, happy and incredibly alive. He had only one regret: that he should have had to lose Marmie and the children to discover what his spirit was.

Michael talked volubly on their way to the temple. "You'll be able to feel all the magical power here once you develop your psychic talents. This city is absolutely teeming with magic. When you're in a death trance, you can walk through the streets and look around and see demons and spirits everywhere. It's one of the great magical capitals of the world, maybe the greatest.''

They reached the *losmen* and went upstairs. Wanda and Dr. Ambara were supposed to have gone out shopping while Randolph was studying with Michael, but when Randolph unlocked the door of his room, he found them sitting there. They looked up anxiously as he entered and Dr. Ambara said, "You're back. I was beginning to worry.''

"What's happened?" Randolph asked. "Wanda? Is everything all right?''

"We had a call from the police in Djakarta. They found our names in I.M. Wartawa's address book. They called Memphis first and then Memphis directed them here.''

Randolph slowly walked across the room. "Have the police discovered what we're trying to do?''

"No," Dr. Ambara said. "But in some ways it could be worse than that. I.M. Wartawa was found dead outside his office early this morning. His throat had been cut.''

"My God!" Randolph breathed. "Do the police have any idea of who might have done it?''

"Well, of course that was what they wanted to know from *me*. They said that three or possibly four men were seen driving away from the building shortly afterward. Americans in appearance, but nobody was sure."

"It's Ecker again, isn't it?" Wanda asked.

Randolph ran his hand through his hair. All the exhilaration of releasing his spirit into the morning sky had been deflated now. "It certainly sounds like Ecker."

"And the probability is, of course, that I.M. Wartawa told him where we are, and why, and with whom."

Michael asked, "Who's this Ecker?"

Randolph went over to the small refrigerator and took out two bottles of beer. "Do you want one?" he asked Michael, but Michael shook his head. Randolph pried open the cap of one of the bottles and drank the beer straight from the neck. Then he said, "Ecker is one of four very tough-looking characters who have been following us all the way from the continental United States. Ecker seems to be the leader, although we've never heard him talk. Maybe he's a mute, something like that. Whatever, they've been sticking pretty close to us and we have reason to believe they might be the same people who murdered my family."

"In which case, they probably want to murder you too," Michael said equably.

"Not necessarily," said Randolph. "They may be doing nothing more than trying to scare me. After all, they haven't done very much to keep themselves hidden. On the flight out from Honolulu, they were positively glaring at me, right out in the open. I was frightened at first that they were sent out to kill me, but the more I think about it, the more likely it seems that they were sent just to keep tabs on whatever I was doing. Maybe to warn me off too. To remind me to behave myself and stop competing with some of my influential competitors back home."

Michael sniffed and took out a cigarette. "He may not have wanted to kill you at first, this Ecker, but if he has been talking to I.M. Wartawa and if I.M. Wartawa has been talking to him, he's going to know that you're attempting to meet your wife and children."

"And?" Wanda asked.

"And nothing," Michael replied, scratching a match on the side of Randolph's closet door and lighting his cigarette. "Except that your wife and children were the only eye-witnesses to their own deaths, the only ones who saw who killed them. And so if *I* were this Ecker character, I'd do everything I could to make sure you never got to talk to them."

SEVENTEEN

Memphis, Tennessee

Waverley Graceworthy was sitting in the huge library of his mansion on Elvis Presley Boulevard playing backgammon with his niece, Gertrude, when the butler came in to announce that Mr. Neil Sleaman was paying him an unexpected visit.

"You'd better show Mr. Sleaman into the study," Waverley told the butler. He reached over and patted Gertrude's blond, braided hair and smiled. "Go to the kitchen, why don't you, Gertie, and ask Mrs. Morris for some of her sand tarts. Tell her you can have a glass of hot, brandied milk to wash them down with."

He walked along the wide, carpeted corridor, his hands tucked into the pockets of his red-quilted smoking jacket, until he reached the study. Usually Waverley referred to the study as his "den," although it was large enough to accommodate a fair-sized family bungalow, complete with carport. There were huge, dark oil paintings on the walls, mostly of Confederate victories: Bull Run and Fredericksburg, and the armored steamboat battle off Memphis in 1862. There was a cavernous fireplace but today the fire was not lit. The temperature at midday had been well up into the low nineties and the night promised to be sticky.

Neil Sleaman was standing by the fireplace holding a thin, black-leather briefcase. He looked pale. Randolph, of course, had been calling him erratically day and night and expecting immediate answers to all his questions.

"Glad you stopped by," Waverley said, offering Neil an armchair. "Is there anything I can get you to drink?"

"A beer would be fine," Neil said.

Waverley went to the fireplace and pushed the button beside the marble surround. "I usually prefer it, of course, if we make our meetings a little more discreet."

"I'm sorry, but I didn't want to tell you this on the telephone and I thought you would probably want to hear about it immediately. Randolph called me only fifteen minutes ago and said he was making arrangements to come back to Memphis."

"When?" Waverley asked. "Not right away, surely."

"On the first available flight. That's Garuda Airlines to Djakarta, then Thai International to London via Bangkok. He could be back here in Memphis by Saturday afternoon."

"Did he give you any idea of why he has decided to come back so soon?"

Neil put down his briefcase as if it hadn't really been worth carrying anyway. "He said that he'd been having some fresh thoughts about the Sun-Taste contract and that he'd probably found a way to solve our problems, that's all."

"Sun-Taste expects him to make up the shortfall by tomorrow, doesn't it?"

"That's correct according to the contract. But Randolph must have spoken to Sun-Taste's president direct from Bali. Randolph's given them his personal guarantee that he can make up the shortfall by the end of next week, and he's also promised that any tonnage that arrives later than originally contracted for will be free of charge."

"Now, let's hold on here," Waverley said, raising his hand to his fine-boned chin. "You've been giving me *your* personal guarantee that Raleigh won't be back on line until Friday at the very earliest."

"That's correct," Neil insisted. "There is no way that even one barrel of processed cottonseed oil can be produced by that plant until three o'clock Friday afternoon. No way at all. They don't even have the new valves assembled yet."

"So how can Randolph possibly suggest that he can make up the shortfall? And how in *hell* can he offer any tonnage for free? He'll put himself straight out of business."

Neil took a sharp breath. "Waverley," he said, "I really don't know, and that's why I'm here. I mean, there's always a possibility that grieving over his family has turned Randolph's mind a little. Maybe he's gone over the edge. But he sounded very calm when he called today. He sounded like he was in complete control of what he was doing."

Waverley frowned. "He can't have found an alternative source of supply. Gamble's is all committed, and the Association certainly isn't going to let him have any. Even if he has managed to find some abroad, he can't possibly ship it to Memphis by the end of next week. It isn't technologically possible. Damn it all, it isn't *humanly* possible."

The butler knocked at the door and Waverley called him in. The butler was English, smooth-faced, plump and exaggeratedly glib. Only another Englishman would have detected the lowliness of his accent and the endless sarcasm of his manner. Waverley thought he was almost aristocracy.

"A beer for Mr. Sleaman," Waverley ordered.

"By all means, Mr. Graceworthy," bowed the butler and withdrew.

"Fine man," said Waverley. "Now listen, where were we?"

Neil perched himself awkwardly on the arm of one of Waverley's hide-covered armchairs. "You did suggest that we wouldn't have any more problems with Randolph once he went off on vacation. I didn't know how or why. I didn't ask. But it obviously hasn't worked, has it?

Waverley pattered his delicate fingers against the surface of the burled-walnut table. It sounded like falling rain on a lonely night in one of Elvis Presley's sad and romantic songs. "I have to make some calls. For some reason, not everything went according to plan. Well, it's a war, isn't it, of sorts? And in wars, mistakes sometimes crop up, misjudgments."

With sudden intuition, Neil said, "You didn't arrange for anybody to beat him up, did you?"

Waverley raised his head. His watery eyes were cold and uncompromising. "My dear young man," he remonstrated and then turned away so that Neil would find it awkward to engage his attention.

But Neil persisted. "You didn't arrange for anything worse than that? I mean, you didn't send Reece after him, did you?"

"Poof," Waverley said dismissively.

Neil stood up. "You sent Reece. I should have known it."

Waverley turned back to him. "So what if I did send Reece? What do you have to be so righteous about? What do you think the Clares did to me and to my family? What do you think Randolph Clare is doing to me now? Would *you* suffer such injustices? Would *you* allow the son of the man who destroyed your personal life to complete the job his father left unfinished and destroy your business life too? Would you? The Clares are like jackals, father and son, feeding on the achievements of others, sucking them dry. They're not creators; they're not initiators. Everybody praises their business acumen; everybody praises their independence and their tenacity. But only I know what scavengers they are. Only I know what predators they are. It was only my pride and my dignity and my sense of humanity to my wife that allowed Randolph Clare's father to remain independent. It was only my sense of justice that allowed Randolph Clare himself to develop his business as far as he has. Now he has gone too far. Now I withdraw my goodwill. Now he has to suffer the consequences of what his father did."

Neil Sleaman was silent for a moment and then he said with surprised respect, "That was quite a speech."

The butler came back with Neil's beer in a tall, trumpet-shaped glass. While he drank it, Waverley impatiently walked around the study tapping the knuckle of his thumb against his front teeth. Neil, with white froth on his upper lip, asked, "Does Orbus know you sent Reece after Randolph?"

"Yes."

"And what does Orbus think about it?"

Waverley gave a shrug. "What Orbus thinks about it is not particularly relevant. For me, this is a personal matter as well as a business matter."

He walked across to his desk. There was a large silver inkstand, a bronze Tiffany lamp in the form of intertwined orchids and two silver-framed photographs, one of Waverley's father, a fine mustachioed man with a stiff white collar, and the other of Waverley's mother, an alluring woman with a feathered hat and dark, curly hair. "Personal," Waverley repeated and lifted his eyes to stare at Neil challengingly, daring him to criticize, daring him to doubt what he was doing just one more time.

"I'd better go then," Neil told him. "I'll give you a call on your answering machine if I hear from Randolph again during the night."

He finished his beer with one last hurried swallow, wiped his mouth with his handkerchief, collected his briefcase and went to the door.

"Neil," Waverley said sharply, and Neil hesitated, his hand on the doorknob. "Never question me again, Neil," Waverley told him.

Neil looked as if he were about to say something but changed his mind. Waverley heard him walk down the hallway and then the unctuous voice of the butler bidding him good night.

Waverley remained where he was, a diminutive figure in the vastness of his den. The light from the Tiffany lamp shone green on his glasses so that for one second he looked as if he had the eyes of a demon. He opened a drawer of his desk and looked inside. It was scrupulously neat: pens, pencils, rubber bands, paper clips, scissors, everything in its allotted slot. At the back of the drawer, however, there was another photograph in a frame matching those of Waverley's mother's and father's. A serious, pretty girl standing outside a white-painted house, a girl whose eyes were strikingly violet and whose hair was the color of touch-me-nots.

Waverley looked down at her for a moment and then angrily closed the drawer. He returned to the library to find that Gertrude had tired of waiting for him to come back for their game of backgammon and had put the set away.

It was a little over an hour later when the telephone rang in the library and the butler announced that Mr. Robert Stroup was on the phone from Denpasar, Bali. Waverley said tersely, "Put him through."

There was a distant, ringing echo on the line but otherwise Waverley could hear Bob Stroup quite well. Bob Stroup was Reece's mouthpiece. The two of them had an uncanny, silent rapport that had been developed through years of boyhood friendship, and climactically when the First U.S. Cavalry Division penetrated the Fish Hook in Cambodia in 1970. Reece had been captured by Viet Cong and his tongue had been sliced out. Stroup had disobeyed orders and penetrated six miles into the jungle to find him. Ever since then, Stroup had expressed everything that Reece wanted to say: accurately, volubly and usually profanely.

"Did you locate Randolph Clare yet?" Waverley asked him.

"We're close, Mr. Graceworthy, I gotta tell you. We're so damn close we can smell him."

"But you haven't actually located him?"

"Not actually, if you want to use that word."

Waverley let out a tiny sigh of impatience. "How long do you think it's going to take to find him?"

"That depends. We've been spreading some money around but the people here are kind of dumb, if you know what I mean. They want to poke into your business but they won't tell you theirs. They're different from Vietnamese, I gotta tell you."

"Do you yet have any idea of why Randolph Clare went to Southeast Asia? Has he been talking to any businessmen? Any food processors? Any fabric factories?"

"Not so far as we can tell, Mr. Graceworthy. I mean, as far as we can tell, he came here for nothing else but to find this guy Michael Hunter, this death-trance addict."

Waverley frowned. "What guy Michael Hunter? You haven't told me about this."

"We haven't?" queried Bob Stroup. Then, "Hell, no, I

guess we haven't. As soon as we found out where Clare was headed, we lit out after him. Straightaway, Bali here we come. I gotta tell you how hot it is here. And the food, how can they eat this shit? I don't care if I never see a grain of rice again in my whole damn life. They eat snakes too, would you believe? Stir-fried snakes. The first thing I'm gonna do when I get back to Memphis is go straight to The Butcher Shop and cook myself a twenty-four-ounce sirloin with two baked potatoes and half the fucking salad bar, I gotta tell you.''

''Bob,'' Waverley interrupted him caustically, ''I want to know about this Michael Hunter.''

''Well, sure, he's a death-trance addict. Well, the word isn't addict but I forget the other word. It means when you're good at something.''

''Adept,'' put in Waverley.

''You got it. Adept. And what he does is, he goes into this death trance and he can talk to people who are dead.''

''He can talk to people who are dead?'' Waverley asked, pronouncing his words with exaggerated care as if speaking to a retarded child.

''The guy we wasted in Djakarta told us all about it.''

''Before or after he was dead?'' Waverley asked sarcastically.

''Before, of course. But he had a full-sized thirty-five-dollar Bowie knife pressed up against his throat so I don't think he was lying too much. He wasn't one of your down-and-outs either. We opened his office up and he had more than twenty big ones in cash. The money had a note with it saying, 'As per Mr. G. Twyford's instructions,' if that makes any sense.''

The hair on the back of Waverley's neck prickled. ''It certainly does make sense. George Twyford is Randolph Clare's accountant. So presumably those twenty thousand dollars were sent to this man you killed as a payment from Randolph Clare.''

''Well, that's kind of the way we figured it,'' Bob Stroup agreed. ''This guy we killed told Clare and his pals where to find this Michael Hunter, and Clare paid him for the information.''

''But twenty thousand dollars?''

Bob Stroup sounded a little embarrassed. ''We laughed at him too, you know, when he first started talking about meeting dead people and stuff like that. But he said it wasn't crazy at all. It really happens. Provided they can rake up the money to pay for it, almost everyone can go meet his dead Aunt Minnie. He said all kinds of people do it. Even big American corporations do it. It's crazy, but it works.''

''Well, Randolph Clare seems to think it works,'' Waverley remarked. ''Otherwise he wouldn't have paid your deceased friend as much as twenty thousand dollars.''

''Well, there you go,'' said Bob Stroup. ''The only hitch is, we can't locate this Michael Hunter. We'll do it, believe me. We'll find him. But he's one of these ghost characters; everybody saw him yesterday but nobody's seen him today.''

Waverley asked, ''What do you think Randolph Clare is trying to do?''

''I don't know. Maybe he wants to talk to his father. Or maybe to his family . . . you know, his wife and his kids. My sister went to a spiritualist right after her husband was killed. Danzarotti, his name was. Her husband, not the medium.''

''Bob,'' Waverley said cuttingly, ''supposing it works?''

''Supposing it works?'' queried Bob Stroup, baffled. ''Well, supposing it does?''

''Bob, who saw you kill the Clare family?''

''Only the woman and the kids themselves, and they're dead, right? Dead men tell no tales. Nor women neither. Nor . . .'' he stopped in mid-sentence. It had just occurred to him what it was that Waverley had been trying to suggest.

''Eyewitnesses,'' he whispered.

''Did you ever take your masks off?'' Waverley asked.

''Right at the end we did, when the woman and the girl were hanging from the rafters. That was something we wanted to relish good, you know, and what can you see from the inside of a fucking ice-hockey mask?''

He hesitated, and even over the international telephone

link, his voice was beginning to sound haunted. "Besides—
you know—they were *dead*, or almost. So what could they
possibly do? Who could they tell? We strung 'em up with
barbed wire, and—"

"That's enough!" Waverley snapped. "The last thing I
want is to hear you incriminating yourself over the telephone. There's no bug at this end but God only knows what
listening and recording devices they have on the satellite.
Chief Moyne was telling me that they have electronic sen-
sors that automatically start recorders going every time a
key word gets mentioned, like 'gun' or 'dope' or something
like that."

"Well, if that's true, you just started them going full-
belt," Bob Stroup retorted with an unexpected crow of
pleasure.

"For Christ's sake!" Waverley rapped at him. "You're
not so stupid that you can't see it for yourself. If this
Michael Hunter really can arrange for Randolph Clare to
talk to his wife and children, what's the second thing he's
going to say to them after telling them how much he loves
them?"

Bob Stroup sniffed. "I guess he's going to want to know
who did it."

"Precisely. He's going to want to know who did it. And
if this Michael Hunter is genuine, the possibilities are that
he's going to find out."

"So we'd better waste him as soon as we find him."

"You bet you'd better. And you don't have much time.
Neil Sleaman called in earlier this evening and said that
Randolph Clare was on the way home. This morning's
flight to Djakarta, or tomorrow morning's flight as far as
you're concerned. Then straight back to Memphis by way of
London."

Bob Stroup asked, "Doesn't Neil Sleaman know where
Clare is? Once we know where Clare is, we can track down
this Michael Hunter too."

"Clare's been careful not to tell Neil where he's staying.
Neil kept asking him but he kept refusing, and Neil didn't
want to push it too hard. I don't think Clare suspects Neil,

but he didn't want anybody to know where he was. Privacy, he said, no intrusive phone calls from the factory. But he's probably making sure that nobody accidentally or not-so-accidentally passes his address on to you and Reece or those other coyotes of yours."

"You want to give me some instructions?" Bob Stroup asked.

"Yes. Find Randolph Clare as quickly as you possibly can and dispose of him just as we arranged. Then find this Michael Hunter and make sure you deal with him too, especially if he has already had the opportunity to speak to Randolph Clare. I don't want him talking to Clare's family after Clare is dead and putting the finger on us posthumously. Then I want you to fly straight back to Memphis on the earliest possible flight."

"Supposing we don't catch up with Clare before he leaves Bali?"

"Let's just say that you had better."

"But if we don't?"

"Give it twenty-four hours. Keep on searching, then fly back here. But I know you're not going to disappoint me, you and Reece. You never do."

He heard a clock out in the hall chime twelve-thirty, a deep Westminster chime, as sonorous as death itself. He thought about Randolph actually talking to Marmie again. It was quite poignant in a way. He had always liked Marmie. He had certainly not borne her any personal malice. But then his eyes strayed across the library to where the Bechstein stood, its lid as shiny as a lake of ink, and on the stand there was the score for Mozart's Fantasy and Sonata in C-Minor, a melody Ilona used to play.

And suddenly he thought to himself, *Ilona*.

"Bob?" he said. "You still there?"

"Still here, Mr. Graceworthy."

"Bob . . . see what you can do to bring me this Michael Hunter alive."

"Alive? That ain't gonna be easy."

"See what you can do. If you need more money, just call me. I'll wire it to you."

"Whatever you say, Mr. Graceworthy."

Waverley put down the phone but sat for a long time holding the receiver in his hand. It was only when his butler came in and asked if he wanted his bath drawn that Waverley blinked and focused his eyes.

"You are well, sir, I trust?" his butler sneered.

"Quite well, thank you. Would you fix me a brandy and soda?"

"But of course, Mr. Graceworthy."

Waverley went over to the piano and slowly picked out the first notes of Mozart's Fantasy. He had never learned to play it the way Ilona did. He had been too old by the time she died, too old and too stiff-fingered. But those few isolated notes always brought back the feeling that she was still somewhere in the house, unseen, unheard, leaving nothing behind her but a softly felt eddy of air.

Ilona, thought Waverley. Could it really be possible to meet the dead? Perhaps Bob Stroup had misunderstood. Perhaps the man he had killed had gabbled out the first fantastic story that had come into his head in a desperate effort to stay alive. Yet Bob Stroup had no imagination whatsoever. That was what made him an excellent killer. And if the man had really said that, Bob would have reported it to Waverley without emotion and without embellishment. A man who had made his way through enemy-infested jungle just to rescue a buddy who had already been given up for dead was not the kind of man who needed to make up stories. He was probably not the kind of man who could.

The butler brought Waverley his brandy and soda. He was slightly amazed to see that Waverley had taken out his handkerchief and was wiping tears from his eyes.

EIGHTEEN

Bali

Randolph was awakened by somebody gently shaking his shoulder. It was just daylight; the light that strained through the bamboo blind was pearly and pink as if the sun were shining through a veil of rose-colored Balinese silk. He turned his head and saw Wanda standing over him, wearing only a shirt with the sleeves rolled up.

"What's wrong?" he asked.

She kissed his forehead. "Michael's waiting for you outside."

Randolph reached for his watch. "Is it five already? I feel like I just closed my eyes."

"You shouldn't have stayed up so late talking to Dr. Ambara."

"Dr. Ambara is an extremely fascinating man."

Wanda retreated from Randolph's mosquito net while he sat up and stretched. Through the smoky muslin, he watched her walk to the window and raise the blind, and it occurred to him that he liked her more than he had ever liked any woman other than Marmie. Wanda treated him with a casual directness and equality in spite of the fact that she worked for him.

He struggled out of the mosquito net and found his clothes. "Something's knocking in back of my head," he said.

"Ten ice juices and Balinese rum, that's what's knocking,'' Wanda remarked. While Randolph had been discussing psychic phenomena with Dr. Ambara on the previous evening, he had developed an almost unquenchable thirst for crushed ice soaked in pineapple and *sirsak* juice and topped up with rum.

He laced his white-canvas shoes. "Okay, I'm just going to the bathroom and then I'm going to the temple. If anybody comes asking questions, lock the door and call the front desk. Did Michael bring anybody around to keep watch?''

"There's a ten-foot-tall Chinese guy in a 'Feed the World' T-shirt.''

"That's terrific. I don't know how long this session is going to take but we'll be back in plenty of time to catch the plane.''

"You really believe they're *that* dangerous? Ecker and those friends of his?''

"They killed I.M. Wartawa. At least it looks as if they did. And everything Jimmy the Rib told me in Memphis is beginning to make a lot of sense. Ecker—or Reece, or whatever his name is—is the Cottonseed Association's strong-arm man. If you don't toe Waverley Graceworthy's line, buddy boy, you're going to end up in serious trouble. I honestly believe that Ecker was sent out to frighten me while I was away on what Waverley Graceworthy thought was a long vacation. Either to frighten me or to kill me. Look at what happened to my limousine when it was supposed to pick me up at Memphis Airport. Anybody who can fix up a stunt like that is obviously quite capable of killing people without even thinking about it.''

Wanda asked, "Why didn't they try to kill you in Memphis if they were going to kill you at all, instead of sending Ecker all the way out here?''

"It's quieter here. Less suspicion. What are the Balinese police going to say? An American businessman loses his family, becomes depressed, hangs himself in his hotel bathroom. All over. And nothing to make any of my friends back in Memphis suspicious. Besides, I think Waverley and Orbus were burning to find out why I came here. Waverley hates my guts, but at the same time, he's incurably inquisitive about everything I do. Did you know that when I was married, he even sent someone around to take one of the menus from the reception? For some reason, he's obsessed with Clare Cottonseed and with me."

Wanda came over and touched his shoulder. Then she bent forward and kissed him. "You will be careful, won't you, when you go into this trance today?"

"I'll try to be," Randolph said. "To tell the truth, I don't know *how* to be careful."

Michael was waiting for him in the *losmen*'s lobby downstairs, leaning against the reception counter smoking a cigarette and talking in Basaha Indonesian to the plump little girl who helped run the hotel with her grandmother.

"*Saudara sudah berumahtangga?*" he asked her. "Are you married yet?"

The girl giggled and shook her head. "*Tidak. Mungkin nanti.*"

"You see," Michael told Randolph. "They all say it. 'Maybe later.' " Then he turned back to the girl, blew her a smoke ring and said, "*Saya akan kembali nanti.*"

The tall Chinese bodyguard whom Michael had brought along to protect Wanda and Dr. Ambara in case they were found by Ecker and his men was standing stolidly by the *losmen* doorway, his muscular arms folded over his breasts. He wore a dirty sweatband tied around his shaven head and one of his eyes was blind.

"Ain't he sweet?" Michael joked as they stepped out into the street.

Randolph asked, "Are you sure we have to do this? I really don't like to leave Wanda and Dr. Ambara alone."

Michael said, "It's imperative. You must have at least one experience of a death trance while you're here in Bali before we try to do it in Memphis. Unless you know what to expect, know what the warning signs are, you won't stand a chance. We'll go to the temple, induce the trance, and then we'll go to the Dutch Reform Cemetery on Jalan Vyasa. It should be quite safe provided you remain completely calm."

They were walking through the street market now, through

the fragrant smoke of a little stand selling peanut butter on hot toast, and coconut cakes drenched in molasses. A man dressed in scarlet silk was dancing barefoot on the sidewalk, leading a monkey on a long chain.

Randolph ran his hand through his hair. "You mean, I'm actually going to see dead people today?"

"Missionaries, most of them, merchants, local politicians."

"How, er . . ." Randolph was embarrassed. "How long have they been dead?"

Michael glanced at him. "You don't have to do it if you don't want to. In fact, it's better if you don't. You should never go into a death trance if you're frightened. The leyaks will sense you right away."

"Well, that's another thing," Randolph said. "About these leyaks—"

Their conversation was interrupted for a moment while they crossed Jalan Gajahmada. Then, as they reached the opposite sidewalk, Michael said soberly, "I hunted leyaks for about a year, maybe for a little longer. What happened was—on my very first death trance—the leyaks killed my *pedanda*."

"That's a high priest, right? A *pedanda*?"

Michael nodded. "He was the same high priest my father had asked to take care of me. He was more than a priest, and he was more than a father. We weren't friends particularly. When you study the ways of Yama, it's almost impossible for you to be friends with your teacher; the stress of the situation is far too intense. But he was all around me, and inside of me as well. As long as I live, my *pedanda* will live too because what he gave me was much more important than food or clothing or education, or even love. He taught me to transfer myself from the world of the living to the world of the dead, and even back to the world of the yet unborn. He made me superhuman in a way, but of course anybody would be capable of the same thing if he could only believe."

"I believe," Randolph said firmly. Michael looked at him and there was no recognition in his expression of the twenty-five-year difference in age between them.

"Do you?" he asked.

"I *believe*," Randolph repeated doggedly.

They reached the Temple of the Dead. Together they eased open the vast copper doors, one of which gave a groan that sounded like a dying man. They closed the doors behind them and walked directly through the derelict outer courtyard to the inner courtyard. This time Michael produced thin silk scarves and laid them over the stones before they sat down. He filled the censers with incense and lit them while Randolph walked around the courtyard examining the shrines: the shrine to Yama, the ruler of hell; the shrine to Dewi Sri, the goddess of fertility; the shrine to Kali, the destructive manifestation of Siwa; the shrine to Dharma, the god of virtue.

The curved emerald roofs of the shrines rose above the walls of the dank and shadowy courtyard into the sun, into the world of the living. But when Randolph turned around, Michael was beckoning him to sit down on his mat, and already the smoke from the incense was blowing through the temple like the breath of the dead.

On the ground between them Michael had laid a large object, the size of a horse's skull, that was concealed beneath a faded scarf of decoratively dyed silk.

"What's that?" Randolph asked.

"The mask of the Goddess Rangda. Do you want to see it? It's very *sakti*, very magical. It's used in dances and trance ceremonies."

Without waiting to hear Randolph's reply, Michael drew the silk away from Rangda's face. Randolph stared for a long time at the Witch Widow's bulging eyes, at her curving, crossed-over teeth, at her feral snarl. She was ferocity, cruelty and sheer blood-spattered terror. A face to be seen only in nightmares.

"Is that what she really looks like?" Randolph asked with trepidation in spite of himself.

Michael covered up the mask. "I've never seen her, not for real, but there are some *pedandas* who have. And, yes—according to them—that's what she looks like."

"Why do we have to have the mask here?"

"Because we're entering Rangda's empire, that's why; the realm of the dead. We can enter it only if we recite the ritual songs and show respect for Rangda. The magic of the mask creates a gate, a way through to the other world. And as long as the mask remains here, the gate will remain open. That's why the death trance is forbidden by Indonesian law, because leyaks can escape through the gate into the physical world just as easily as we can enter into the spiritual world."

"Is there any way you can prevent that from happening? I mean, suppose leyaks come through the gate without our knowing it while we're on our way to the Dutch cemetery."

Michael shook his head. "They can't do it here, it's sacred ground. That's why I always try to enter the death trance from the inside of a temple. Leyaks cannot walk here. The only being who can come close is Rangda herself, and she rarely does, especially if you take care not to disturb her leyaks while you're in the trance."

He paused and then said seriously, "The only time I've ever known it to happen was during my first death trance. Rangda possessed the mask and used it to kill my *pedanda*. So here's a word of extra advice . . . when we come back out of the trance and you find yourself sitting here, stay away from the mask until you're sure the gate to the other world is closed and everything is safe."

"What about the dead themselves? The spirits?"

"What about them?"

Randolph settled himself on the floor. "I don't mind telling you that I'm just as scared of them," he told Michael.

"What do you have to be scared of? The dead won't harm you. The dead will be overjoyed to see you."

"But they're *dead*."

Michael said, "It was your burning desire to see your Marmie again that brought you here. Do you still want to see her or have you changed your mind? *She's* dead, remember. She's one of the dead, and she'll be just like the people you're going to see today."

Randolph shut his eyes and lowered his head. "Oh; God," he murmured. "Sometimes I wonder what the hell I'm doing."

"Whatever it is, you're paying for it," Michael said, deliberately trying to be businesslike and mundane.

Randolph wrapped his arms around his knees and shouted at Michael, "I'm scared! Don't you understand that? I'm scared shitless!"

Michael raised his hands, their palms toward Randolph. He stared at Randolph and his face was utterly serene. "You're not frightened," he said, and his voice had an extraordinary metallic quality; it was as if he were speaking from a great distance. "You're not frightened at all. You're about to enter the world of the dead, but the world of the dead is nothing more than the other side of the mirror. One side bright, one side dark. But nothing to be frightened of, ever, because the dead are as happy to meet the living as the living are to meet the dead. These are not ghosts, Randolph. These are real, ordinary people, the kind of people you could pass in the street and never even glance at. The only difference between them and you is that *they're* dead and *you're* still alive. But you'll be dead one day just like they are, and when you're dead, will you expect the living to be afraid of *you*?"

Randolph closed his eyes but Michael ordered, "Look at me. *Look* at me. And breathe deeply. Get rid of all of that panic. Get rid of all of that chaos. Your mind's like a traffic jam. Unlock it. Calm it down. Stop worrying."

It was almost ten minutes before Randolph was sufficiently calm for Michael to start his chanting. Even then, Randolph could feel transient scurries of panic in the corners of his brain, like sudden bursts of tumbleweed blowing across a landscape that was supposed to be desolate and utterly still. But Michael obviously considered that he was relaxed enough to enter a death trance and began to sing the sacred songs and tap his foot in time with the magic music, the music that was there but wasn't, and gradually he coaxed Randolph to follow him into a state of other being.

The *kendang* drums beat their complicated rhythms. The *ceng-ceng* cymbals rang. Randolph closed his eyes not because he wanted to, but because he had to, and he could hear the chiming of gongs, the staccato of tapping sticks, and the scuffling of a hundred feet through the courtyard.

"We can walk now among the dead," sang Michael. "We can see quite clearly the ghosts of those who have gone before. Our eyes are opened, both to this world and to the next. We have reached the trance of trances, the trance of the dead, the world within worlds."

Randolph felt the stones rise beneath his feet as if they were made of freshly kneaded dough. He heard insistent whistles and talking, and shadows flickered in front of his eyes, the shapes of masks and faces and gesticulating arms, like in the *wayang* shadow theater. He was sure he could never attain the spiritual frenzy required of a trance, and yet he was overwhelmed by the jangling music, the relentless beat of the drum and Michael's continuing chants.

They were still chanting when a taxi—a dented green Mercury with a smoking exhaust—drew up outside the temple on the opposite side of Jalan Mahabharata. Inside, wedged uncomfortably and sweatily in the backseat, were Richard Reece, *aka* Richard Ecker; Jimmy Heacox; and Bob Stroup. In the front seat sat a girl wearing a shocking-pink T-shirt and grubby white shorts, her hair twisted up with a batik scarf. She was Jennifer Dunning, the girl whom Michael called Mungkin Nanti, Maybe Later.

"Is this the place?" Bob Stroup demanded.

"This is the place," Mungkin Nanti said flatly. "If Michael is giving your friend any death-trance lessons, this is where he'll be."

"Looks like the fucking Castle Dracula," Jimmy Heacox remarked.

Richard Reece of course said nothing but stared at the gates of the Pura Dalem with cold, milky eyes.

"You'd better go carefully," Mungkin Nanti warned. "When he's in one of those death trances, he's amazing. He can move so fast you can scarcely see him. One second he's right in front of you and then he's waving at you from way across the street and you didn't have time to blink. It's time, something to do with time. In a trance, time goes different. That's what he told me anyway."

Reece touched his fingers against Bob Stroup's shoulder. As if the silent man had somehow managed to communicate a complicated message, Bob Stroup asked, "What is this place?"

"It's a temple," Mungkin Nanti told him. "The monks don't use it anymore for some reason. They call it the Temple of the Dead."

Reece nodded to Bob Stroup and the three men climbed out of the taxi. Bob Stroup said to Jennifer Dunning, "You go back home. And thanks for your help." He peeled twenty U.S. dollars from a large roll and handed them to her. She took them reluctantly.

"You're not going to hurt him, are you?" she asked, her eyes worried.

"Hurt him? Why should we hurt him?"

"Well, all I want you to do is to stop him from going into any more death trances."

Bob Stroup smiled and closed the taxi door. "What we said we were going to do—what we agreed on—that's just what we're going to do and no more. Now why don't you get on home? You don't want your boyfriend to know it was you who told us where he was, do you?"

The taxi drove off. Reece and Stroup and Jimmy Heacox stood in the sunlit street for a moment, looking around, checking *warong* stands and shops for potential eyewitnesses, each smiling with that peculiar kind of mirthlessness that tightens the face of men who understand their incontestable power over the rest of humanity, a power that stems simply from the fact that they have no fear of pain and no fear of death. They have seen it all before and they have decided they don't care.

Reece gave a nod of his head, and they crossed the street to the gates of the Pura Dalem. Bob Stroup turned the handle and announced, "It's unlocked."

Reece held out his hand and Jimmy Heacox passed him a green sports bag. Tugging back the zipper, Reece produced three white ice-hockey masks, which they fitted over their faces. They pushed open the heavy copper doors and edged into the outer courtyard one by one, glancing quickly from side to side to make sure no one was lying in wait. Then they closed the doors behind them, pausing for a second to listen, and drew Colt automatics from their combat jackets. The only sound was the clattering of the pistols' slides as each of them chambered the first round and cocked the hammers.

Reece beckoned and swiftly they crossed the derelict outer courtyard until they reached the *paduraksa* gate, which led to the sacred inner temple. Incense smoke was billowing out of the gate, twirling across the outer courtyard and through the broken-down *bale agung* and *bale gong* pavilions, where the local villagers had once met and the temple orchestra had once played. But there was no music here today. Only the rustling of dried leaves in the faintest of morning winds. Only the muffled sounds of traffic in the city streets. Only the strange, shrill calling of mynahs and parakeets.

Reece stepped through the inner gate and then lifted his hand. Michael and Randolph were sitting only twenty yards away, half-hidden by the incense smoke, each swaying repetitively back and forth. Michael was chanting the ancient death-trance mantras in Sanskrit, the language of the high priests, in a high, warbling pitch that seemed to set the air trembling. His voice sounded almost like a musical saw, reaching a vocal weirdness that neither Reece nor Stroup nor Heacox had ever before heard in their lives, not even in the jungles of Cambodia.

"What the fuck's he doing?" Heacox whispered hoarsely. "He sounds like the cat got his balls."

Bob Stroup said, "The old man made it one-hundred-percent clear that he wanted the kid taken alive. You got that, Jimmy?"

Heacox said nothing. As far as he was concerned, it didn't matter whether the kid lived or died. Who cared, so long as he got his bonus at the end of the trip? He sniffed and screwed up his nose in disgust at the smell of the incense.

Although it was silent in the real temple—in the temple that manifested itself in the physical world—there was crashing gong and cymbal music in the temple that manifested itself in the world of the dead, the temple that Randolph and Michael were now entering. There were drums, whistles and tapping sticks, and the deep, shuddering booms of the *gangsa*. Randolph, his eyes tightly closed, was hurling himself furiously backward and forward now in time to the drumming. His mind was exploding with noise, detonating with janglings and boomings and scintillating ringings. He could no longer think of who he was, or why he was, or what it was that compelled him to sway with the music. He was beyond the threshold of reality and approaching the darkness of absolute trance.

There was one moment when he was very frightened. The floor of the temple felt as if it were dropping away from underneath him, as if it were vanishing into empty, echoing space. Then the universe collapsed around him in great thundering blocks of noise and color, deafening avalanches of darkness and mass. He was sped through time and perception so fast that streaks of dazzling light hurtled past his eyes like meteors and then burst apart into a glittering white flower with silver-showered petals that unfolded and bloomed and swelled until it revealed that he was back on the temple floor, his eyes open now, staring at Michael.

The music had stopped. The temple was silent. Randolph looked around and then back at Michael.

Leaves stirred on the temple floor like gray and desiccated skin.

"What's wrong?" Randolph asked. "What's happened?"

Michael smiled. There was a strange, bright light in his eyes.

"Can we try again?" Randolph asked. "Is it me? Is it me that's wrong? Do I have to have more practice?"

Michael said, "Nothing is wrong. Nothing is wrong at all."

"I don't understand."

"It is very easy. You have attained that state which you came out here to Bali to attain. You are in a death trance. Your mind is guided very much by mine, of course, but nonetheless, you will be able to see everything I see and just as clearly.''

Michael's voice sounded strangely taut and flat and his phraseology was completely different than before. No more straight, direct, matter-of-fact statements in that nasal American-Balinese accent of his. Instead, a kind of placid Oriental politeness; Kane out of *Kung-Fu*, only far more elegant.

''Follow me,'' Michael said and his words seemed to blossom inside Randolph's brain. Together they rose from the temple floor and walked back across the inner courtyard to the *candi bentar*, the split gate.

With their backs pressed against the carved stone walls, hiding well out of sight behind the curves of the gate, Reece, Stroup and Heacox—three white-faced demons from a different kind of dream—watched them pass and not one of them could believe what he saw.

Randolph and Michael appeared to be almost transparent. Although they were walking slowly, they reached the outer gates of the temple in less than a blink, and then suddenly the gates were opened and they were gone.

''What in hell?'' Heacox demanded. ''I didn't even get time to take a bead.''

''You heard what the girl said,'' Stroup told him. ''They're into one of these trance things. She said they were fast.''

''So what the fuck do we do?''

Reece lifted a finger to Bob Stroup and nodded toward the inner courtyard of the temple where the mask of Rangda now lay deserted.

Stroup spoke for him. ''The girl said that if they want to get out of the trance, they have to come back to the same place they went in. So all we have to do is wait for them here. Then we pop Randolph and take the kid.''

They advanced cautiously into the inner courtyard where they prowled around, their automatics stuck in their belts. Stroup bent forward and peered at the incense; then he walked around the shrines.

''You gotta believe these people. They're even worse heathens than the goddam VC.''

Heacox approached the mask of Rangda, edged around it in curiosity for a while and then lifted the silk covering with the muzzle of his pistol.

"Jesus, it's my mother-in-law."

Reece snapped his fingers sharply, which meant to leave the mask alone.

"Don't touch nothing," Stroup said by way of explanation. "If you mess around with anything here, Clare and the kid may not be able to get back and then you're going to have to explain that to His Highness, Mr. Waverley Graceworthy."

"Gives me the fucking creeps, this stuff," Heacox complained.

They circled around the inner courtyard one more time. They peered into every leaf-silted corner. While he was examining an erotic bas-relief on the side of one of the shrines, however, Bob Stroup thought he saw something flicker out of the corner of his eye. A shadow, no more than that, close to the mask of Rangda. His reflexes were so high-strung, however, that he twisted around fast, ducked onto one knee and covered the mask with his automatic before the others realized what was happening.

Reece whipped out his automatic too. They waited tensely, and then Reece gave Stroup a ducking motion with his head that meant, "What the hell's going on?"

"I could have sworn I saw something. Just there, beside the mask. Like somebody moving, just for an instant."

"Nerves," Heacox said. "There ain't nothing there."

Stroup was completely unmoved by this skepticism. "There was something there. I saw it. A shadow, I don't know."

Heacox walked across to the center of the courtyard with his hands planted on his hips. To make fun of Stroup, he waved his arms from side to side through the empty air as if he were feeling for the Invisible Man. "I don't feel nothing yet," he said loudly. "No, I definitely don't feel nothing at all."

Reece pointed quickly across the width of the courtyard to indicate to Stroup that if anybody *had* been there, he would have had to walk right in front of all of them to reach the mask. A flap of his hand said, "Maybe a bird? Maybe a butterfly?" Trigger-happy GIs had fired whole belts of M60 ammunition at rustling insects in the jungle trees. They were understandable, these jitters, at least to anyone who had been there. And even after ten years, you never got rid of them completely.

Slowly Stroup pushed his automatic back into his belt. "Could be you're right. Maybe a plane passed overhead, or a cloud or something."

Heacox picked up the mask of Rangda and arranged the silk scarf around it so that its face was showing. "Now it *really* looks like my mother-in-law. Gives you the goddam creeps, doesn't it? I mean, these people worship these things. They really believe they're real. Can you imagine saying your prayers every night to something with a face like this?"

The Goddess Rangda glared at Heacox with unadulterated viciousness, her eyes protruding, her lips drawn back, her curved fangs shining.

Stroup said a little nervously, "Put it down, Jimmy."

"It's a mask, that's all. They put them on their heads and they jump around in them to scare the shit out of their kids."

Reece gave a quick shake of his head and Stroup translated, "Put the mask down, Jimmy, will you? Richard wants you to put it down."

Heacox tossed the huge mask up into the air, caught it and then challenged both Reece and Stroup with a lopsided grin. "Don't tell me you're scared of it? Come on, Bob. Don't tell me that. How about you, Richard? Chicken?"

As a last defiant gesture, he lowered the mask over his head and shuffled from side to side, shouting, "Grrr! I eat fat-assed Americans like you for breakfast! With stir-fried noodles!"

He laughed harshly and raised his hands to remove the mask. But his laugh suddenly changed and he let out a horrifying scream, the kind of scream that Bob Stroup had not heard since three of his men had dropped into a *punji* trap full of sharpened stakes in Vietnam. Heacox clawed wildly at the sides of the Rangda mask and staggered around the courtyard.

"Jimmy!" Bob Stroup shouted and caught hold of him. For one moment Stroup found himself staring straight into Rangda's face and he could have sworn he felt a chilly blast of sour breath. But then Heacox buckled and collapsed and the mask hit the stones of the courtyard with a hollow, wooden sound and rolled away.

As it rolled, the mask left a batik pattern of bright scarlet blood on the ground. It came to rest against the plinth of a nearby shrine.

Stroup turned around slowly to stare at Jimmy Heacox. He had seen some horrific injuries during the war: men with half their bodies blown away, yet still capable of smiling at you; men with no arms; men with no legs. But he was completely unprepared for the sight of Jimmy Heacox. Even Richard Reece, when he came up and stood beside him, looked apprehensive and the two of them were silent and unmoving for almost half a minute.

Heacox's head had been torn off his neck, leaving nothing but his larynx and his tongue: a long ribbon of red, torn-off tongue, like a grisly necktie.

"Holy shit!" Stroup breathed at last. And then they turned simultaneously toward the mask. Reece made the gesture they had used during silent advances through the jungle to indicate that there might be booby traps around.

Stroup frowned at the mask in disbelief. "A booby trap? What kind of booby trap can tear your head off? There wasn't any kind of explosion."

They approached the mask cautiously. Reece prodded it with his foot, trying to roll it over so they could see inside it. Eventually they pressed the soles of their boots against it to try to topple it away from the shrine. They jumped back as a sensible precaution against a rigged explosion, but also out of fright. They could deal with danger they understood, but this was something different. Both of them knew there was no antipersonnel device ever invented that could have torn off Jimmy Heacox's head like that. Reece made a

quick sign to Stroup that the way Heacox had been decapitated reminded him of a shark bite.

"Something with teeth anyway," Stroup agreed.

They bent forward and peered inside the open neck of the
mask. Stroup took off his mask so he could see better. But
the sunlight at this corner of the courtyard was quite bright
and the illumination inside the mask was enhanced by the
two glowing pinpoints that shone through the Goddess
Rangda's eyeholes.

"It's empty," Stroup whispered. "Where the hell's his
head?"

Reece kicked the mask again but it was obvious that it
was totally empty. Jimmy Heacox's head had been torn off,
devoured, and was gone.

"I never saw anything like this," Stroup said in wonder.

Reece looked back at the body and shook his head in a
way Stroup understood to mean, "The stupid jerk should
have done as he was told and left the goddam mask alone."

"He was scared of it," Stroup remarked. "He was only
trying to prove to himself that he was tough."

Reece nodded toward the place where Randolph and Michael had been sitting, where Stroup had glimpsed the
shadow. He did not have to make any gestures for Stroup to
know what he was thinking. This death-trance business was
a lot more hair-raising than either of them had realized. A
lot more difficult too. And even if they *did* manage to bring
the kid home for Mr. Graceworthy, would Mr. Graceworthy
thank them for it? Christ Almighty, a mask that could bite a
man's head off? People who could walk across a courtyard
faster than you could even lift your gun to take aim at them?
Devils and demons and who the hell knew what?

Stroup scratched the back of his neck and stared around
the temple. "We gonna stay?" he asked. "Supposing there's
worse."

Reece, behind his expressionless mask, indicated that
they had a job to do, a job for masters who would not be
patient if they failed. Heacox had disobeyed the first two
laws of safety and survival: *Do not touch unless you have
to, and then do not touch until you've checked.* And maybe

here in the Temple of the Dead there was one more law, even more important: *Do not touch until you understand it.*

What neither Reece nor Stroup knew was that the shock of Rangda's attack on Jimmy Heacox had rippled through the realm of the dead like a minor earthquake, rousing up fear and funeral debris, disturbing corpses in their graves, making ashes shift in urns. The dead suddenly raised their faces to the sun that never shone and listened, and through the world of veils and half-forgotten memories, there was a sharpened rustling sound. The leyaks had been alerted. Eyes glowed. Feet hurried through leaves and bone dust.

Randolph and Michael had just reached the corner of Jalan Vyasa, opposite the plain brick wall that surrounded the Dutch Reform Cemetery. Randolph had found their progress there hypnotic. They had walked in a curious gliding motion through the streets of Denpasar, and the sunlight had seemed blurry, as if his face were covered with a translucent scarf. Noises had been strangely indistinct. Yet he had been able to see Michael clearly, and he was aware of a sharply heightened sensitivity, not to the everyday things around him, but to feelings and emotions in the air. At one street corner he had suddenly sensed regret. Not his own, but the regret of a woman who was sitting at a second-floor window staring out over the market and fanning herself.

Michael had said, "You feel it? That's good. She has just lost her husband; there are still complicated emotional ties between him and her. Eventually they will unravel, you know, but right now they're still strong enough for you to be able to pick them up."

Now, on the corner of Jalan Vyasa, both Randolph and Michael felt a sickening, prickly sensation, a sudden lurch of uncertainty.

"What is it?" Randolph asked as Michael lifted his head to listen and concentrate.

"Something's happened," Michael told him anxiously. "Something not too far away."

"What do you mean, something's happened?"

Michael listened a little while longer but then shook his

head. "It's hard to say. Some kind of disturbance. There's a smell of leyak around the place."

"What does a leyak smell like?" Randolph wanted to know.

"I'll tell you what," Michael said as they crossed the street. "There's one group of Balinese who call themselves the Bali Aga, which means the original Balinese. They live on the shores of Lake Batur, which is very secluded, and they keep up all the ancient customs most of the Balinese have forgotten. One of the customs they've retained is that of lying their dead in the open, without coffins, and simply allowing them to fall to pieces. Well, if you go to their cemetery on a warm, humid day, when Lake Batur is thick with mist, and if you breathe in, that's what a leyak smells like."

"Sounds like a pleasure I could happily do without."

They reached the gates of the Dutch cemetery and flickered between the green-painted iron palings as if they were ghosts themselves. A wrinkled old man in a pink turban turned his head as he heard the gates squeak behind him, but they were gone by then. They passed the trim brick gatehouse, where three Dutch women in black were waiting for somebody, holding armfuls of flowers. Then they glided along the well-weeded brick pathway between rows of headstones so blindingly white that they appeared to Randolph to be shining through a fog. At last they turned off to the right beneath overhanging frangipani trees where the graves were older and less well-kept, and where the creeper had been allowed to grow wild along the cemetery wall. The sons and daughters of the dead who rested here were themselves dead, and so these dead were beyond remembrance.

Randolph followed Michael, his heart beating wildly. His mouth was dry, his ears sang and he was chilly with perspiration. Symptoms of fear, he thought. Indications of abject terror. It was frightening enough, entering this neglected part of the cemetery, without anticipating that you might actually meet the spirits who occupied it. He wiped his face with his hands and the salt sweat stung his eyes. The cicadas seemed to be deafening and the black cemetery birds hopped about and screeched over the graves.

"Now," Michael said, lifting one hand.

They stopped, side by side, where the brick path ran into gravel. Randolph looked around fearfully, excited and not knowing what to expect, not knowing what he would see or how he would react.

The spirits of the cemetery appeared beneath the dancing shadows of the trees with such sad grace that Randolph found it impossible to be frightened. They were indeed, as Michael had said, ordinary men and women and children. They approached silently and stood among the headstones only a few feet away, their hands by their sides, staring at Randolph and Michael with an expression of curiosity and longing.

"These are really . . . the *dead*?" Randolph whispered.

Michael nodded.

Randolph took one or two careful steps forward. The people of the cemetery followed him with their eyes, turning around to watch him as he came among them. There were old men in black frock coats and with white hair that waved in other winds. There were soldiers with cropped heads and khaki uniforms, and eyes that spoke of inexperience and sudden death. There were women, their faces white with suffering, their starched bonnets reflecting the glow of immortality. There were children, some of them tiny, some with rickety legs, some with puzzled faces bloated by tropical disease.

Randolph walked farther into their midst and turned around and around so he could see all of them. He was so moved that he found the sweltering atmosphere of the graveyard almost suffocating. His chest seemed to be aching for air. His heart seemed to be aching for pity.

A young dead girl in a black dress came forward through the grass. Her cheeks were thin and her eyes were lambent and dark. She raised a hand toward him as if she were unable to believe that he really existed, a living being in the world of the dead.

"Can you speak?" Randolph asked her hoarsely, his voice thick with emotion.

Michael said, "They're Dutch but most of them speak a little English."

"You've seen them before?" Randolph asked. "You've actually heard them speak?"

The girl in the black dress said, *"We are all dead, sir. Can you save us?"*

Randolph turned to Michael in desperation. "What can I tell her? What can I say?"

Michael gently shook his head. "There isn't anything you can say."

Randolph looked back at the girl and said, "Tell me your name. Your name. Who are you?"

"Natalie, sir. Natalie Van Hoeve."

Randolph slowly put out his hand, his palm turned toward the dead girl, his fingers spread. Natalie watched him and then raised her own hand in the same way. They both hesitated for a moment and then their fingertips touched, the dead and the living, the spiritual and the mortal. Randolph could feel her fingers, the delicate touch of them, but a cold tremble went through his body, a tremble that shook him to the core, not just his flesh, but his soul as well, and everything he had ever believed in.

Because if these people were still here after all these years, sadly wandering in this cemetery, where was the Lord their God? Where was their place in heaven?

Randolph drew his fingers away from Natalie's and said quietly, "Bless you, Natalie. I hope you find peace."

Then he went through the crowds of the dead—because there were thirty or forty of them now, and ever more gathering—and he touched them one by one. He felt their coldness and he felt their hopelessness, and the worst feeling of all was his own hopelessness because he knew that he himself would be dead in not many years to come and that all he could look forward to was emptiness, and longing, and eternal regret.

Michael had stayed where he was on the pathway, watching Randolph carefully. He understood exactly what Randolph was feeling; he had often felt the same way himself. It was too early for him to explain to Randolph that what people were in death was nothing more than they had been in life. To the passionate, passion; to the fulfilled, fulfillment. To the plain and the ordinary and the hopeless, an immortal existence like most of these people in this Dutch Reform Cemetery.

Randolph was still walking among the dead when Michael suddenly called his name. Not loudly but in a tone marked by its urgency and by its note of warning. Randolph turned around at once. Michael was pointing toward the dark, creeper-entangled wall of the cemetery where the trees overhung the graves so heavily that it was almost impossible to see the stones.

"What's wrong?" Randolph asked. He began to retreat toward Michael, the host of the dead silently following him.

"I'm not sure. I thought I saw something."

"What? What is it?" Randolph asked. He felt seriously alarmed now. It had been traumatic enough to touch the hands of people who had been dead for forty years, but to think there might be real demons around was terrifying.

"What can you see?" Randolph asked, straining his eyes toward the distant shadows beneath the trees. He wished he had his glasses.

Before he could say anything else, Michael seized his sleeve. "Run!" he shouted and began pulling Randolph back along the pathway.

Randolph stumbled and almost fell. "What is it? For God's sake, tell me!"

"Leyaks!" Michael barked.

The dead spirits in the cemetery began to mill around in rising panic.

"What about them?" Randolph shouted. "What about all these people?"

"They're dead!" Michael retorted.

Randolph hesitated. He could see the girl called Natalie raise her hands in horror, and for the first time, he could see the leyaks, gray-suited, ashen-faced, ten or eleven of them emerging from under the trees. A terrible moan of fright went up from the men and the women in the cemetery and the children began to shriek and cry.

"How can we leave them?" Randolph begged. He had sudden visions of massacres that he had helplessly witnessed on television: Vietnam, Lidice, Petrograd. Now he had the chance to save some of the victims, or at least to save their spirits.

But Michael darted back, snatched at his sleeve again and screamed at him furiously, "They're dead, for Christ's sake! They're dead! There's nothing you can do! Now run or you won't stand a chance!"

Randolph looked back at the dead. Behind them he saw the eyes of the leyaks burning in their faces like coals smoldering in the grates of hell. He saw something dark hurtle through the air; it might have been a child. Then Michael was wrenching at his arm, pulling him helter-sketler along the brick pathway toward the cemetery gates.

Although they ran with all the swiftness that had startled Reece and Stroup, the leyaks ran equally fast. They were still more than fifty yards from the gates when Randolph glanced anxiously to the right and saw the glowing orange eyes of two leyaks as they ran parallel to them between the rows of headstones. He turned and looked quickly behind and saw five or six more, their gray faces contorted in hunger and fury, their eyes alight.

Nobody in the cemetery apart from Randolph and Michael could see the leyaks because the creatures belonged to the realm of the dead. The Dutch women in their black coats had found their husbands and were now promenading solemnly between the tombs, carrying their sprays of white flowers, unaware that only three pathways distant they were being passed by the fiercest of ghouls. They turned with disapproving frowns as Randolph and Michael ran by, but somehow Randolph and Michael were little more than shadows themselves, and the sound of running feet.

The cemetery gates were still agonizingly far away, and beyond the gates there was still the street to be negotiated before they reached the temple. Randolph began to gasp for breath. He was fit but he had not run as far and as hard as this since he was twenty years old. The blood began to thunder in his ears and his heart pumped wildly and he knew he was close to having to give up.

The leyaks who had been running parallel to them now began to edge their way nearer, hurdling the rows of headstones one by one. The leyaks behind them were gaining, and another group appeared on their left-hand side.

Randolph gritted his teeth and tried to force one last burst of strength from his body but it was too much. His right knee gave way; he staggered, almost regained his balance and then pitched onto the brick path, grazing his hand and lacerating the side of his chin.

He saw Michael stop, turn, hesitate. "Run, for God's sake!" he gasped at him. "Don't worry about me!"

Almost at once he felt a heavy body hurtle on top of him, and then another, and the next thing he knew, there were savage claws tearing at his face, teeth ripping at his clothes. He screamed in terror, thrashing and rolling and trying to beat off the leyaks. Their stinking breath blasted into his face; their eyes burned incandescent in front of him. He felt fiery pain as one of them raked its claws all the way down the inside of his thigh, and then a third leaped on top of him and sank its teeth into his bicep.

Oh dear Jesus, he thought, *they're tearing me apart*.

NINETEEN

He could hear somebody shrieking. He could hear snarls and furious roars, and then suddenly he was tossed sideways across the path. A hand touched his shoulder, a friendly hand. And then he was being pulled upright, onto his knees at first and then onto his feet. He staggered forward blindly, his face smothered in blood, one of his arms dangling uselessly, and then he collapsed again.

A cloth was wiping blood from his eyes. He looked up and saw Michael. "Have they killed us?" he asked through swollen lips.

"Hurry!" Michael pleaded, his voice that of one who knows it might already be too late.

Numbly Randolph looked around. He could not believe what he saw. The cemetery path was crowded with the Dutch dead and they were throwing themselves at the leyaks, scores of them, men and women, beating at the beasts with upraised fists, jumping on their backs to try to bring them down to the ground, shrieking in anger and overwhelming the leyaks.

"My God," Randolph whispered. "My God, Michael, they're doing it for me."

With blazing eyes, the leyaks tore into the spirits of the Dutch dead, tearing and snatching and biting. Yet the Dutch continued to press forward and to pull the leyaks down, pressing on in hopeless but almost happy self-sacrifice.

"Come on," Michael urged, and Randolph struggled to his feet. But he found it impossible to take his eyes off the grisly struggle going on in the middle of the cemetery. Although there were so many of them, the Dutch had no chance against the leyaks. The creatures were demonic berserkers, mindless and vicious, the snarers of souls. Their filthy, hooked claws ripped through spiritual tissue, tearing the spirits of men and women into tattered shreds. There was no blood but the injuries were hideous nevertheless. Randolph saw an old Calvinist preacher fall to the ground with half his face clawed away. He saw a beautiful young girl pirouette and collapse, her leg savaged by the teeth of two ravening leyaks. He saw a soldier caught from behind by one leyak, while another snagged open his stomach.

The shrieking was the shrieking of those souls who had been torn too badly to drag themselves away and who knew that the leyaks would carry them back to Rangda's lair, where they would be devoured. There was no final peace for souls devoured by Rangda. They would be ingested into her black and slippery system with their consciousness intact, forever.

Randolph turned to Michael in desperation. The horror of this struggle was that to the real world, it was silent and invisible. The black-dressed mourners continued up the path toward their dear departeds' graves as if nothing were happening. And the pain of it was that so many of these dead people had given up their immortal souls to save Randolph's life.

"Come on," Michael said in a voice that was now gentle and encouraging. "Come on, Randolph. They can't last much longer. You owe it to them to get away."

Randolph nodded and turned. Following close behind Michael, he limped, staggered and stumbled the distance to the cemetery gates. There he clung to the railings for a moment, racked with pain, shivering, and heaving for breath, but when Michael said, "Come on," again, he managed to push himself upright and follow him out into the Jalan Vyasa.

The last face he saw was Natalie's. She had torn herself away from the struggle and run after Randolph to the cemetery gates. "*Don't forget me!*" she called. "*Don't forget me!*"

But then three leyaks were on her and Randolph saw their mouths gape open in ferocious hunger and tear at the girl's neck.

He did not need any further encouragement to limp his way along Jalan Vyasa and back toward the Temple of the Dead. Shoppers and stall-keepers noticed their passing but when they looked again, the pair was gone. They stumbled their way through the strange, foggy light of the world of veils, past fragrant *satay* stalls and long batik scarves that blew gently and silently in the hot morning wind.

"Can you make it?" Michael asked.

"I think I'm bruised and bitten more than anything else. Come on, keep going, I can make it."

They turned the last corner into Jalan Mahabharata and Randolph hobbled the length of the street until he saw the stone-carved guardians of the gate, with their thick moss coverings. But there were still twenty yards to go when Michael reached out, took his arm and said, "Hold it. Something's wrong. The temple gate is open. Somebody's been there."

They approached the temple cautiously. A moped blurted past, the odd, slow-motion effect of its motor sounding to Randolph like drums and death rattles and magical sticks. Michael pressed himself against the green-copper doors of the temple and made a quick survey.

"It's Ecker," he said. "Ecker and another man. They're waiting for us in the inner courtyard. They've both got guns."

"How did he find us?" Randolph panted, leaning against the wall.

"I don't have any idea. But the minute we reenter the real world. out of our trance, they're obviously going to try to kill us."

Randolph glanced anxiously behind him but so far there was no sign of the leyaks. "What can we do?" he asked. "I don't know whether I prefer to be shot or torn to pieces. It's kind of academic, isn't it?"

Michael bit his lip. "There's a chance that we could lure Ecker out of there. The leyaks aren't going to be long though. It must have been Ecker disturbing the trance gate here that alerted them. The leyaks will know where to find us."

Almost as he spoke, two gray-suited figures appeared at the far end of Jalan Mahabharata and began to walk quickly toward them. Michael looked in the other direction and saw another leyak approaching from the opposite end of the street.

"We don't have any time," he told Randolph. "Stand in the doorway there and wave your arms, *slowly*, mind you, real slowly, because you're still in the death trance and Ecker won't see you properly if you're too quick."

"What are you going to do?"

"I need a mirror," Michael replied, and without any further explanation, he jogged quickly across the street to the Sambal Restaurant, a small run-down Indonesian *rumah makan* with grubby plastic blinds, and a patriotic painting of Soekarmen, the governor of Bali, propped up in the window.

The leyaks were closer now; Randolph could see the orange smoldering of their eyes. He took a deep, painful breath, pushed open the temple door a little farther, lifted his arms and began to wave and shout as slowly and as deliberately as he could.

"Ecker! Reece! Whatever the hell your name is! I'm over here! I'm over here!"

He saw Reece turn in amazement, Reece with his white ice-hockey mask. He saw the other man turn around too. Another blank, white face. They were almost as frightening in their appearance as were the leyaks, and he knew now that they were just as determined to destroy him.

"I'm over here!" he yelled at them. "What are you, chicken? Are you chicken, Reece? Are you only brave enough to kill women and children? Come on and get me if you're so goddam tough!"

He glanced back into the street anxiously. The leyaks were less than seventy yards away now and approaching fast. There was still no sign of Michael. He had disappeared into the doorway of the restaurant and showed no sign of coming out again. Randolph hoped to God that he hadn't decided to save his own skin, leaving Randolph caught between three flesh-tearing beasts from the world of the dead and two cold-blooded killers from the world of the living.

Reece and his henchman began to run across the court-yard toward Randolph, their guns raised. Randolph was caught between Reece's slow-motion mortal running and the irresistibly rapid advance of the leyaks. He checked the street again, desperately frightened now that the leyaks would reach him well before Reece did.

He stopped shouting and waving his arms and stood half-in and half-out of the temple doorway, his head lifted, and thought to himself, *This is it. My God, I can't escape from this.* He had always known that he would have to die but he had never imagined that death would approach him like this, like three black express trains rushing in on him from all sides.

He could hear the dusty sound of the leyaks' feet on the sidewalk, the snarling undertone of their breathing. He could hear Reece shouting something at him: a long, slow, indistinct blurt of sound. He saw Reece stop only a dozen feet away and raise his automatic.

It was at that instant that Michael came sprinting and leaping across the street; he was carrying in upraised arms a large, dazzling mirror. With his sneakers scuffling on the sidewalk, he hurtled himself around, pushed Randolph away from the temple door with his back and held the mirror up toward the oncoming leyaks.

"Come and get us, you stinking corpses!" Michael screamed at them. "Come on, come on, this is what you wanted! Come and get us! Good fresh flesh for your Mistress Rangda!"

The effect of the mirror on the leyaks was extraordinary. They stopped only a few feet away and raised their hands to protect their eyes, edging off as if in sudden terror.

"What's happened?" Randolph asked. He was pressed against the wall, well out of Reece's line of fire. "Why have they stopped?"

"They're frightened," Michael panted. He lifted the mirror higher and waved it at the leyaks threateningly. "They think I've gotten hold of a picture of them and they're frightened. There's only one way you can destroy leyaks and that's to get a picture of them and then burn the picture in front of their eyes. They don't realize that this is a mirror."

"How long is that going to hold them off?" Randolph wanted to know. "And what the hell are we going to do about Reece, or Ecker, or whatever he calls himself?"

Just then Reece appeared at the temple doorway, his gun lifted, and stared at Randolph and Michael through the slits in his mask. Although his face was covered, it was obvious that he was astonished at what was going on. To him, the leyaks were invisible and all he could see was that Michael was waving a large restaurant mirror from side to side and Randolph was leaning against the temple wall, his shirt and pants torn, his face covered in congealing blood.

Reece took off his mask and Bob Stroup did the same. Reece nodded to Stroup and Stroup said, "Let's get inside. I don't know what the fuck you're trying to do but you're going to attract too much attention out here."

Michael worriedly licked his lips and said to Stroup, "Hold this mirror for me. Then I'll come in. Randolph—" and with a jerk of his head, he indicated that Randolph should step inside the temple. Randolph eased himself away from the wall and obediently shuffled through the gate.

"I ain't holding no mirror," Bob Stroup said indignantly.

Reece cocked his automatic and raised it so it pointed directly at Michael's head. Only Michael and Randolph could see the three flame-eyed leyaks who were now trying to shuffle their way closer to Michael on three sides, hoping that one of them would be able to jump on him before he could destroy the "picture."

"Listen," Michael urged Bob Stroup. "You know what's going on here, don't you?"

"Some kind of screwball religious ceremony or something."

"The death trance, don't you understand that?" Michael

had to enunciate his words very slowly to make himself comprehensible.

Reece made two or three quick gestures and Stroup said, "Okay. One of our friends just got killed here while you were away. He put on that mask thing you've got lying there in the courtyard and it chewed his goddam head off."

So that was it, thought Randolph. They had interfered with the sacred mask of Rangda. No wonder the leyaks were alerted so quickly. And with the sharpest of pains, he thought of Natalie.

Michael insisted, "You have to hold the mirror for me while I get inside the temple. Otherwise the same thing is going to happen to all of us."

Bob Stroup was annoyed and baffled. "Do I believe you or not?" he demanded of Michael. "I mean, what is this shit? There's nothing out there. The street's empty. What do I have to hold that goddam mirror for? What are you trying to do? You trying to make me look like an asshole?"

God, thought Randolph, *don't worry about that. You look like one already.* He was almost ready to collapse from shock and pain.

After a tense and uncertain moment, Reece gestured that Stroup should go along with Michael and take the mirror. Stroup tucked his automatic into his belt and took the mirror sullenly. Michael took one quick step backward, onto the sacred ground of the temple, and then gripped the back of Stroup's combat jacket.

Stroup had been out of the leyaks' reach in the real world, but Michael was still in the realm of the dead and his grip on Stroup's clothing was just enough to draw an infinitesimal part of Stroup's spirit into the realm of the dead with him. It was similar to the way in which Michael had guided Randolph's spirit out of his body and into the skies above the temple. It was insubstantial and indefinite, but since the leyaks had the fiercest appetite for living spirits, for them it was enough.

"Will you let go of my—" Stroup snapped, annoyed and twisting around to shove Michael off.

As he did so, he turned the mirror away from the leyaks

and in one screeching second of terrifying rage, they flung themselves like wolves onto his shadowy spirit and literally began to tear the life out of him with guzzling teeth, snatching claws and flaring orange eyes.

Stroup screamed and fell into the street as if he had been shot. The mirror smashed across the sidewalk, a hundred silver knives. Michael quickly jumped back into the temple, clutching a long, bloody scratch on his hand where one of the leyaks had caught him a glancing blow. Reece, tongueless, grabbed Michael and shook him, but then stopped and stared in horror at what was happening to his lifelong friend, the man who had saved his life.

None of Stroup's physical body was in the realm of the dead, only his spirit was. He twisted and jerked and screamed as the leyaks tore his spirit into shreds, yet there were no physical wounds on him, no blood, no gashes, no bites. He looked as if he were suffering an agonizing epileptic fit, but the leyaks were savaging him just as viciously as if they were a pack of wild animals, and just as fatally.

It took no more than a minute. Stroup lay still. Then, as quickly as they had first attacked, the leyaks hurried away. Only one of them turned around at the corner of the street to stare back at Randolph and Michael with lighted eyes. There was an expression of demonic hatred on its ashen face that Randolph would have nightmares about for weeks to come.

Reece lowered his gun and walked out into the street. He knelt down beside Stroup and felt his pulse. He gently slapped Stroup's cheeks, but Stroup's head fell sideways against the gritty ground and they knew he was dead. A broken man, lying amid the fragments of a broken mirror. Reece uttered two or three strange, glottal cries and then stood up. With a wave of his gun, he indicated that Michael and Randolph should carry Stroup's body into the temple and close the door.

Michael said to him wearily, "I'm sorry about your friend. Believe me, it wasn't my fault. You don't understand what you're dealing with here."

Reece took no notice and prodded him with his gun,

urging him to hurry. At last they managed to manhandle Stroup's body through the gates and lay him down among the dried-up leaves in one of the temple's broken-down pavilions.

Michael said to Reece, "We didn't kill him. It wasn't us. There are spirits out there. Ghosts, if that makes it easier for you to understand. They killed him. He shouldn't have turned around. It was only the mirror that was keeping him safe."

Reece's mouth tightened with suppressed frustration and emotion. His cold eyes darted from Michael to Randolph and back again. His instructions from Waverley Graceworthy had been quite explicit: kill Randolph Clare and bring Michael Hunter back to the United States alive. But there had been explicit conditions too. Randolph Clare was supposed to be killed so that his death looked like an accident and Michael Hunter was supposed to be brought out of Indonesia without any complications from the immigration authorities.

Bob Stroup had been essential to the carrying out of these conditions. Not only had Bob Stroup understood exactly what was wanted, he had been able to express in words every nuance of Reece's feelings. But now Bob Stroup was lying dead, Jimmy Heacox had been decapitated by that gruesome mask, and the only accomplice Reece was left with, Frank Louv, had been as mad as a goddam hatter ever since Khe Sanh, when a stray fragment of shrapnel had taken away half his brain.

What was more, for the first time since he had been captured by the VC in Cambodia, Richard Reece felt frightened. He could deal with muscle, he could deal with knives and guns and broken glass. But what had happened here at the Temple of the Dead was the kind of thing that could turn a guy's guts into clear-running water. If Randolph and Michael had not been standing there watching him, he would have dodged out of that courtyard as fast as he could run and there wouldn't have been a leyak alive or dead that could have caught him.

He pushed his automatic back into his combat-jacket pocket and buttoned up his jacket. He looked at Randolph and Michael with an expression like Barre granite, and then he lifted one finger. A warning. *Don't think that you've seen the last of me, my friends, because just as sure as bears do what bears do, in the goddam woods or out of them, you're going to see me again, and I'm going to make you suffer for what happened here today. You know, like totally suffer.*

He turned and walked with a quick, muscular gait out of the temple, hesitating for just a moment by the gates and then disappearing south on Jalan Mahabharata.

Randolph collapsed on the floor of the courtyard but still Michael refused to let him rest. "Randolph, we have to get out of this trance. We may be safe from the leyaks but the Goddess Rangda could still get to us unless we're careful. And besides, you've stayed in the trance too long. There's a danger you'll never get out of it."

Randolph allowed Michael to half-carry him across the outer courtyard, through the *candi bentar* and into the inner temple. There they saw what had happened to Jimmy Heacox. Michael helped Randolph down to the floor of the courtyard and then walked across to give Heacox's body a cursory and disgusted inspection. Heacox's exposed tongue was already alive with glistening blowflies. Michael turned to look at the mask, which was lying on its side only a few feet away, staring with malevolent hatred at the sky.

"What happened?" Randolph asked. He kept his eyes averted from Heacox's body.

Michael circled around the mask of Rangda cautiously. "The mask is very magic. How can I put it? It *is* Rangda in a way, as well as a representation of Rangda. It guards the gate, as well as helping us to create it. Rangda does not discourage the living from entering her realm, not by any means, but she makes damn sure that you do it with respect, and on her terms."

Randolph wiped blood from his nose. "How come she let *us* through but killed this guy?"

Michael gingerly draped the mask in its ritual silk scarf and carried it back to the center of the courtyard. "That's because—like all truly evil beings—the Goddess Rangda is completely unpredictable."

Michael returned and sat down, studying Randolph carefully.

"Remember too that it's only a mask, even if it is a magic mask. The Goddess Rangda herself is something else. Something a hundred times worse."

Randolph felt that he was going to faint soon. The Temple of the Dead seemed to grow dark and he could have sworn that he saw movements in the shadows: figures, ghosts. The day was so humid now that sweat was streaking the dried blood on his cheeks and he did not know if he was shivering from cold or from shock.

"One question," he said. "When you went hunting leyaks, how did you kill them?"

"With a Polaroid camera," Michael said simply. "Provided you can stay out of the leyak's way long enough for the picture to develop, you're in business. You hold the picture up in front of him and set fire to it with a cigarette lighter."

"And what happens when you do that?"

"Believe me," said Michael, "you don't want to know what happens when you do that."

Michael began to recite the words that would bring their bodies and their spirits together again and restore their mortality. "O Sanghyang Widi, we ask your indulgence to leave this realm . . . fragrant is the smoke of incense that coils and coils upward toward the home of the three divine ones."

Randolph closed his eyes. He felt as if the whole world were being compressed, with himself in the center of it. Everything became darker and darker, and slower and slower, until he thought that Earth itself must be coming to a halt. When he opened his eyes, he was still sitting in the courtyard and Michael was getting to his feet.

"Is it over?" he asked thickly. His head pounded and his right arm felt as if it were burning.

"It's over," Michael assured him. "I want you to stay right there while I go find a taxi. We have to take you back to the *losmen* and see how bad you're hurt."

"The flight's at three."

"Let's just see if you're fit to take it."

Randolph reached up and held Michael's sleeve. "Listen," he said, "I know we ran into some trouble today with those leyaks. But if Reece and those other two hadn't interfered, it would have been all right, wouldn't it?"

Michael shrugged. "Probably," he agreed. "The Dutch Reform Cemetery is always a pretty quiet place."

"I want to do it again," Randolph said. He raised his head and looked Michael directly in the eyes to show him that he meant it. "I want to do it again, and I want to see Marmie this time."

Michael gently pried Randolph's fingers off his sleeve. "Let me go find us a taxi."

"You know something?" Randolph said. "You're a pretty rare kind of person."

"Maybe. Most of it was inherited."

Randolph gave Michael as much of a smile as the pain in his arm would allow. Michael was so much like his own sons could have been. It was strange, he thought as Michael padded off on his soft-soled sneakers to find a taxi, that when he had confronted Reece, knowing full well that Reece might be the man who had killed Marmie and the children, he had felt no rage, not even a sense of revenge. He had seen Reece for what he was, a hired killing machine, cruel and violent, but thoughtlessly violent. Randolph had regarded Reece with nothing more than stunned curiosity. He reserved his anger for the men who had thoughtfully and with utter malice employed him. When he returned to Memphis, he would have his pound of flesh from them. Yes, and all the blood that came with it.

He thought he heard Michael coming back. His mind suddenly rushed in on itself and he fell sideways onto the stones.

TWENTY

Memphis, Tennessee

Dr. Ambara came away from the window, allowing the fine lace curtains to fall back, and said, "You should be able to go out today. I think those stitches will hold."

Randolph took off his glasses and set them on his breakfast tray. He had had a good breakfast of corned-beef hash and poached eggs and now he was reading *The Wall Street Journal* while he drank his coffee.

"How long before you can take them out?" he wanted to know.

Dr. Ambara looked even darker than usual, silhouetted against the window. "What you want to know is, how long before you can attempt another death trance."

Randolph sipped his coffee and waited while Dr. Ambara packed away his surgical instruments. When the doctor was silent, Randolph asked, "Well?"

"Well what?"

"How long before I *can* attempt another death trance?"

Dr. Ambara shook his head. "I don't know. The injuries you suffered were quite severe. You were lucky not to lose the use of your right arm altogether. Perhaps a month. Perhaps six weeks."

"Are you sure I couldn't try it any earlier? I mean, once the stitches are out—?"

"No," said the doctor, sitting down on the side of the bed. "It is not just your body that needs to recuperate. It is your mind too. The emotional experience you went through in Bali was enough to send many normal people into life-long psychotherapy. You saw the dead, Randolph; you saw demons. And now you lie here in bed in Memphis and although it all happened far away, it has left you with scars.''

Randolph picked up his glasses and began folding and unfolding them. ''Well,'' he said with resignation, ''I guess I did ask you to take care of me.''

Randolph had suffered the worst of his agonies during the long journey back from Bali to the United States. Dr. Ambara had patched up his wounds as well as he could but by the time they reached London, Randolph had been running a high temperature and shivering and shaking like an agued horse. Only a massive injection of tetracycline had kept his infection and his temperature under control but he had insisted on returning to Memphis, even after Dr. Ambara had warned him there was a risk of septicemia, even of death.

It was Monday now. The doctor had cleaned and stitched Randolph's wounds and dosed him with sedatives and antibiotics. This morning's breakfast had been his first real meal, and even though his lips were still swollen and he ached all over, he had thoroughly enjoyed it. He had realized, very early this morning, just after the sun had slanted into his bedroom and awakened him, that he was no longer grieving for Marmie and the children, at least not in the same way as before. He had seen Natalie, the Dutch girl, and touched her, and he knew now that he would see Marmie in the same way, and touch her too. And although he had lost his children, he would be able to hold them again and assure them once and for always that he loved them.

There was something else too. He was sure, after everything that had happened, that it was Waverley Graceworthy and Orbus Greene who had sent Reece and his rat pack after him to Indonesia, maybe to kill him, maybe to do no more than frighten him, but certainly to make sure that the Cottonseed Association asserted its supremacy over Tennessee's cotton-processing industry and that Waverley Grace-worthy at last had his petty revenge on Randolph's father.

"How's Michael?" Randolph asked. "He's not too upset?"

"Oh, I think he's settling in fine," replied the doctor. "You have to remember that this is the first time he has ever been to America. It seems to me that he's walking around in complete amazement, trying to understand what it was that made his father into the kind of man he eventually became. How can a man from a country like America become a mystic? There is not much mysticism in Memphis."

"Well, maybe there is now," said Randolph, grimacing as he adjusted his pillow. "Have you two discussed the idea of your possibly seeing your late wife?"

Dr. Ambara colored. "Yes, we have. We may attempt a death trance later in the week, but I don't want you to think I'm keeping you in bed in order to preempt Michael's attention. You *do* need the rest, and your stitches *do* need to heal."

"Come on, I understand," Randolph said. "If it hadn't been for you, I wouldn't even have known about death trances."

"Well, maybe that would have been a blessing," Dr. Ambara said philosophically.

At that moment there was a brisk rapping at the door and Wanda came in, dressed in a pair of tight white pedal-pushers and a dark-blue silky blouse. She looked remarkably pretty and attractive.

"You're looking almost human again," she told Randolph.

"I feel like Frankenstein's monster. All I need now is a bolt through my neck."

"Neil Sleaman is outside. He'd like to see you."

"All right," Randolph said. "Would you ask him to wait for ten minutes while I finish my breakfast. See if he wants a cup of coffee."

"You've had calls from Mr. Graceworthy, Mr. Trent and Mr. Petersen. Also, your Cousin Ella called and she wants you to call her back as soon as you can. It's something about the funeral, nothing important."

"I see we're back in business," Randolph commented

"I beg your pardon?" Wanda asked.

"Wanda," Randolph said earnestly, "you went all the way to Indonesia with me and now we've come back. All this while you've been patient, understanding, loving, honest, open, and attractive beyond all description. Now that we're back at work, I don't want you to think I've forgotten any of that, because I haven't."

Wanda was silent for a moment, a little smile touching her lips, her eyes looking away in a mixture of modesty and self-satisfaction. "Thank you," she said at last and turned and left the room.

"Good girl," said Dr. Ambara, unexpectedly letting out a short laugh.

"When are you seeing Michael?" Randolph asked.

"Later today. He wants to teach me some of the basic mantras."

"Well, just make sure that nobody follows you."

"I'll be careful," Dr. Ambara promised. Michael was registered at Days Inn on Brooks Road under the fanciful name of Husain Qizilbush, the cover he had taken in case Reece or any other Cottonseed Association hirelings tried to find him. Randolph was no longer prepared to give Waverley Graceworthy or Orbus Greene the benefit of the doubt. They were killers as far as he was concerned.

Dr. Ambara left and Neil Sleaman came in carrying a cup of coffee.

"Neil," Randolph said. "How are you doing?"

"Fine, thank you, Mr. Clare. Surprised to see you back so soon. And—my God—you sure took a pasting in that taxi accident, didn't you?"

"Superficial cuts mainly," Randolph said casually. "Do you mind taking this breakfast tray off the bed for me?"

Neil carried the tray over to the other side of the room and then pulled up a chair and sat close to Randolph, parking his cup of coffee on the bedside table.

"We had a slow start out at Raleigh," he said. "There was trouble with the valves, like I told you. And then some of the staff downed tools until there was a security inspection. You know, they were afraid of more explosions. But everything's running pretty good now. The only problem is, we can't possibly catch up on lost production. Not for nine or ten weeks at best. We don't have the oil and we don't have the processing capacity."

Randolph sat up a little straighter to distance himself from Neil Sleaman's Binaca-flavored breath. "The problem is solved, I told you," he said.

"Well," Neil said with a slight grimace of irritation, "I'd sure like to know how you did it. We were working all week to come up with some kind of an answer and . . . well, there was no answer. We've fallen way behind on our production schedule, and that's it."

Without changing his expression, Randolph said, "The Cottonseed Association is going to help us."

Neil stared at him. He exhaled a sharp, disbelieving snort and then sat back in his chair, planted his fists on his hips and snorted again. "The Cottonseed Association?"

"That's right," Randolph replied, trying not to sound smug.

"Well, I'm sorry, Mr. Clare," Neil said, "but the Cottonseed Association won't help us out, never in a million years. Orbus Greene still has not replied to that deal you tried to make, and the way I hear it, he isn't going to either. Times are too tough, Mr. Clare, and the Cottonseed Association isn't going to help you survive as an independent. They won't do it. They'd rather see you—"

"Dead?" Randolph interrupted.

"I wasn't going to say that. I was going to say bankrupt."

"Nevertheless, the truth is that they would rather see me dead."

"You're serious?"

"I'm very serious," Randolph replied. "And what's more, I have evidence. And that's why the Cottonseed Association is going to help us out, because if it doesn't, I'm going to take that evidence to the chief of police and have Waverley Graceworthy and Orbus Greene indicted for homicide and conspiracy."

"I'm sorry, Mr. Clare," Neil replied, shaking his head. "I really don't think this is going to work. I mean, there is no conceivable way in which any member of the Cottonseed Association could have been connected to your family's homicides. Chief Moyne said that himself, and I have to say myself that you seem to be getting . . . well, I wouldn't say paranoid but—''

"Oh, paranoid, am I?''

"I'm sorry, sir, I didn't mean to be impertinent. But you can't blame everything that's happened on the Cottonseed Association. It just isn't realistic.''

Randolph asked suddenly, "Have you heard of a man called Reece?''

Neil colored but vigorously shook his head.

"Let me tell you something about this man called Reece,'' Randolph said. "He's a mute, a Vietnam veteran and a hired enforcer for the Margarine Mafia. Reece and three other gorillas followed me all the way out to Manila, to Djakarta and to Bali, and when I got to Bali, they threatened my life and nearly succeeded in killing me. It was only through luck and through the efforts of friends that I managed to escape alive.''

Neil said nothing but tried to meet Randolph's unrelenting gaze without flinching.

Randolph said, "I can produce a witness who can connect Reece with Waverley Graceworthy—Jimmy the Rib— and I can produce plenty of other evidence that connects Reece with the murder of my family and also with the murder of an innocent man in Djakarta.''

Neil said, "I hate to make this point, sir, but if you can do that . . . why don't you do it right away? I mean, I'm not trying to moralize or anything, but surely it would be indefensible to use this evidence simply to get all the cottonseed oil we need rather than to bring Mr. Graceworthy and Mr. Greene to justice?''

Randolph frowned at him. "My intention, Neil, is to do both. First to squeeze them, then to see that they get what they deserve.''

"I see.''

"You don't seem very happy about it,'' Randolph commented.

"Well, sir, there is one snag for sure."

"Yes? And what's that?"

Neil said, "My briefcase is in the other room. You'll have to excuse me while I get it."

Randolph waited impatiently, and when Neil returned, he was carrying a newspaper clipping from the *Press-Scimitar*. He handed it to Randolph without a word.

The headline read, "Black Gangster's Legs Amputated In Bizarre Beale Street Slaying." Randolph read the text quickly, then looked up at Neil questioningly.

"They found him just after you left for Indonesia," Neil said.

"Well, they sure did," Randolph said bitterly. He read aloud the last two paragraphs of the news report. "Chief of Police Dennis Moyne said that the killing was 'more than likely' the work of black fanatic groups exacting revenge for previous acts of violence that the deceased had perpetrated against them. He discounted reports that several white men had been seen leaving the victim's apartment after the slaying, alleging that these reports were nothing more than 'ill-informed and ill-intentioned gossip.' "

Neil said, "I'm sorry. It was just unfortunate."

"For Jimmy, yes."

"I'm sorry."

Randolph handed back the clipping. "Why should you be sorry? You never knew him, and there are probably plenty of people on Beale Street who are quite happy that he's dead. He wasn't what you might call a bundle of fun."

"I'm sorry because it kind of cuts the ground from under your case against the Cottonseed Association, doesn't it?"

Randolph frowned. "Oh, no. Jimmy the Rib's evidence was only minor, only circumstantial. The real evidence comes from eyewitnesses."

"Eyewitnesses? Eyewitnesses to what?" Neil wanted to know. His face was pale and he kept folding and unfolding the news clipping, first this way and then the other, with thin, agitated fingers.

Randolph said, "Ask Waverley if he'd like to meet me

Wednesday morning, say ten o'clock at the Clare Cottonseed Building.''

"Well, I'll try," Neil said doubtfully.

"Tell him to bring his attorney," Randolph added. "We might be drawing up a contract."

Neil took out a small leather-covered notebook and jotted down Randolph's instructions with a gold ballpoint pen. Then, without lifting his eyes from the page he said, "I really would find it a help if you could tell me a bit more about what you have in mind. I mean, I really don't think that an unsubstantiated threat against the Cottonseed Association is likely to make them change their minds." He paused and then added, "I know for sure that Waverley Graceworthy does not take kindly to threats, especially from the Clare family."

Randolph was tempted to say something caustic in return but he held his tongue and said, "Just fix up the meeting, would you? And tell Wanda about it. She'll want to make all the arrangements."

"Yes, sir."

"All right, you can go now."

"There was one more thing, sir."

Randolph looked up.

Neil, flustered, said, "Apparently you came back from Indonesia with a gentleman called Michael Hunter."

"That's correct. How did you know?"

"Well, I make it my business when you're away to check every company expenditure over fifteen hundred dollars, and an extra air ticket from Bali to Memphis was charged to our travel account in the name of Michael Hunter. I assumed that he was a guest of yours, sir, so obviously I didn't query it."

"You were right," Randolph told him. "He is a guest of mine. I personally authorized the payment of that ticket."

"Is Mr. Hunter, er . . . is he staying here now?"

Randolph raised an interrogative eyebrow.

"What I mean is," Neil stammered, "is he here now, in the house? Staying with you? I ask only in case he would like somebody to show him around Memphis."

"No, he's not here now," Randolph said. And for the first time, he was convinced not just by Neil Sleaman's behavior since the fire out at Raleigh, but by the man's sheer naked anxiety, that he was betraying him.

None of the evidence Randolph had was conclusive; none of it would stand up in court. But from the moment Stanley Vergo had suggested that the fire out at Raleigh was not accidental until Neil Sleaman had shown him this news report about Jimmy the Rib, two and two had been making four, and four and four had been making eight.

Why should Jimmy the Rib have been murdered—after all his years of precarious survival in the toughest districts of downtown Memphis—just after he had spoken to Randolph about Reece and the Cottonseed Association? Several white men had been seen leaving the building, just like three or four white men had been seen leaving the building when I.M. Wartawa had been murdered.

And who was the only person with whom Randolph had discussed his meeting with Jimmy the Rib? Chief Dennis Moyne of the Memphis police, the very man who had dismissed allegations that white men had been seen leaving the building and had laid the blame on black extremists.

And who was the only person with whom Randolph had discussed his meeting with I.M. Wartawa? Neil Sleaman, who was now trying to find out where Michael Hunter was staying.

Neil had defended Waverley and Orbus and the Cottonseed Association just once too often, which was evidence enough for Randolph of where his loyalties lay. Neil had been in charge of Clare Cottonseed's production department when the factory at Raleigh caught fire, and Neil had been in charge of making sure the plant got back in business. In spite of Neil's logical-sounding explanations, there had been nothing but technical delay, all of it just a little too technical to make sense.

There was only one question that stuck in Randolph's mind like a jagged piece of glass, a question he could not seem to crack. Why was Waverley Graceworthy so determined to destroy him, to destroy not only his corporation, but his family? Surely business alone had not driven him to murder. Hanging people and shooting them and cutting their legs off simply for the sake of a cottonseed-processing contract? Well, damn it, that seemed more fantastic than leyaks, and death trances and the Witch Widow, Rangda.

Yet Reece had probably murdered Marmie and the children on Waverley Graceworthy's instructions, and Reece had probably murdered Jimmy the Rib on Waverley Graceworthy's instructions, as well as I.M. Wartawa and God only knew how many other innocent people. And there was no doubt in Randolph's mind that Neil Sleaman was part of this conspiracy to exterminate everyone and everything that had anything to do with Clare Cottonseed. He had no proof. As far as he was concerned, he needed no proof. He had only to look at Neil sitting beside his bed, pale and confused and guilty, the epitome of Judas, to know that it was true.

Nonetheless he spoke quietly, with no evidence of anger, and he gave Neil Sleaman one more opportunity to prove that he was loyal.

"Mr. Hunter is staying at the Shelby Motel on Summer. I didn't want him here for reasons of security."

"Ah, the Shelby," Neil nodded. "Would he like a tour, do you think? I mean, this is a pretty interesting time of year what with the Beale Street Music Festival, the Cotton Carnival and the International Barbecue Contest."

"Well, no, Neil, I don't think he's the kind of person who would go for a tour," Randolph replied. "He's what you might call a spiritual type."

"Maybe he'd like to see the Mid-South Bible College."

"I don't think so. Thank you for your consideration anyway."

Neil was very agitated now. "Would he like to see Beale Street? Or maybe Mud Island? It seems a pity he should visit Memphis and never see Mud Island."

Randolph smiled and shook his head.

"Okay," Neil said. "I was only trying to be hospitable."

"Surely," Randolph acknowledged.

As soon as Neil left, Randolph picked up the telephone and asked Charles to put him through to 386-3311. Charles

knew better than to ask what the number was or why
Randolph was calling it. The phone rang two or three times
and then a voice said, "Shelby Motel. How can I help
you?"

Randolph said, "I want to make a reservation. A double
room in the name of Michael Hunter. Yes, tonight."

Later that morning Randolph climbed painfully out of bed
and Charles helped him to the patio, where he read for a
while, drank two or three small cups of black Mocha coffee
and watched the wind ruffling the azaleas. He supposed that
he should have felt deeply grieved by Neil Sleaman's be-
trayal, in much the way he should have felt deeply vengeful
against Richard Reece. But he felt that Neil and Reece were
only stick men, treacherous and dangerous certainly, but
motivated only by money, not by malice.

It was the Cottonseed Association that was at the heart of
the darkness: Waverley Graceworthy and Orbus Greene.
Against them Randolph felt a righteous hunger for revenge
that would have to be satisfied before he could ever find
peace.

They had killed his wife and children; they had tried to
kill him too. In return, they would have to be punished.
And since they had succeeded in butchering almost everybody who might have been a witness against them, there
was only one place Randolph could go for evidence: into
another death trance to talk to Marmie.

Close to lunchtime, Wanda came out onto the patio. She
was wearing a pale-blue linen business suit and she looked
very smart and efficient.

"Well," he smiled, shading his eyes from the sun, "the
ideal secretary."

"I brought you some papers to sign. Sven Petersen wants
to tie up that cattlecake contract with Southern Feeds."

"Sure. Just bring me a pen."

Wanda sat down opposite him, laid the papers out on the
wrought-iron table and showed him where to sign.

"You know," she said, "I really appreciated that compliment you paid me this morning."

He squiggled "Randolph Grace" and then looked up. "I

meant it. Besides, it wasn't a particularly easy compliment to pay. When you really mean something, the words never seem to come up to what you're trying to convey."

Wanda watched him sign his name two more times.

"Is that it?" he asked, and she nodded.

"You know something?" she said. "I feel guilty about the way I keep thinking about you."

"Why should you?" he asked in the gentlest of voices. "I think I feel the same way about you, and I don't feel guilty."

"But Marmie, and the children—"

"They're still there, and just as soon as these stitches come out, I'm going to go talk to them. Wanda, I love Marmie. I loved her before she was killed, I love her now, and I will probably love her forever. But that doesn't mean that I can't have feelings about you too."

He was silent for a moment and then said, "It may not be fair of me to ask you to wait for a while. You have your own life to lead, and I can't control it. But the time will come when I can give you all the attention you deserve . . . provided you can accept that I was once married to a lady called Marmie and that she didn't leave me because I stopped loving her, and that I once had three children called John and Mark and Issa and that somewhere in this universe I always will."

Tears glistened in Wanda's eyes and she stood up, bent over him and kissed his forehead. "I'll be back tomorrow with some more papers. Neil told me about the meeting with Waverley Graceworthy."

Randolph grasped her hand. "I love you," he said unaffectedly. "But there's one thing more. I suspect that Neil may be thinking of leaving us. I'm not certain, but it could be that another processor has offered him more money. So for the time being, could you make sure to be careful of what you tell him? Don't talk about me, for example, or Michael or Dr. Ambara. Don't talk about any confidential memos that may pass over your desk. Don't make him feel that he's been marooned, but don't let him know anything particularly confidential either."

"All right," Wanda said. She kissed him again and left.

Randolph sat in the midday sunshine and listened to the sounds of the birds and the insects. He thought he heard a boy shouting in the distant shrubbery; it was a voice just like John's, but when the breeze dropped for a moment, he realized it was only a dog barking.

"Oh, God," he said sadly.

TWENTY-ONE

Michael was stretched out on his bed at Days Inn watching "The Price Is Right" when Dr. Ambara knocked at the door.

"It's me, Ida Bagus Ambara."

Michael swung off the bed, shuffled across the floor, rattled back the door chain and opened the door. He was wearing only bright-red undershorts and smoking a cigarette. His hair was tousled and he looked as if he had not slept well.

Dr. Ambara quickly closed the door behind him. "It's all right, I wasn't followed."

"Pity," said Michael. "I could use some excitement."

Dr. Ambara looked at him questioningly through thumb-printed glasses but Michael reached for his shirt and said, "It's okay, Doctor. I was only joking."

"Randolph is much better today," Dr. Ambara reported. "He sends you his salutations."

"As long as he keeps on sending his money as well."

Dr. Ambara took off his coat. "He's not cynical about you, you know."

"I know," Michael acknowledged, "and I'm not cynical about him. It's just that you don't want to go through a death trance like that every day of the week."

"What does that mean?"

Michael stood by the window buttoning up his shirt and

314

looking down at the bright, glittering blue of the Days Inn king-sized swimming pool, where blond heads bobbed up and down and tanned bodies stretched out under the sun. Trying not to sound too negative, he said, "It means that every day of the week is far too often. In fact, once in a lifetime may be too often."

Dr. Ambara was loosening his striped necktie. "What are you trying to tell me?"

"I don't know." Michael breathed smoke and then crushed out his cigarette in an ashtray. "I guess I'm trying to tell you that I'm all washed up."

"You mean you don't want to take me into a death trance to meet my Ana?"

Michael ran his hand through his hair. "I don't know. Maybe I'm feeling cooped up. Maybe I need to get drunk. Maybe it's just that I've arrived in America and half of my personality has suddenly found that it's home. I've been down by the pool listening to young people talking. I've been watching television. I've been standing out front just watching the cars go by. A whole part of my personality is home, Dr. Ambara, and suddenly the temples and the death trances don't seem so important anymore. Well . . . it's not that they aren't important, it's just that I see them in a different perspective."

Dr. Ambara said gravely, "You mean that they have diminished in your esteem?"

"No, Doctor, not diminished, but somehow they seem to be different."

Dr. Ambara took off his glasses and carefully wiped at the corners of his eyes with the tips of his fingers. "What about Randolph? Will you take him into a death trance to meet his family?"

"I guess I'm going to have to. A contract is a contract, after all; and unless he pays me, I won't ever get back home."

"Do you want to go back?"

"I'm not sure. I haven't seen enough of America to be able to judge. But I have to take him into that one last trance, and I'm sorry, Dr. Ambara, I really am, but that's the last trance I ever want to do."

Dr. Ambara swallowed, lifted one hand helplessly and dropped it again. "So I don't get to meet my Ana after all."

Michael said hoarsely, "I'm sorry. I've been sitting here all morning wondering how I could tell you."

"Well, it's not your fault," said the doctor. "I should understand fear more than anybody."

"You're right," Michael replied. "It's fear. Two bad death trances in a row, and the leyaks seem to be getting more cunning too. I'm not sure I'm going to be able to survive many more trances."

Dr. Ambara said, "I have learned most of the chants and the mantras. Is it possible that I could enter the death trance alone?"

"Are you kidding? Your very first death trance?"

Dr. Ambara stood up, his hands clasped in front of his chest. "I have studied this subject very thoroughly, Michael. I know theoretically what to do even if I am something of an innocent when it comes to the practicalities."

Michael took out another cigarette and lit it. He stared at Dr. Ambara through the smoke. "You know what the practicalities are, don't you? These practicalities you're something of an innocent about?"

Dr. Ambara said nothing but remained standing in the same position, a position that seemed to be one of supplication and devotion, but also of determination.

Michael said, "The practicalities are leyaks, real leyaks, who can tear your lungs out. And the Witch Widow Rangda, who can do ten times worse."

"I know of all these dangers," Dr. Ambara said quietly. "I know of all the demons, and of all the difficulties."

"You'll die," Michael assured him. "You'll die and Rangda will eat your soul. You'll spend the rest of eternity as one screaming soul inside one screaming cell inside the blackest, most disgusting body in any demonology anywhere, period. Listen, Doctor, do you seriously want to be part of some raddled witch's septic ovaries? For ever and ever and ever?"

"I thought you would help me to find Ana. I thought that was part of the agreement."

"The only agreement is that I may try one last death trance, and on the other hand, I very well may not. And since Randolph Clare is the man who's footing the bill, I think *he* has the right to meet his family, don't you? Instead of your meeting your Ana? Believe me, this is nothing personal, Dr. Ambara. If I thought I could handle it, I'd do it for you. But that last death trance, that was just about the ultimate. I was two feet from being chopped liver that time, and believe me, my guardian spirit was trying to *tell* me something right then, like 'Stay away from Rangda and stay away from the leyaks. Stay on your own side of the grave, where you belong.' "

"But if I attempt the death trance on my own?" Dr. Ambara persisted.

Michael shook his head. "Even if you manage to get into the trance without killing yourself, the leyaks will immediately pick up your jitters and your inexperience. You'll die, Dr. Ambara, believe me."

"But the power of Rangda is not as great here as it is in Bali."

"That's only a guess. Nobody has ever tested it out."

"Perhaps this is the time."

Michael shrugged. "I can't stop you," he said, "but you could take a camera along for protection if you think it could help."

"Well, I'll see," said Dr. Ambara, knotting his necktie again and pulling on his coat. "I'm disappointed of course, but maybe this is all for the best."

"Yes," Michael said. "Maybe it is."

He opened the door and Dr. Ambara hurried out and along the blue-carpeted corridor. Michael stood there watching him for a moment, then went back into the room and chained and bolted the door behind him. Through the window he could see Dr. Ambara walk quickly across the courtyard beside the swimming pool and toward the parking lot.

Michael had never admitted his fear before, not as openly

as this, and never to a man like Ida Bagus Ambara, who was not much more than a stranger. Perhaps his first real admission of cowardice had been his promise to Mungkin Nanti that he would never try death trances again. Both of the last two trances had affected him as would a serious car accident, and it was going to take a supreme effort of will for him to enter any more. With a grim smile, he thought, *I'm a burned-out pedanda, a half-caste high priest with nothing to look forward to but a Balinese government pension and a lifetime of selling plastic sandals.*

He finished his cigarette and then went through to the bathroom to brush his teeth. Even in the flattering lights of the hotel mirror he looked thin and haggard and haunted, a man who only recently had seen death in all its grisly glory.

He splashed his face with cold water and then dabbed it dry with a hand towel. It was just then that there was another knock at the door and he called, "Who is it?"

"Mr. Qizilbush? This is room service. I have those drinks you ordered."

Michael went across and loosened the chain. "I didn't order any drinks. You must have the wrong Qizilbush."

Immediately the muzzle of a .45 automatic was thrust through the crack in the door and a thick voice demanded, "Take off the chain. Open up or we'll blow your head off."

Michael jerkily did as he was told. The door burst open and two men came in waving automatics. He recognized one of them as Reece; the other he did not recognize at all. He was short and thick-set, with a prickly shaved head and bright-blue eyes that stared with a kind of incandescent madness. This must be Frank Louv, Michael thought, the fourth man in the quartet that had followed Randolph Clare to Bali and back.

"So, we got you," said Louv. Reece said nothing but twisted Michael's arm behind his back and pushed the muzzle of his automatic against the side of Michael's head.

"You been giving us trouble, you goddam slant," the mad-looking Louv grinned at him. Then he jabbed his gun into Michael's genitals, so viciously that Michael gasped and tried to jackknife forward, until Reece forced his arm back up again.

"Good thing that doctor friend of yours led us here, ain't it?" asked Louv. "Not that he *knew*. I mean, he was trying his best to shake off any tails, but what was he looking for? Cars, that's what he was looking for. It didn't occur to him to look for a motorbike, now did it? It never does, not to car drivers. That's what we call psychology."

He paused, looked around the room. and then gratuitously jabbed Michael in the genitals a second time.

"That sure hurts, don't it? Just like my ass hurts from riding around on that motorbike following that stupid doctor friend of yours. Listen, if it hurts, don't blame me. Blame him. Next time you see him, punch *him* in the balls, tell him he owes you."

Michael spat his cigarette onto the carpet. The mad-looking man ground it out with his brown-leather motorcycle boot.

"You must have something," the man said. "Mr. Waverley Graceworthy wants you real bad. What are you, a slant or only half a slant? Mr. Waverley Graceworthy wants you alive, alive-o, and undamaged. So why don't you slip into some strides and we can go meet him face-to-face. Believe me, Charlie Chan, you'll enjoy it."

Slowly, reluctantly, Michael began to dress. Reece pushed the curtains aside and stared down at the swimming pool. Michael had the feeling that he was considering how easy it would be to pick off the swimmers, one by one, with a high-powered rifle.

Frank Louv nudged Michael with his automatic. "You ready? There . . . don't forget your cigarettes. What kind of brand is that, Lion? Some kind of slant cigarette? Mr. Graceworthy said to treat you good. Guys like you, I used to waste in the Delta and take some pleasure in doing it. How can you trust anybody who's half American and half slant? I used to think, should I shoot the American half of them for being traitors or the slant half of them for being slants?"

He seemed to think this was hugely amusing because he

let out a high whoop of glee and danced an abrupt little fandango.

Reece came away from the window and waved his hand to indicate that they should leave.

Michael said, "I have friends, you know that? You people are going to run into a hard time when my friends find out what has happened to me. This isn't Bali."

"You're too right this isn't Bali," grinned the mad-looking Louv. "This is Memphis, Tennessee, and in Memphis, Tennessee, Mr. Waverley Graceworthy is the undisputed king of the mountain, so believe me, we ain't going to be running into no hard time, especially not from wimps like Mr. Randolph Clare."

Reece made a signal to Louv to shut up. Then they walked Indian file out the door and along the corridor until they reached the elevators. Louv said, "My piece is in my pocket, Mr. Half-Slant Hunter, and believe me, I ain't concerned about using it."

Michael said something in Sanskrit. The mad-looking man snarled, "What did you say? When you talk around me, friend, don't you go using none of that Chink lingo."

The elevator door opened and Michael obediently stepped inside. "I was saying a prayer," he told the man. "I was praying that when you die, the great god of gods, Sanghyang Widi, should force-feed you for all eternity on cockroach shit."

As Michael was being taken to Waverley Graceworthy, Randolph was slowly and painfully getting dressed, against Dr. Ambara's instructions. He was already bored with sitting on the patio and lying with his feet up on the sofa, and there were two things he intended to do. One was to visit the processing plant out at Raleigh to see how Tim Shelby was managing; the other was to lay some flowers on the graves of his family.

He called Herbert and Charles and between them they helped him out to his limousine. Charles settled him in the backseat and gave him a throw for his knees.

"I'm not an invalid," Randolph protested.

Charles said, "You still have to take care of yourself.

You're the only one we have left. Mrs. Wallace made some of those cookies you like, special. They're in a jar in the cocktail cabinet.''

"Tell Mrs. Wallace she's an angel."

"I'm not telling Mrs. Wallace nothing like that," Charles muttered.

Herbert drove out of the driveway and into the glare of the afternoon. "Your doctor isn't going to be too pleased about this, Mr. Clare," he commented as they headed toward the William B. Fowler Expressway.

"He's my doctor, not my mother," Randolph replied. He leaned forward, opened the cocktail cabinet and poured himself a large glass of Jack Daniel's. Then he opened the Swedish-crystal cookie jar and helped himself to three of Mrs. Wallace's finest. Herbert's eyes watched him in the rearview mirror. "I tasted those when they came out of the oven. Some cookies, huh?"

"My secret weakness," Randolph chuckled.

He spent an hour out at Raleigh inspecting the rebuilt wintering plant. The factory was back at full production now, and Tim Shelby had it running twenty-four hours a day, with some of the men working double shifts.

"If we don't have any outside help, how long do you think it will take to make up the contract?" Randolph asked as they sat in Tim's office after the inspection.

"Two months, maybe six weeks."

"It seems to me you took a long time getting back into full production, nearly a week longer than you first predicted."

"We had trouble with the valves. Neil had to get replacements for them in Germany. That took up most of the time."

Randolph swilled his whiskey around in his glass. Tim had a friend who gave him a dozen bottles of Chivas Regal every birthday, so there was always a good supply on hand for visiting dignitaries. Randolph asked, "What exactly was the trouble?"

"I'm not sure. They kept blocking. Neil had one of the fitters from Woodstock working on them."

"Why didn't your own fitters work on them?"

"Our own fitters were pretty much tied up replacing the pipework and the refrigeration unit."

"Any trouble there?" Randolph asked.

"No, sir, just with the valves."

"Did you ever see the valves for yourself?"

Tim Shelby frowned. "No, sir, I can't say I did. I'm not sure what you're trying to get at here."

"I'm not sure either," Randolph said. "Did you know the fitter who Neil brought over from Woodstock?"

"No, sir, he wasn't familiar to me personally."

"Did any of your staff know him?"

"I'd have to check that out."

Randolph finished his drink. "Okay," he said. "I know it's a chore, but would you check to see if any of your people recognized that fitter or knew his name. I'm going to Forest Hill now. I should be back home around four o'clock. Let me know if you've found out who he was."

Tim Shelby stood up. "I guess Neil would know who the fitter was. He drove him over from Woodstock himself."

"Did he? Well, that was considerate of him."

"I guess he just wanted to make sure we got the plant back into business as soon as possible."

"Yes," Randolph said, "I guess he did."

Herbert drove him to Forest Hill Cemetery and there under a May sky that was almost purple, he bowed his head over the graves of Marmie and the children, graves that were still unmarked but that would eventually bear the names of Randolph's wife and the names he and she had so joyously written only a few short years ago on crisp white birth announcements.

He stood for almost ten minutes beside the graves, but after his experience in the Dutch Reform Cemetery in Denpasar, he felt that his gesture was oddly hollow. Marmie and the children no longer inhabited the bodies that lay beneath the ground, although they were here somewhere, maybe close by. He looked around at the rows of surrounding tombstones and wondered if Marmie and the children could see him, maybe even hear him.

"Marmie?" he said, clearing his throat. A Tennessee

warbler landed suddenly on Marmie's wooden grave marker, ruffled its bright-green back and sang *chip, chip, chip-chip-chip* at him.

"Marmie," Randolph repeated, "if you can hear me at all, if you can see me, I want you to know that I haven't forgotten you for one single minute. I want you to know that I've discovered a way to see you again, to touch you again. It won't be long now, no more than a week, and then we'll be together."

He swallowed. His throat was suddenly dry although his eyes were filled with tears.

"Marmie, listen to me. I love you."

An old man in a fawn cotton suit and an old-fashioned skimmer suddenly appeared from behind a nearby monument. He stared at Randolph for a moment and then at the warbler perched on Marmie's grave.

"You trying to teach that little feller to talk?" he inquired.

Randolph took out his handkerchief and blew his nose, shaking his head at the same time. The old man came closer and stood next to him, admiring the warbler as if it actually belonged to Randolph and was so well trained that it followed him around.

"He's a cute one, ain't he?" he remarked.

"I guess."

"You know what they say about songbirds that fly around cemeteries, don't you?"

Randolph found himself looking at the contrast between the old man's soft, withered neck and his crisp starched collar. "No," he replied. "What do they say?"

"They say that they sing all the songs that come rising out of the graves when the dead are buried. A song don't die, you see, like a human does. A song comes rising out of the grave and a bird catches it, that's what, and keeps it, to sing again. One day when all the human race is dead and there's nothing but birds left alive, all the beautiful music that was ever written and ever sung will still be heard because the birds will be singing it, although there won't be nobody to listen."

He paused, sniffed and said, "What you teaching it?"

Randolph shook his head. "I'm not teaching it anything, I'm afraid. I only wish I could."

He returned to the limousine. Herbert was waiting patiently, listening to the Memphis Chicks on the radio. He switched off the game as Randolph approached but Randolph asked, "What's the score?"

"Hunsaker just struck out."

"Get me Neil Sleaman on the phone, will you?"

"Sure thing."

After a short while, Randolph was put through to Neil Sleaman's secretary, Janet. "Is Neil not there?" Randolph asked.

"No, sir, I'm sorry, sir. He called a taxi and went out. I don't know where he was going."

"Janet, could you do me a great favor? Could you call the taxi company and ask where they dropped him off? Then call me back right away?"

"Yes, sir, for sure."

Herbert started up the limousine. "Where to, Mr. Clare?"

"Home," Randolph said.

They had been driving for only three or four minutes, however, when the car telephone bleeped. Randolph picked it up and said, "Janet?"

"Yes, sir. I just called the taxi company. They said that Mr. Sleaman was taken to the Shelby Motel on Summer. He was met there by several other people. The taxi driver recognized Mr. Orbus Greene's car, although he couldn't tell if Mr. Orbus Greene was there or not. Apparently the car has darkened windows."

"Thank you, Janet. You're quite amazing."

"My father-in-law used to work for the taxi company, sir."

"That accounts for it. Send them a bottle of champagne on office expenses."

"Yes, sir. Domestic or foreign?"

"They're taxi drivers, Janet, not gourmets."

"Very well, sir, domestic."

Randolph put down the phone and sat back with a feeling of bitter satisfaction. He had always hoped that Neil would

be smarter than that, smart enough to realize that Clare
Cottonseed was soon going to grow into one of the greatest
names in international business circles and that he was going
to grow along with it. Smart enough to understand that
Randolph himself, for all of his friendliness and his willing-
ness to trust people whom he probably shouldn't, had an
underlying strength that rarely failed him, and a sense of his
own value as unshakable as reinforced concrete.

He could only suppose that Neil had succumbed to
Waverley Graceworthy's spurious air of Southern tradition
and to the promise of payments far more generous than he
deserved. It was ironic in a peculiar back-to-front way that
Neil should have turned out to be just the kind of cheap
wheeler-dealer that he looked like. If anything had given
him away, it was those snappy suits and that bolo tie.

Herbert turned the limousine into the driveway of Clare
Castle, and there, as Randolph had half-expected, was OGRE
1, Orbus Greene's long, black limousine.

TWENTY-TWO

Orbus spread his bulk over Randolph's three-cushion couch. He sat with his feet wide apart, yet they were surprisingly dainty feet for a man his size, and they were smartly encased in two-tone Oxfords of white and brown. His belly nestled in his lap like a schoolroom globe.

As he spoke, he devoured cookies almost continuously, his chubby pink hand moving back and forth from dish to mouth with the sort of flowing, practiced gestures that reminded Randolph of a weaver.

"Well," he said, glancing up at Randolph from time to time, "you think you've outsmarted us, don't you?"

"I think you've outsmarted yourselves," Randolph retorted, leaning back in his armchair, his eyes flickering from dish to mouth, watching Orbus eat.

"I admit that young Neil has plenty to learn," Orbus told him. "He should have realized that Mr. Hunter was too valuable an asset for you to announce his whereabouts to a professional minion like himself. He should have realized you were testing him. It's his *manner*, you know. That's the problem with Neil. Too damned greasy by half. You always get the feeling that if you shake hands with him, you'll come away with your fingers all covered with hair oil."

Randolph sat silent for a while and then stood up. He walked around to the back of the couch so Orbus would find it difficult to turn around and look at him.

"Why didn't you answer the proposal I made for the Cottonseed Association to help me meet the Sun-Taste contract?"

Orbus swallowed noisily. "That was Waverley's decision. You must understand, Randy, that Waverley wants your internal organs, and he wants them hanging out to dry on his front fence."

"Why?" Randolph demanded. "Why so badly?"

"Who knows why? He always says it's personal. There isn't any question, though, that he was prepared to tolerate you while Clare Cottonseed was running at a loss, and he was prepared to accept you when you when you were running at a moderate profit. The existence of one reasonably successful independent company could only help encourage more business for everybody, that was what he used to say. But Sun-Taste was just too much success. If you could get and keep Sun-Taste, it would mean that you were becoming one of the big boys, like Brooks and Gamble's and Dillons. Brooks' last two quarters have been poor-to-disastrous, and so have Waverley's. Well, you know that for yourself. But let me tell you something: the day Waverley heard that Sun-Taste had decided on Clare Cottonseed, believe me, he was hysterical. I mean, he went ape."

Randolph said nothing but walked around the couch until he was confronting Orbus again. "So Waverley, for some mysterious personal reason—"

"As well as for a perfectly understandable business reason," Orbus interjected.

"All right then. But for some combination of reasons, mysterious and understandable, Waverley wants me eliminated. Not just bankrupted, but six feet under the ground."

"That's what I've come to see you about," breathed Orbus. He picked up the last of the cookies and shoved it in his mouth.

"Would you like a few more?" Randolph asked.

"I shouldn't," Orbus said.

Randolph rang for Mrs. Wallace and then said, "Where's Neil now? Was he too embarrassed to come here with you?"

"You could say that, but I didn't really want him along. What I'm going to say to you now, I want to be private, and stay private."

"Go on."

"Well," Orbus wheezed, his voice more high-pitched than ever, "it is my understanding that you have some sort of evidence that connects Waverley Graceworthy with Richard Reece, and Richard Reece with what happened to your family up in Canada."

"You know about Reece?"

"Certainly I know about Reece. I've been complaining to Waverley about Reece ever since Waverley first employed him. Reece is a maniac. Reece has no morals at all, good or bad. If you tell him to push somebody's teeth down his throat, that's just what Reece does, and what's more, he waits for the teeth to go through that person's system and come out the other end so he can push them down twice just to show he's done a good job. There's a whole gang of them, all vets, all crazy. God only knows how Waverley got to know them, but they treat him like the Emperor Napoleon."

Mrs. Wallace knocked at the door and Randolph invited her in. He indicated the empty cookie dish and said gently, "Mr. Greene finds your cookies every bit as desirable as I do. Do you think he could have another batch?"

"There are twenty-four to the batch." said Mrs. Wallace coldly.

Orbus heaved himself around and smiled at her. "That's okay," he told her generously. "I didn't want too many anyway."

When Mrs. Wallace had gone. Randolph said, "The fire at Raleigh was definitely sabotage then?"

Orbus nodded.

"And what about my family?"

"They were supposed to be frightened, that's all. Threatened, tied up, robbed. The trouble was, Reece went bananas."

"Why are you telling me this? You realize that you're implicating yourself in anything up to a dozen deaths? My family, Jimmy the Rib, the three men who died at Raleigh,

I.M. Wartawa; who knows how many more?'' Randolph held his fists clenched tight to control himself.

Orbus suddenly asked, "This room isn't wired for sound, is it?"

Randolph shook his head.

"All right then," Orbus said. "I'm a tough businessman. You know that. I've been head of Brooks Cottonseed for as long as I can remember, and I was mayor of Memphis in the bad old days when this city was nothing but sweat and shit and niggers and gangsters with faces like cans of economy ham. I've done my share of grafting and I've done my share of bullying, and there are plenty of people who wouldn't mind seeing my substantial person floating in the Mississippi facedown, along with the unborn babies and the dead dogs. I went along with Waverley when he was hiring Reece simply to lean on people, to hurry up payments and that kind of thing. I approved of that. Now and then one or two members of the Cottonseed Association would get out of line, politically or businesswise, and then Reece and his boys would go around and remind them where their allegiance ought to be. I didn't object to any of that. That's necessary, that kind of enforcement, in this city, even today, even with it all smartened up. But when Waverley went after you, he must have told Reece something a hell of a lot different from what he told *me* he'd said because I don't approve of killing, not anybody, certainly not for the sake of business, and I especially don't approve of killing innocent women and children who don't have anything to do with what their husbands or fathers might have been playing at. I'm a Christian, Randy, you know that; and while there might be no particular commandment against intimidation, there sure as hell is one against murder, which is exactly the name of the game that Waverley's been up to."

Randolph listened to Orbus with a gradually growing coldness. He had thought after the funeral that if he could find out *why* Marmie and the children had died, somehow his mind would become more settled and he would be able to accept their deaths more easily. But now that he knew Waverley Graceworthy had ordered them killed for nothing more meaningful than a margarine contract, he felt a frigid rage that seemed to crystallize the structure of his bones and turn his skull into aching ice.

Orbus sensed Randolph's shock and he tried to be sympathetic.

"Listen to this, Randy. Waverley found out from Reece and his boys what you were doing in Indonesia. At first he ordered you killed, both you and this Michael Hunter. I don't know how you managed to get away; Reece was the only witness and you can't say that Reece is exactly the world's greatest raconteur. But whatever . . . Waverley knows that you can go into some kind of trance where you can talk to people who are dead. He also knows that you need Michael Hunter to help you do it. He's worried that you're going to get Michael Hunter to help you talk to Marmie and that Marmie is going to put the finger on Reece and give you some clues that might just stand up in court."

Randolph nodded and said huskily, "Well, that's exactly it. The death trance is real. I've experienced it for myself. You see, I've got plenty of circumstantial evidence, even though one of my witnesses was killed—"

"That black guy? Jimmy the Rib?"

"That's right. But if it comes down to it, *you* can substantiate Waverley's connection with Reece now. That's if you're willing to testify. And all I need do then is to go into another death trance, find Marmie and see what she remembers about the night she was murdered."

Orbus looked up as the door opened and Mrs. Wallace came in with a fresh dish of cookies. "You're a lady," he told her and shook out his handkerchief to wipe the sweat from his face. Mrs. Wallace pinched in her cheeks and walked out again without a word. She obviously thought that to offer her cookies to Orbus Green was the culinary equivalent of throwing pearls before swine.

Orbus resumed eating. "Obviously, I'd prefer *not* to testify," he told Randolph with his mouth full. "In fact, one of the reasons I'm talking to you now is because I don't want my name mixed up in any of this. If Waverley wants to behave like a homicidal maniac, is that my fault? But, well, let's see how things go. Reece might confess. He can write even if he can't speak. And there has to be somebody, somewhere, who knows that Waverley has been paying Reece for services over and above normal friendly conversations, somebody who might testify instead of me.''

Randolph was going to say something caustic to Orbus about his cowardice but decided against it. Any man who could allow himself to grow to Orbus's size and unashamedly sit and cram cookies into his mouth while he was discussing brutal homicide was obviously far beyond shame. All that Orbus was holding onto now was his blurry sense of right and wrong. It was all right to threaten, but it was wrong to kill. Perhaps Orbus could sense that his heavily labored heart was close to the end of its efforts and wanted to die redeemed. Randolph did not know, and did not much care either. The only people who would mourn the passing of Orbus Greene would be the proprietors of Memphis's restaurants.

Randolph asked, ''How about a glass of Madeira to swill those cookies down?''

''Well, you don't hear me arguing,'' replied Orbus. Randolph went over to the cabinet and came back with a brimming glass of dark dessert wine; Orbus tasted it and then gulped it down.

''What were you doing at Shelby's Motel?'' Randolph wanted to know.

Orbus wiped his mouth with his handkerchief. ''What I was doing at Shelby's Motel was expecting to collect Michael Hunter.''

''But?''

''Well, you know for yourself, don't you? He wasn't there. Somebody had booked a room in his name—it was you, wasn't it?—but nobody ever checked in. Of course Neil panicked. He realized then that you had set him up. It would have been funny if it hadn't been so pitiful.''

Orbus ate another two cookies and then said, ''You probably won't believe this, but I've been telling you the truth up until now—even so far as it casts no credit on me—so there's every reason for you to give me the benefit of the doubt. The reason Neil and I went to collect Michael Hunter was to keep him safe from Waverley.''

"Go on,'' Randolph said in a noncommittal voice.

"Waverley, you see, had given special instructions to Reece that Michael Hunter had to be taken alive. Waverley had changed his mind from the time when he wanted him dead. Mind you, he hasn't changed his mind about *you,* he still wants *you* dead. Anyway, Neil and I could think of only one reason Waverley would want to keep Michael Hunter alive, and that was to force him to take Reece into one of these special trances so he could deal with Marmie. You know, deal with her for good and all. You have to believe me, Randy, that man wants to see you buried. Don't ask me why. But I have only to whisper the name 'Randolph Clare' within ten feet of that man and he starts to shake like a rabid schnauzer. He hates you like *hell*.''

Randolph said, "Let me get this straight. You and Neil were going to 'collect' Michael Hunter just so Waverley couldn't get him?''

Orbus gave an undulating shrug. "I'm not discussing motives here, Randy.''

"What you really mean is, you were thinking of playing us both off. Waverley and me, using Michael Hunter as a hostage.''

"This is business, Randy. In business you have to take every opportunity that presents itself.''

"Except that *this* opportunity turned out to be a bluff, and you and Neil Sleaman were left with egg on your face and your pants around your ankles. And now you've come to me sniveling for sympathy and babbling about commandments and Christianity. God Almighty, Orbus, if you really had any guts, why didn't you come and tell me about Reece as soon as you heard that Marmie was dead? Why didn't you warn me then? Reece nearly killed me in Bali. How many tears would you have managed to squeeze out of those fat eyes of yours if Reece had succeeded? If they'd flown me home in a box? How Christian would you have felt about Marmie then? All you're worried about now is your own guilty implication in Waverley's madness and the fact that

Michael Hunter and I might very well bring back the evidence that will put you right where you belong, in the state penitentiary.''

Orbus lowered his head and looked sorry for himself. To demonstrate to Randolph how deeply contrite he was, he refrained from taking another cookie, an act of contrition that Randolph failed to notice.

"Randy, you misjudge me." Sorrowfully.

"I don't think so, Orbus. Go on, tell me what you would have done if you and those goons of yours had actually found Michael Hunter at the Shelby Motel.''

Orbus heaved himself to his feet. "Let me tell you something, Randy. I've come here today of my own free will and I've committed myself. So don't push it, okay? The deal is simply this, that if you keep my name out of this business, you'll get all the help you need and more besides. Not just information, but cottonseed oil too, to get you out of this fix with Sun-Taste. And after that, a new beginning for both of us. Maybe a working partnership between Clare Cottonseed and Brooks Cottonseed, completely outside the Association. Come on, Randy, we're talking mutual benefit here. We're talking forgive and forget. The future, not the past.''

"And Waverly?"

Orbus guffawed. "Waverley? Waverley's cracked.''

"So you want me to go into a death trance and find the evidence that will get Waverley indicted and Reece put away, after which you and I will start talking about working partnerships, and the future, and forgive and forget?''

Orbus winked at him. "The cottonseed business is a *pie*, Randy. The fewer hungry people there are to sit down and share it, the larger the slices.''

Randolph found the moral and physical excesses of Orbus Greene so overwhelming that he was speechless, unable to answer the man, unable to make any kind of decision about his offers. What do you say to a man who would scarcely have stopped masticating long enough to hear that you were dead and yet who was desperately begging you to help him avoid a punishment he richly deserved?

Randolph said, "Let me think about it, okay? I'll call you later."

"And what will you do about Neil?"

"Nothing for the time being, apart from suspend him."

"He has a very earnest personality. He's very willing. I hope you don't do anything to crush his sense of personal worth."

Randolph laid a hand on Orbus's massive shoulder just to irritate him. "What would it take to crush *your* sense of personal worth, Orbus?"

Orbus laughed. "Mount St. Helens, I should think."

Orbus's attendants were waiting for him outside, studiously picking their teeth. One of them opened the limousine door while the other three heaved Orbus inside as if he were so much blubber. He made himself comfortable and then turned to Randolph and said, "You take care of yourself, Mr. Clare. Whatever you think about me, I'm harmless. Corrupt, possibly. Self-serving, undoubtedly. Cruel, more than likely. But nobody has ever died to further my career and nobody has ever died because I felt vengeful. So a word to the wise and the wildly romantic: watch out for Waverley."

The bodyguards glared at Randolph as they climbed into the limousine. Then the doors slammed and with a slewing of gravel, they drove around the drive and through the gates. Randolph stood on the front steps watching them go. Then he turned and went back inside.

"That man," complained Mrs. Wallace, coming through the hallway with the empty cookie dish. "I don't know what to make of him."

"Me neither," Randolph admitted. "I don't know whether I hate him or like him in a strange sort of way."

"He's a beast," Mrs. Wallace declared unequivocally.

"The world is running with beasts," Randolph replied.

As Randolph returned to his library, Dr. Ambara was sitting in the living room of his single-story house in Germantown, naked, his legs crossed, his palms facing upward, attempting to enter the death trance. The blinds were drawn but the afternoon sunlight illuminated in muted amber the sisal carpeting, the simple bamboo furniture, the Balinese clay pottery and the *lamak* hangings. On the wall behind the sofa there was a large painting of a half-naked duck shepherdess, done in the style favored by American tourists. On the mantelpiece above the fireplace there was an intricate selection of root carvings in pale teak: attenuated nudes, lions with wings, and dragons.

Dr. Ambara's glasses lay beside him on the carpet. Three or four books of Hindu ritual were propped up before him so he could read the Sanskrit mantras as he proceeded. There was a small mask of Rangda on the coffee table, a mask he had bought on impulse four years earlier at the Djakarta airport. He had draped it with silk and surrounded it with wilting azalea flowers and smoking joss sticks.

He was very frightened, but also very determined. If Michael Hunter refused to take him into a death trance, he would have to enter it by himself. Randolph Clare had entered it and survived, and he was a Westerner. Surely a calm and disciplined Indonesian could enter the death trance with the greatest of ease, arousing no leyaks and talking to any dead spirit he wished.

Dr. Ambara began to sway slowly back and forth, humming the magic mantra *Om* to begin with but then reciting the words of the Sanskrit chant of the dead. He closed his eyes and rocked like a grieving woman, backward and forward, backward and forward, but he found it difficult to empty his mind and every now and then a noisy motorcycle would go past and break his concentration.

"Take me into the world of the dead, O Sanghyang Widi. Let me speak with those spirits who have entered heaven before me. O carry me into the smoke, O Sanghyang Widi."

He went on and on, repeating the same mantras over and over again. He thought of nothing but Ana; and then he thought of nothing but emptiness; and then suddenly he was sliding backward across a lake of ink under a black sky, faster and faster, and the real world began to rush away from him like a rapidly shrinking bubble.

He saw stars bursting over his head; he heard grinding noises like cliffs colliding with cliffs. He heard screams that were hardly human, if they were screams at all; and then the world began to rumble and shake, and huge chunks of blackness began to collapse on him and bury him, until at last a single dazzling silver ring touched the inky surface of the lake and spread outward and outward, one ring after another, brilliant ripples that never connected, like a Chinese metal puzzle.

He opened his eyes. The sitting room seemed almost the same except that the sunshine was foggier somehow, and the blinds seemed to blow far more slowly in the afternoon breeze. He slowly stood up, naked and brown and thin, and looked around in wonder. He was quite sure now, from the way in which Randolph had described it to him, that he had entered the death trance. He moved across the room as if he were swimming, raised the blind and looked out into the street. Cars were driving past like cars in a dream; a scrap of newspaper tumbled over and over in the road with the measured grace of an unfolding flower.

Dr. Ambara turned away from the window and crossed over to the bamboo chair where he had left his clothes. He found dressing difficult; his clothes clung to his skin as if they were highly charged with static electricity. But at last he managed to finish buttoning his shirt, slip on his mules and walk through the hall to the front door.

There was a color photograph of Ana in the hall, over the telephone table where the dried flowers stood. He had gathered and dried those flowers himself the week after Ana died. He stared at her for a moment: that dark, oval-shaped face; that black, braided hair; those red lips that were just about to break into a smile, and those eyes that had looked at him every day for three years and had never seen him.

He could almost smell her perfume sometimes at night when he lay in bed. He could almost feel her stirring in her sleep. The worst agony of all was to call her name and then wake up and realize that she would never answer, never again.

He opened the door and stepped out into the hazy sunshine. He did not live in the best part of Germantown, and he had never attempted to have his name put forward for the Farmington Country Club or the Memphis Hunt & Polo Club. But he lived in a smart collection of new pine houses not far from the Neshoba Community Center, within easy reach of U.S. 72 and just ten minutes away from the Hindu Garden of Temples, where Ana's deified soul was now resting.

In accordance with Hindu practice, Ana's body had been cremated and her ashes scattered on the Mississippi. Twelve days later, a second funeral, a *nyekah*, had been held in order to release her spirit from her emotions and her earthly thoughts. Her purified spirit remained in the Ambara temple, a temple which, because the Ambaras had been childless, would never contain any other than her spirit and that of Ida Bagus Ambara. Dr. Ambara often wondered who would mourn him when he was dead, who would cremate him and make sure that all the offerings were made to Yama, the god of the dead.

He glided through the streets beneath the dappled shadows of newly planted sugarberries and September elms. Children were playing on the sidewalk and they lifted their heads and turned around as he passed by, sensing that somebody had disturbed their games but not quite understanding who. A scruffy brown-and-white spaniel barked at him but then stopped abruptly, cocked its ears and uttered an apprehensive whine.

The afternoon was glaring and hot but Dr. Ambara felt curiously chilled. A slightly built figure with glasses and a bronze-colored Thai-silk shirt, he moved through the noisy streets of Germantown like a half-remembered spirit. He was keeping as calm as he could, remembering what Michael had said about arousing the leyaks. But all the same, he felt a tightening sensation in his chest, a feeling of terror and happiness together, and a dizzying feeling of triumph, too, that he had managed to enter the death trance unaided. Perhaps he had omitted some of the necessary prayers; perhaps he had failed to recite the sacred mantras in the traditional order; but his sheer obstinate belief had carried him through from the world of men into the world of spirits, and his sheer obstinate belief was keeping him there, an inexperienced and frightened explorer in the land of the dead. The streets he crossed were not "Real Germantown" but "Death Germantown," and his passing stirred up long-past memories as well as dust.

He reached the Hindu Garden of Temples. It was a small garden, a quarter of a mile back from Hacks Cross Market, overshadowed by sassafras and surrounded by a high chain-link fence. He passed through the open gates and went along the concrete pathway around the Temple of Prayer. The sun glared from the temple's whitewashed walls. The temple had been built five years earlier by Hindus living in and around Memphis; it was a simple block building based on the plans used for the local health clinics but altered by the architects to give it the proper proportions of the *vihama*, a perfect cube, with a *sikhara* sanctuary that was exactly twice its height built close by.

Dr. Ambara walked swiftly and silently through the gardens, between rows and rows of elaborately carved stone shrines. As he did so, he became aware of blurred white figures standing beside each shrine, each figure with its head covered, not moving but waiting patiently next to the memorial where its deified soul had been laid to rest. As he approached, he tried to look into their faces, but one by one the figures turned away from him, as if ashamed to be seen by a mortal.

Dr. Ambara hesitated for a moment and then said a short prayer to Siva, the Hindu god of destruction and re-creation, the god that he, as a high-caste brahmana, personally favored. *O Siva, smile on me. O Siva, protect me.* Then he glanced around, half-expecting the figures to turn and face him. But they remained unmoving and speechless, their robes blowing white in a silent and mystical wind.

He was only two pathways from Ana's shrine now, and he knew that he should have been excited and glad. Yet a strange coldness settled over him, an inexplicable feeling of dread. Something was wrong, although he could not understand what it was. There were no leyaks here as far as he could tell. The death trance had not wavered, and his belief in seeing Ana remained unshaken. Yet the white figures beside each shrine were so mute that they somehow seemed threatening now, and he passed each succeeding figure with increasing fear until he was almost running; he turned around again and again to look behind to see if the figures were staring at him as he hurried past.

At last, however, he reached the end of the row where Ana's shrine stood, only twenty yards away. It was a miniature temple modeled on the Pura Puseh in Batubulan, where Ana had been born. And there in front of it, her head bowed, stood a white-draped figure. Dr. Ambara knew that at last he had found his dead wife.

He whispered, "Ana," and cautiously walked toward her. Then he said, "Ana," even louder and held out his arms.

The figure did not turn around. She remained standing in front of her shrine with her head bowed as if deep in meditative prayer.

Dr. Ambara's footsteps slowed. The hot afternoon wind rustled in the leaves of the sassafras trees. He halted only two feet from his beloved Ana, unsure now, half-inclined to turn around and run away.

"*Ana.*" A name spoken so quietly that it was scarcely audible over the sound of the insects and the distant murmur of traffic on the highway.

"Ana, this is me. Ana, my beloved."

Slowly, carefully, Dr. Ambara reached out to touch Ana's shoulder. His heart was whipping wildly against his rib cage and he felt cold and sweaty at the same time. A sudden gust of wind seemed to ripple through Ana's white robes and through the robes of all the other figures standing watch over their shrines. Then Ana turned her head to look at him, and at the same time, she lowered the shawl from her head. Dr. Ambara stared at her in utter terror because this was not Ana at all. Instead, he found himself confronted by an ashy-colored face with snarling gray teeth and eyes that burned as ferociously as blast furnaces.

He knew then that he had been deceiving himself, that he had blundered into the death trance as an amateur, and that the leyaks must have been following him ever since he left his house. He had probably recited his mantras so clumsily that, unaided, he could not have entered into the death trance at all. Rangda and her running dogs had helped him and then they had accompanied him here to the Garden of Temples, every step of the way slavering, salivating and licking their lips in anticipation of a living spirit.

"Siva, preserve me," he said with utter simplicity. His terror was so great that he was unable to cry out. He knew that they would tear him down and drag him to Rangda; he knew that he would suffer unspeakable agonies for all eternity. He dropped to his knees on the pathway.

The leyak who had been standing beside Ana's shrine approached him, snarling quietly. There was a moment's pause and then its right hand arched back and raked across Dr. Ambara's face. Dr. Ambara felt the claws as hot as fire, and muscle snapping away from his cheekbone. Then the leyak clawed at him again with both hands and blinded him. Dr. Ambara accepted his mutilation submissively, almost philosophically. He was fully aware that there was no escape, and he was fully aware that if he struggled, the leyaks would rip him to pieces here and now. He tried to think of Ana and of ecstasy, of life everlasting and of Siva, and he tried to forget that the skin of his face was hanging down in bloody tatters and that the leyak's filthy talons had ripped into one eye and burst it and dragged the other eye out of its socket onto his cheek.

He stayed where he was, kneeling, and recited his prayers. He was still praying when the leyak who had blinded him was joined by three other leyaks who seized him with vicious claws and began to drag him away.

He cried out once, out of despair. Then he allowed the leyaks to take him back to their mistress without complaint.

TWENTY-THREE

Waverley Graceworthy entered the double doors of the conservatory and walked across its Turkish-tiled floor with neat, precise, clicking footsteps. He reached the white-painted cast-iron bench where Michael was sitting, stopped and drew back his cream-linen coat to reveal a canary-yellow vest with a gold watch chain attached.

"Well, then, here you are," he said as if he had been searching for Michael all over the house. He took off his Panama hat and hung it on an iron torchère. Michael, who was sitting hunched forward and smoking a cigarette, raised his eyes cursorily but did not reply. A few yards away, Reece was watching over him, filing his nails, smiling and tilting his chair back and forth. Reece was wearing a "Memphis Showboats" T-shirt instead of his combat fatigues, and his masklike face was unusually contented. Waverley had rewarded him well for bringing Michael back to Elvis Presley Boulevard.

Waverley nodded and Reece got up and brought a chair over for him. Above their heads in the white-iron framework of the conservatory, birds fluttered and sang and the sun shone saffron through the elaborately patterned glass. Waverley's conservatory was spectacular. Built onto the back of his house in 1914, it was a hundred-foot-long cathedral with a spire, an upstairs gallery and two winding staircases, one at each end. Rare tropical and subtropical

341

plants had been brought from all over the world, including the finest collection of palm trees in the mid-South: rattans and doums, coco de mer and raphia. Waverley admired palms because they were useful and profitable as well as attractive; they yielded everything from vegetable ivory to sago.

"You should feel at home here," he told Michael, leaning on his cane. "The atmosphere is not dissimilar to Bali, I shouldn't suppose."

Michael nipped out his cigarette and flicked the butt on the floor. "In Bali," he said, "people have respect for each other's freedom."

"But, my dear friend," said Waverley, "I have no intention of keeping you here against your will. The only reason Mr. Reece brought you to see me in a rather more pressing manner than usual was because I was somewhat concerned that you might have misconstrued my intentions."

"I don't think so," Michael said. "Reece here—or Ecker, or whatever he calls himself—has already killed one man that I know of and probably several more, and he tried to kill me, and from what I understand so far, he did all of it on your instructions."

Waverley pursed his lips. "Richard does tend to be impetuous."

"You call wholesale murder *impetuous*?"

"Perhaps impetuous isn't quite the word. But Richard is certainly no more than headstrong. Correct, Richard?"

Reece grinned and attended to his nails.

Michael said to Waverley, "All right then, what the hell's happening here? You've dragged me to this place for some reason; don't you think I ought to know what it is?"

Waverley nodded. "Commendably direct of you. I like directness. That's why I can never bear to do business with the Japanese. I brought you here because I understand that you have a very unusual talent. I understand that you are capable of meeting and talking to people who are no longer with us, people who have gone on to a higher spiritual plane, so to speak."

"You mean the dead," Michael put in.

Waverley raised his hand to indicate that "dead" was a word which, for reasons of taste, he preferred not to use.

"I understand that you can not only achieve this remarkable condition yourself, but that you can guide others into it." Waverley paused and then said, "For recompense."

Michael remained where he was, hunched forward on the bench, his hands clasped together, his grubby sneakers tapping out a soft rhythm on the tiled floor.

Waverley said, "Some years ago—thirty-one years ago, to be precise—I lost my dear wife after a series of family misfortunes."

He paused again and swallowed, and then he took off his glasses. "Her name was Ilona. She was a woman of extraordinary beauty and charm and grace. I always knew that I would miss her deeply, but I had no idea that my grief for her would never fade and that it would forever be a burden to me, a heavy weight that would never leave my heart. I miss her as much today, Mr. Hunter, as I missed her in nineteen fifty-three, the year she died, and I have to tell you that I would give anything to see her again."

Although the request itself remained unspoken, Michael knew this was a clear demand for him to take Waverley into a death trance. He sat back, reached into his shirt pocket and shook the last Lion cigarette from a crumpled pack. As he propped it between his lips, Waverley snapped his fingers to Reece and said, "Light him." Michael, however, ignored Reece's proferred Zippo and lit his cigarette himself with book matches.

"Well?" Waverley asked at last.

"Well what?"

"I wish to see Ilona again. Will you help me?"

Michael shook his head. "I'm already committed."

"You mean to Randolph Clare?"

"You've got it. And besides, I don't much care for your way of doing things. All this violence and guns and leaning on people. A person who does things the way you do wouldn't be safe in a death trance. Too many negative thoughts going on in your head, too little calmness, too little repose. The leyaks would come after you the moment you passed through the gate.''

"The leyaks?" Waverley queried. "Now what on earth are leyaks?''

"Take it from me," Michael said, "you don't want to know what leyaks are, not now, not ever.''

Reece made two or three quick gestures in sign language. Waverley frowned as he tried to interpret them and then looked back at Michael and asked, "Demons? Is that what he's trying to say?''

"Demons of a kind, yes.''

"Mr. Hunter, I'm not sure that I believe in demons.''

"You'd believe in leyaks if one of them started to rip your heart out.''

Waverley stood up and walked in a little circle around the conservatory floor. "So there's danger," he said thoughtfully. "Well, I'm sure that even demons can be overcome if we handle things properly. You've been into these death trances before, you've met these demons. How do you usually cope with them?''

"I run," Michael said.

Reece tugged at Waverley's sleeve and gave him a brief description in sign language of what had happened at the gates of the Temple of the Dead in Denpasar, when the leyaks had been pursing Michael and Randolph and Michael had used the mirror to fend them off.

Waverley said to Michael, "I didn't quite understand all of that but apparently you used a mirror.''

Michael said, "The only way to defend yourself against a leyak is to take his picture and then burn the picture in front of him. There was a time when I actually used to go hunting for leyaks, a little matter of revenge I guess you could call it. In those days I used to take a Polaroid camera with me. It was risky, but it worked pretty well. Think of the priests who used the same principle in the old days, before photography. They used to take pen and brushes with them and try to sketch the leyaks' portraits. Most of the time they were butchered before they managed to finish even a rough outline. There's a famous sketch in one of the private vaults of the Museum Bali: a leyak half-drawn on a sheet of paper spattered with dried blood. That was brought back over a hundred years ago from a death trance by one of the most famous of all *pendandas*.''

Waverley waited for Michael to continue but when Michael fell silent, he said a little sharply, ''The plants in here are very rare, you know. They don't much care for tobacco smoke.''

''Did you see me offer any of them a cigarette?'' Michael retorted. ''If you don't want any smoke in here, sir, I suggest you let me go.''

''Well, well, smart remarks,'' Waverley said tightly. ''But I regret that I cannot—or will not—release you until you take me into a death trance with you.''

Michael shook his head. ''I'm not doing it. I already made up my mind last week. I'm going in for only one more death trance, and that's the trance Randolph Clare asked me to do. At least his mind is clear and calm, not fucked up with killing people the way yours is. Taking somebody like you into a death trance would be suicide for both of us.''

''Even with a camera?'' Waverley asked, trying hard to control his temper.

''In a death trance you have to use your camera the same way a deer hunter stalks a deer. You have to pick your leyak and you have to take his picture before he realizes what you're doing, and then you have to keep out of range of his claws and his teeth long enough for the picture to develop, and then you have to hold it up in front of him and you have to burn it and make sure it burns quick. Believe me, it isn't a picnic.''

Waverley said, ''You'll be very well paid. Whatever Randolph Clare has offered you, I'll double it.''

''No go,'' Michael insisted. ''It doesn't matter how much money you pay me. If I get killed, it won't be worth it.''

''I could have you killed right now,'' Waverley told him coldly.

''Well, I'm sure you could,'' Michael agreed, although not with bravado. He was intimidated by Reece, and he found Waverley disconcertingly polite and cruel and unpredictable. But there was little option. To enter into a death trance with Waverley Graceworthy would be nothing short of offering himself to Rangda as a sacrifice. All he could possibly look to for survival would be the sheer spiritual and geographical distance that lay between Bali, "the navel of the world," and Memphis, Tennessee, "the city of good abode." Perhaps the distance was great enough to allow entrance into the realm of the dead without arousing the leyaks.

After all, as far as Michael knew, nobody in Memphis or anywhere in the continental United States had attempted to enter a death trance, certainly not recently, and so the leyaks probably had had no interest in it as a feeding ground. The nearest place in the Western Hemisphere that leyaks preyed was Haiti, where voodoo adepts still entered a kind of death trance and gave the leyaks occasional live spirits to snare. In Haiti, of course, they called the leyaks by another name, zombis.

Waverley said, "You're thinking, aren't you? You're weighing the odds. Perhaps it's not quite as dangerous as you were trying to suggest."

"It's not only how dangerous it is," Michael told him, "but I have another obligation to meet, one to Randolph Clare."

"Randolph Clare is not the kind of man you should be doing business with, not in Memphis," Waverley advised sternly. "Randolph Clare is—how shall I put it?—something of a pariah."

Michael stood up unexpectedly. Reece banged the two front legs of his chair on the floor and stood up too, instantly threatening.

"It's still no go," Michael said.

"This is very unfortunate," Waverley told him. "Unfortunate for me, of course, because I still wish to meet my Ilona again, but even more unfortunate for you because I shall have to keep you here, locked up, until you agree to take me."

"You can't hold me here. That's kidnapping," Michael challenged.

"My dear boy, I can hold you here for as long as I like, and there isn't a single damned thing you can do about it. Who's going to come looking for you? Your precious Randolph Clare?"

"I have plenty of friends in Bali," Michael retorted. "If they don't hear from me soon, they're going to start checking with the American Embassy. I have friends at the embassy too."

Reece communicated something to Waverley in sign language and Waverley suddenly smiled.

"I hope all your friends in Bali aren't as reliable as your American girlfriend."

"Who are you talking about?"

"The pretty one."

"Jennifer Dunning? What about her?"

"According to Richard, Miss Dunning was the one who told him where to find you when you were in your death trance."

Michael stared at him and then at Reece. "What kind of crap is that?"

Reece grinned and made a suggestive circle between finger and thumb. Then he uttered an extraordinary throaty laugh that sounded like a baby choking.

"You're all crap, do you know that?" Michael snapped at him. "You and him, the both of you. A couple of crocks of crap."

"Richard assures me that he's speaking the truth. It *was* Miss Dunning who gave you away."

Michael hesitated for a split second; then his sneakers squealed on the tiled floor as he dodged, feinted and made a dive for the nearest doorway. Reece was after him instantly, vaulting over the white-iron bench. Michael reached the door and was struggling with the handle when Reece caught up with him.

"Don't hurt him!" Waverley called.

Reece hooked his arm around Michael's neck and then gave him a devastating punch in the kidneys. Michael dropped to the floor, hitting his face against the tiles and chipping one of his front teeth. He lay there paralyzed for almost half a minute, staring in helpless agony at Waverley's approaching shoes. Waverley stood over him for a moment—two handmade golfing shoes in pale-beige kid, and immaculate trouser cuffs—and then he prodded Michael with his cane.

"I want you to do what I ask, my friend, and take me into a death trance."

Michael shook his head. Bloody saliva trailed from his mouth to the grouting on the floor. "No," he managed to say.

"Very well," Waverley said. "Richard will conduct you upstairs, where you will be locked in without food until you change your mind. That is all I have to say on the matter."

Reece jostled Michael to his feet. Michael was white-faced and gasping for breath. He stared at Waverley with violent disbelief. "I can't understand someone like you wanting to go into a death trance," he said harshly.

"Oh?" inquired Waverley.

"People want to go into a death trance for one of two reasons. Either they're after money or they want to express their love for someone they lost. Occasionally they're out for revenge, but not often. Well, it seems to me that you already have plenty of money, and it also seems to me that you're quite capable of getting whatever revenge you feel like here on earth, in the real world, without taking it beyond the grave. That leaves love. But you? *Love?* You don't even love yourself."

Reece began to twist Michael's arm but Waverley held up his hand to restrain him. He studied Michael and then said in a peculiarly dreamlike voice, "You may be right. Maybe I don't love anybody, not even myself. I lost the capacity to love when I lost Ilona. I loved Ilona and nobody else. You are right, yes. But I wish to enter the death trance so that I might find that love again, that love I lost."

Michael said adamantly, "Believe me, it won't be there. The love has to come from you, not from the spirit you're trying to find. Spirits don't experience emotions in the same way we do. The only love you'll ever get from a spirit is your own love, reflected back at you."

"Will you take me?" Waverley demanded, abruptly petulant.

"No," Michael whispered.

Waverley nodded his head and Reece grasped Michael's arm even more tightly, pushing him out of the conservatory, through the doorway and into the house. While Michael was being locked up, Waverley paced up and down, gently touching the leaves of his plants, admiring his brilliant tropical flowers, stopping now and then to look around.

Reece returned, continuously flexing his muscles like a National Guard gym instructor.

"An obstinate boy," Waverley commented. Reece made a face and grimaced.

"Well, never mind," Waverley went on. "He's bound to cooperate sooner or later, if only to regain his freedom. Do you think he's right about the death trance being dangerous or is he exaggerating?"

Reece made a cutting-his-throat gesture with his finger and reminded Waverley of what had happened to Bob Stroup and Jimmy Heacox.

"Ah, yes," Waverley said, "but they were *tampering,* weren't they? Hunter and Randolph Clare managed to get out relatively unscathed, no thanks to you, and it seems to me that with better organization, the death trance would probably be very much safer. Polaroid cameras, he said. We'd better arrange for Williams to go buy some, with plenty of film."

Reece looked dubious. Waverley turned on his heel, smiled at him and then gave him a playful chuck under the chin with the tip of his cane. If anybody but Waverley had tried to do that to him, Reece would probably have broken his neck.

"You find the idea of ghosts and spirits rather terrifying, don't you?" Waverley gibed. "You faced up to flame throwers, didn't you? And mortar bombs, and sharpened bamboo spikes. You even managed to survive after your tongue was cut out. But ghosts and spirits, they really unnerve you. Demons and vampires and loogaroos!''

Waverley laughed and smacked his cane noisily on the floor. ''Well, my friend, you're just going to have to swallow your fear because we can do some good for ourselves in the spirit world. We can silence that Marmie Clare before Randolph can get to her and start digging up evidence to show that it was *you* who disposed of her, and that you have connections with *me*. And we can also talk to my beloved Ilona and prove what I have suspected for forty years. This time without any doubt, without any prevarication, and then we'll have Randolph Clare right there, squeezed, ruined, and that will be even better than killing him.''

Reece listened to this and nodded, although he was used to Waverley's thin-voiced braggadocio by now and he knew that Waverley could never tell the truth to anybody, especially not to himself. Waverley had just said ''my beloved Ilona'' with deliberate sarcasm, but Reece had heard him on other occasions when he had argued and shouted to himself and then cried Ilona's name out loud like a man begging a woman. The tragedy of Ilona's death as far as Waverley was concerned was that she had left him no pride and, as with many men of short stature, pride to Waverley was everything, even above money. Even above God.

Reece made a laconic gesture that meant, ''I could still kill Randolph Clare and then we wouldn't have to risk going into a death trance.''

But Waverley said, ''No, Richard. Not now. There are already too many people who have us under suspicion, and if Randolph Clare were to die now . . . well, I'm not sure that even Chief Moyne could protect us. If you had succeeded in disposing of him in Bali, that would have been a different matter, especially since he was involved in something illegal. But now it's too late. And besides, this way is far more complete and far more discreet. And—how shall I put it?—far more *artistic*. Yes, it's quite artistic.''

While Waverley was talking to Reece, Randolph was trying to discover what had happened to Michael. He had painfully climbed out of bed and gone down to the library, where he was sitting at his desk in his blue-silk bathrobe, telephoning everyone who might have some idea of where Michael had gone, and why.

Dr. Ambara's phone rang and rang and nobody picked it up. The Indonesian office on Madison Street had never heard of anybody called Hunter. "We have a Han Tah, sir, if that is of help." None of the airlines had received a booking in the name of Michael Hunter, although Sunbelt Airlines was going to fly somebody called Eli Hunter III to Phoenix later that evening. And the desk clerk at Days Inn, where Michael had been staying, had entered his room with a passkey but reported "everything normal, sir. His baggage is still here, so he couldn't have checked out, and as you know, his accommodation has been paid for a month in advance. Maybe he just took a walk."

In the end Randolph called Wanda, who had gone back to the office to finish the Petersen contract.

"Michael's missing," he told her.

"How could that be? I called him this morning and he was quite happy."

"Did he say he was going to go for a walk, anything like that?"

"He said he was thinking of going for a swim later on. And he promised faithfully that he was going to call me before he went down to the pool. He was very serious about his security."

Randolph rubbed his eyes. "He couldn't have been followed, could he?"

"I don't think so. We did everything we could to make sure nobody knew where he was."

"I've been calling Dr. Ambara but I can't raise him. Dr. Ambara wouldn't have told anyone, would he? I mean, he wasn't strapped for money or anything like that? If Orbus or Waverley had offered him twenty thousand dollars to tell them where Michael was hiding out, you don't think he would have taken it, do you?"

"No, sir, I don't think he would have," Wanda replied confidently.

It was then that Randolph's second phone extension began to blink. "Hold on for a moment," he said. "And I'm sorry, I didn't mean to be disloyal to Dr. Ambara, but you know, the way this thing seems to be going—"

He picked up the extension and said, "Yes?"

It was Charles. "The Days Inn for you, sir. They said that you asked them to call if they had any information about Mr. Hunter."

"Thank you, Charles. Could you put them on?"

It was the same desk clerk to whom Randolph had spoken only twenty minutes earlier. He said flatly, "This probably doesn't signify anything, Mr. Clare, but one of my cleaners saw Mr. Hunter leave the hotel this afternoon with two men. He kind of noticed the men because they were both dressed in some sort of Army uniform and they both looked— well, I can only quote what my cleaner said, sir—'hard-bitten.' Please forgive me if they were any friends of yours, sir."

"No, thank you, they weren't, and you did very well to call me."

"Thank you. Mr. Clare. We try to help."

Randolph got back to Wanda. "You're not going to believe this. Reece has got him. One of the hotel cleaners saw him leaving his room this afternoon with two men in combat jackets."

"Oh, my God. Then that means Waverley Graceworthy has him."

"That's what it looks like."

"But without Michael, you won't be able to make your case against the Cottonseed Association, will you? If you can't get into another death trance and if you can't talk to Marmie . . ."

Randolph was silent for a moment. Then he said, "It's not my case against the Cottonseed Association that matters so much."

Wanda said sympathetically, "I know."

They both realized, without sharing the thought out loud, that Waverley Graceworthy was quite capable of killing Michael and making sure his body never came to light. And if Michael were dead, there was no hope of Randolph's producing any fresh evidence against Waverley, and no hope of his ever seeing Marmie.

Randolph suddenly thought to himself that the prospect of seeing Marmie just one more time was the only inspiration that had kept him going these past two weeks and that even the survival of Clare Cottonseed was nothing beside that one burning hope. He took out his handkerchief, wiped his eyes and shakily transferred the telephone receiver from one hand to the other.

"What are you going to do?" Wanda asked.

"I'm going to call Chief Moyne, for beginners."

"Chief Moyne and Waverley Graceworthy are bosom buddies. You told me so yourself."

"All the same, there's been a kidnapping here. That's a serious offense and Dennis is going to have to take some kind of action. He can't ignore it."

"All right then," Wanda agreed. "But will you call me back and tell me what he said? I'll stay at the office until I hear from you."

"I'll get straight back."

Randolph asked Charles to locate Chief Moyne for him. When he did so within two or three minutes, Chief Moyne sounded agitated and out of sorts. "Randy? I'm just about to rush out of the office. We have the fireworks tonight and the Cotton Carnival Ball, and I'm fifteen minutes late already. Charlotte will just about kill me."

"Dennis, this is more important than the Cotton Carnival Ball."

"Tell that to Charlotte. She's been dressing up for it for the past two weeks."

"Dennis, when I came back from Indonesia last week, I brought a friend with me. A young half-caste, an Indonesian-American. He was staying at Days Inn on Brooks Road. This afternoon when I called him, he was gone."

There was a long silence. Then Chief Moyne asked with obvious vagueness, "What's that you said? Who? I'm sorry, Randy, I wasn't really listening there."

"Dennis, my friend has been kidnapped. He was last

seen by one of the hotel cleaners, who saw him being escorted away from the hotel by two men in combat jackets.''

"Kidnapped?" asked Chief Moyne in perplexity.

"Well, what do you call it when a man is forcibly taken away from his hotel room by two known thugs?"

"Er, well, this is all pretty woolly," Chief Moyne replied. "Hey! I guess I shouldn't be saying 'woolly' on the night of the Cotton Carnival Ball, should I? Two men in combat jackets, you say? But was there any clear evidence of forcible abduction?"

"I told my friend to stay in that hotel room and not to move out of it until I gave him permission."

"Oh, yes? And how old was your friend?"

"I don't know. Twenty-two, twenty-three."

"Well, I'm sorry, Randy, but no matter how strongly you told your friend to stay in that hotel, he was over the age of consent, right? And he could walk out of there anytime he felt like it. I mean, you understand that, don't you? When a *kid* gets kidnapped, that's pretty straightforward, but when an adult goes walking off with two other adults, with no sign of weaponry or physical coercion, well then, that's different."

"How did you know there was no sign of weaponry or physical coercion?" Randolph demanded.

"Because you never mentioned it, that's why. And because the very first thing you would have said was, my friend was taken away at gunpoint, or with a rope around his neck, or with his arm twisted behind his back."

Randolph said, "Dennis, you're not being very helpful. Those two men answered the description of two of Waverley Graceworthy's hired heavyweights. One of them calls himself Reece, or Ecker. I have every reason to believe that Waverley has kidnapped my friend."

"Waverley?" laughed Chief Moyne. It was difficult for Randolph to tell over the telephone whether the man's mirth was genuine or synthetic. "Now why in the world would Waverley want to kidnap anybody, especially some half-caste guru from Indonesia?"

"I never said he was a guru."

"Aren't they all gurus? Now listen, Randolph, I really have to run. Maybe we can talk in the morning."

"I never said he was a guru, Dennis. Who told you he was a guru?"

Chief Moyne blustered, "You said it yourself. A half-caste guru, that's what you said. Now why don't you come around to see me tomorrow, when we can discuss this rationally?"

"I can't come around to see you tomorrow because my friend has been deprived of his liberty tonight, and besides, that Waverley Godalmighty Graceworthy may take it into his head to get rid of him."

"What kind of implication is that?" Chief Moyne wanted to know.

"It's probably slanderous," Randolph retorted. "But I can prove it, and if you ask me, so can you. Waverley Graceworthy has been pulling your strings too damned long, Dennis, and it's time you stopped dancing."

Chief Moyne said quietly, "I choose to forget that remark, Randy. I can understand that you made it in the heat of the moment."

"I don't want you to forget it, Dennis. I want it to burn in your brain like a branding iron."

"Listen, Randy," Chief Moyne said, uncomfortable now, "let me send you one of my senior officers. Maybe you can talk it out with him."

"I don't need to talk about it, Dennis. I know what's going on; I wasn't born yesterday, and I'm not about to die tomorrow. I want you to send a team out right now, and I want you to surround Waverley Graceworthy's home, and I want my friend brought out of there alive."

Chief Moyne blew a long, slow breath. "Well, I'm sorry, Randy. I can understand your ire, but I couldn't do anything like that, not without a properly sworn warrant, and even then, I'd be risking my job."

"Believe me, Dennis, I'll break you for this if it's the last thing I do," Randolph warned him. "We were supposed to be friends, you and I. We've had dinner together, gone fishing together, watched ball games together. I respect you—or at least I used to respect you—because you were always independent and you always upheld the law, no matter what. No matter what, Dennis, you always did! And now listen to you. My friend has been kidnapped and you know as well as I do who's responsible. And yet you won't move. You're frozen. Because, Jesus, Dennis, you don't move one inch these days unless Waverley Graceworthy gives you the nod.''

Chief Moyne said in a voice scarcely his own, ''My daughter had cancer, Randy. You know that. She was three years at Baptist Memorial before she died. So, you know, don't talk to me about respect.''

''You won't do it, then? You won't go out to Waverley's house and get my friend?''

''No, sir.''

Randolph licked his lips and found they were dry. He was beginning to feel that he was standing on an island that was gradually being cut away underneath his feet. Inch by inch, turf by turf, until there was nothing left but the black and threatening sea.

He said gently, ''You go off to your ball, Dennis,'' and then he put down the phone.

He sat at his desk for a minute or two before picking up the phone again and calling Wanda. ''You were right about Chief Moyne. He won't respond. Waverley paid his daughter's hospital expenses.''

Wanda said, ''I didn't know that. What happened to his daughter?''

''She died,'' Randolph said bitterly.

TWENTY-FOUR

Michael woke up and it was dark. He groped around until he found a bedside table and then a lamp. He switched on the light, sat up and looked around. He had been dreaming that he was in Bali, in the room he used to live in with his mother after his father had burned himself to death. The roof had been constructed of corrugated iron, and every morning the roosters had walked across it with a scratching, metallic sound that had frightened him.

But he was not in Bali. He was lying on a single bed in a small room at the far end of the upstairs corridor in Waverley Graceworthy's mansion. He touched the walls and wondered if the room had ever been used to imprison anybody else because there was no wallpaper, just bare brown plastering, and someone had scratched a long row of marks into it as if marking off the days. Or even the weeks?

There was a basin with a faucet that constantly dripped, a small window covered by slatted plastic blinds, a table with a battered top and a chair with a broken back. Michael climbed off the bed and went across to the window, where he parted the blinds and peered out, but there was little to see. A large triangular section of tiled roof, the side of a dormer window and the glow of one of the carriage lamps that illuminated Waverley Graceworthy's driveway. The silhouetted top of a large cottonwood tree. The reflected red gleam on a window of an automobile's taillight.

Michael tried to open the window but the sash had been screwed into the frame. He stared out for a while longer, then let the blind snap back and went to sit on the edge of the bed. He said a prayer to Sanghyang Widi, and to Yama, and he wished he had learned the sacred art of making himself invisible, which his old *pedanda* had always claimed that he himself was unable to do. Total sublimation of the self, total denial of the ego, total humility both physical and spiritual, that was the secret. Then the body would simply vanish.

He had smoked the last of his cigarettes. Well, he had wanted to give them up anyway. He had started smoking after his first serious accident with leyaks. His *pedanda* would have frowned on him for smoking, but by then he had lost his aspirations to be a priest. He had lived only for the sake of living, for finding out what he was supposed to be doing in this world, a half-caste Balinese-American living in Denpasar with no money, very little skill and a natural ability to talk to the dead. It was not the sort of curriculum vitae that guaranteed success in any walk of life. "Oh, yes, and what did your father do?" "He set fire to himself because he couldn't understand why he shouldn't."

There was no mirror in the room and Michael began to wonder what he looked like. Pale probably, with tousled hair and a fifteen hours' growth of beard. He knew he was sweaty. The room was insufferably close and he began to imagine that he could not breathe. He took shallow, panting breaths, hoping they might help him eke out the oxygen longer. He wondered what it had been like for those Indonesian women who had been bricked up inside their husbands' shrines. He had seen death from both sides of the grave and he still found it frightening and difficult to understand, an extraordinary transition from flesh to spirit, a dismemberment of body and soul, always tragic and always perplexing. Perhaps the most tragic and perplexing part about it was that the dead were not safe even when they were dead. The world of the living and the world of the dead were equally crowded with princes and predators. Death, like life, was a swarming hierarchical pyramid of privilege and pain, of attainment and punishment, of agony and rishes, at the top of which the gilded gods resided with their serene and idiotic smiles.

It was the gradual erosion of his faith in the gods that had made death trances more dangerous for Michael. He knew that Reece and his men had not been entirely to blame for what had happened at the Dutch Reform Cemetery in Denpasar. His own lack of celestial purity had alerted the leyaks too, and that was the reason they had not only been swarming close by, but lying in wait for him at the very place he intended to go.

He went to the washbasin after a while and splashed his face with cold water. He drank a little of it out of his cupped hands. He was just drying his face on the shoulder of his T-shirt when the door was noisily unlocked and opened and Waverley Graceworthy came in, closely followed by Reece.

"Well, well," smiled Waverley. "I hope you've been comfortable."

Michael said, "I could use a cigarette."

Waverley gave Reece a backhanded beckon and Reece tossed Michael a fresh pack of True with a mocking smile that seemed to mean, "Sorry they're not your regular dog-shit brand." Waverley watched Michael patiently as he tore open the pack, tapped out a cigarette and lit it.

"I came to ask you if you might have changed your mind," Waverley said. "It does seem rather foolish, doesn't it, for you to spend day after day incarcerated here when a simple favor would not only make you wealthy, but ensure your release?"

"Do you honestly think I trust you to let me go?" Michael asked.

"My dear friend, you have my word on it."

Michael shook his head. "The answer is still no. All you're offering me is a choice of ways to die. At least if I suffocate to death in this room, or if you decide you've had enough of me and shoot me, my soul will go to heaven and the chances of my being devoured by the Goddess Rangda will be slight rather than certain."

Waverley sat down on the edge of the bed. "I do find it amazing that you actually believe in these things. The Goddess Rangda! Now *she* sounds fearful!"

"Take it from me, she is fearful."

Waverley traced a pattern on the floor with the tip of his cane. "And the answer is still definitely no?"

"The answer is still definitely and positively no."

"Well, you know, that gives me some difficulty," Waverley said. "And the difficulty is that your patron, Randolph Clare, has been making inquiries about you and insisting that the police department search my premises in the rather optimistic belief that they might find you here."

"What's optimistic about that?" Michael asked. "I am here, aren't I?"

"You are at the moment, dear boy. But whether you will still be here when the police make their search tomorrow depends entirely on you."

Waverley paused for a moment and then added, "The chief of police is an excellent chum of mine, you see, and he believes that he has been able to stall Mr. Clare for tonight. But Mr. Clare, for all of his trespasses, still has money and influence, and if he demands that a search be made . . . well, the chief will have to do it, and I will have to accede to it."

Michael said, "Put that into plain English."

"It's very simple. If you don't agree to take me into a death trance by seven o'clock tomorrow morning, you and Reece will be taking a scenic drive together and only Reece will be coming back."

Michael smoked his cigarette in silence. Then he blew out a last sharp blast of smoke and crushed it out on the vinyl-tiled floor. "The answer is still no."

Waverley sighed and stood up. "Well," he said, "you have eight hours to think about it. Seven hours and fifty minutes, to be precise."

Waverley and Reece left the room, locking the door behind them. Michael eased himself back onto the bed and lay there staring at the ceiling, his head propped on his hands. There was an elaborate crack in the plaster that reminded him of the outline of Buddha's face. Buddha, the peaceful. Michael had seen death but he wondered what it was going to be like to die. He had never asked any of the spirits he had met whether it hurt or whether you simply closed your eyes, then opened them again and discovered that you were dead.

Less than a quarter of a mile away, outside the gates of Waverley's mansion, a black Cadillac limousine drew up to the curb on Elvis Presley Boulevard in the shadow of a trailing sassafras. Randolph, in the rear seat, leaned forward and tapped Herbert on the shoulder. "Stay here for an hour. If we're not back by then, call the police. The best man to speak to is Captain Ortega, if he's around."

"Yes, sir," Herbert said and then turned around to say, "Are you sure this is wise, what you're doing? I hope I am not impertinent in asking."

Wanda was in the back of the limousine with Randolph. Randolph was wearing jeans and a black turtleneck sweater. Wanda was dressed in black-corduroy slacks and a dark-blue blouse. Randolph carried a flashlight, although at this moment he would have preferred a gun.

Randolph said, "Herbert, you're right, this is probably crazy. But the police are not helping us find Michael and by the time they do, Waverley will probably have moved him someplace else or killed him."

"Well, you're the boss," Herbert said. But he tapped the digital clock on the Cadillac's dash and said, "One hour only. Sixty minutes and no seconds. Then I call for assistance."

"You got it," Randolph told him and climbed out of the car, with Wanda close behind.

They crossed the highway until they reached the gates of Waverley's mansion. The gates were closed and they opened only from inside the house but Randolph knew from previous visits that Waverley had no security cameras or alarms on the grounds. The house itself was well-protected, with three Dobermans prowling the courtyards, but Wanda had brought along something they hoped would distract the dogs: ten pounds of sirloin steak from Randolph's freezer, hurriedly defrosted in the microwave.

Together they walked along the brick perimeter wall of Waverley's property, trying not to be conspicuous. It was a humid, airless night and the trees in Waverley's grounds stood as still and silent as if cast out of bronze. In the distance, off to the northwest, Randolph could hear the faint crackle of fireworks as Memphis celebrated King Cotton. An occasional car slashed by along the boulevard, paying them no attention. Randolph prayed that they could get into the grounds before a police car came past. A man and a woman walking along Elvis Presley Boulevard at close to midnight with a flashlight and ten pounds of steak would undoubtedly be liable to questioning, if not to summary arrest.

"Here," he said. They had reached the corner of the property where the front wall and the side wall were joined by a tall pillar of large stone blocks. Because time and traffic pollution had eroded the pointing between the blocks, it was comparatively easy to climb up, using the crevices for toe and finger holds.

Randolph glanced around and said, "You go first. I'll help you up."

He tossed the plastic bag full of meat over the wall. Then he lifted Wanda as high as he could until she managed to catch a grip on the stone blocks. It took her only a few seconds to scrabble her way up to the top and roll herself over. Randolph heard her drop down lightly on the other side.

Randolph was about to climb up the wall himself when a car appeared, driving slowly north. It drew up beside him and the window went down. There were three men in the car, heavy-set and serious-faced. The man in the front passenger seat beckoned to Randolph and said, "Hey, buddy."

Randolph walked over but kept his distance.

"Did we pass the Elvis Presley home yet?" the man asked.

"It's back about a half-mile," Randolph told him. "There are plenty of signs you can follow, but it's closed at night."

"Oh, that's okay. We're in Memphis for a convention and our wives made us promise to visit Graceland and lay a few flowers on the memorial, so what we're aiming to do is drive past and toss these roses over the fence."

The man in the backseat held up a bunch of bedraggled yellow roses.

"I always tell my wife the God's-honest truth," said the man in the front passenger seat.

"Well, that's very wise," Randolph said and stood on the sidewalk watching while the car U-turned and headed south toward Graceland. As soon as its taillights had vanished, he ran back to the corner of Waverley's property and began to scale the wall.

It was more difficult than he had imagined. He was still stiff and bruised from his encounter with the leyaks, and Wanda was ten years younger than he and played regular games of squash. He heaved and grunted, tearing one of his fingernails as he neared the top, but at last he managed to swing first one leg over the copingstones and then the other. He dropped down into the darkness of Waverley's gardens like a big black bear falling out of a tree.

Wanda was crouched, waiting for him. "Sssh!" she hissed. "I just saw somebody walking around the side of the house."

"We'll try to get in through the kitchens," Randolph suggested, brushing himself off. "Waverley likes to eat late so they may still be open."

"I'm surprised he didn't go to the ball. He doesn't usually miss it, does he?"

"He doesn't usually kidnap somebody like Michael either. I've been thinking about that, you know. I'm beginning to wonder if he doesn't want to use Michael for some devious scheme of his own. I mean, if he were thinking of having Michael killed, he would make sure that he stayed well away, wouldn't he? He'd probably go to the ball just to establish an alibi."

They bent over and ran as quickly as they could through the undergrowth, pushing aside rhododendron branches and kicking away entanglements of creeper. At last they reached the bushes close to the northwest corner of the house. From there they would have to cross thirty yards of open driveway to reach the shadow of the kitchen wing.

"Anybody around?" Wanda whispered.

"Not that I can see."

"No dogs? I'm afraid of dogs."

"I don't think so. I must say that after leyaks, the idea of being attacked by dogs seems almost enjoyable."

Although they left the cover of the bushes as quietly as they could, their footsteps sounded ominously loud in their ears and Randolph stubbed his toe against a small hummock in the tarmac driveway when they were only a third of the way across. But they reached the kitchen wing without anybody's seeing them and they pressed themselves against the white-painted wall, breathing deeply and praying that their luck would hold.

"This doesn't say much for Waverley's security," Wanda whispered.

Randolph pressed a finger to his lips. "Don't let's start congratulating ourselves until we're in there."

He was just about to lead the way around the corner, toward the brightly lit kitchen door, when he heard the door open and the chef speak loudly to one of his assistants.

"First he says out, then he says in. First he wants fish, then he changes his mind and wants veal. First sauce, then no sauce. What's the matter with his brain today? You take a man who can make so much money, you think he get his brain straight. Look at all this snapper, straight in the trash."

The assistant said something inaudible in reply and then the door was slammed. Randolph listened to hear if the chef locked it but as far as he could tell, the key remained unturned, the bolts unshot. Cautiously, he peered around the corner.

There was a row of garbage cans, then two concrete steps, then the kitchen door. Its glass panes were opaque and it was impossible to see the inside of the kitchen clearly, but Randolph could make out the distorted image of the chef as he crossed from one side of the room to the other. Then abruptly the chef disappeared. One of the kitchen lights was switched off and Randolph heard a brief clatter of pans as they were stacked.

"Come on," he breathed to Wanda and together they tiptoed past the garbage cans and up to the door. When Randolph pressed his face against the glass, he could distinguish a large, white-topped table with a rack above it for *bains-maries*, kettles and ladles, and beyond that, an illuminated gas range. To the right of the gas range there was a closet and then the dark rectangle of an open door.

Randolph grasped the door handle and slowly turned it. The door swung open without a sound. Waverley Graceworthy obviously believed in keeping his hinges well oiled. On soft-soled golf shoes, Randolph stepped into the kitchen and Wanda followed. They closed the door behind them.

"No dogs yet," Wanda breathed. "I hope I don't have to carry this steak around all night."

They hurried quietly to the open door at the far end of the kitchen. Only one pan was simmering on the gas range. It smelled like chicken broth. Randolph peered around the door to see if there was anyone outside; then he tugged Wanda forward and into the corridor.

"I hope you know your way around," she said.

"I'm making this up as I go," he told her.

The corridor was twenty yards long, its walls painted with dark-green gloss. They made their way along it until they reached a paneled oak door that had been left ajar.

"Probably one of the dining rooms," Randolph suggested.

"Let's just hope that Waverley hasn't decided to have a late supper in here," Wanda whispered back.

Randolph hesitated and bit his lip. "Well, if he's in there, he's in there. This looks like the only way into the house."

Gently he reached forward and eased the door open a few inches. The dining room beyond was dimly lit and paneled with the same pale oak as the door. Randolph could see the glint of reflected light from a gilt frame and the sparkle of a crystal decanter. He pushed the door open all the way and stepped inside.

The table was laid for one. There was a white Brussels-lace placemat, a napkin in a silver-gilt napkin ring, a crystal glass for white wine and a service plate edged in gold. A lone candle dipped and flickered in a tall silver candlestick but there was nobody in the room. Presumably the chef had gone to tell Waverley's butler that the master's dinner was almost ready. Not the snapper, the veal, and without the sauce.

Randolph and Wanda negotiated the dining room, making sure to leave the door behind them open an inch, the way they had found it. Then they went through to the main hallway, the only part of the house Randolph so far remembered from his previous visits. It was in darkness except for a huge chandelier that hung from the main ceiling, its electric candles turned down to a glimmer. There was a strong smell of lavender floor polish, and an electric floor polisher stood on the opposite side of the hallway close to the sitting-room doors. But there was nobody around—at least not for the moment—and Randolph and Wanda were able to make their way to the foot of the stairs undetected.

"We'll search the house from the top down," Randolph whispered, looking around anxiously. "Keep an eye out for locked doors."

"Suppose we find one?" Wanda asked.

"Then we tap on it and see who's inside."

"Isn't that dangerous?"

"Of course it's dangerous. Just coming here is dangerous. But if anybody answers—anybody who isn't Michael—all you have to say is something like, 'Sorry, maid,' and get the hell out. Just remember that Waverley has a major-domo, a butler and a valet, and maybe ten full-time ladies who don't do anything but clean the place. Even *he* won't know if you're a maid or not unless he gets to take a look at you."

Wanda took Randolph's hand. "Randolph, I'm scared. Could we call it a night?"

"Come on," Randolph chided. "We're here. We have to give it our best shot."

She glanced up the dark, forbidding staircase. "All right," she said at last.

They climbed the stairs side by side until they reached the second-floor landing. There were huge Persian carpets hanging on either wall, and sculptures of women and strange beasts. The upstairs corridor extended directly in front of them, unlit except for a double wall lamp at the far end, which was almost a hundred and fifty yards away. The length of the corridor was carpeted in patterned Stark rugs, and that isolated wall lamp gleamed on what looked like an endless succession of polished brass handles.

"You take the left side, I'll take the right," Randolph said.

Slowly, pausing every now and again to listen, they progressed down the corridor, grasping each door handle, holding their breath and then turning it. If the door could be eased open, they would quietly close it again. If it was locked—and almost a third of them were—they would rest their heads against the white-painted panels and call softly, "Michael? Are you in there? Michael?"

They were two-thirds of the way up the corridor when Randolph thought he heard something from behind one of the doors. Underneath his sweater he was sticky with sweat and he wished to God he had worn a T-shirt. He held up his hand for Wanda to stop turning handles and he listened again.

"Did you hear something?" Wanda whispered.

"I'm not sure." He bent his head closer to the door and called, "Michael? This is Randolph. Can you hear me, Michael?"

There was an aching quiet. It was so quiet that Randolph could even hear the popping of distant fireworks.

Then there was a scuffling sound somewhere along the corridor behind them and Randolph turned to see Reece standing on the landing, holding two Dobermans on short leashes.

Randolph turned the other way, and into the twin circles

of light cast by the wall lamp stepped Waverley Graceworthy and the mad-looking man, Frank Louv, who had helped Reece kidnap Michael from Days Inn.

Waverley Graceworthy walked forward with a smile and held out his hand. Randolph remained where he was and refused to take it.

"This is an honor," Waverley said with the utmost courtesy. "Mr. Randolph Clare, the wealthy, independent cottonseed processor, paying an unheralded midnight visit to the humble home of one of his greatest rivals."

"I think you can spare the sarcasm," Randolph replied. Louv snuffled and let out a grunt of amusement. As the man came closer, Randolph could see that he was swinging a chain-jointed cosh in his hand.

Randolph said, "I called Dennis but he was unable to help. A little matter of the Cotton Carnival Ball. I'm surprised you didn't go yourself, Waverley. You usually like to make an appearance."

"I was planning to," Waverley said. "I was just about to have my supper and then go up there to present the awards. Unfortunately, business matters have somewhat delayed me. One must attend to business before one attends to pleasure."

Randolph said, "I want you to release Michael Hunter."

"I beg your pardon?" Waverley tried to look baffled.

"You know what I'm talking about. Your hired bullies here took Michael Hunter from Days Inn this afternoon. They were seen and identified. If you don't have him here, I'd like to know where he is, and I'd like to have him released."

Waverley smiled, a smile of pure lemon and vinegar. "My dear Randolph, I scarcely think that you and Miss Burford here are in any position to make demands, do you? I have caught you red-handed, or red-footed, shall I say, trespassing on my property with intent to commit goodness only knows what kind of theft, or arson, or crime against my person."

"Waverley, you kidnapped Michael Hunter and I want him back. Otherwise I'm going to call the police straightaway and have this palace of yours ripped to pieces from top to bottom.''

Waverley was smiling at Wanda now. He could sense her anxiety about the Dobermans, which were slavering and straining and scratching their claws against the polished floor. "How would you like me to order those dogs released?" he asked gently. "They are attack-trained; they used to work for the SWAT squad before they were discharged as too dangerous. Reece likes them though, don't you, Reece? Reece would do anything for those dogs, and those dogs would do anything for him. Why, if Reece were to point at Miss Burford and say *kill*—''

"That's enough, Waverley," Randolph interrupted. "I think you and I ought to sit down now and have a discussion about this. Let the girl go back to my car; it's parked right outside. Then we'll see what kind of deal we can work out between us.''

Waverley slowly shook his head. "Not interested, Randolph. Not interested in deals. The time when you and I could make deals together, that's all over. Besides, your car is no longer outside. It's parked in my garage, and your chauffeur is sitting in my cellar with his hands shackled to a drainpipe and a gag over his mouth.''

He smiled again and then said with satisfaction, "Dennis warned me that you might try something ridiculous, and indeed you have.''

Randolph refused to be impressed. "You can't hold anybody here against his will, Waverley. It's lunacy. You can't hold Michael, and you can't hold me, and you can't hold Wanda and Herbert. I've never known anything so damned unbelievable.''

He started to move but Reece brought the Dobermans closer and they snarled in echoing stereo, their saliva mottling the corridor walls.

"I think you know something *very* unbelievable," Waverley said, completely unfazed. "I think you know all about this magical Hindu death trance. Now *that's* unbelievable, but I'm assured that it's just as real as the fact that I'm holding you here and that I don't have the slightest intention of letting you go.''

"And what exactly do you hope to achieve?" Randolph demanded.

Waverley slowly smoothed his hands together as if he were rolling out a thin sliver of clay between his palms. "I hope merely to tidy up a business that has turned out to be rather messy and complicated. It's all your fault, really. You know, Randolph, you're a stubborn man. When your factory out at Raleigh caught fire, you should have taken the hint right then and there. Orbus did warn you, didn't he? Of course Orbus is not always as persuasive as he might be, but just the same, you're an intelligent man. You should have seen the writing on the wall. Especially after that very unpleasant business with your family."

"What did you expect me to do? Retire? Abandon my life's work? Commit suicide?"

Waverley shrugged. "All three of those options were viable, at least from the Cottonseed Association's point of view. Unfortunately, *very* unfortunately, you decided not to take any of them, and so here we are, in a messy and complicated situation, you just as stubborn as ever and me wondering what on earth we can possibly do about it."

Randolph said, "You've got Michael here. I want to see him."

"He's perfectly well," Waverley assured him.

"I would still like to see him."

"Well, as matter of fact, Randolph, that's exactly what we intended to do now in any case. You see, my dear fellow, Michael has proved almost as uncooperative as you have, and it's quite clear that he's going to need a little persuasion."

"A little persuasion to do what?"

"To take me into a death trance, of course."

"To take *you* into a death trance?" Randolph asked in perplexity. "What do *you* want to go into a death trance for?"

Waverley Graceworthy looked at Randolph for a long time over the tops of his wire-rimmed glasses. His eyes could have been pale-blue stones lying at the bottom of an ice-cold stream.

Eventually he said, "I wish to talk to Ilona, my wife."

"Ilona? But Ilona died almost—"

"Thirty-one years ago, yes. An overdose of sleeping pills. One of the greatest tragedies the Graceworthy family has ever had to endure."

"But why on earth do you want to see her? Surely you've gotten over her death by now. And, Waverley, I have to tell you, those death trances can be highly dangerous. I almost got myself killed. I'm still covered with bites and bruises. Look at me." He rolled up the sleeve of his sweater. "Look at my arms. Did you ever see bites like that?"

Waverley looked away. "I am quite aware of the risks, Randolph."

"Then why do you want to do it?" Randolph demanded.

"I want to do it because something happened in a nursing home in Little Rock, Arkansas, in February of nineteen thirty-seven and I want to know what it was."

Randolph stared at him and then lifted his arms as if he were invoking the judgment of Moses. "Are you crazy?" he asked. "What the hell are you trying to say?"

Waverley's voice was lifeless. "I am not trying to say anything. I want to know what happened, that's all. I want to know if the rumors were really true."

"What rumors?"

Waverley pointed a sharp finger at him. "My bride of only three years went to the Cardinal Nursing Home in Little Rock, Arkansas, in February of nineteen thirty-seven, in secret, without my knowledge, and when she came out of that nursing home, she had a letter from the doctor saying she could never have children. I have no heirs, Randolph. I have nobody to whom I can pass on this house; I have nobody to whom I can pass on my money, or my pride, or my family name. I was robbed of that by a bride who secretly took herself off to a nursing home in Little Rock, Arkansas, and only God and the devil know what went on there. An abortion? Maybe. But was it *my* child who was aborted? An operation on her fallopian tubes? An ectopic pregnancy? Who knows? She never explained it. She never would. And after that she would disappear sometimes for weeks on end and then just as suddenly turn up again, always expecting me to love her just as I did before."

He paused, breathing hard as if he had been running.

"I asked her again and again, 'What's happened? Where have you been? Do you love me? What happened in Arkansas?' And she would never answer me, not directly. All I got was hints, strange looks and offhand suggestions. And rumors, yes, plenty of rumors. Friends at the Cotton Exchange, always ready with a sympathetic frown, the offer of a drink and, 'I hate to mention this, old buddy, but wasn't that Ilona I saw the other day out at Lucy with you-know-who?' "

Randolph and Wanda exchanged glances but remained silent. Waverley seemed to be talking more to himself than to them, a bitter soliloquy that he must have repeated over and over again.

"The last years were terrible," he said. "I knew she didn't love me; I knew she had given her heart to some other man. But I tried so hard to keep her. I tried so hard to make her understand how much I adored her. But then she started taking the pills and the drinks, and she fell apart in front of my eyes."

He hesitated and then said, "In the end she was so ill that I told her to go back to the man she really wanted because I couldn't stand to see her die. But she wouldn't—she refused—knowing that if she did, I would find out who it was."

Another pause and then with grief as abrasive as fragments of broken glass, Waverley said, "She died. She took her own life. It was April sixteenth, nineteen fifty-three. A Thursday afternoon. I came home from the office late and there she was, lying on the bed just like one of those medieval effigies, pale, her hands crossed over her breasts. And I came into the room and everything went slow, very slow, so that it seemed to take me hours and hours to reach her. She was cold. *Cold!* You never felt anything like it. I kissed her and her lips were like marble. And it was all because of this other man and all because of what she had been through at the nursing home in Little Rock, Arkansas."

Randolph said in a measured voice, "You have suspicions then of who Ilona's lover might have been? And you think you know what might have happened out at the clinic?''

Waverley appeared to recover himself; a certain sharpness return to his eyes. "Yes," he said and whacked his cane on the floor. Randolph was reminded of the Bob Dylan song about the negress, Hattie Carrol, who was killed by a blow from the cane her employer "habitually carried" and for which crime he was given a six-month sentence.

"I suspect that my wife's lover was your father, and I suspect that what happened at the Cardinal Nursing Home at Little Rock was that my wife gave birth to you. I further suspect that your father and his wife then adopted you and brought you up as a Clare in spite of the fact that your mother was a Graceworthy."

Waverley's voice was trembling now, and he kept rapping his cane against the floor. "I suspect that when you were born, there were complications and that because of those complications, you sterilized my wife and denied me the sons and the heirs that should have been mine. That's what I suspect and that's what I've been suspecting for over forty years, and this is the first chance I'm going to have to prove it . . . in a death trance. I'm going to ask that woman, I'm going to ask her straight to her face, and if she tries to deny it, then by God, I'm going to know that she's lying. And you, Randolph, you! You couldn't stay peaceful, could you? You couldn't make your living quiet and cooperative, oh no, you had to show the Cottonseed Association that Clares were the best and screw you, Charlie. And all the time I used to look at you and think to myself, *That's Ilona's only son; that's the only son of the only woman I ever got to love.* You look like her and you talk like her, and sometimes when I see you make that gesture with your hand, that kind of sideways gesture, I know that's *her*, that's Ilona, and when you do that, I don't want to hurt you for anything. But then you duck your head a little and talk all serious, and that's your *father*, and I could kill you for that. You think it's painful, do you, to lose your family, to lose your wife and to lose your children? Well, I can tell you all about pain. I never had that wife, I never had those children. Your father killed all of that before it could ever exist, and the weapon he killed it with was *you*.''

Waverley shook his head as if time and history were amazing, as if love were inexplicable. ''He used you to sterilize my wife, and he used you to taunt me with after he was dead. 'Lookit, here's the son *you* should have had, Waverley, except that he's mine!' And I hate to say this, Randolph, but I watched your progress through school and through college, and I felt some kind of real bond with you, some genuine understanding. That is, until your father's personality started coming out in you, that overbearing spirit, and you built up your cottonseed plants and you built up your production capacity; and you know as well as I know, Randolph, that if Clare Cottonseed continues to grow at its present rate, the Cottonseed Association is going to be looking at bankruptcy within four years and more than four and a half thousand people are going to be out of a job.''

Randolph was shocked through and through but he looked Waverley straight in the eye and said, ''This is insane, Waverley. This is really insane. Why don't you call off these dogs and let Michael free? Then let's you and I sit down at a table and talk this thing through. These—*rumors*—they're just ridiculous. I don't know where they came from but how could you possibly believe them? How could you possibly *want* to believe them?''

Waverley lowered his eyes. ''When I talk to Ilona, I'll find out for sure.''

''And what if Michael refuses to take you to see her?''

''He won't,'' Waverley said bluntly. He raised his head, snapped his fingers at Reece and pointed to Wanda. ''If he wants this young lady of yours to stay alive, believe me, he won't.''

TWENTY-FIVE

They brought Michael down to the living room just as the gilded clock on the mantelpiece was striking one. Waverley was infected with an extraordinary euphoria. He marched up and down the room like a marionette, rapping the floor with his cane, rapping the tables with his knuckles. Randolph stood in the corner by the fireplace, apprehensive and quiet. Reece was over by the French doors, admiring the exhibition he had set up on the patio outside.

"Ah," Waverley said as Frank Louv brought Michael into the room. "You know Mr. Clare, don't you?"

Michael and Randolph looked at each other, each trying to convey what had happened by something approaching telepathy, but it was scarcely necessary. The consequences of Michael's kidnapping and Randolph's break-in were glaringly obvious.

"Mr. Clare came to *rescue* you," Waverley said as if he were talking to a five-year-old child. "He climbed over the wall and broke into the house, but unfortunately for him—ah, unfortunately for him!—we always have plenty of people on watch and he was observed, from the very moment he climbed over the wall, and he was caught! And here he is. Well, he doesn't look pleased, does he? But then, would you if the same thing had happened to you?"

Michael said, "I was asleep. Is this what you woke me up for?"

Waverley laughed and slapped Michael vigorously on the back two or three times. "You must come to the patio door; then you might understand."

Tugging Michael's sleeve, Waverley led him over to the French doors, which had been opened wide. The floodlights that surrounded the house had been switched on and the lawns looked as bright and artificial as a Hollywood movie set. There were three marble statues arranged around the patio: a muscular Adonis; a voluptuous Diana, complete with dogs; and a bad copy of Michelangelo's "Dying Slave." In the center of the brick-paved patio, tied with cord to a folding chair, sat Wanda. At her feet, their tongues hanging out like scarlet rags, lay Reece's dogs.

"You'd better explain this to me," Michael said guardedly.

"My dear fellow, there's nothing to explain," Waverley smiled. He was almost jolly. "I want you to take me into a death trance, and the persuasive part about it is that if you continue to refuse, Mr. Reece or his friend here will whistle to the dogs and Miss Burford will have to suffer the consequences. Those dogs are Dobermans, in case you don't recognize them, and they're trained to attack. They are capable of savaging Miss Burford to death in a matter of minutes, I assure you. And it will all be your fault."

Michael turned to Randolph, who told him apprehensively, "He means it, Michael. If you don't take him into the death trance, he'll have her killed."

Michael ran his hand through his hair. Randolph thought that he looked exhausted. He wanted to ask Michael about Dr. Ambara but Waverley and Reece were hovering too close, anxious to hear Michael capitulate.

"Well?" Waverley asked. "Let's give it three minutes, shall we? And then let's set those dogs loose. Your choice, Michael."

Michael lifted his eyes as if the answer to everything was written on Waverley's ceiling. Then he looked down again and sideways at Waverley. "I need my mask. I need my incense too," he said tonelessly.

"Your mask?"

"I brought it with me from Indonesia. It's in a large

gray-polyethylene sack back at Days Inn. You'll find it in the closet. The incense is in a purple box, top left-hand drawer of the bureau. You won't mistake the mask. It's very big, about as big as this—'' he stretched out his hands. ''It's red and white and gold, a kind of papier-mâché with artificial hair glued to it.'' He looked at Reece and said, ''The teeth are artificial too, except when they choose not to be.''

Reece looked away. He had tried to persuade himself night after night that he had been suffering from hallucinations that morning in Denpasar when Jimmy Heacox had put his head into the mask. On the other hand, he was pretty sure tht he hadn't been and that—magically, impossibly— Jimmy's head had been bitten off and digested by something that did not even exist, not in the real world anyway, while what was left of him had been spat out onto the temple floor like so much offal. Jimmy's grisly, protruding tongue had been left hanging out as a warning to others: *Never mock the Witch Widow Rangda; never speak her name disrespectfully; never betray her or fail to do her bidding.*

The next hour passed as slowly as if the mechanism of Waverley's clocks had been lubricated with treacle. Waverley obliged his captives to sit side by side on a small colonial sofa from which they could look through the French doors at Wanda. Michael smoked eight cigarettes; Randolph remained motionless and silent, trying to preserve his energy; Reece made an enthusiastic job of flossing his teeth, sawing the floss back and forth between his molars.

It was well past two o'clock when the mad-looking Louv returned from Days Inn carrying a huge bundle wrapped in one of the hotel blankets. He set it down in the middle of the living-room floor and then delved into his pocket and took out two boxes of incense sticks. ''I had trouble getting that stuff. The night clerk wanted fifty just to open the fucking door. In the end I told him to open it for free or I was going to open *him*. Back to belly. The stupid bastard.''

Waverley had been out of the room for most of the time, but now he was sitting in the corner on a small Queen Anne chair, his legs neatly crossed. He stood up and approached the mask with undisguised fascination.

"Stay away," Michael warned.

Waverley stepped back. "Whatever you say, my dear fellow. Are we ready to enter the death trance almost at once?"

Michael said tiredly, "Let me prepare. Do you have any dishes, anything I can use for burning incense?"

"My butler will bring them."

Michael asked for Randolph's help in dragging aside the sofas and the coffee table so the center of the room was clear. As they moved about, he leaned close to Randolph's ear and murmured, "When we're gone, follow us."

"What?" whispered Randolph.

"Follow us into the death trance. You know how to do it."

"But what can I do even if I manage it?"

Michael gave Randolph a weary smile. "I'll show you once we're there. Don't be afraid. And remember, you might get to see Marmie and the children. This might be your last chance."

Randolph nodded his agreement. The butler had come back into the living room with four Spode dishes that Michael set down ritually at each corner of the room and then filled with sticks of incense. He lit the incense with great concentration and the smell of sandalwood and jasmine began to drift across the floor. Louv sniffed and went into a fit of sneezing. "Smells like a Saigon flophouse," he protested.

Michael took no notice of him. Instead, he approached the mask and cautiously tugged aside the blanket. Then he tore open the polyethylene to reveal the mask itself, still draped in scarlet silk but with one eye glaring out at them like the eye of hell itself.

"So this is the notorious mask," Waverley said in fascination as Michael carefully laid it down in the center of the floor. "Is this the same mask that—" he mimicked with a twist of his hands the removal of a man's head.

"This is the same mask," Michael acknowledged without

taking his eyes off Reece. Reece grimaced in disgust and looked the other way.

The mask of Rangda was arranged according to custom: her face covered with silk, her curving teeth invisible. To cover her face was a mark of respect for the most terrible of all the goddesses. *O Rangda, we shield our eyes from your ferocity. O Rangda, we drape thee and dress thee; thou art the bride of death; the widow of darkness; we lay flowers for thee; we worship thee; we light incense for thee at the four corners of the world.*

Michael sat down on the floor, his legs crossed, his palms lifted upward. He indicated with a nod that Waverley should do the same. Reece came forward and helped Waverley to struggle into position; they could hear Waverley's knee joints click.

Michael was about to begin his recitation of the sacred mantras when Waverley tapped Reece on the side of the leg with his cane and said, "You too. You're coming. You don't think I'm going to enter any death trance without protection, do you? And where are those cameras? Did Williams get back with those Polaroid cameras?"

Reece held up a brown canvas camera bag and showed Waverley the two SX 70s inside.

Michael leaned forward. "*He's* coming?" he queried, pointing at Reece.

Waverley asked, "There isn't any problem, is there?"

Michael shook his head. "If he's going, I'm not going, and that's final. If the leyaks don't kill me, he certainly will."

"Reece!" barked Waverley.

Reece had hefted out of his jacket his .45 Colt automatic and pushed back the slide. Now he pressed the cocked and loaded pistol against Michael's nose. Michael pushed the gun away with a gentle finger and said, "Okay. That's fine. You want to come, you come. Sit down next to Mr. Graceworthy and don't worry about emptying your mind. That must have happened years ago."

Randolph recognized one of Michael's bouts of nervous silliness but there was nothing he could do to help him.

Louv kept guard over Randolph with his chain-link cosh, swinging it around and watching in satisfied disbelief as Michael began to chant the words that would take Waverley Graceworthy and Richard Reece along with him as companions into the world beyond the veil.

They were one and a half miles south of Forest Hill Cemetery, where both Ilona and Marmie were buried, but Michael knew from his experience in Denpasar that ordinary time and distance were totally different in the death trance. Distance was what they made of it, time had already passed them by. As soon as they had passed into the realm of the dead, they would be able to walk to Forest Hill like flickering ghosts, faster than the mortal mind could understand.

"O Sanghyang Widi," Michael chanted, and Frank Louv snorted and pretended to blow his nose to conceal his amusement.

"Can you believe this stuff?" he appealed to Randolph.

Randolph shrugged and continued to watch with deep anxiety as the incense smoke trailed across the living room and Michael chanted the mantras, sweat already glistening in the furrows of his forehead. It would be necessary for Michael to more than redouble his previous efforts if he was to take two people into the death trance with him, particularly people who were spiritually unprepared, unbelieving and hostile. It was possible that he might not be able to manage it, in which case Reece would almost certainly kill him and then turn on Wanda and Randolph. Waverley preferred that his revenge on Randolph be "artistic," but if that was denied him, Randolph did not doubt that he would be quite content with violence.

Randolph glanced across the living room toward the open French doors, where the fine lace drapes stirred and curled in the warm night breeze. Wanda had lowered her head out of exhaustion and fear, but the two Dobermans remained alert at her feet, their ears pricked up and their red tongues lolling, and Randolph knew it would take only a whistled command from the mad-looking Louv for the dogs to jump up and savage her. Louv did not need a gun to keep Randolph and Wanda imprisoned; the dogs were more than enough.

Now Michael began to rock back and forth, and Waverley and Richard Reece, with some embarrassment, began to imitate him.

"Empty your minds," Michael repeated. "Empty your minds of everything. Of hope, and fear, and mistrust. Empty your minds of all feelings of revenge. Empty your minds of confusion and accusation and resentment. Your minds will have to be calm, as calm as the sky, as calm as the surface of a bright-blue lake."

Waverley closed his eyes, followed by Reece. They rocked backward and forward, over and over again until they were all three swaying in the same hypnotic rhythm, the incense smoke curling between them softly like the ribbons that drift over a Hindu funeral procession, through the fields and down to the ocean.

Michael sang each of the mantras of the death trance twelve times. Waverley was quivering now as if he were cold, and Reece's head was thrown back, his mouth gaping open as if he were high on heroin or cocaine. Michael was concentrating so hard that a trickle of blood could be seen in one nostril and his clothes were clinging to him wetly.

"O Sanghyang Widi, take us into the realm of the dead; O Yama, receive us; O Barong Keket, protect us."

Then Michael sang the mantras for the thirteenth time, the magical number of the merak roofs on the shrine of Yama, and an extraordinary tremble passed through the air. As Randolph stared at the three men sitting on the floor in front of him, they seemed to grow curiously distorted, as if their bodies had been stretched. Michael opened his eyes and stared at Randolph, his face like that of someone seen in a carnival mirror. Michael opened his mouth and appeared to be saying something but Randolph was unable to hear him.

"What the fuck's happening?" Louv wanted to know. "Look at those guys, they look like they're squashed. Reece! What the fuck's going on?"

He walked over to Reece, who was still kneeling on the floor. Reece had stopped swaying now and his eyes were open, but he did not seem to be able to focus and one side of his face was wildly out of proportion, like that of a medical freak.

"Reece!" Louv shouted.

"Don't touch him!" Randolph warned. "He's all right; he's gone into the death trance. He looks that way because time and space are different in the death trance. The way you see things is different. Believe me, he's okay."

"Jesus," swore Louv, stepping away.

Michael stood up, his image wavering as if viewed through water. Then Waverley stood up, and Reece. Frank Louv took another pace back, then another. "Jesus," he repeated, more in awe than in fear.

Silently, quickly, in a strange, translucent flurry, Michael and Waverley and Reece walked toward the living-room door, opened it and disappeared. It was all over in a moment, and then Randolph was left with Louv, Wanda and the panting Dobermans. Louv sat down on the arm of the sofa, shook his head and said, "I never seen anything like that. Not ever. They was just like ghosts."

"They went into the world of the dead, that's all," Randolph explained.

"That's all? Are you kidding?"

"I've done it myself. It's something like being hypnotized. You can actually meet people who are dead . . . their spirits, or their ghosts if you like."

The mad-looking Louv ran his hand through his thinning hair, agitated and nervous.

Randolph nodded toward the open French doors. "Are you supposed to keep her tied up like that the whole time they're gone?"

Louv sniffed, cleared his throat and said, "Oh, yes. Yes. Sure. Those are the orders."

"You like working for Mr. Graceworthy?" Randolph asked.

"Sure I like working for Mr. Graceworthy."

"I guess he pays pretty good."

"He sure does. I used to work for Midas, you know, fitting mufflers. But this pays double."

"More interesting too, I'll bet."

"It sure is. Gets rid of your what's-its-names too. You know what I mean, when you're all up tight."

"Latent aggressions," Randolph suggested.

Louv swung his cosh around and around. "That's it, something like that. When you've been out in Nam, I mean you can't unlearn all that stuff. I was in III MAF at Chu Lai. That changed my life, that war. Made me a different person. When I got back here, all I could get was a job in a supermarket, collecting carts from out of the parking lot; then that job at Midas. And all the time, you know, I was trained for handling an M-Sixty and for breaking people's necks with my bare hands."

Randolph rubbed the back of his neck to ease the tension building in his muscles. "So you found your vocation at last," he said.

"Sure did."

"It's a pity you went to Waverley Graceworthy first. I could use a talent like yours."

The cosh went around and around unceasingly, but Randolph could tell that Louv was waiting to hear what he had to say.

"I've been looking for a head of security for almost six months now," Randolph said. "A top man, trained by the military, to run all my security operations. Also to make sure that none of my competitors try to get funny."

Louv stopped swinging the cosh. "What kind of money are you offering?" he asked. "Just supposing that anybody was interested, that is."

"Eighty-five Gs, plus expenses. Plus a handgun of course, with a full permit."

Louv thought about that. Then he started swinging the cosh once more.

Randolph said, "Of course there would have to be some kind of a transfer fee, a kind of bonus, to attract the right man."

"Really?"

"I was thinking of maybe fifty."

"Fifty thousand?"

"What do you think?" Randolph asked. "Fifty cents?"

"And this job." Louv asked obliquely, "would this job be head of security? I mean the real top banana in security, not under nobody else?"

"You've got it," Randolph told him.

There was a long silence. Louv stood up, walked across to the French doors and sniffed distastefully at the warm night air. Then he came back, smacking the end of the cosh into the palm of his hand.

"You can take somebody's head off with one of these," he informed Randolph, a preoccupied expression on his face.

Randolph decided to take the plunge. "Do you want the job or don't you?" he asked.

"I'd need some time to think it over."

"There isn't any time to think it over. You get the job only on the condition that you accept it right away."

The man sucked in his breath. "Well, I don't know about that. You've seen what Mr. Graceworthy's like when he loses his temper."

"If you take the job and if you let me out of here right now, nobody is going to have to worry about Mr. Graceworthy, ever."

"I only got your word for that."

The man walked up and down the room a few more times, swinging his cosh and smacking it into the palm of his hand. On his fourth crossing of the patterned carpet, he stopped beside the silk-draped mask of Rangda and said, "That's some face, wouldn't you say?"

"Well," Randolph replied cautiously, "it's supposed to be scary. It's supposed to frighten people away."

"Oh, yeah?" The man lifted one corner of the silk scarf and stared eyeball to eyeball at Rangda's grotesque snarl.

"Phew," he said, shaking his head. "That's really some face."

"They deliberately make it scary so you won't be tempted to put your hand into its mouth."

Louv looked at Randolph narrowly. "Why should anybody be stupid enough to put his hand in its mouth?"

"I don't think stupid is quite the word for it. By tradition.

they always place a piece of gold in the mask's throat. I think it has something to do with giving the actor who wears it a golden voice, some kind of superstitious rubbish like that. But it's a hefty piece of gold. Every mask has one. Maybe ten or eleven ounces, and what's the price of gold?''

"You're putting me on," the man said slyly.

"Try it and see," Randolph smiled.

"This is a put-on, right? You think I'm some kind of stupid putz who goes around sticking his hand in masks, looking for gold.''

"You've got my secretary guarded by attack dogs, you've got me covered by a cosh that could take my head off my shoulders. Do you think I feel like making jokes?''

"Yeah, and what if Mr. Graceworthy comes back and wants to know where's the gold? What kind of trouble is *that* going to get me in?''

"Mr. Graceworthy doesn't know about the gold, and my friend Michael Hunter isn't going to tell him, for sure, and this is quite apart from the fact that Michael Hunter probably won't be coming back. You know how Mr. Graceworthy works. Mr. Graceworthy employs people like you and Reece, and that speaks for itself.''

"So what you're saying is, if I was to take the gold, and if the dogs weren't too obedient all of a sudden so that you and she could get out of here without having your asses gnawed off, then nobody would be none the wiser? You're talking a deal here, right?''

Randolph nodded. "You've got it. And it's all in your favor too. If there isn't any gold there—which there is of course—but if there isn't, you don't lose anything. And if there is, I still have to trust you to let us go free.''

"And this ain't no put-on?" the man asked again with a surprisingly amiable smile.

Randolph shook his head emphatically.

The man hesitated for a moment, then knelt on his hands and knees and peered between Rangda's curving fangs.

"It's pretty dark in there. I don't see no gold.''

"It's right at the back," Randolph assured him.

Slowly, carefully, Frank Louv inserted his hand between

Rangda's curling lips and into her mouth. Randolph coughed out of nervousness and the man looked up at him and said, "No funny business, right? Otherwise I whistle up those dogs."

"You have my word," Randolph told him. Cold perspiration ran down inside his armpits.

"I can't feel nothing so far," the man reported.

"Farther in," Randolph urged him.

"What kind of a shape is it? Any special shape?"

"Well, they usually make it in the shape of a—"

The blistering roar that came out of the mouth of the Witch Widow's mask made even Randolph's scalp turn cold. The eyes swiveled, the fangs stretched apart and the mad-looking Louv shrieked in fear. He tried to snatch his hand away but then Rangda's jaws snapped together and there was a sound like someone cracking the ribs of an umbrella.

The man screamed again—a long, ululating scream this time—and tried to wrench his arm away from Rangda's tightly closed teeth. He tugged and tugged, screaming and whimpering and almost laughing from pain; then his arm suddenly came free and he held it up. It was bitten off just below the elbow, with veins and sinews hanging from it like bloody vermicelli. His face was shocked and ashen-gray.

"Jesus, my arm. Jesus, my arm . . ." He kept babbling and waving the stump at Randolph as if he were threatening to hit him with it. Blood splattered everywhere; his arteries were spouting like faucets turned on full blast.

The mask roared again and the man staggered away from it, terrified. "Jesus, dear Jesus!" he shrieked, then tripped and collapsed and lay on the carpet shuddering.

The Dobermans outside on the lawn immediately stood up, their fur bristling, their ears perked up, their tails erect. But Louv, trembling and crying as he was, was unable to whistle the command that would make them attack.

Randolph crossed the room and stepped through the French doors. Wanda, tied to the chair, stared at him in horror.

"The mask," she cried hysterically. "The mask actually bit him!"

Randolph tried to sound calm. "It happened before, in Denpasar. Almost the same thing. The mask isn't actually Rangda, that's what Michael said, but it's kind of a personification of Rangda, which means that it can bite just as she does."

"Oh, my God," Wanda whispered. "You have to get us out of here."

Randolph approached the chair but the Dobermans shifted around and growled at him, warning him off. He took another step and then another, but this time they pounced forward and barked at him furiously.

"They were told to guard me," Wanda said desperately.

"They don't have to take their instructions so goddam seriously," Randolph complained. Behind him, on the blood-patterned carpet, Frank Louv tried to get up on his knees but collapsed again.

"The meat!" Wanda exclaimed. "They took the meat away from me when they tied me up. They left it on the landing upstairs."

"Wait," Randolph said, "and keep calm. They won't bite if you keep calm."

"What about the mask?"

"The one thing the mask *can't* do is walk."

"Oh God," Wanda said. Randolph hurried back into the house and leaped up the stairs three at a time. He reached the landing just as Waverley's butler was distastefully picking up the plastic bag of sirloin steak from one of the tapestry-covered chairs. He stared at Randolph in surprise.

"What the 'ell are *you* doing up 'ere?" he demanded, his upper-class English accent slipping away like water.

"Collecting my property," Randolph told him and grabbed for the bag of steak.

The butler tried to tug the bag away but Randolph shoved him hard in the chest with the flat of his hand, and then again, and the butler released his hold.

"Just stay out of this," Randolph told him. "It's more than you can handle."

The butler, winded, could do nothing more than watch in amazement as Randolph ran back down the stairs, skated

across the hallway and into the living room. Outside th
French doors, the Dobermans were pacing nervously an
growling and yapping, and when they saw Randolph, the
barked even more furiously.

"Here, dogs," Randolph called. "Here, dogs! Dinne
time!" He reached into the plastic bag and clawed out tw
or three pounds of warm, wet steak. He held it up so th
dogs could get the scent of it and then he tossed it over t
the far side of the lawn.

The dogs hesitated, uncertain of what to do. They ha
been ordered to guard Wanda but their attention had bee
diverted by the mask's attack on Frank Louv, and nobod
had told them what to do next. Randolph threw anothe
handful of meat and shouted, "Go on, dogs. Dinner, fo
God's sake!" and at last their appetites overcame thei
confusion. They leaped away across the grass and bega
wolfing down the steak.

Randolph wrestled with the knots that tied Wanda to th
chair; in the end he had to twist one of the chair's arm
sideways and break it off in order to free her.

"Listen," he said as he yanked at the last of the cord, "
promised Michael that I would go after him into the deat
trance."

"But you can't!" Wanda protested.

"I have to. This may be my last-ever chance."

"But Randolph—"

"Please, Wanda, I know what the risks are. What I wan
you to do is to go down to the cellar, find out where Herber
is and ask him to drive you home. Don't take any nonsens
from the butler, or from any of the other servants if they tr
to stop you. Call the police if anybody gives you trouble
Go home, please, and wait for me there."

"Randolph, you can't do this. It's far too dangerous. An
that mask—"

"I know what I'm doing," Randolph reassured her
although—if he had allowed himself to admit it—he wa
just as frightened as she was. "All I want you to do is to g
someplace safe so I don't have to worry about you. Now
please."

Wanda held his arms for a moment, her face white and streaked with tears. "Damn it," she said, "I love you."

Randolph kissed her forehead. "And I love you too. So stay safe, and I'll be back."

"Say that as if you mean it," Wanda replied.

They went into the living room. Frank Louv was lying facedown on the floor and when Randolph leaned over him, he could see that the man had stopped breathing and that his eyes were wide open and staring.

"Is he dead?" Wanda asked. When Randolph nodded, she looked across at the mask of Rangda and shuddered.

Randolph said, "Off you go, and lock the door behind you. I'll lock the French doors and take the key with me when I go after Michael. Whatever anybody says to you, don't let him in."

Wanda gave Randolph one last, long look, as if she wanted to imprint his image on her mind forever, and then left, turning the key in the living-room door. Randolph closed and locked the French doors and then went over to the middle of the room, where the mask of Rangda was glaring at the sofa, and knelt down cross-legged in the way Michael had taught him.

He bowed his head; he emptied his mind. He let all the furious, frightening, jangling thoughts of the past few minutes tumble out of his brain like fragments of colored sand tumbling through an hourglass. An inner calm began to envelop him, shining and pale and infinitely restful. He wondered if Waverley and Reece had been able to find such calm, but then he let even that gritty little piece of thinking tumble away with the rest of the colored sand.

He spoke the words of the sacred mantras. He heard the gongs ringing again, and the *tip-tap-tapping* of the sticks. He heard the furious, irritable shaking of the *ceng-ceng* cymbals and the slow, deep tones of the *trompong*.

He was not an adept but he believed, and on the strength of his belief he was drawn slowly and silently into the realm of the dead. Blackness gradually rose up around him like the petals of a night-colored lotus and then closed over his head. He heard echoing whispers, and the ground beneath

him seemed to dissolve, shrinking away like the black sands
of Krambitan, shrinking and shrinking until he was balanced
on nothing but a single grain. The universe spun around
him. The stars came out, one after the other, then more and
more and more, whole galaxies of stars, stretching in every
direction for unthinkable light-years; and there he was, in
the center of all of these galaxies, the lord of the stars, the
lord of time, the master of all space.

The universe tightened. The stars crowded together. Then,
like a glittering fireworks display, they burst apart, and
Randolph opened his eyes and found himself sitting on the
floor of Waverley Graceworthy's living room, in front of
the mask of Rangda and the body of a dead man.

He rose up quickly and moved like a figure seen in
dreams, across the room, through the French doors and out
onto the spotlit lawns.

The Dobermans raised their heads from their gory supper
and one of them yowled, but Randolph glided past them so
swiftly that all they did was to sniff, lick their jowls and
return to the torn meat.

Randolph walked around the side of the house until he
reached the driveway. He was just in time to see the front
gates of Waverley's mansion open and three cars glide
toward the house. He recognized the first car, a long, black
limousine with the license plate OGRE 1. Behind it came a
silver New Yorker carrying on its door the crest of the
Memphis police department, and Randolph, pausing by the
side of the driveway, could see that Dennis Moyne, looking
serious and unhappy, was sitting in the back with two of his
senior deputies. Behind Chief Moyne's car came a Memphis
patrol car without lights.

Randolph had no time to stop and see why Orbus Greene
and Dennis Moyne had suddenly turned up. He walked on
down the driveway until he reached Elvis Presley Boulevard; then he turned north in the direction of Forest Hill
Cemetery. The fireworks had finished now; the night was
quiet. An occasional car drove past with the strange slowness of everything perceived in a death trance; a plane

crawled across the sky, its lights flashing in a slow, measured rhythm. Even the cicadas sang a deep, blurred song.

It took him only five or six minutes to reach the cemetery. The main gates were closed for the night but a small
side gate was open and he walked through. He knew where
Ilona Graceworthy was interred; the Graceworthy vault was
only sixty or seventy yards from the Clare family tomb. He
flickered between the rows of headstones, between the obe-
lisks and the angels, a half-real figure in an unreal world.
Above his head the sky was humid and overcast and the
lights from the city were reflected on the clouds. The headstones gleamed unnaturally white in the darkness, like the
teeth of skeletons protruding from the soil. There was no
wind. The sassafras trees were silent, not even sighing as
they frequently did for the dead.

He reached the end of the row of headstones where the
Graceworthy vault was located, and suddenly there they
were: Michael, looking strained and agitated; Waverley, his
face unnaturally flushed; Reece with his cameras and his
disdainfully cold stare, his automatic pushed into his belt as
if it could protect him from the dead. Michael had laughed
scornfully when Randolph had suggested taking a rifle into
a death trance to hunt the leyaks. "How can you kill
something that's already dead?"

Waverley was calling Ilona. It occurred to Randolph that
they had probably just arrived, Waverley being older and
slower than the others. Randolph stepped quietly back and
pressed himself against the coldness of one of the tombs so
that Reece would not be able to see him, and he listened and
watched in frightened fascination.

"Ilona! Ilona, I beg you! Where are you, Ilona? It's
Waverley. I want to talk to you! They said I could talk to
you!"

There was no reply. Randolph glanced quickly around the
cemetery and realized that there were no spirits here, at least
none that he could see. Perhaps all the spirits in Forest Hill
had moved on to other destinies, to new incarnations, to
other lives.

Waverley repeated, "Ilona! Ilona, my love!"

For a long time nothing happened. Waverley called "Ilona!" two more times but his voice sounded broken and hopeless. Michael remained where he was, his head bent forward. Reece was shuffling his feet, sniffing and looking around belligerently. Reece's image seemed to constantly waver and change as if he had not managed to completely manifest himself into the realm of the dead.

Randolph pressed closer against the tomb, breathing slowly and evenly. Whenever Reece turned away, he allowed himself a quick look around the cemetery to make sure there were no leyaks, but in the artificial twilight created by the light-pollution from downtown Memphis, no eyes burned, no ashen faces appeared.

When Randolph turned back, however, he saw something remarkable. The wrought-iron gates in the front of the Graceworthy vault were being opened from within by dead-white hands. The rusted hinges grated like the teeth of men in agony. And then, as Waverley Graceworthy stepped back in dread, a woman appeared: a woman in white with a face of white. A woman with dark, impenetrable eyes; long, dark hair; and a coronet of tangled flowers.

Randolph shook with simple fear. The woman stood in the gateway of the Graceworthy vault, one hand still resting on each open gate, and she stared at Waverley as if she were trying to draw everything out of him: his soul, his feelings, his very life essence.

"Ilona," Waverley whispered, loud enough for Randolph to hear. He dropped suddenly to his knees on the pathway.

"Ilona, this is Waverley. This is Wave, my darling, your own dear Wave."

The woman remained silent and unmoving.

"Ilona, I wanted to tell you that I loved you. Ilona, I loved you, do you hear me? I always loved you, and I love you still."

The woman slowly came forward across the neatly cut grass, her bare feet making no impression. Reece took two or three steps away from her and fumbled in his bag for his Polaroid camera. Michael saw what he was doing and waved irritably to tell him that Ilona was not a leyak and that they were in no danger.

Ilona laid her hand on Waverley's head. *"You loved me?"* she asked in a voice as cold as quicksilver.

"I loved you always."

"You never loved me. Why do you trouble me now?"

"Ilona," Waverley begged and raised his head; Randolph could see the tears glistening in his eyes. "Ilona, please forgive me."

"There is nothing to forgive," Ilona said. *"You meant nothing to me, ever; you mean nothing to me now."*

"That can't be true. Why did you stay with me, why did you keep coming back to me?"

Ilona smiled. Randolph stared at her and was suddenly unnerved by the feeling that this woman, this spirit, this walking apparition from the grave . . . *this* was his mother come to life again. He resolved then that—Reece or not—he was going to talk to her.

Waverley insisted, "You never left me, did you? You must have felt something for me. Even after you had his child, you came back."

Slowly Ilona shook her head. *"You never understood me, did you, Wave? You never understood anybody. I came back to you only because he couldn't leave his wife and because I didn't want anybody else. You gave me a home, you gave me money, you didn't demand too much. I had to sleep somewhere at night when I wasn't with him. I had to have somewhere to hang my clothes. Perhaps you think I was weak. Perhaps you think I should have left you and made a new life on my own. But after the child was born, I felt closer to him than ever, and at least when I was with you, I could keep on seeing him. I could see the baby too, and you will never know how much that wrenched my heart. But he brought the baby up so well. He brought him up to be wholesome and moral, and I was never ashamed of him. He was mine."*

Randolph left his hiding place beside the tomb and stepped out into the open. He walked slowly toward Waverley and Ilona, ignoring Reece as if he didn't exist. Reece drew out his automatic but kept it pointing upward; he was spooked now, afraid that mortal weapons would not be of any use. Michael, surprised, came hesitantly forward too, but Randolph raised a hand to wave him away.

Ilona turned as Randolph approached. Her dark eyes stared at him unblinkingly; her hands, which had been slightly lifted, fell slowly to her sides. Randolph walked up to her so they were scarcely three feet apart and looked, for the first time, into his mother's eyes. The flowers that formed her coronet were wild flowers, and they were dead.

"*It's you,*" Ilona whispered.

Randolph nodded. "I never knew until today. Waverley told me. Father never did."

"*Father,*" repeated Ilona gently and reached out her hand to touch Randolph's hand. "*I never thought I would ever hear you say that to me, either living or dead.*"

A single tear sparkled in her eye, as bright as a diamond.

Down on his knees beside them, Waverley stared from one to the other. "Then it's true," he said hoarsely. He groped for his cane and tried to get up. He almost lost his balance and Reece came over and helped him. Waverley leaned on Reece's arm, white-faced and shaking. "It's true! It's really true!"

"You knew it all along," Randolph said. "What's making you so upset now?"

"Because," Waverley breathed. "Because I always prayed that it was my own meanness, my own suspicion, my own small-mindedness. I always prayed that it wasn't true."

He turned aside, a glint of light sparking in his glasses. "I always prayed that she loved me," he said mournfully.

Ilona stroked Randolph's hand, separating each finger, caressing the line of each vein.

"*Do you know something?*" she asked, her voice sweet and cold like chilled white wine. "*Families are not parted by death. I understand that now. Mothers and sons, fathers and daughters, nothing can ever untie them.*"

She leaned her head against Randolph's shoulder. She was intensely cold and her hair seemed to crackle with static electricity. Randolph was frightened, but also very moved.

"My son," she breathed, and even her breath was cold. *"My son, I have held you at last."*

It was then, however, that Michael laid his hand on Randolph's shoulder and said, "Randolph," urgently.

Randolph raised his head. Waverley and Reece had turned away from the Graceworthy vault and were making their way uphill.

"What's the matter?" Ilona asked. *"Where are they going?"*

Michael said, "Quick, Randolph. They're looking for Marmie."

Randolph took Ilona's ice-cold fingers between his strong warm hands. "I have to go," he told her. "Later I'll try to come back. I promise you."

"Randolph!" Michael urged him. "If they find her, and if they start threatening her . . . Well, you know what Reece is like."

"Mother," Randolph said desperately and kissed the cheek of the dead woman who had given him life. Then he turned away and ran after Michael.

TWENTY-SIX

When they reached the crest of the hill, they stopped among the rows and rows of gleaming white headstones. Waverley and Reece were some distance behind but even so, they were nearing the site where Marmie and the children were buried and Waverley was shrieking at the top of his voice, "Marmie Clare! Marmie Clare! Let's have a look at you, Marmie Clare!"

"She won't come out for that kind of screaming," Randolph panted.

"She's a spirit now," Michael reminded him. "Spirits don't feel the same kind of hostility that living people do."

"I'm going to kill that bastard," Randolph vowed, aware that those were the most vicious words he had ever spoken in his life, even more vicious because he meant them.

Randolph and Michael started jogging again, through the chilly marble forest of angels and spires and blind-eyed effigies of Christ. They could still hear Waverley screeching out for Marmie, his voice sounding like the cry of a buzzard, or a crow. "Marmie Clare! Marmie Clare! Let's see you, Marmie Clare! Come on, Marmie, where are you hiding?"

But then Michael looked quickly to one side and said, "Randolph!"

Randolph halted abruptly. "What is it?"

"There! Look, and there!"

Randolph shielded his eyes and peered into the grainy gloom. "I don't see anything. What is it?"

Michael held his shoulder and directed his gaze to a tall catafalque in the near distance. Randolph saw nothing at first but gradually he detected a slight movement, an inky shape detaching itself from the shadow of a tomb and pouring itself into the shadow of another.

"Do you think somebody's watching us?" he asked. "Police maybe? Security guards?"

"Leyaks," Michael said.

"Leyaks? But I thought America was safe!"

"There, look, and there! And *there*!" Michael ordered.

This time Randolph saw the sultry burning orange of slanting eyes. This time he saw the ash-white radiance of grisly faces.

"My God, you're right. Leyaks."

Michael said, "Ambara, it must have been. Have you talked to Dr. Ambara?"

"Not since yesterday morning. I couldn't raise him. Why? What does Dr. Ambara have to do with it?"

"I wouldn't take him into a death trance. I said it was too dangerous and that I was going to do only one more and that it would be for you. He was pretty angry about it. He said he was going to try it on his own."

"You didn't stop him?" Randolph asked incredulously.

"How could I stop him? I'm not his *pedanda*. He's a grown-up man, or at least he *was*. That's what he must have done though, gone into a death trance and aroused the leyaks. Now they're really after us. Look, there must be a hundred of them out there!"

Randolph asked tightly, "What the hell are we going to do?"

"Run," Michael said. "And I mean *run*."

"But Marmie and the children! If Waverley calls them out, the leyaks will get them too! Damn it, Michael, they'll be torn to pieces!"

"Randolph, they're dead already; there's nothing you can do about it. Now come on. Let Waverley get what he deserves. Reece too."

Randolph hesitated. Waverley, fifty or sixty yards away, was standing in front of the Clare tomb now, rapping his cane on the path and shouting, "Marmie Clare! Marmie Clare! Come on out, Marmie Clare!"

Unseen by Waverley or Reece, dark and threatening shapes were altering the skyline of tombstones, shapes that had deathly white faces and eyes that flared orange with incandescent hatred. The tribe of leyaks, the children of Rangda; scores of them rustling through the cemetery, hungrily converging on live spirits and dead souls.

Michael pulled at Randolph's sleeve. "Last time you were lucky. But not this time, buddy boy. Look at them, Randolph! If we don't get out of here, we're going to end up as dead as they are! Do you want to be one of them? A leyak? A zombi, for Christ's sake?"

Randolph was about to edge away, about to abandon Waverley and Reece, when a chill ran down his backbone and he stood up straight, staring, and there was nothing Michael could do to pull him away.

"It's them," he said in a haunted voice, not caring if Michael heard him or not. "Michael, it's them."

Michael let go of Randolph's sleeve, stood where he was and stared. With the greatest of grace and simplicity, in ordinary clothes, hand in hand, Marmie and John and Mark and Issa had appeared and were standing in a line in front of Waverley and Reece.

Marmie, beautiful Marmie, with her hair looking just as it had on the morning he had left her. John, even taller than he remembered. Mark, with that mischievous smile. And his beloved Issa.

Randolph walked toward them along the cemetery pathway, ignoring the advancing shadows of the leyaks, and the tears were running down his cheeks. He felt devastated; uplifted but also terrified; his mind bursting with the extraordinary powers of the human spirit. Because he found that he couldn't call out, he raised his arms, and as he did so, Marmie and the children caught sight of him and their faces lit with sudden joy. Randolph ran now, ran toward them, and then they were together again, and he was holding them, and even though they felt cold, they were his, their spirits were his, and he loved them as he had never loved them before.

"Marmie," he breathed, his voice unsteady. "Marmie, it's dangerous here. You have to come with me, all of you. You have to come now."

Marmie could not stop touching him in disbelief. *"How did you get here? Randolph, you're still alive! How did you get here? I can't believe you're here!"*

"Come on," Randolph urged her. "John, Mark, Issa, we have to get away from here!"

"Dad," frowned John, *"what's wrong? Dad, what are you doing here?"*

"We can't leave," Issa pleaded. *"We can't."*

Now Waverley stepped forward, his cane resting on his right shoulder like a rifle. "This is extraordinarily touching, isn't it? What a night for reunions! Mothers and wives and children."

Reece stepped forward too, and he was smiling. Marmie stared at him in horror. Then she reached out and clutched her children closer. Issa stared too, in abject fear.

"Why is he here?" Marmie whispered.

Issa began to weep.

"Why is he here?" Marmie repeated, almost screaming.

Waverley said, "He's here for my protection, that's why he's here."

"He raped me!" Marmie shrieked. *"He raped me! He raped my daughter! And then he tortured us, and then he killed us!"*

Randolph had to take hold of Marmie's icy wrists to prevent her from rushing across and attacking Reece with her bare hands.

"He raped us and raped us, and then he wound barbed wire around our necks, and while we strangled in agony, he took off that mask of his and laughed! Demon!" she fumed at him. *"Demon!"*

Michael came up now and pulled at Randolph's shoulder.

"We have to leave, Randolph, and we have to leave right *now*! They're all around us. Come on."

Marmie whimpered in Randolph's arms. From a scream, her voice dropped to a whisper. "*Make sure that he suffers, Randolph. Make sure that he pays for what he did. When he was watching us die, Randolph . . . when he was watching us die, he was smoking a cigar . . . listen to me, Randolph . . . he was smoking a cigar and he dropped it. You know that knothole in the floorboards . . . he dropped it down there and he cursed because he dropped it down there. But it went under the floorboards, Randolph . . . and he couldn't get it out. . . .*"

Reece shoved Randolph away from Marmie and held his automatic up close to Randolph's face. Marmie backed away from him in fear even though he had already taken everything from her that she could surrender: her body, her sexuality, her very life.

Waverley said in a precise but peculiarly deranged-sounding way, "We want you to know, Marmie, my dear, that if this husband of yours ever attempts to contact you again, if he ever attempts to winnow out evidence against us by talking to you, we will injure him so severely that he will spend the rest of his days in agony. Not dead—because that would afford him the ineffable bliss of meeting you again—but painfully crippled."

Marmie said nothing but shook her head from side to side, traumatized even in death by the sight of the man who had killed her.

"Waverley, there aren't any words for you," Randolph said.

Waverley beat a tattoo on the ground with his cane. "You took away my wife, you took away my children. I did the same to you, Randy. It's called poetic justice."

Michael said, "They're here, Randolph."

Waverley asked, "Here? Who's here?"

And it was then that the leyaks rose out of the darkness, white-faced, snarling, more than fifty of them, with raging eyes. Randolph drew Marmie and the children closer, and he could feel their fear mingle with his. They were completely surrounded; there was no escape.

"The lykas," Waverley breathed in terror. "Randolph! Is *that* what they are? The lykas?"

"Leyaks," Michael corrected him. "And everything I said about them is true. You are just about to discover what it feels like to be eaten alive."

Waverley, stunned, reached out to Reece for support but Reece backed away and let him stagger.

"The camera," Waverley hissed at him. "Damn it, Reece, the camera! Use it! The camera!"

The leyaks edged closer. Marmie, collecting herself now, said, *"I've never seen them before, Randolph, but I know what they are and I know where they come from. I also know what they will do to us."*

"We're together," Randolph said. "At least this time we're together."

Issa said, *"I'm frightened, Daddy. Oh, Daddy, I'm so frightened."*

One of the leyaks lashed out toward Reece with its claws. Reece, seizing the moment, stepped back and took a flash photograph of it. The Polaroid camera whined and a blank white print was fed out. Startled by the flash, the leyaks drew back a little, allowing Reece just enough time. The leyak's image gradually appeared on the photograph and then Reece held it up between finger and thumb and waved it at the leyak contemptuously. The leyaks shied back even farther. They had crowded so close together that they were obviously unsure of which of them had been caught by Reece's image-maker, and when he took his Zippo out of his pocket and flicked it alight, they stumbled back with their hands over their eyes.

Reece had been trained in Vietnam. He knew how to survive and he knew how to pick his moment. As soon as the leyaks cowered back, he barreled his way through them, pushing them aside in all directions, and then he was off running. Waverley tried to hobble after him but Michael seized his arm and held him back.

"Let him go! They'll probably run him down anyway. You deserve what's coming to you, you creep."

There was an odd comic-book bravado in the way that Michael spoke, and Randolph—clinging to his family, grasping John's hand and pressing Issa's head against his chest—suddenly understood what it was that made it possible for people to live out their lives. He suddenly understood that dignity was not just a word, not just a quality, but the essential ingredient of human existence.

The leyaks clustered nearer again. They made a shuffling, rustling sound as if they were flaking to pieces as they walked. It was like the sound of ashes in a Hindu funeral pyre when the relatives rake through them for the bones of the person they loved.

Waverley took two or three uncertain steps toward the leyaks. Randolph and Michael and Marmie watched him. The leyaks watched him too, their eyes flaming orange with a lust for flesh.

"They're not attacking," Michael murmured to Randolph in perplexity. "They've got us cornered but they're not attacking."

Randolph did not know what to say. He simply held on to Marmie and shook his head.

It was then that they felt a deep, resonant rumble. The leyaks gnashed their teeth and raked their claws in the air but seemed disinclined to come any closer. As the rumble grew louder, some of the marble urns began to rattle and the lids on the tombs started to vibrate. A marble angel toppled from her pedestal and fell to the ground, breaking in two.

Randolph turned to Michael and shouted, "What's happening? Michael! What's happening!"

But Michael had covered his face with his hands and was slowly sagging to his knees, and even Waverley was wheeling around in terror.

"Daddy! What is it?" Issa screamed.

And for a second time Randolph thought, *I've failed her. For a second time I've allowed her to suffer. Oh, God, take care of my precious children. Oh, God, preserve their souls.*

The rumbling grew so loud that they could hardly bear it.

Their teeth vibrated and their bones seemed to buzz, and it seemed as if the whole cemetery was going to be split apart. A huge granite tomb cracked with a report as sharp as gunfire and a tall spire shattered into pieces and collapsed. Dust rose into the air, the dust of broken marble mixing with the dust of long-dead lives.

Michael was shouting, "Barong Keket! Barong Keket! Save me, Barong Keket!"

But the holy name of the Lord of the Forests was not enough to hold back the huge, dark apparition that now bore down on them. Across the cemetery, blotting out the twilight, blotting out the skyline, massive and black and rumbling and stinking of death, came something as huge as a tidal wave and as terrifying as hell itself.

Issa screamed. Marmie held her hands to her head and stared in hypnotic horror.

The apparition approached them and rolled back the darkness that covered its face. Then it roared—an appalling, shuddering roar—and more tombs collapsed.

Randolph had seen the face on the mask but he had not been prepared for anything like the face itself. A face as wide as a car, with bulbous eyes that were not painted this time, not varnished, but glutinous and real. A nose with cavernous, gaping nostrils. A dripping mouth with vicious fangs that were curved and gleaming and as strong as elephant tusks.

Most frightening of all was the apparition's crown. Around her forehead, instead of hair, hundreds of human heads protruded, living human heads, each screaming and weeping in endless torment. For one moment Randolph glimpsed the screaming face of Dr. Ambara among them, and he knew that what Michael had said earlier had been true. Dr. Ambara, rest his soul, had brought the leyaks here.

"What is it?" Waverley asked querulously.

Michael slowly took his hands from his face. "The Witch Widow Rangda," he said over the rumble of the apparition's arrival. "It looks like she has come to collect her souls in person."

Waverley looked at Randolph and then at Michael. At last, turning his back on the huge black bulk of Rangda, he approached Marmie, and John, and Mark, and Issa. He was pale but calm. He took off his glasses and tucked them into his pocket.

"I beg your forgiveness," he said huskily. "If it were not for me, you wouldn't be here now, exposed to this danger. I cannot change myself; I cannot feel contrite. But I have been the author of everything evil that has happened to you, and if it is possible for me to put it right, I shall."

He held out his hand to Randolph and said softly, "Forgive me if you can. It may be no use."

Waverley then turned back and directly confronted the huge, glaring presence hovering over them. The ground began to shake and thunder rumbled through the cemetery. Lightning crackled everywhere, illuminating in fitful flashes the distended, staring eyes and the long, curved teeth and the mouth that dripped with a distillation of human juices. Rangda, the goddess of death, the carnivore of the cemeteries, an ancient evil as old as the planet itself.

"Have me and all my malevolence!" Waverley screamed up at Rangda. "Have me and let these others free! You will have your fill with me, my lady. I will be enough to satisfy your appetite."

"My God, he wants it," Randolph breathed. "He *wants* Rangda to take him; he *wants* to suffer."

Michael stood up and watched Waverley in fascination, still fearful for his own life but gripped by the spectacle of one man offering himself that others might go free. Waverley could see for himself what his punishment might be, that of crowning Rangda's forehead, and he suspected there were worse punishments that remained darkly invisible.

Rangda reached down from the blackness of her cloak and even the leyaks hissed and cowered back. Waverley, however, remained unflinching, his head lifted, his eyes still challenging the Witch Widow to take him as her sole sacrifice.

"Dear God," whispered Marmie, and at that moment the goddess seized Waverley in her scaly claws and lifted him to her mouth.

Her fangs gaped open. Waverley—perversely or bravely,

or simply because he was too frightened by what was happening to him—remained silent. No scream as the first curved fang plunged into his stomach. No scream as his arms were ripped out of their sockets. No scream as the last of the old-style Southern gentry disappeared from sight between those voracious lips, leaving nothing behind but a momentary runnel of blood.

Randolph and Michael waited, numb and shivering, while Rangda loomed over them.

Michael said, "She's going to take us too. I know it. Say your prayers, old buddy. This is eternity coming up."

Rangda darkened the sky over their heads like an electric storm. They waited and waited, but then at last the Witch Widow drew down the blackness that covered her face and turned away. At that, the leyaks began to disperse, slowly at first but gradually in increasing numbers, their eyes narrowed until they were no more than slits of orange fire. Within five minutes the cemetery was deserted and the darkness of Rangda had thundered away toward the southeast.

Randolph sat with Marmie and the children on the edge of a broken tombstone and talked for the rest of the night.

"I want you to know that I love you dearly," he told Marmie, and she listened with that sweet, distant smile he had always adored. "I'm going to go back now, and I'm going to live out the rest of my life, and I'm going to enjoy it to the full. But that life will always be dedicated to you—and to you too, John and Mark and Issa—and you will never die because you will always be here, inside of me."

A light rain began to fall across the cemetery as dawn broke. Randolph urged, "Wait for me, Marmie. I'll come back someday and then we'll be together for all time."

But suddenly Marmie was gone, and so were the children. He stood up and called, "Marmie?" but they had completely vanished.

Michael had been waiting for him in the shelter of a tree. "A new day," he said. "The death trance is over."

Together they walked back in silence along Elvis Presley Boulevard until they reached Waverley Graceworthy's mansion. As they approached the entrance, walking under the dripping trees, they were surprised to see that OGRE 1 was still parked in the driveway, as were Chief Moyne's car and the Memphis police patrol car. There were also three other police cars, their lights flashing, and two station wagons from the Shelby County coroner's office.

They approached the front door just as four policemen and two medics struggled out of the doorway with a gurney on which a massive shape was covered with a heavily bloodstained sheet.

"What happened?" Randolph asked. He lifted the sheet and saw that underneath it lay Orbus Greene, or what was left of Orbus Greene. His white suit was almost black with blood, and huge chunks of raw flesh had been bitten out of the side of his body. His face was like beaten beef. Randolph's stomach tightened and he let the sheet fall back.

"Ah, Mr. Clare," said a familiar voice. It was Captain Ortega from downtown, a smart young career-detective with a handsome Latin face and a briskly clipped mustache. "You came just in time for a terrible tragedy, I regret. I must please ask you to keep this confidential for the moment. We have kept it from the media so far, until we understand it better."

A police officer came past carrying a dead Doberman in his arms. He threw it noisily into the trunk of his car and then went back into the house.

"What the hell happened here?" Randolph asked. He was shaken and tired and bewildered.

Captain Ortega took his arm. "Mr. Graceworthy kept some very fierce guard dogs on the premises," he confided. "It seems that last night Mr. Orbus Greene and Chief Moyne, as well as several other persons, including two policemen, paid a visit to Mr. Graceworthy, perhaps a social call after the Cotton Carnival Ball. Whatever it was, it seems that Mr. Graceworthy was not here and the result was that the dogs attacked the guests and killed them. Nine dead people in all, each very seriously savaged. One of them even lost an arm, an arm we cannot find anywhere."

He took out a small inhaler and squeezed it up each

nostril. "Of course we have put down the dogs. They were too dangerous to even take back to the city pound. But we are still anxious to trace Mr. Graceworthy. You have no notion of his whereabouts?"

Randolph slowly shook his head. "If I hear from him, do you want me to let you know?"

"That would be helpful," smiled Captain Ortega·as another gurney was wheeled past. Randolph recognized a silver-skull ring on the hand that dangled from underneath the sheet: one of Orbus Greene's bodyguards.

He asked abruptly, "Do you mind if I use the phone? My chauffeur was supposed to meet me here and he seems to be late."

"By all means," said Captain Ortega.

Herbert said he would pick them up in fifteen minutes. While they waited for him, they spent the time in Waverley's gardens, walking and talking.

"Leyaks, of course," Michael said quietly. "No dogs could have done that."

"You mean they went through the gate and came back here?"

Michael nodded. "Waverley Graceworthy's living room is not sacred ground, after all. The leyaks were probably chasing Reece and came bursting into the real world right where all these people were sitting. Nobody had a chance."

"And what about the leyaks now?"

"Well, that's the danger. They're loose in the real world, who knows where? And of course they have to kill to survive."

Randolph asked, "You're not thinking of going leyak-hunting again?"

Michael took out a cigarette. "Not me," he said, shaking his head.

Randolph was silent·for a moment and then said, "I have some staff vacancies. The vice-presidency in charge of production just happens to be free. I'm letting Neil Sleaman go."

Michael shook his head again. "Maybe I'll take up taxi driving," he said, half-smiling.

Randolph was thoughtful. "I knew a taxi driver once," he remarked. "In fact, he was the one who put me on to Reece. Do you know what he used to think? He thought that Elvis Presley faked his own death just to get some peace from his fans."

"Good theory," Michael said, nonchalantly blowing a smoke ring.

Randolph nodded. "I wonder what happened to that taxi driver. I never heard from him again."

Michael said, "Usually that's the best way."

FOOTNOTE

On March 27, 1985, Richard Stevens Reece was appre-
hended by police in Gary, Indiana, on charges of assault.
His particulars were sent to the Federal Bureau of Investigation, who determined that he was also wanted by the Royal
Canadian Mounted Police in connection with a multiple
rape-murder at Lac aux Ecorces in the Province of Quebec.

Reece was extradited to Quebec, where he was tried and
found guilty of homicide. The evidence that principally
decided the jury was a cigar butt that was found beneath the
floorboards of the cabin where the rape-murders took place.
Saliva on the cigar butt matched samples of Reece's saliva,
and also samples of semen taken from the bodies of the rape
victims matched Reece's.

Richard Reece was sentenced to life imprisonment. He
hanged himself in his cell on the morning of July 9, 1985,
leaving a note that said simply, "Fish Hook."

THE BEST IN HORROR